Merridy Christmas

Ashley Maureena

Published 2022
Printed in the United States of America
ISBN: 978-1-7328725-4-7
E-ISBN: 978-1-7328725-5-4
Library of Congress Control Number: 2022920867

Cover design by Ashley Maureena

For information, please write:
Ashley Maureena
PhoenixCrossFire Press
1200 Jupiter Rd
#942154
Plano, TX 75094

www.ashleymaureena.com

Dedicated to those I lost during the writing of this book: my father, John; my great-uncle, Gale; my grandmother, Carolyn; and my mother-in-law, Lorraine.

Please note that this book deals with certain topics, including: sexual assault, forced abortions, and PTSD. These topics may be traumatic for some readers. If this is you, I first wish God's ever-loving embracing around you and your life. Also please proceed in knowing characters do overcome these situations, but the journey may be difficult for you to read. I love all my readers.

Sincerely,

Ashley

Table of Contents

Part One: The Audition

Chapter 1 15

Chapter 2 27

Chapter 3 31

Chapter 4 48

Chapter 5 57

Chapter 6 66

Chapter 7 76

Chapter 8 81

Chapter 9 94

Chapter 10 100

Chapter 11 106

Chapter 12 114

Part Two: The Contract

Chapter 13 121

Chapter 14 128

Chapter 15 135

Chapter 16 142

Chapter 17 147

Chapter 18 154

Chapter 19 166

Chapter 20 179

Chapter 21 192

Chapter 22 198

Chapter 23 203

Chapter 24 209

Chapter 25 219

Chapter 26 236

Chapter 27 244

Chapter 28 256

Chapter 29 263

Chapter 30 279

Chapter 31 292

Chapter 32 298

Part Three: The Performance

Chapter 33 311

Chapter 34 315

Chapter 35 322

Chapter 36 327

Chapter 37 337

Chapter 38 343

Chapter 39 352

Chapter 40 363

Chapter 41 373

Chapter 42 379

Chapter 43 387

Part Four: The Album

Chapter 44 401

Chapter 45 413

Chapter 46 424

Chapter 47 433

Chapter 48 442

Chapter 49 453

Chapter 50 458

Author's Notes

Acknowledgements

Appendix: Song Credits

To every thing there is a season, and a time to every purpose under the heaven: a time to be born, and a time to die; a time to plant, and a time to pluck up that which is planted; a time to kill, and a time to heal; a time to break down, and a time to build up; a time to weep, and a time to laugh; a time to mourn, and a time to dance; a time to cast away stones, and a time to gather stones together; a time to embrace, and a time to refrain from embracing; a time to get, and a time to lose; a time to keep, and a time to cast away; a time to rend, and a time to sew; a time to keep silence, and a time to speak; a time to love, and a time to hate; a time of war, and a time of peace.

Ecclesiastes 3: 1- 8

Part One: The Audition

Chapter 1

"I know this is awful timing, with your project and everything, but I'm in a bind." An auburn-haired woman sighed. Her eyes drifted down to a skating rink. The Dallas Plaza's rink sat at the middle of the mall, four stories below where they stood. "In a month, they'll start putting up the garland, and wreaths, and lights... and that giant tree."

"Largest indoor Christmas tree in America," her friend agreed. She played with her ebony twists while staring at the scene below with her friend. "But singing in front of that giant Christmas tree is certainly a big deal. It has opened a lot of doors for others."

"Right! See Kara? That was my first thought, so I signed up for the audition."

"Even though they asked if you could ice skate?"

The first woman blushed. "Yeah... I mean, it just had a disclaimer that the performer must be able to skate in order to perform. I said yes because I plan on being able to skate by the time of the performance." Flustered, she turned her full attention to her friend. "I didn't lie. I'm sincere. I knew you could skate... and, I'm really, really desperate."

Kara laughed at her friend. "Of course, Merridy. I just have to give you a hard time. Let's head down."

The two women linked arms and walked to the nearby escalators. "Thank you, Kara. This means a lot to me. You're always there for me."

"And I always will be, Merridy Christmas." She bumped her friend with her hip. "You do the same for me as well." They went to the skate rental on the ground floor of the Plaza. "Two size nine's, please," Kara told the teenage boy behind the counter. The boy pulled out a pair of size nine skates, and placed on the counter. When he did not move to get another pair, Kara forced a smile. Through her teeth she clarified her statement, "Two pairs of size nine's, please."

Merridy stifled her giggles as they walked away with the skates.

"Can you imagine that? Does that boy order one shoe at a time? Yes, I would like a size ten left foot shoe, and a size nine-and-a-half right foot shoe," she mocked a voice. "Kids these days." She sat on a seat to change into the skates.

"We were dumb when we were kids. Well, I was. But I suspect you were too," Merridy joked. She sat next to her friend, staring at the ice skate in her hands.

Kara knelt before her friend to assist her with the ice skates. "Few more laces than you're used to."

"Certainly. Guess it helps with the ankles." Merridy rotated her feet to become acquainted with the feeling. "And certainly not basketball shoes."

"Tell me about it." Kara stood on her own skates and held her hands out to Merridy. "My parents would have preferred me in the basketball sneakers. They both played college ball. It's how they met."

Merridy took her friend's hands and slowly stood. "How do you stand on these so easily?"

"Practice." Kara took a step toward the rink. "Like the practice I'm going to make you do."

"I already feel it in my calves." She took a step onto the ice and nearly slipped instantly. Her eyes remained glued to her feet.

Her hands clutched desperately at Kara's firm grasp. "I can't do this."

"Yes. You can," Kara sternly told her. "Look up."

Merridy jerked her eyes to meet Kara's, but her feet still slipped on the slick surface of the ice. Her ankles felt weak. "I can't…"

"Stop thinking about it, Merridy." Kara pulled her further onto the ice. "You didn't over-think when you learned to walk. Learning to skate will be the same."

"I was a baby when I learned to walk. How am I supposed to remember the techniques I used when I was a year old?" she countered.

"You're over-thinking…" Kara reminded her in a sing-song voice.

Merridy sighed and struggled to clear her mind.

"Tell me what song you are going to sing."

"I was thinking of singing 'O Holy Night'. It's such a beautiful and powerful song." Merridy continued to hold Kara's hands as her friend led her further onto the ice.

Kara nodded. "The message is needed, and the vocal range needed to perform it will certainly show off your talents."

"Maybe so, but even if no one cares about how well I sing, I want them to hear that message. Isn't that what my Sunday school teacher says about her teaching? Especially when she gets nervous that she's not eloquent enough?"

"True." Kara laughed. "I've always had performance anxiety. I can't imagine singing."

"And I can't imagine teaching." Merridy barely noticed they were nearing center ice. "What led you to teaching anyway? Hockey to marketing and teaching seems like a big jump."

"I was always interested in marketing," Kara responded. "In high school, I did all the marketing for my friends' bands. And when I was on our hockey team, I did it for the booster's events. No matter how much my parents disapproved."

"Your parents disapproved of you marketing?" The new skater finally straightened her ankles without overly-thinking about it.

"My parents disapproved of me playing hockey," Kara replied. Her words were terse. The tone caught Merridy off-guard.

Hesitantly, she asked, "Why not?"

Kara's brow furrowed. She wanted to keep Merridy distracted, but also did not want to bring up her past hurts. "Let's just say hockey wasn't the normal sport of choice in their community."

"They wanted you to play basketball like they did," Merridy nodded in understanding. "I guess parents want to push us in the same directions they took."

"It was more intense than that... there was a lot of guilt, and using the past." Kara noted Merridy began pushing her leg forward with more control. "It's a whole convoluted situation. But the result was no mom or dad in stands for any hockey games."

"That's horrible," Merridy stopped skating in her shock at the revelation. "I'm sorry this is bringing up bad memories for you." When she squeezed her friend's hands, Merridy suddenly realized that she stood center ice. "Oh no."

"Merridy..."

"When did we get here? How did we get so far?" Her legs began to buckle. "Oh no. My ankles are weak. I'm gonna fall..."

Kara secured her grip on her friend's hands. "You were doing so well Merridy! Don't fall now!"

The pep talk encouraged Merridy to find her balance and stand firm. The frown on her face indicated to Kara that she finally found her determination.

"There it is. You found it." Kara nodded. "Hold on to that feeling girl." She pulled slightly away from Merridy, allowing her grasp to loosen. "Now I'm going to pull back and you move toward me on your own."

Merridy nodded her head. "Okay, I can do it." She skated forward slowly at first, then quickly as she began to lose her balance. Kara reached out and caught her. "I made it."

"Very good, you're doing well!" The two shared a laugh. "Let's do it again," Kara began to suggest, but was cut short by her cell phone ringing. "Okay, hold on to my hand and work on your balance while I see who's calling. It better not be work. I need just one day off..." She tugged her phone out of her pocket and noted the number. "It's my boss," she said, half defeated.

"You should take it. That's really important if they're calling on a Saturday."

"But..." Kara stated. They were in the middle of the rink, and Merridy relied on her for support, metaphorically and literally.

"It's okay," Merridy reassured her. "I will stay here and practice my balancing. Ankle strength." Merridy gave a giant grin, and Kara knew there was no point in arguing with her.

"I'll be quick," Kara reassured her before rushing away on the ice. "Hello?" she called into the phone.

Merridy took a deep breath and surveyed the area around her. "If I stay really still and balance, I should be okay," she told herself. She attempted to maintain her newfound determination, but it began to fade as more and more groups of people found their way onto the rink. "Oh no, maybe I can

19

make it to the wall and just hold onto the rail." She slowly moved one foot forward, then another, but a group of teenagers moved toward her in the opposite direction. The collision of the phone-immersed group and the inexperienced skater created a commotion. Merridy cried out as she lost all sense of balance and direction. She plummeted to the hard ice below.

"Easy there."

Before Merridy could reach the ice, she felt two hands grab her flailing arms from behind. The owner of the voice lifted her back onto her feet and kept sturdy hands on her arms. "Are you alright?"

"Yes, thank you." Her voice echoed defeat. "I was just trying to get to the rails."

"What happened to your helper-friend?" One of the hands released Merridy's arms in order for her savior to skate around and face her. "You were showing decent progress."

Merridy took in the man who helped her. He wore a baseball cap low over his brown eyes. His face was half covered with a trimmed beard. He donned a hoodie as well and draped the hood over the top of his cap. Despite his anonymity, his smile was sincere. "Thank you, all progress is credited to her. She's a former hockey player, and I'm unable to tell that puck-thingy from a turnip." She eyed the crowd for any sign of Kara. "Um, my friend had an emergency call she had to take." She shook her head. "That's why I was headed to the rails. I thought they could stable me while I kept practicing. It's important I learn to skate."

The man nodded. "In a rush to get to the Olympics?"

"I am certainly *not* an athlete," Merridy laughed. "But I have an audition to sing, on ice. And if I can't skate out to the stage and stand still long enough to sing, then it doesn't matter how well I sing."

He released his grip on her and crossed his arms across his chest thoughtfully. Merridy attempted to keep her balance on her own again. "And can you sing well?"

She grinned sheepishly. "I like to think so..." She slipped slightly but caught herself. "Much better than I can stand on ice."

"Lucky for you, *that* is something I can help with." He held his hand out to her. "Name's Jacob."

"Merridy." She shook his hand gently.

"Merridy?" he repeated her name with a chuckle. "That's certainly a new name."

She felt a blush in her cheeks. "And my last name is Christmas. Try having a name like that."

"Merridy Christmas. That's actually pretty cute." Jacob winked. "For a singer."

His jovial attitude allowed her to relax. "I suppose. Merridy is a combination of 'melody' and 'merry'. Maybe I was meant to be a singer. Or it could be worse. I have twin cousins named Holly and Jolly in England. Holly loves it; she became a designer. Jolly, not so much. He goes by Lee. And has some anger issues, which is to be expected, when you name a boy Jolly Christmas."

The commentary caused Jacob to belly-laugh. "Come Miss Merridy. I can show you how to skate while your friend deals with her emergency call." He held his hand out to her again, but this time in order to lead her, rather than greet her. "I'm from Vancouver. Grew up on the ice."

"Explains the maple leaf on your hat," she joked and accepted his lead.

"Too on the nose?" he asked. "I was afraid of that." He led her slowly on the ice, providing as little help to her balance as possible. "You know, in my family, we learn to ice skate when we learn to walk."

"And in mine, we learn to ride horses as soon as we can stay straight in the saddle."

He turned to her, "Seriously?"

She giggled. "I thought we were making Canadian versus Texas jokes. Though my parents do have a ranch southwest of here."

"And my family is a hockey family." He nodded his head. "We're both fairly stereotypical, aren't we?"

"Texans with a ranch. Canadians that play hockey... do you play hockey?"

The question caught Jacob off-guard, and he cleared his throat. "I do some work with a local team."

"At least you're doing what you grew up loving?"

"I'm certainly living the dream." He paused and knelt in front of Merridy. "Let's work on these ankles. That will help you tremendously." Casually, he adjusted her stance. "Is singing your dream?"

"It's absolutely all I've ever dreamed of doing. We lived in a small town, and I would sing at my church there. I sing at my church here too." She sighed. "It's a lot harder to be noticed in the city than in that little town. I'm hoping this audition will be my chance."

"I hope it goes well for you." He patted her leg. "Do you feel more stable?"

"Actually, I do." She clapped her hands together happily. "You are amazing. Is this what you do, teach people how to be stable on ice?"

He stood up with a grin. "I've been known to help children on the ice. You'd be my first adult to help."

"I do like being a first. Even though the gift of giving free skating lessons to an adult is probably a little less rewarding than helping a cute kiddo."

"What do you mean?" he asked with a puzzled tilt to his head.

"You know, how we're blessed when we bless others, the act of giving is its own reward. It's my life philosophy. I've just never been on the receiving end of the giving from my fellow man." She giggled. "It feels a little weird. I prefer to give than get."

Jacob smiled broadly. "I feel the same way. I'd rather sneak a gift into someone's hands and let them just enjoy the treat than be given something crazy... like a watch that can feed ten families for a year."

His sentiment caused Merridy to smile with a slight blush. He seemed sincere with the statement, and that sincerity sent electricity through her. She pushed her hair back from her shoulders in order to refocus on the task at hand. "Okay. I can do this. One foot in front of the other."

"I'll be right next to you," Jacob reassured her. He skated alongside the hesitant woman. "What is this audition for?"

"For the tree lighting ceremony, here." She nearly reached out for him, but regained her balance and continued forward. "The last two local acts who performed here have gotten record contracts. It's a very big deal. A lot of people watch the celebration."

"If you get a record deal, what kind of music would you record?" He gently placed a hand on her elbow as she began leaning too far one direction. "Rock? Country?"

"Honestly, I love so many genres. I would experiment with different sounds, certainly." She threw both arms straight out to her sides in order to catch her balance. "But I do know that I would sing my faith. Whatever genre someone wants to call that. Christian? Gospel?"

He nodded. "I can't imagine it will be easy for just any record company to accept that decision."

"You're probably right. It will be hard. And that might be why some start off in pop or country, and then are finally able to tell the record company that they want to speak their faith. I don't know." She managed to skate a bit and stop on her own. "But I'll never know what dealing with a record company is like if I don't learn to skate." She turned to Jacob with a smile. "How was that?"

"You are catching on pretty quick for a lady that nearly kissed the ice a few minutes ago." He tucked his hands into his hoodie's front pocket. "I'm genuinely impressed."

"Guess I'm just determined to figure this out." She cheerily smiled at him. "Maybe by the end of this session I will be able to do a triple lutz."

"I can't even do that," he laughed.

The two skated slowly around the rink for several minutes, exchanging stories of their childhood in order to distract Merridy as she found her rhythm skating. "With a last name like 'Christmas', I have to know, is it your favorite holiday?"

"Absolutely!" Merridy answered giddily. "I love everything about it: the music, the decorations, the food. What about you? Is Christmas big where you're from?"

"Oh yes. The lights are incredible there. And of course, there's a North Pole, Santa's village, and, oh, the German market was a favorite of mine. It felt like I was teleported right into Europe. Like the old Christmas stories and movies."

"Like the Nutcracker!" Her enthusiasm caused him to smile.

"Heh, yes, like the Nutcracker. Or at least the first part, before the trippy dream. It's nice. Fancy party, dancing, giant life-sized toys. My mom loves that ballet. She keeps saying she's going to host a party like that someday." He altered between lightly touching her elbows or shoulders to help her keep balance and shoving his hands in his pocket. "I hope she knows a magical toy maker, for my sake."

"I'm not one for fancy parties, but if there's a magical toy maker involved, count me in." She slipped slightly, but Jacob caught her before she fell, once again. "Though your pretty magical yourself, knight-in-shining skates."

"I guess they're right. Not all knights wear armor." He helped her stand firm on her skates once more before glancing at his watch. "Oops."

"What is it?"

"I'm very late, to quote the White Rabbit, for an important date." He glanced at Merridy and the exit to the rink. "I'm really sorry Merridy. Maybe we can continue this at another time. When is your audition?"

"Next week," she sighed.

"Hmmm…" He pulled his phone out of his pocket. "That doesn't give us a lot of time. And I would stay if I could, but, I'll really be in trouble if I'm any later." She noted a picture of Jacob and a beautiful woman on his phone's lock screen as he used his thumb to unlock the phone. "If I'm not being too forward, I would love to get your number so I can text you my schedule, and we can train some more. I work at a rink in South Hills this week."

"South Hills? That's perfect. I live there." Merridy smiled. "Thank you so much for helping me Jacob." She accepted the phone from him and input her number. "I'm sorry you're going to be late today on my account."

"No worries. It was my pleasure to be your knight-in-shining skates." He took his phone and shoved it back in his pocket. "Shall I escort you to the railing?"

"The exit would be nice. My ankles can't take much more." She linked her arm in his as he patiently skated with her to the exit.

Chapter 2

Kara rushed back to the skating rink entrance in time to see Merridy turn her skates into the rental booth. "I am so sorry lady!" she told her friend.

Flushed in the cheek, Merridy turned to her with a smile. "No need to apologize Kara! Your job is really demanding... and, I had a good time on the ice." The flush in her cheeks intensified. "And I met someone."

"Met... someone?" Kara repeated. Her eyebrow arched. "Like a... boy?"

"He was a guy, yes. He was helping me learn to skate." Merridy held up a finger. "And yes. He was 'absolutely gorgeous' because I know you're going to ask."

"Ooooooh," Kara joked. "Merridy getting her flirt on!"

"Haha." Merridy followed Kara away from the rink and to the nearby coffeeshop. "Hard to flirt when you're flailing around on ice like an infant. But he *did* ask for my number so we could plan another training session."

"And you weren't flirting?" Kara asked with a laugh. "Sounds like you were ma'am."

"If flirting is being my natural, clumsy self, then sure." She jabbed a playful finger into Kara's shoulders. "And what about you? What big thing happened at work that they had to call you on your off day?"

Kara waved her hand dismissively. "Oh *that*. That was just me getting put in charge of our big anniversary marketing campaign for next year."

"You did!" Merridy stopped walking to jump up and down in excitement. "Yes! I knew you would! I told you they'd recognize your talent." She pulled her friend in for a tight hug. "It's everything you've been working toward. I'm so proud of you."

"Thank you. It means a lot to hear that." Kara wrapped her arms around her friend and sighed. "This means I'll be really busy with this project. All the meetings, the storyboards..."

Merridy patted her back. "I understand my friend. I know it's going to be crazy, and intense, but you'll also be the happiest lady ever because it's what you wanted. You've put everything into your career."

The two parted from their hug. "Yes. I guess I really have." She smiled. "I have so many ideas flooding my mind."

"Then best we get you to a seat so you can start writing them down... while I enjoy a nice hot chocolate with my ankles propped up."

"You have got to start working out and strengthening those ankles." Kara linked arms with her best friend and headed toward the coffeeshop's plush couch. "But in the meantime, while I'm brainstorming, I could use some music. Like the sound of you telling me all about this guy you met."

"Don't get too excited. He told me he was late for a date, and his lock screen had him and a beautiful woman on it." Merridy offered her friend a frown. "I saw when he got his phone out. She was gorgeous, Kara."

"As are you." Kara shook a finger at her. "Don't jump to conclusions though. Date can mean many things. Could be a business transaction. Could be piano lessons. Could be tea with his sister - who *could* be the beautiful woman on the phone screen."

"Despite the fact they looked *nothing* a-like?"

"Maybe... cousins?" Kara edited her statement with a hopeful smile.

Merridy shook her head. "I'm just going to be grateful that someone who trains kids in hockey is taking time to help me. I'll need a juvenile-level training, for certain." She flagged a nearby waitress. "Besides, it takes some of the awkwardness out of it right? He'd be touching my legs and ankles and such. Now I can just look at him as a teacher. And focus on my training, and my music, and..."

"Your marketing." Kara buried herself back into the couch. "Oh Merry-Berry. I will still find time to do your marketing. I promise. We'll get your name out there before the event."

"Don't worry about that Kara! Your work is far more important. I can do some of my own marketing." Merridy offered a huge smile to her friend. "I mean, I don't understand that world like you do. But if you point me in the right direction, I can do the heavy lifting."

Kara pulled her bag between them and slipped out her tablet. "I was going to book you a professional photoshoot with a friend of mine that owes me a favor. We need to do a little shopping for your shoot. And then I can set up your page and website... Okay, I know, I need you to pick some songs to record a video of you singing."

"I thought you were about to suggest for me to go shopping. I can do that..." Merridy ordered her drink with a grin. "Unless you think my sense of style is outdated."

Her friend tossed her the tablet. "There is a certain look I think we should shoot for."

Merridy perused the pictures her friend had collected. Photo-after-photo of elegant yet wholesome women modeling a boho-chic wardrobe filled the screen. "I do like these clothes. I would totally wear them." She flipped a few more pages, noting the semi-smug look on her friend's face. "But you already knew that. That's why you picked them."

"The best way to market you is by being true to you. I'm not going to suggest you be anything other than what you are inside." Kara produced a small notepad from her purse and began jotting notes. "That's my plan with this company too. Be true to the company's values. Not just any company reaches 150 years old in America. And there's a reason they did." Her words began to mumble as she leaned closer to the notepad, deep in her brainstorming.

A smile passed on Merridy's face as she watched her friend's creative process at work. She wished such sparks of inspiration could hit her as they did her friend. Instead, she would stare for hours at her piano or guitar, hoping a song would hit her, and receiving only a line and a chord. Her eyes drifted back to the tablet. She knew her friend would want to go shopping with her, and, therefore, she decided to focus on deciding which songs to practice for her first videos.

Chapter 3

"You're late."

Jacob rushed into the ornate hall of a downtown luxury hotel. The sounds of a string quartet echoed from the Grand Ballroom, and past the double doors he could make out a mingling of sequined gowns and black ties. But in the hallway, a fierce figure stood between him and the party. She wore a sinfully red strapless gown with a slit high on her jutting right leg, both arms akimbo with painted nails digging into her hips. Despite the red-carpet makeover, anger exuded out of her. "I know," he replied. "That's why I texted you that I was running late, and that I was sorry."

"That doesn't change the fact that I had to show up *alone*, getting pictures *alone*..." She shook her head. "Do you know what that does to our image? My image? The rumors that could start..."

He slumped his shoulders slightly as she continued her rampage. "I'm sorry Ameleah. Sorry for images and rumors, and heaven forbid I ever arrive late anywhere." He shoved his thumb toward the direction he came from. "The press is still out there. They asked why I came separately and I told them... I was late. Because you're a punctual person, and I'm not. Hence my nickname. Shouldn't that stop *any* rumors?"

Ameleah eyed him. With her false lashes and heavy mascara, her narrow eyes appeared like a giant mass of darkness. "You know you're not good with the press. Why wouldn't you consult me first?"

"Because you were in there," he pointed at the ballroom, "and I was out there." His finger quickly pointed behind him. "Now can we get in there," the fingered returned to pointing at the

31

ballroom, "and leave this argument out here?" The finger finally pointed to the floor he stood on. "This *is* a function hosted by *my* team."

"Fine." One of her hands flailed out in a motion of frustration. "Take my arm, and we'll go in together as a proper couple." She held an arm out for him to take.

He hesitantly took it. "Or just as a couple, Ameleah." He walked into the room hoping to avoid the sharp side-eye she gave him. He knew if he could smile and say a few greetings alongside her, he would finally be released to see his best friend and his brother, both of whom played for his team. Subtly, she pulled him toward a group of older gentlemen with younger women on their arms. Each woman was more beautiful and wore more expensive clothes and jewelry than the next.

"White Rabbit!" shouted one of the men with a handclap on Jacob's back. "Was afraid you wouldn't be able to make it when I saw Miss Ameleah here alone."

"Oh, you know me, I always show up late in the game!" Jacob joked. He felt Ameleah's arm stiffen around his, and he stopped his chuckling. "But yes, I was on the ice and lost track of time."

Ameleah plastered a smile on for the group. "That's my Jacob. He adores the ice. If it wasn't for me, he'd practically live in an igloo."

The group shared a laugh, though Jacob only shyly smiled at the sentiment.

"Speaking of which, we are looking at homes in Stargrove," Ameleah announced to the group. "Mr. Branson, isn't that where you live? Is it a lovely neighborhood?"

Jacob steadied his breathing and kept a fixed smile on his face.

"Quite lovely, quite lovely," the man replied back. "Will you be buying a pre-built home, or one of the available lots? I always recommend purchasing a lot and getting an architect to design a one-of-a-kind piece. And of course, the material selection would be higher-end than you get in a pre-built model."

"Of course!" Ameleah hastily agreed. "I couldn't imagine living anywhere someone else lived. The high-rise I'm in now was brand new when I moved in. But, a little too small for a power couple. Wouldn't you say dear?"

"Um," Jacob responded. He suddenly thought of the cozy craftsman home he grew up in. He adored the details in the wood paneling and the love put in the handmade tiles of the bathrooms. "I guess?" It was all he could offer Ameleah. Her glare came swiftly, and faded just as suddenly before the others could note it.

As if they sensed his aura of dread and misery, his teammates found him. "Jacob! Buddy!" His best friend, Terry Sanger, walked through the group to throw his arms around his neck. The rapid and fierce hug broke the hold Ameleah had on Jacob's arm. "Come with us. We're taking a group photo of the team." With his back to Ameleah, Terry offered Jacob a wink. "Team captain has to be front and center."

A sigh of relief escaped from Jacob. "Of course!" He kissed Ameleah on the cheek. "Sorry, dear, duty calls." He followed Terry away toward the opposite end of the ballroom. "Is there really a team picture happening, or...?"

"Not yet," Terry responded with a wink. "But there will be once we round up all the guys."

The team captain cast a worried glance over his shoulder. Ameleah's cold gaze pierced him despite the distance put between the two. "We'll need one, or she will flip."

"Or you can man up and tell her to stop treating you like you're her property." Terry shrugged. "Your choice. But this is exactly why I don't get into committed relationships."

"You don't get in committed relationships because no woman would put up with you," Jacob joked. He walked up to his brother, Eddie, and a few of the other players who huddled together away from their spouses and significant others. "Yo, Eddie, team photo at the far wall."

Eddie stroked his beard. "By the far wall? You mean where the food and drinks are?"

"With you, it's always where the food and drinks are," Jacob sighed. He patted his own belly. "Working on the dad-bod already?"

The fellow teammates laughed at the joke. "Laugh all you want," Eddie defended himself, "but she finds my beard and body gorgeous." He motioned for his friends to follow them to the far side of the wall. "Let me guess, we're running away from Ameleah?" he discreetly asked his brother.

"Why Eddie, how could you guess?" Terry asked from Jacob's other side. He poked his head around Jacob in order for Eddie to see his mischievous grin. "Is it how quickly he's walking, or how he's working hard and pulling the captain card to gather everyone together?"

"It's because at the last three functions, he's done all he can to avoid her."

"What?" Jacob asked. He stopped walking. "That's not true."

Eddie patted his brother's shoulders. "Rosella's baby shower. Where were you? Where was Ameleah?"

"That was a baby shower. I'm not going to sit with her at a baby shower…" Jacob frowned. "We were all upstairs playing pool while the women did whatever women do at baby showers."

"Season opener," Terry countered. He pushed his finger into Jacob's chest. "You did all you could to stay away from her, but she kept snaking into every picture the press took of you."

Jacob frowned. Perhaps the two guys who knew him best had valid points. "Look, I just needed a little breathing room. The season just started. There's a lot of pressure on us to win the Cup this year. And I'm trying to stay focused on getting the Art Ross this year."

"You're trying to win the Art Ross every year," Terry reminded him. "Every. Year."

"The more goals I get, the more goals the team gets, and the more wins we get. It's not a bad *goal*." Jacob grinned. "Get the pun?"

Eddie stared at him and shook his head. "Never again, little brother."

"I don't know, buddy," Terry continued. "If I didn't know any better, I would think you're finally seeing how Ameleah uses you. Took you forever. Late as always, White Rabbit."

"She's not using me," Jacob defended Ameleah. "We don't see eye to eye on everything, but we *do* care about each other." He noted the last group of team members walking their way and waved them over. "Maybe it's the public eye just getting to her. It's changing her. But when I get the chance, we'll talk. I'm sure it will all work out." He frowned. "Being late to this didn't really help my case though."

"Why *were* you late?" Terry asked. "I mean, it's your natural state, but you've always got the best excuses."

Jacob rolled his eyes. "I was helping someone, if you must know."

"Uh-huh," Terry stroked the stubble growing on his chin.

Before he could ask more details, the entire team gathered around Jacob. "Let's take your photo. Everyone huddle together," one of the event photographers directed. After several minutes of pointing the group of rowdy men in the right directions, the flashes of cameras began to surround them. The antics of his fellow teammates caused Jacob to laugh, and he finally felt comfortable for the first time since arriving at the gala.

"Nice," Ameleah told him as the group began to disperse. She stood behind a photographer. "I'm sure it will be all over Twitter."

"I think the morning news is here too..." Jacob began.

"Excuse me, could you take our picture?" Ameleah asked the photographer she stood next to, effectively cutting off Jacob from talking. "You're with the monthly, correct?"

The photographer flashed his badge with an affirmative nod.

"Excellent," Ameleah stated. She wrapped an arm around Jacob's waist. "We're big fans of the monthly. Smile for our friends, Jacob." Her other hand fell to her hip, and she flashed a well-rehearsed smile to the camera. Jacob followed suit. "I believe our seats are at that table, with the big donors. Everyone wants a team captain, of course."

"Of course. Guess that means Terry is at the other table." He noted his friend finding his place at the other head table. That was always the case at donor-based events. The bigger the star, the more the people paid to sit at a table with them. Jacob never felt like a 'celebrity athlete'. He simply played the sport

table with their favorite hockey celebrity, and *you* are standing them up. You have an obligation."

"I also have a bladder," he replied. "I was coming back. This is why I said 'excuse me'. That's the polite thing to say, isn't it? I don't announce to people 'Hey I have to go to the bathroom.' Or is that the chic thing to do now?" He folded his arms angrily across his chest. "And do you hear yourself? They paid to sit with *me*? My obligation? Did you not listen to my speech?"

Ameleah's gorgeous face contorted with her rage. "Of course, I listened to your speech. I was impressed. I'm wondering who your speech writer was... is that why you were late?"

His hands flew up to his head in frustration. The fingers traced through his slicked-back, dark brown hair as he took in long, deep breaths. "I can't believe you. That was no speech writer. That was from my heart. That is how I feel." He frowned. "You used to be that way, Ameleah. What happened?"

"What happened?" she yelled. "Nothing *happened*. I still *care*. Did you miss when my name was called out? I gave twenty-grand to this pet project of yours. That is a lot of *caring*." She turned back to the ballroom. "And I *won't* be spoken down to or insulted, when I am here, trying to help you please your donors and maintain a good image. It takes a lot of work to groom you. Cover for you." Her hand landed on the ballroom door. "I expect you back in your seat in ten minutes. Try not to be late, *White Rabbit*."

Jacob stood, stunned. Another buzz on his phone broke his trance. "Groom me?" he muttered. He continued to the restroom, fumbling with his phone to read his messages.

'Oh dear. Turnip Girl? Is this my new nickname now? I hope not, though I guess it's better than Radish Girl. Say that too fast, and it sounds like Rash Girl. But yes, she is the former hockey player, and she is one of the best people I know, so you might be right! And I can't help that I don't know hockey. My family grew up playing football and riding horses, you knew that from earlier today. I could tell you all about football – I could probably be a pretty efficient referee. But hockey? I'm not even sure what our team is called. Tornados? What's your nickname anyway?'

'Sorry. That may have been too forward to ask you your nickname? I'm not very good with words. My foot is put in my mouth a lot. So, so sorry. I'll stop bugging you. Except to say thank you, one more time. Thank you!'

Jacob paused outside of the restroom door, smirking at the text messages. Despite having met the woman only briefly that day, he could imagine her cheeks blushing while typing the last message.

'My nickname is White Rabbit. And that's
not too forward at all, Turnip Girl. I look
forward to you becoming a world-famous
musician. Everyone will be shouting your
name 'Merridy! Merridy! Merridy!' and I
will simply laugh and say 'Turnip Girl'. ;)'

'And by the way, the hockey team is
called Texas Twisters. Like a tornado.
I'll give you a few points for being close.'

He smirked at his own cleverness and tucked the phone in his
pocket. By the time he had finished and washed his hands, the
phone buzzed once more.

'That explains your random quote earlier.
I was curious if you were a Wonderland
fan, then I caught myself saying
'curiouser and curiouser', which then
made me Alice. Hey can my nickname be
Alice instead of Turnip Girl? I mean, it's
nicer to be an Alice than a root vegetable
that I've never even had before.'

'Absolutely not. You don't get to pick
your nicknames. And Alice fell chasing
the White Rabbit. You didn't fall because

45

the White Rabbit caught you. It just
wouldn't be right.'

'Very true. I guess instead of a knight-
on-shining-skates, that makes you a
rabbit-on-shining-skates. Probably why
you're a good skater too. Rabbits have
those huge feet. Compared to Turnips,
who are known for their prowess on the
ice. Haha.'

Jacob laughed at her response. He glanced at his watch and
noted the time. Three minutes to get back in his seat according
to Ameleah's demand. His eyes drifted between the watch and
his text messages. "What are you doing?" he whispered to
himself. "You met this girl today. Your girlfriend of seven years
is in there waiting for you to return." He sighed deeply and
headed back to the ballroom.

'I have to go silent for a bit. I'm at a
charity ball thing and have to talk with
some donors. Not my favorite fancy
events, but I guess it is for a good cause.
My Sunday is pretty booked too, but I
have an early practice on Monday. Would
you be up for some skating lessons that
afternoon? Whenever you're free after
2?'

A momentary pause followed his message.

> 'I understand. It's your very important date. :) Monday works for me. How about 3. The rink in South Hills. I'll meet you there. Have a great night and weekend!'

Satisfied with the response, he returned to his chair precisely at the ten-minute mark. Ameleah mouthed a silent 'thank you' to him and discreetly drifted her hand over to his thigh. He covered her hand with his and remained distracted throughout the rest of the event. On one hand, he held his girlfriend's hand. But the other hand stayed fixed over his phone.

Chapter 4

Kara and Merridy walked down the sidewalk from their church to the downtown shops and restaurants of South Hills. "After our visit to Evelyn, we could do a photoshoot," she suggested. "Since you're wearing one of your new outfits. We'll still do the professional shoot later, of course."

"I suppose it must be done to overhaul my profile." Merridy pointed out the art-deco front of their friend's café. "Downtown would be a cute place to do the photos. Plus the park." She lifted the guitar case in her other hand. "I also picked out what song I'm going to do for my first video. It's one we did this morning, so I have a few practices under my belt."

"Oh really?" Kara grabbed the door handle of the coffeeshop they were headed to and held it open for Merridy. "Which one?"

"Thank you, and 'It is Well'." Merridy noted the woman behind the coffeeshop counter. "Hey, hey Evie!" She cheerily called to the woman. "How are you sweetie? We miss you on Sunday mornings." She hurried around the counter to hug her friend.

"I miss being there. But I have the church livestream playing while I work." Evelyn turned to Kara. "Hey sister."

"Hey darling." Kara hugged Evelyn tightly. "The place is empty," she added with concern. "I know it's been slow, but..."

"Well, yes..." Evelyn sighed. "It's been getting a little worse each month. I've been thinking about leaving since spring. I saw it coming, but I just don't know where to go, how to fund it, what to do with the house. And, I found out the rental agreement has me stuck here through the end of next year unless someone can take over my lease. And there's no going

48

out of business clause. And there's no fixed rate on the rent, apparently?"

Kara exchanged a worried glance with Merridy.

"Everyone's favorite Seattle-based coffee company is now a block away, has a line of customers constantly, and they can hire dozens of employees. All I have is me – and I can't even give myself a salary. It's killing me to see all these people moving to South Hills, and instead of bringing me more business, it's made me lose the business I had."

Kara hugged her again. "It's a factor which city governments never think of when encouraging population booms. Chain stores and restaurants move-in and run out the small businesses."

"It's so hard," Evelyn's voice broke. "I miss Zeke, Kara. I miss him so much. Your brother was better at this. He was the businessman."

The mention of her brother caused Kara to bite her lip. She refused to give into the feelings of loss and emptiness that filled her heart every time she thought of her family. "We will figure out something," she told her sister-in-law. "We're family after all, right?"

Evelyn sobbed at the sentiment. "Yes, we're family. But, Kara, I can't ask you to take this on. You shouldn't burden..."

"Quiet," Kara interrupted her. "My brother wasn't the only one with business-sense. Now, let's have some lunch. You hungry, Merridy?" She shot her friend a significant glance.

"Absolutely," Merridy responded, understanding the meaning of the glance. "And super thirsty."

Wiping her eyes with her sleeve, Evelyn stepped behind the counter. "In that case, what can I get you ladies?"

"I am going to need the egg white spinach wrap, a side of the mixed berry parfait, the strawberry salad, a cheese Danish, a large mocha latte with 2%, a medium orange juice, and two bottles of water." Merridy grinned at the awe-struck Evelyn. "I didn't have breakfast."

Evelyn smiled. "Thank you, Merridy. That will be $35.10. Will you be paying with cash or card?"

"Card, ma'am." Merridy handed her card over to Evelyn while Kara glanced over the display of already fresh baked goods.

"Here are your two waters and a glass of orange juice, ma'am." Evelyn handed Merridy her drinks. "Your food and latte will be out shortly."

"I'll go get us a table," Merridy told Kara with a wink. She dropped the water bottles in her over-sized bag and took her orange juice and guitar case to a table by the window.

"You know what," Kara said. "I'll need that egg white spinach wrap too, the overnight berry grains, four madelines, a large pineapple hibiscus on ice, a large caramel macchiato, a bottle of water, and I'm about to have a business meeting so I'm going to need a half-dozen of those lemon poppy muffins."

Evelyn gasped at Kara.

"And I'll be paying with cash," Kara finished. She handed a hundred-dollar bill to Evelyn. "The change can go in the tip jar."

"Kara..."

"And can I get a pre-order of muffins to-go for the morning? I'll need some to take to my office. I'm on breakfast duty this week."

Evelyn's eyes began watering at the kindness Kara was showing her. "We can certainly arrange that." The two worked on the next morning's muffin order before Evelyn turned to make their drinks and food. Kara joined Merridy at the table with her bottle of water and lemon poppy muffins.

"You're a good person," Merridy told Kara.

"So are you," Kara responded back. "You ordered a fair number of things." She began peeling the wrapper off one of the muffins. "Evelyn was always an amazing baker. That's where her heart is, I think. The coffee was always my brother's passion. I think he picked it up while playing ball in Europe."

"Basketball?" Merridy asked with a surprised squeak.

"Yep, in a European league."

"Wow, I had no idea." Merridy grabbed a muffin. "I knew he had been to Europe because he told me about Italy a lot. I didn't realize it had been for that. Your family is gifted with athleticism and business-sense."

Kara sadly examined the empty café. "I wish he had had a little more sense to have a solid plan for Evelyn. Why would he sign a rental agreement for such a long term but without a fixed rate? I didn't think such a rental agreement would be possible." Kara sighed. "I miss him so much. He was my supporter, no matter what, and no matter from where. When he moved back to the States, I was so excited to have him near again." She thoughtfully took a bite of her muffin. As she chewed, she pulled her tablet out from her bag. "Keeping this place going has to be eating through the insurance money. If she could find a sub-lease or at least break even to cover operational costs and living expenses until the lease expires, she could sell the house and relocate to someplace smaller and cheaper."

"Does she want to leave?" Merridy asked. "I mean, what if we could just bring her business? Get the word out there. Maybe she wouldn't have to leave."

"When she brings our food, I'm going to ask her to sit down and tell me what she wants. And I will help her get there." She shoved the rest of her muffin in her mouth. "These are really good," she added, in between her chewing.

Merridy laughed. "Yes, they are." She smiled toward Evelyn who carried a loaded tray to the two. "As is all the food Evie makes!"

"Thank you Merridy." She began setting their food and drinks on the table, listing them as she went. "I think that's everything. Enjoy your meal ladies."

"Wait, Evie," Kara told her with a hand on her arm. "Please sit and talk with us."

Evelyn glanced around the café and the sidewalk outside. "I guess I've nothing else to do." She pulled a third chair up to the table.

"Tell me, do you want to stay here, in South Hills? In this location? If business could turn around, would you want this place?"

The question Kara posed caused Evelyn to lower her head in thought. "I wanted to, at first. I wanted to keep this place going in honor of Zeke. His hopes and dreams were in this place. He loved South Hills, and this downtown space, and he was so proud of this coffee. He wanted to make an unlimited coffee bar." She shook her head. "He was all about the coffee and the perfect roast, because of Italy and Spain, you know." Her lips quivered from the held-in tears. "I want a bakery. A proper bakery, where I can make weddings cakes, and the coffee doesn't have to be the perfect roast because that's not why people come. I'm not good with coffee. And honestly, there are too many bakeries in South Hills to compete with. It's just as bad as the influx of corporate coffeeshops. I want to find a quiet, small town out in the country and open a bakery there, and just live a simple life. The city is here now, and I was never much a city girl."

Kara reached a hand out to Evelyn. Her sister-in-law took her hand and squeezed it tightly. "I thought as much Evie. I can see it in your eyes. This isn't the world you belong in anymore. You always loved the quiet life. You just fell in love with a globe-trotting city boy."

They exchanged a giggle. Merridy even joined their laughter before asking, "What's the game plan Kara? I know you're already thinking of something."

"First step is putting a notice out there that you're looking for a sub-lease. But we won't take just any sub-letter. Some people smell the desperation and try to stick you with covering partial lease. It's, ridiculous, to say the least. In the meantime, we increase business to at least cover your costs. We'll work on your online presence, do specials of the day so you're offering a smaller menu daily – quality instead of quantity, and I think live music several times a week would draw people in. Folks love drinking fancy coffees and eating carbs while listening to music."

"I can't pay a musician, Kara," Evelyn laughed.

Merridy snapped her fingers. "I know just the lady who will do it for free." She met Kara's smiling eyes. "This is perfect, for us both, Evie. I get a recurring gig, and you get free entertainment."

"I think the basic plan is settled. I just have a bit of work to do on my end," Kara grinned. "Now, I have a lot of food to eat, and a lot of social media work to do. Evie, you have a menu to work on. Daily specials for the next week, both food and drink. Then cut your old menu down a bit as well. Merridy… well, you eat too."

The plan made all three excited and hopeful. Evelyn hurried to her kitchen to begin assessing the most popular menu items. Kara blindly ate her meal while her eyes were glued to her tablet screen. And Merridy stared at her blank phone while she shoved berries in her mouth. Every ounce of her wanted to message Jacob that she had a new gig. But the text message from the night before was clear that he was too busy to communicate today. The thought made her sigh.

"What's wrong buttercup?" Kara asked her without looking up from her tablet or food.

"I was just thinking about…" Merridy shook her head. "Never mind. It's silly."

"You were thinking about your man," her friend corrected her. "That was certainly the longing, pining sigh of early relationship butterflies."

"He's not my man, and we're not in a relationship," Merridy shot back. "He's just, kind of fun to talk to. We didn't text much last night. But what we did say was pretty fun."

Kara finally allowed her eyes to drift from her screen to Merridy. "Ladybug, you were *beaming* last night. I've not seen you that giddy in a long time. I'm happy for you."

The sentiment caused Merridy to blush. "I was laughing, maybe. I don't know about beaming. He kept calling me Turnip Girl because I told him I didn't know a hockey puck from a turnip when he helped me skate. And he said his friends call him White Rabbit because he's always late."

"White Rabbit?" The familiar name caused Kara to tilt her head in contemplation. "And his name was Jacob? What was his last name?"

"Um…" Merridy paused. "You know, I don't know his last name. I guess that's scary, if you think about it."

Kara's fingers swiftly tapped on her tablet, and she held the screen up to Merridy. "Is this your White Rabbit?"

An image of Jacob in a black jersey with the number '14' emblazoned on it filled the screen. "Yes! That's him! How did you…"

"Oh, my, goodness, Merridy!" Kara exclaimed. "Your White Rabbit is famous. He's Jacob Kenway. He's the captain of the Texas Twisters, our professional hockey team."

"What?" Merridy squeaked. "He said he helps kids learn to skate, and that he worked *with* a hockey team. He didn't say he was a hockey superstar!"

Kara took her friend's hands in hers. "Listen, he probably liked the idea that you didn't know who he was, and you were treating him like any other person. And honestly, he does help kids learn to skate. It's one of his charities. And he does work *with* a hockey team, aside from the Twisters. He works with Team Canada. He's an Olympic gold medalist. He's…" Kara's excitement waned. "He's also dating Ameleah Antoine, the swimmer-turned-model-turned-designer."

The revelation made Merridy's face turn pale. "Oh."

"I'm sorry, Merridy. But, he really does seem to be a genuinely nice guy in everything he does. I don't know a single story that mentions otherwise. He fights on the ice, but even the guys he fights love him as a fellow player. Fans love him. To be fair, I think his intentions to help you are honest. He really *does* want to help you." Kara frowned. "I'm sorry I was pushing you into a more romantic light with him. I was hoping for the best."

Merridy pulled her hands back. "No. No, it's okay. Like I said before, he wasn't my man, and I even thought he was with someone. I bet it was the girl on the phone lock screen I saw. I think I knew, in my gut, that he was a taken guy just helping stranger." She waved her hand and turned back to her food. "Nothing more to think about. I have to finish this food, figure out where the stage area will be in here, make sure my teeth are clean, makeup is good, and we have a photoshoot and video to finish while the lighting is good." She lowered her fork from her strawberry salad and turned her attention to the Danish. "Glad I ordered this guy."

Chapter 5

The arena cheered as the final buzzer sounded. "Twisters win it! 3-2 thanks to a late goal by Jacob Kenway!" Jacob nodded his head in acknowledgement as his teammates patted his back and shoulders in celebration. "Another last minute save by the White Rabbit!" the announcer continued.

Jacob steadied his breathing and skated over to his coach. "Good job, kid." His coach winked and nodded to him before turning his attention to the other team's coach.

"Gather up guys," Jacob called out for his team to line up. They formed a line to high-five the other team in the tradition of good sportsmanship. He shared a mumbled 'good game' and masculine hug with the other team's captain before disappearing to the locker room. He tossed his gear to their allocated places and peeled his sweat-soaked jersey off. "Geez, finally," he sighed. He leaned back against the wooden frame of his hutch with a sigh.

The blinking light on his phone caught his eye. A surge of hope hit him. Before any of his teammates entered the room, he grabbed the phone and swiped to check his messages. Hope dissolved as swiftly as it had come. He noted missed messages from Ameleah and his mother. None from Merridy. He checked the message from his mom first.

"Hi, Snickerdoodle. Your friend Ameleah just reached out to me about visiting? I didn't know you were moving in together and getting serious enough for her needing to 'get to know me better'. Does your old mum not get the inside scoop anymore? Anyway, I won't respond to her until we talk. Hope you see this after the game. Love you, cookie.'

Jacob stared at the phone, dumbfounded. His anger began to boil within, overwhelming him to the point he barely noted the rest of the team and a few reporters entering the locker room.

"Man of the hour!" Terry shouted. He rubbed Jacob's hair and kissed the top of his head. "They're all lining up for you."

"Sure," Jacob curtly responded.

Terry's joviality stopped as he noted Jacob's dark expression. "What's wrong, bro?" He began removing his soak-stained uniform.

"I'm reading missed messages from Ameleah."

"Ooooh!" Terry halted the progression with his uniform and spun around. "Yo, Eddie! You need to come over here for this!"

Jacob did not even wait for his brother to arrive before reading the texts out loud. "Message One: Hey, I secured us an appointment with an architect from New York. He's flying down to meet us Monday afternoon. Mark your calendar."

Eddie sat in the chair next to Jacob. "No, what day and time works for you?" he asked.

"Message Two: Since we're building a house together, we are going to need a storage unit for some of your things, or send to those poor people donation places. Your 'aesthetic' doesn't mesh with my vision. It's critical for when I invite the design magazines over for the tour."

"Whoa!" Terry shouted, shocked at both the audacity and condemnation within the message. Other teammates, intrigued by the commotion, gathered around.

"Message Three: Perhaps you need to contact your mom for a luncheon? With the engagement, it's important I get to know her."

His brother scratched his head. "You're engaged?'

Ignoring the questioning, Jacob continued with the reading. "Message Four: Why aren't you responding? Message Five: I left your mom a message myself. Seriously Jacob, I feel more like your social assistant than your fiancée." The comment made those listening snigger chortle amongst themselves. "Message Six: Why are you silent? Is this still about that incident last night? When you came back, I thought everything was settled." Jacob finished the message with a scream and threw his phone at the open duffle bag in his locker hutch. "What is wrong with her?" he shouted. "I never proposed! I never agreed to move in together! She's deciding everything for me!"

His outburst, though justified, made Terry turn to the few reporters in the locker room with wide eyes. "Alright, members of the press, we request you to please leave. This is a private affair, and we request the courtesy of you not reporting on it… if you want to maintain your access to the after-game locker room." Terry and a couple of other teammates and trainers ushered the reporters out of the room.

Jacob punched the wall of his hutch in his frustration and roared more profanity aimed at Ameleah's behavior.

"How are you going to respond to her?" Eddie casually asked. He had his phone in his hands, and his thumbs flew across the screen. "I'm letting mom know you're not engaged to Ameleah and to ignore the crazy bat."

"I don't even want to speak to her. How do I respond to that? Anything I say would..." He paused, staring angrily at the phone in his bag.

"Lead to a break up?" Eddie completed his younger brother's sentence. "After that, probably not the worst outcome. Why are you bent on keeping this going? She's hot, yeah, but she's not the only hot fish out in the Dallas sea."

"it's not that. We used to have something." Jacob sighed. "When she was just focused on her swimming, everything was fine. And it wasn't the worst when she started modeling. But now... she's focused on making everyone else happy except us." Speaking it aloud permitted Jacob to steady himself, though it did not ease his frustration with Ameleah. "Tell Terry he's up for the press conference." Without showering, he threw a t-shirt on, grabbed his duffle bag, and slid out of the locker room by the back door.

He felt his phone buzz once more, and he held his breath. He hoped it was his mom responding about Eddie's text, and not another message from Ameleah. He did not know if he could maintain the recently attained composure if it was from Ameleah. Gingerly, he lifted the phone out of his duffle. It buzzed again before he could see the screen.

'Hey lady – wanted to let you know Evelyn is in a tight spot. We're going to try to have an event at her place. I'll be playing. Would you be able to help out with a sound system? Can I rent them from the church?'

'Oops! You are clearly not Jessica nor are you a lady! So sorry – yikes – hope you're having a good Sunday!'

The messages caused him to smile. Merridy was a welcome distraction, and the contents of the message intrigued him.

'You caught me. I'm not Jessica. And I don't have a sound system on hand. The day went… interesting. Good and bad. What's going on? What's happening with your friend? Anything I can help with? I wouldn't mind hearing you sing at an event.'

He paused before hitting send. "Is this because I'm mad at Ameleah, or because I'm serious?" With a few moments of deliberation, he slowly pressed 'send'. Shoving the phone into his bag again, he hurried into the arena's underground parking lot. "What do I do? What do I say to Ameleah?" Frustrated, confused, and angry, he ran his fingers through his hair. "What do I say to Merridy?" In his search for his keys, he felt the phone buzz again. Retrieving both from the duffle, he opened his trunk and threw the bag inside.

'Again, I'm really sorry for texting you. I know you said you were busy today. But my friend owns a coffeeshop in downtown South Hills that's not doing well since her husband passed away and competition moved in. If you ever wanted to grab a cup of coffee there, I'm sure that would help. And if you really wanted to see me perform there, I will let you know when the event is. Won't lie... it would be pretty cool to see you there. :)'

Jacob fell into the driver's seat with a sigh. He tossed the keys and phone into his cup holders and stared at both without starting the car. Her message caused the continuance of his dilemma. Merridy appeared to be a genuinely amiable and munificent person. Clearly, she was loyal to her friends and cared about their well-being, and all while trying to pursue her dream. Potentially, even, at the cost of spending time on the pursuit of that dream. Her sweet nature and authenticity allured him. Why? Because they were the same qualities that he wished Ameleah still possessed.

Seven years ago, he met Ameleah at a charity event for Dallas athletic afterschool programs. She spoke of the importance of swimming for all ages. She cared about funding a multi-pool natatorium for the city's youth to train and compete. She truly cared. Now the natatorium was falling into disrepair with no water in the basins, and she had no knowledge of it. She did not care to have knowledge of it. The altruistic spark in her slowly faded the more she toured the modeling circuit and spent time with her extended family in France. She returned to

Dallas to begin her own fashion company with a pseudo-Parisian accent and a different outlook on life. He wanted the Ameleah of seven years ago.

Reaching up to press the 'on' button of his car, he sighed. He had to speak with her. Once his systems booted up, he gave a voice command to call Ameleah.

Within moments, she answered the call. "Where have you been? I've been texting you for hours."

"I'm sorry. I was beating Winnipeg," he seethed. "Hard to text you when my phone is in a bag in the locker room, and I'm on the ice in front of twenty-thousand people."

There was a pause on her end. Finally, she offered a snort. "I guess I should apologize for forgetting you had a game today."

"You guess?" He bit his lip to maintain composure. "I guess that's as close to an apology as you're capable of. Ameleah... we need to talk."

"Yes, we have a lot to do. I am arranging my vision board now for the meeting with Mr. Merriweather tomorrow. He's English, but I think he really will do justice for the French chateau I'm picturing..."

Jacob propped his elbow against his car door to fidget with his hair. "Ameleah, we are not moving in together."

"But..."

"And we're not engaged."

Audible silence festered over the car's speakers.

"I never asked you to move in with me. You suggested it, publicly, in front of others. And I don't want to build a chateau or any other gaudy mansion. And I absolutely never, ever, proposed to you. The fact that you are telling people I have, my own mother, in fact, is an incredible over-step. Not only is it not true, it ruins what should be a magical moment I'm allowed to plan and execute. The proposal is all the guy has."

"We have been together for seven years, Jacob. People expect us to be taking next steps."

"I do not care about what people expect. I care about what is right for us. And maybe if you were the same Ameleah you were when we first started dating, we would be engaged. But you're not, and I might not be the same Jacob, either."

Crying echoed in his car. "Are you… are you breaking up with me?"

He pondered her question. Was he? "I don't know. Sometimes I feel like we should, but then I remember the good times Ami. I want to find those again. Maybe… maybe, we need counseling?"

Her crying calmed slightly. "I can do that."

"Apologies to Mr. Merriweather. If you send me his number, I will call him and cancel…"

"No," she quickly interrupted him. The cries fading faster. "I will handle him. And… I will find us a counselor."

"And Ami, this time ask me what my schedule is. Don't book an appointment for me, please. I had plans already tomorrow afternoon. I couldn't have made the architect meeting anyway."

"Oh…okay. I need to go. This is a heavy conversation for the telephone." The line clicked, indicating her hang up.

Jacob turned to his phone sitting in the cup holder. A deep sigh left him, and he realized his breathing had been restrained during the whole conversation. "Now, to deal with the other problem." He picked up his phone and the open text message from Merridy.

'Hey, I text wrong people all the time. And I was busier earlier, but I'm free now. And that is awesome what you are doing for your friend. I will have to check out the coffeeshop.'

He hesitated in contemplation for his next message.

'I need to tell you something. Because I feel like you are a genuine and honest and nice person. And I don't want to be a jerk that kept anything important hidden. I don't just work with a hockey team. I also captain the Twisters. I am a hockey celebrity, even though I don't want the title. And it was really nice that you had no idea about any of that. But you're going to find out soon enough, and I wouldn't want you to be angry at me for not telling you. Or telling you I have a girlfriend, in case I... seemed to lead you on in anyway. I don't want to be that guy. I really do want to help you skate. If you're still game.'

Fingers crossed; he sent the second text.

Chapter 6

Surrounded by an army of pillows and teddy bears, Merridy sat on her bed with a laptop opened to one side, her phone on another side, and a guitar in her lap. She silently strummed a few chords while staring at the picture on her laptop. Jacob posed on the red carpet for a sports award show. His arm wrapped around the waist of the blonde-haired, blue-eyed, tall, elegant Ameleah Antonie hurt her heart more than she cared to admit. But she could not stop staring at the picture.

"It was only twenty minutes," she chided herself. "And a couple of text messages. What did you think would happen? Mr. Right would fall into your life like an apple on your head?" She focused on the guitar strings, changing chords. "You said you'd give the desire of my heart, and I thought it meant whatever I want..." she sang. She paused and opened a memo pad on her laptop. She typed the words and noted the chord she had been playing.

Her phone dinged. She attempted to ignore it. Her hand drifted to the guitar's strings but once more the phone buzzed. Exasperated, she grabbed the phone and reviewed the messages. Reading the confessions from Jacob caused her to sob. She only had herself to blame. Never once did he lead her on, if she were to be honest. Any potential for romance had only been in her rampant imagination. Yet, the wild fancies of her imagination were enough to cause her turmoil and remove any ability she had to think rationally. With an unintelligible screech, she fell over onto her stuffed animals to cry. Her guitar slipped down to the side of her bed.

After several minutes of ugly crying, she finally calmed herself enough to steady her breathing. "He's being honest," she told herself. "More honest to you than you are to yourself." The truth, she knew, was that she needed his help desperately. She still had the most important audition of her life, and she needed his help to succeed. Merridy closed the picture of Jacob and Ameleah. "Remember, you thought he was taken when he got your number. You stupid girl. You only met him yesterday."

Before she could respond to the text, she stood and walked around her bedroom briefly. The movement allowed her to regain her composure. Once she felt sufficiently like her normal self again, she returned to her seat and picked up her phone.

'I appreciate your honesty with me. To be honest myself, this afternoon my bestie pieced it together. I was telling her that you called me Turnip Girl. When I mentioned you were called White Rabbit, she figured it almost immediately.'

'And I'll be even more honest, the fact I found out you are a celebrity did make me nervous when I accidentally texted you.'

She stared at the phone, considering a third message, but not wanting to appear nervous or too eager.

'I thought my nickname might have given it away. Or at least would eventually. I'm glad there's no ill-will. Maybe after skating practice, I can get you a coffee

or five at your friend's shop. Token of
my good faith.'

'I would like that. Though you don't have
to buy. You never did anything wrong. In
fact, YOU are helping ME.'

'I am certain I will cash in on the favor.
Always good to have a musician 'owe you
one' I think.'

'Oh, I see now. Very cunning, sir.'

'I've been known to have a few 'hat tricks'
up my sleeve. =P'

'Is that... a hockey reference? Ok, if
we're going to be friends, maybe I should
learn about the sport.'

'You don't have to. I'm certain there's
other hobbies I have. When I figure
them out, I'll let you know. :) What are
you up to tonight?'

'I'm working on updating my social media
profiles. Or I was. Then I got
distracted with two lines of a song I'm
trying to write. But that fizzled out too.
Guess I should go back to the social
media stuff.'

Merridy turned to look at her laptop and opened her minimized
social media. Her video that Kara filmed and edited was still
uploading.

'Though the video I'm trying to upload is
taking forever. I don't know if I should
stop it and try again. I'm trying really
hard to be patient.'

'A video? Is it of you singing? I might
have to cyber stalk you.'

'Yeah. It's a music video. My friend is a
marketing genius and filmed and edited it.
She also took a bunch of pictures of me
all day to update my 'look'. It's the worst
feeling being a model. I know it's

necessary, but it's nothing I think I can get used to... how do you do it?'

                    'I didn't. I haven't. Hope I never will.
                    My girlfriend loves it, but I'd be happy to
                    avoid every camera ever.'

'That makes me feel better, actually.
People always act like it's easy to be in
the limelight. Or that the limelight is the
end goal. But it's not, for me. I just want
to do what I love and share it with
others.'

                    'It will never be easy being in the
                    limelight. Best you know that now. I wish
                    someone had told me.'

                    'In other news, do you like dogs?'

'Of course I do!'

She sat her laptop on her nightstand. The progress-circle had moved a few percentages which granted her the peace of mind that the video was still uploading correctly. The guitar was returned to its stand, and she dimmed the lights of her bedroom with an app on her phone. Although the hour grew late, she sensed that she and Jacob would be texting even later, and she made to get comfortable amongst her pillows and stuffed animals. The thought of staying up late to text a friend amused her; she had not done such a thing since college. Another 'ding' indicated Jacob's message. A picture of a massive, fluffy brown and white dog greeted her.

'This is Porthos. He's an American Akita.
Since he's been all up on me here at home,
I thought he wanted to say hi.'

'HELLO PORTHOS! OH MY GOODNESS
HE IS SO HANDSOME AND FLUFFY! I
ADORE HIM! <3'

'I love that he's named after a Musketeer
too!'

'Yes. He's the handsomest good boy.
Possibly part bear. And all of my dogs
have been named after Musketeers. He's
certainly a true Porthos though.
Outgoing, friends with everyone – and
loves food.'

'I don't know what I want to discuss first.
All the adorableness of your puppers or
your knowledge of Dumas' work.'

'I think my puppy's adorableness speaks
for itself. Do you see those eyes?'

Merridy giggled when Jacob sent another picture of him and Porthos curled up on a bed. The dog almost seemed as big as him. She grabbed one of her teddy bears and took a selfie with it. Captioned, 'the only snuggle bear I have', the picture was sent to Jacob.

'You can borrow mine. Be careful though
– he farts.'

The message caused Merridy to burst out laughing, and she let Jacob know.

'I have to know – why the Musketeers for
your dogs?'

'Oh that. :) I read an abridged version of
'The Three Musketeers' when I was a kid
and thought it was cool. I wanted my own
special musketeer that would protect me

like they protected the king. My first
dog as a kid was a shepherd named Athos.
Actually, he was appropriately Athos too.'

'Handsome, noble... but a little broody?
Did your dog have a drinking habit?'

'If water were booze, he'd be exactly
Athos.'

'Alright, tell me about your Aramis and
D'artagnan, if you've had them.'

'Well, luckily my Aramis was not the
womanizer at all. That would have been
awkward. He was a shepherd too. And
my D'artagnan was the only smaller dog I
had. A Jack Russell terrier. His tiny
energy is why I skipped Porthos at the
time and named him after the youngster.
He's actually still alive, but staying with
my mom. They have a bond, and I couldn't
split them apart.'

'That is adorable. I can picture a little terrier jumping around just like an eager D'artagnan. :) Is your mom still in Canada?'

'She and my dad are, and both of my sisters. My brother is on the same team as me, thankfully. I say thankfully, but sometimes it's not so thankful. He's my OLDER brother. And you know how that can go.'

'I am blessed to be an only child – so I don't know how that can go first hand. But I've heard the stories!'

'Lucky you!'

'Sometimes lucky. But it also means I got all the parental attention – for better or worse. Though we did get a dog, a mutt who was part retriever I think, and I named him Johnny. Johnny would sometimes get blamed for things I broke. But he was a good sport about it. And he

was too cute for my mom to stay mad at
for long.'

They began exchanging stories about their pets and childhood. She then questioned his preference for Dumas again, circling back to the inspiration for his dogs' names. They then discussed French literature, all literature, and, consequently, a gauntlet of other media-based entertainment such as movies, television shows, plays, and music. Hours passed until she eventually had to cede that she was too old to still be up at 2am on a school night when she had a 7am conference call. He agreed with the sentiment; his practice started at the same time.

Her eyes drooped reading his final response. Within moments, she was fast asleep with phone still in hand.

Chapter 7

Jacob stumbled into the locker room of the training rink in South Hills. The rink was open to the public, and, on team practice days, fans could watch from the available limited seating. Luckily, there were few fans in the stands at the early hour. He did not mind the morale boost from the fan base, but after yesterday's game, he wanted the team to stay focused – even if he could not be.

"Hey," Terry greeted him. He noted his friend's tired-expression. "Geez, you've seen better days. How did everything go after your storm out yesterday? You fix things with Ameleah?"

"What?" Jacob asked. "Oh, yeah. Ameleah. Yes, she's cancelling the meeting with the architect, understands we're not engaged, and knows we're not moving in together. And she's finding us a relationship counselor." Jacob calmly put his gear away. "Tried to remind her of who she was back then. I want to get back to that."

Terry nodded. "She was pretty awesome back in the day. Little more carefree, and a little less 'what will the press say about every little thing I do'," he attempted to mock her voice. "I blame it on France. She was great until she went there."

"You know, I thought the same thing yesterday," Jacob agreed. "Must be true." He stifled a yawn.

"Did you stay up late dealing with her?" Terry asked him.

"Hmmm?" Jacob asked drearily. "Dealing with who?"

"Ameleah."

Jacob shook his head. "Oh. No. I was up late talking with a friend." He smiled. "Was actually the perfect way to calm down after the whole Ameleah thing."

A high-pitched gasp left Terry as he feigned indignation. "You have a friend other than *moi*?"

His sarcasm earned him a towel thrown at his face. "In fact, I have many other friends than you. She was just the calming and wholesome conversation I needed last night."

"She?" Terry exclaimed. He moved closer to Jacob with a mischievous smile on his lips. "Who is this 'she' that you stayed up late talking to? Do I know her? Have I met her? Is she cute?"

"Whoa," Jacob told him. He put a calming hand on his friend's shoulder. "You don't know her, and she's a friend. I can't judge her cuteness."

"I can. Show her to me." He nodded his head at Jacob's phone. "Show me a pic."

"I don't have a pic of her on my phone."

"You know I will bug you about this all day."

A sigh of defeat left Jacob. "Fine. Here." He used his phone to search for 'Merridy Christmas' on his social media network. Her page popped up, and he clicked her picture for Tyler to see. She stood on the steps of a gazebo with her hands wrapped around one of the posts while leaning back. Her auburn hair flowed in the breeze as did her broomstick skirt. The laughter on her smile and in her eyes made Jacob grin; she was better at being a model than she gave herself credit for. "That's her. She's a friend I'm helping."

"Dude," Terry remarked. "She is *adorable*. She has that plus-sized, girl-next-door, your-mom-will-love-her, waiting-until-marriage, charm." He snatched the phone from Jacob's hand. "Are you going to introduce me to her?"

"No!" Jacob responded and recovered his phone from Terry. "I mean, she's coming over after practice so we can work on her skating. But I'm not hooking you up to date her."

His friend stroked his chin thoughtfully. "Why not? You're with Ameleah. You're not with her. Right?"

"Of course," Jacob quickly answered. "It's just... she's nice. And you are a notorious... how do I put it nicely? Heartbreaker?" Jacob winked. "I'm not losing her as friend because you come on too strong."

Terry feigned innocent, but could not sway Jacob. "Alright, I won't ask her out. But I am meeting her when she comes. What is it that she does? What's the profile about?"

"She's a singer. She's trying to become a professional singer." Jacob gave a half laugh. "That's how we met." He highlighted his Saturday meeting Merridy. "And I have to get her going stable on ice before Saturday. It's a tall order, but she's so determined, I think she can do it."

"Huh," Terry softly said, eyeing Jacob as he spoke. "So, she's the person you were helping and made you late." He slowly nodded his head. "Sounds like quite the woman. Let's hear her sing."

Jacob scrolled down the screen. "She was uploading a video last night. Here it is. Guess the song she's singing is called 'It is Well with My Soul', or that's what the video is called. I don't really know it." He clicked the button, and it started with Merridy playing her guitar alone on a park bench.

When peace, like a river, attendeth my way,
When sorrows like sea billows roll;
Whatever my lot, Thou has taught me to say,
It is well, it is well, with my soul.
It is well, with my soul,
It is well, it is well with my soul.

The scenery changed as she now walked across a bridge over a pond. She no longer played the guitar, though it could still be heard.

Though Satan should buffet,
Though trials should come,
Let this blest assurance control,
That Christ has regarded my helpless estate,
And hath shed His own blood for my soul.
It is well, with my soul,
It is well, it is well with my soul.

Returning to the park bench, the video showed her playing a guitar solo on her acoustic. Jacob was impressed. She spoke of her ability to sing, but her musicality on the guitar was equally impressive.

But, Lord, 'tis for Thee, for Thy coming we wait,
The sky, not the grave, is our goal;
Oh trump of the angel! Oh voice of the Lord!
Blessed hope, blessed rest of my soul!
It is well, with my soul,
It is well, it is well with my soul.

As she entered the final verse, she now had background vocals. Listening hard, Jacob could determine all the vocals were Merridy singing at different octaves to give the end a dramatic effect.

And Lord, haste the day when my faith shall be sight,
The clouds be rolled back as a scroll;
The trump shall resound, and the Lord shall descend,
Even so, it is well with my soul.
It is well, with my soul,
It is well, it is well with my soul.

The video ended with a peaceful, fading shot of the cloud-dotted blue sky above the park.

"Pretty song," Terry responded. "Pretty voice. Pretty girl." He arched an eyebrow at Jacob. "Looked pretty professional."

"Her friend does marketing and helped her with it." Jacob shrugged his shoulders. "Think she wanted something decent out there before the audition for her portfolio." He turned off the screen and slowly lowered his phone to his bag. "She did have a pretty voice," he whispered an agreement.

Terry walked away to his own duffle bag to change for practice. "Man, are you sure I couldn't...?"

"No," Jacob laughed. He commenced to changing his clothes.

Chapter 8

Jacob had told Merridy to come at a time after practice that allowed for him to shower and freshen up, but still he rushed through the whole routine, eager to see her after the hours they spent texting. His mind had been preoccupied all of practice too. The ease of speaking with her, and how transfixed he had felt watching her video, all of it tugged at his stomach. He attempted to deny the feelings. His conversation with Ameleah had been sincere: he wanted to attempt fixing their relationship. And yet, he felt drawn to Merridy. The dilemma agitated him, caused his hands to shake, and his stick work during practice suffered. Yet, he did not want to cast Merridy away from him. He wanted anything but that.

Before he sent his confessional text, he had thought to simply get through the week, fulfill his promise to teach her, and then part ways. But he could not bring himself to do it. His confessional text tested the waters of her personality. And he continued to be surprised at her positive attitude, sincerity, and humor. She even loved his dog.

He grabbed his bag and decided to take it to his car while he waited for Merridy to arrive. The walk might prove useful in distracting his mind, he hoped, or at least clarifying the correct path to take. But when his phone began ringing, he hurriedly grabbed it, thinking it was Merridy. "Hey, I'll be..." he started.

"Jacob! Darling!" Ameleah shouted over the phone. The background noise was immense. "I had to let you know, that Mr. Merriweather could not cancel his flight. He came to Dallas anyway, and I am at the airport to meet him. Are you certain that whatever it is you're doing cannot wait? We can have a lovely dinner at the club..."

An audible, perturbed sigh left Jacob. "No, Ameleah, I can't cancel... much like Mr. Merriweather, apparently. You two enjoy lunch or dinner or whatever it is."

"But Jacob..." she began.

He tossed his bag into the trunk and slammed it shut. "Ameleah, did you even get a hold of a relationship counselor?"

"I... I couldn't find one I liked," she stammered. Her voice held a hint of anger. "Look, I have to go. If you insist on finding a relationship counselor, then find one." The phone clicked off.

Incredulously, he stared at the blank phone. Only a day before, under threat of a breakup, she had been eager to find a counselor for them. Now, she dismissed it with contempt. The phone's screen lit up, distracting him, and he noted the text from Merridy. She had arrived at the rink. He glanced around the parking garage, hoping to spot her. The search was futile. She probably had parked on the ground floor, and most of the players parked in reserved parking on the third floor. He sent a quick message to let her know he would be right there, and, with skates draped over his shoulder, he hurried into the practice arena.

She stood at the floor-to-ceiling plate glass window that separated the arena hall from the rink. Her eyes intently stared at the ice and ignored anyone else around her. The bag on her shoulder appeared to be an oversized purse, but he noted the skates sticking out of them. Her hair was pulled back in a ready-for-business bun. Her dress was a long-sleeve, short-skirt cotton knit, and she wore leggings under it to keep warm on the ice. Jacob paused in his approach to study her. Clearly, the woman had come with the purpose to conquer her need to skate. But her determined stance and girl-next-door outfit caused a wave of panic to flood over him. His mouth, suddenly at a loss for words, sat slightly open.

Was that the same girl that told him her favorite movies were musicals but she never had gone to one? Or that she adored dogs, and lamented that her lease agreement would not allow her to have any pets? And was she the one that told him all about her friend's dilemma with the coffeeshop, with her heart truly breaking over her friend's agony? How could she be the same girl he only met two days before?

"Mah... Merridy!" he finally shouted, words once again forming on his near-lifeless tongue. "Good, you found it."

She turned to him with a wide smile, and he felt his tongue do a belly-flop into the pit of his stomach. "Hi! You know, I've driven past this place so many times, but I've never been inside. I had no idea the big-shot professionals came here to practice."

"Yep, that's us. Big-shots." He pointed his thumb back to where he had come from. "Our executive offices are here, on the other side of the parking garage. Where all the corporate magic happens that keeps us playing. I go in there sometimes because they have an air hockey table. And all forms of hockey are great entertainment." He winked at his sentiment, and slightly swelled with pride that she laughed at his joke.

"*Air hockey*," she stated with a shake of her finger, "is a form of hockey that I'm pretty sure I could compete with you at."

His eyebrow lifted, "Is that so Miss Christmas? I'll have to take you up on that some time." He paused in front of the door to the rink, uncertain if he should greet her with a handshake or hug. One felt too informal, and the other felt far too intimate. He opted for a smile and a beckoning hand wave toward the rink. "Come inside. Let's get laced up and give this a go."

The two entered the rink and began changing into their skates. "At the behest of my friend Kara, I worked out on the elliptical as much as possible and did strength exercises for my legs, especially my ankles. Hoping I'm a bit more prepared today, though not sure what two evenings of workouts will accomplish immediately." She glanced at him with a blush. "Except to realize that I was out of shape more than I thought."

"Not everyone can live at the gym like I do," he offered. It was true. An athlete's job required time at the gym. Her job, did not. Workouts were in addition to the time she spent on her job and her extra work at building a music career. He began to marvel at her ability to balance all that she did in a day. "But if you ever want a workout buddy while I'm in town, I'm always game. You can be my spotter."

"I'd be perfect at that. You know, I can bench press a solid three-hundred pounds." She said the statement so matter-of-factly that Jacob nearly missed the sarcasm. But then she laughed. "You'd be putting your life in God's hands for sure with me as your spotter." She finished lacing and walked toward the ice with wobbly baby steps. "I'm in much more capable hands with yours on ice, than yours in mine in a gym."

"Oh, I'm sure your hands are very capable in other areas." Jacob paused at the statement, afraid that it might be taken the wrong way. "I mean, with like, music." He cleared his throat. "I saw the video you uploaded. It was really well done. Your friend is talented with the filming and editing. And the girl singing was pretty decent too."

Merridy blushed at the compliment but kept her face turned away from Jacob. "Thank you. And yes, Kara is really amazing at what she does. I wouldn't have gotten far in my adult life without her. She's certainly one of my heroes."

"She sounds fantastic. Hopefully, I can meet her sometime." Jacob stood to join Merridy on the edge of the rink. "You ready to become a master ice skater?"

"I'm ready to learn how to skate on my own without falling?" she responded with hope.

Her response caused Jacob to laugh. "That's attainable. Come on." He grabbed her hand and led her onto the ice, less slowly than on Saturday. "Remember everything you learned."

She wanted to protest the speed at which he dragged her onto the ice, but found that her feet seemed to carry her better at the faster speed, much like when she learned to ride a bicycle. She swallowed her protest. He began instructing her at rapid pace on her stance and technique, and she focused on his every word in order to reach her daily goal on the ice. Maximum effort was put into ignoring his hand in hers, or on her arms, shoulders, or legs. The day was to be about training – not about an imagined attraction that could go nowhere.

An hour passed on the ice before Merridy finally felt comfortable skating to Jacob without aid for a distance of five yards. "Yes! Look at you. Only on your second day!" he congratulated her. Without a second thought, he threw his arms around her for a tight hug. "I'm proud of you."

His hug warmed her heart. She closed her eyes and for a moment indulged in the feel of his embrace and the smell of his cologne. "Thank you. It's all due to your work, your help, with me. I couldn't have done this without you." She finally pulled back from his hug. Her eyes drifted up to his own which sparkled with his smile. "I'll always be in your debt." The sparkle in his eye disappeared briefly, she noted. They hastily scanned her face, and she wondered for a moment if he struggled with feelings akin to hers.

But the sparkle returned, and he grinned impishly. "Good. Like I said, musicians are the best to keep in your debt." He winked, and released her from his hug. "Do you feel confidant? Do you think you can practice on your own?"

She frowned. "I think so, yes, but…"

"I mean, we can do some more this evening. And later this week, but I don't want to end *this* session if you don't feel *that level* of confidence."

"Oh, okay, I nearly panicked." She giggled nervously. "Not that I'm needy, but I feel needy."

"And a little hungry?" Jacob asked.

She placed a hand over her stomach and nodded. "I could probably eat."

"I heard about a great coffeeshop downtown. If you'd like to go." He offered his hand to her in a sarcastic, grandiose gesture that caused her to laugh.

"I would love to." She took his hand. "Shall I meet you there?"

"Guess that depends," he started while leading her to the rink's exit. "Do you want to keep training tonight? If so, I can just drive us there and back."

Butterflies formed in her stomach, but she mouthed, "Okay. I do want a bit more training today."

"I admire your tenacity," he complimented her. They changed from their skates to their normal shoes. "Anyone going through this much work deserves to win their audition."

"Hard work doesn't always equate success," Merridy informed him. "Many auditions go to people who put in less work. I've seen it all my life." She tossed her skates into her tote bag.

Jacob tied his skates' laces together to hang over his shoulder. "I would prefer if everything were merit-based. Success, jobs, relationships…" his comment faded at the word. "Anyway, let's go get some coffee and grub." He abruptly walked away toward the parking garage.

She hastily grabbed her bag to follow him out. "Are you okay?" she asked. "That, got to you..."

"Personal problems. I mean, is it okay if I talk about my relationship?" he grimaced. "I've never had a friend, that was female, that wasn't related to me. Is it weird to talk about my dating life?"

"I don't think so," she responded. The truth was, she did not want to think about him having a girlfriend. But she cared about him and wanted to be supportive. "I mean, I'm not the smartest when it comes to dating. I hardly get past the first few dates with guys. Take any advice I give or whatever with that in mind."

"Wow, really?" He glanced at Merridy. Her mouth formed a thin line. No hint of a smile, no shine in her eyes. "I don't understand how that's possible. You're awesome."

"Maybe. But I think it's because I keep falling for the wrong guys. Mama's boys, overly-macho jerks, know-it-all's, or they're already taken."

He silently continued to his car at her last comment. He wanted a woman's opinion about Ameleah not seeking a counselor, but he felt that there was an awkward tension between them that could not handle her name being mentioned. Perhaps he would call one of his sisters or his mom about the situation. "I'm sorry," he whispered. "I won't talk about it. There's other things more deserving than that."

"Sorry, no, if there is a situation you need help with, or something you need to get off your chest, please do it. I'm your friend, Jacob. I'm here to help."

"There is something bothering me, but I should just talk to my sisters or something." He unlocked his car and opened the passenger door for Merridy. "It's not a big deal, Merridy."

She stopped on the other side of the open car door. "What's wrong, Jacob?" The sternness of her face dissolved. "Let me help you for once today."

He frowned. "It's just... I'm having issues with Ameleah, my girlfriend. We're growing apart. She's focused on her image, popularity, wealth... she can't remember someone's birthday but can tell you exactly how many followers she has." Jacob noted his voice rising. "Sorry. I'm trying to get through to her. Remind her of how she used to be. I asked her yesterday if she wanted to go to counseling. She agreed, said she'd find a counselor. But then today, she told *me* to find a counselor." He shook his head. "I don't understand why the sudden change."

Merridy carefully considered her next words. She felt a selfish happiness that there was trouble between Jacob and his girlfriend. But at the same time, she did not want him to suffer. Nor did she want to be seen as 'the other girl' or be used as a rebound from a failed relationship. "I cannot confess to understand such a change of heart. Perhaps she's sensing the rift growing between you, too. And maybe it's scaring her." She took a step away from the car. "Maybe you should be going to coffee with her instead of me."

"Get in the car," Jacob responded to her sentiment with an eyeroll. "One, I promised you coffee already. Two, we got more training to do, and I'm not doing it on an empty stomach. And three, she's having dinner with some architect from New York." He nodded to the car. "So, get in and don't think spending time with you effects my issues."

She sighed. "Only if you promise it won't." She slipped into the car.

Jacob closed the door and walked to the driver's side. He already knew that Merridy's presence *did* affect his relationship. However, the relationship problems surfaced long before he ever met Merridy. "I want to reassure you," he continued, climbing into the driver's seat, "that any problems between Ameleah and myself have been happening for some time. And you're a welcome friend. I've enjoyed talking with you. I hope you've been enjoying it as well."

"Of course, I've enjoyed talking to you." She smiled. "I wouldn't have done it otherwise."

"Then in that case... let's go talk over a meal." He started the car to accentuate the statement.

While he drove to downtown, Merridy noted the inside of his vehicle. Leather seats, wood paneling, and a giant central navigation screen indicated a high-end luxury vehicle that cost more than two or three years of her annual salary. She had recognized the emblem on the car as they had approached it. It was a high-performance electric vehicle. "Beautiful car." She ran a finger over the leather of her seat. Her own vehicle was at least sixteen years old, held together by prayers and a wonderful mechanic. Kara's car was a newer model, only a couple of years old; yet it still could not touch the price tag of Jacob's vehicle.

"Thank you. It was my first real splurge that I picked for myself. Suits and wardrobe and my image stuff – that was agents and, you know, *others*." She assumed he meant Ameleah. "But my car, this was me. Before this baby, I was still driving my first car. It was a beautiful 1956 convertible, red and white, that my dad owned. He and I worked on it together when I was a kid. Loved that car."

"What happened to it?"

He laughed. "The only one who loved it more than me was my dad. He retired last year. Wanted to know if I could part with it so he could go cruising down the west coast with my mom in their glory years."

"Awww, that's sweet."

"I guess. But that meant I had to get my own set of wheels. I made an investment in an electric. They're a little pricey, especially with all the bells and whistles I got for this one, but I am hoping it lasts a long time." He grinned. "I think my friend, Terry, is on his third car in the same number of years. I don't know how he does it. No time to get to know the car – grow a relationship with it."

"True. I've had my car since I was sixteen, and it was a few years old when I got it." She shook her head. "But I know every little quirk about it. Like when she's going to break down before she even has a check-engine light on."

"That's how it should be." He patted the steering wheel. "Still learning this gal. But it's been fun getting to know her." He shot a side-eyed glance to Merrdy. "She's got a lot of features I enjoy that my previous ride didn't have. Makes me wonder why I held on to the old ride as long as I did."

"Yeah?" she asked. "You had a classic '56 convertible. Men would kill to have such a beauty. You loved her. She was a one of a kind..."

"But this new one has comfort that the other could never provide. Sometimes it's about being comfortable, not having a prize to show off. Plus, this new car is gorgeous too, in her own right. And look at this console. Beautiful navigation – it knows where it's going so that I can't get lost."

"Was that a problem for you?"

"Constantly." He pressed a few buttons on the navigation screen. It showed a map to the coffeeshop with the GPS indicating the next turn. "This town changes often with all the people moving here. And I'm constantly traveling all year long... easy to get lost with all that commotion."

"I agree. The town seems more 'hustle and bustle' now than when I first moved here. And that was less than ten years ago." She pointed out of the passenger window to the highway they passed under. "It's almost like when you cross under this expressway, everything slows down a little bit."

They crossed from the regular concrete street to a historic brick-paved road that stretched through the main thoroughfare of South Hills' downtown. Jacob pulled into an empty parking spot in front of the coffeeshop. "Quaint," he said, eyeing the shop. "And I don't mean that in a condescending way. It's colorful, unique, and cozy. Love it. Reminds me of back home."

"Yeah, it seems everything in the new part of South Hills is cookie-cutter. The same shopping centers are built over-and-over with the same look and the same stores." Merridy opened her car door. "And it's those chains and big-box stores the majority of people go to. I don't understand."

Jacob followed her to the door of the coffeeshop. "Especially when I hear most people say they want to support small businesses. But what do they do? Money talks more than anything." He opened the door for her. "And I'm guilty of it too."

"I think we all slip into it. Familiar name breeds confidence." She walked into the near empty coffeeshop. "Good evening Evie!"

The haggard red-head looked up from the tablet she worked on. "Hey Merridy! I'm trying to work on the new menu. Do you want to check it out?" Her eyes drifted to the man next to Merridy. "Oh, hello."

"Hello," Jacob responded. He stepped forward and offered his hand to Evelyn. "Jacob."

"Nice to meet you Jacob. I'm Evelyn." She shook his hand. "Welcome to my little establishment."

"It smells delicious." He glanced around and noted the one customer drinking coffee and reading an e-book in the corner. "And it's a beautiful place."

"Would be a bit more beautiful if there were a few more customers enjoying it."

"We'll fix that!" Merridy cheerily reminded her. "Friday night this place will be packed." She glanced at the tablet. "Let's see the new menu. We're starved." She received the tablet from Evelyn to look at the new options. Jacob leaned in closer to review as well. His proximity caused Merridy to blush.

"Everything sounds good," Jacob confessed. "I've not had anything but a protein shake today." He began placing a large order with Evelyn, and then insisted on paying for Merridy's coffee and wrap as well.

"You didn't have to," she told him as they walked to a table.

He shrugged. "I didn't have to. But I wanted to." He pulled a chair out for her. "Now, tell me everything about Friday. What do you have planned so far?"

Merridy began pointing out the area she had earmarked for the stage and listing the songs she planned on performing. "Kara is working on a flyer tonight to put online and around town."

"Forward it to me. I'll put it out on my account." He produced his phone from his pocket. "In fact, I need to take a picture of my meal and tag this place. That's what those influence people do, right?"

"Influencers?" Merridy giggled. "I didn't think you had it in you."

"For a worthy cause I do. But I might need help." He shifted his seat from across the table to the seat at her side. Evelyn brought their meals to them, and Merridy helped Jacob post a picture to his account. "Hopefully that stirs some attention."

She placed a hand on his. "Thank you, Jacob," she whispered.

He blushed at the sentiment. "Just using this celebrity power for good." He lifted his fork to his mouth. The two dined together, sharing another long-winded conversation. Eventually, well after the sun had set, they returned to the rink for a second training session.

Chapter 9

The counselor's office hummed with emptiness as Jacob sat alone on the plush leather couch. The woman in the chair across from his sat upright with proper posture. She shook the pen in her hand in a frustrated fidgeting motion but never struck her notepad with the apparatus. All remained silent. He shifted uncomfortably, and the leather squeaked. "I'll try calling her one more time," he apologetically offered the counselor.

"No need Mr. Kenway. She did not respond to your last four calls or dozens of text messages. Now, please tell me, does this happen frequently?"

Jacob arched his eyebrows. "The world runs on Ameleah's schedule, according to Ameleah. It's been like this since she returned from Paris."

"What happened in Paris?"

"I wish I knew." Jacob shook his head. "She gave up swimming, decided to do modeling, there was a bunch of shows or something in Paris. She never really told me what she was modeling. And when I asked to come visit, she would tell me that she could not spare a moment between photoshoots and travel schedules. She stayed with her family, some cousins that still lived in Paris." He placed his hands out innocently. "I messaged her constantly. The responses I would get were short and rare."

"And how did that make you feel?"

"Worthless. Like we weren't a couple anymore." He stared at his hands. "I was in the running for an award that year, and it would have been nice to have someone cheering me on. That's what I always thought being a couple was – mutual support in our goals." He picked at a scab of dead skin on one of his hands. "Like I said, I wanted to be supportive of her career too when she was in Paris. But now that she's back, I don't know. It's getting harder to support her career."

"Why is that?"

He sighed at the constant questions from the counselor. Apparently, he was getting therapy whether Ameleah arrived or not. "I think it's her career that's changing her. I understand – she's a model, a designer. It's a lot of networking and portraying a certain image. But it feels like it's been at the cost of her true self." The dead skin scab fell off. "She used to be an athlete, a swimmer, who cared about being the best in her field, and about using that image to help others. Help kids. That's what led me to like her. We had a joint cause in the children."

"Maybe you fell in love with the idea of what you thought Ameleah was rather than Ameleah herself."

Jacob stopped fidgeting with his hand to narrow his eyes on the therapist. "Or maybe I fell in love with an Ameleah that no longer exists."

"In my many years of observation, people do not change who they truly are. They only become truer to themselves and seek the desires of their internal self as they grow older and more mature." She stared down the bridge of her nose to write a few notes on her pad.

"What would you suggest if two people are seeking their internal desires, and it may no longer be aligned?" he asked hesitantly.

"I believe you know the answer to that."

He frowned. "I thought you were a relationship counselor meant to help us recover our relationship, not push us to separation."

"I am here to help you find the correct path for you both, whatever that path is."

Jacob's brows furrowed at her revelation. This was not what he expected when he read her reviews and booked an appointment. Before he could respond, the door of the office burst open. Ameleah flitted inside with a purse and two shopping bags draped on her arms. "Terribly sorry I am late. I got caught up in a meeting that ran longer than expected." Her impromptu arrival startled the therapist. "Sorry, your receptionist insisted on calling to let you know I was coming but I told her I was already penciled in." She plopped on the couch with an exasperated sigh. "What have I missed?"

"Jacob was just informing me of how different your relationship has been since you stayed in Paris."

The therapist's revelation caused Ameleah to side eye Jacob. "Why?" she angrily asked him. "Paris was the best thing that happened to me. My career was sky-rocketed thanks to Charles Lee." She turned back to the therapist. "That's *the* Charles Lee Laban."

"I have heard of him," the therapist let her know.

"Yes, Charles Lee Laban," Jacob mused. "The celebrity-creator. What does he even do?"

Ameleah rolled her eyes. "Stop being dense, Jacob. He's a highly sought-after advisor."

"Is that why you had no time for me when you were in Paris? Getting all that advice?" He refused to even look at Ameleah. His shoulders had become rigid with frustration at her attitude.

"I had photoshoots, runways, interviews… I was very busy."

"Because I don't know what a full schedule is like? You can take time for a one-minute text message. Am I not even worth a minute of your time?" The sincerity of his question hit Jacob hard. Everything he felt lately seemed to hang on her answer.

"Are *you*, the one who is late to our events, asking *me* if you're worth a minute of my time? I don't know Jacob, am I worth a minute of *your* time?"

"I was late to a press function. I'm not late to us. Not when it counts. Not when it's private and personal, and meaningful." He finally allowed himself to look at Ameleah. "I have always wanted to be there for you, Ami."

She narrowed her eyes at him. "Except when it comes to my career, our future, and our home. Oh, and what about Monday? You chose to be not with me then, right?' She pulled out her phone and showed him his social media account where he had checked-in to Evelyn's coffeeshop that night. "Too busy at some dive coffeeshop to bother having dinner with me?"

"I grabbed a meal in-between the other stuff I was doing."

"What other stuff, Jacob?" the therapist asked. He nearly forgot about her presence.

"Pro-bono skating lessons," he responded.

Ameleah laughed at his response. Not a jovial laugh, but one mired in condemnation. "Pro-bono skating lessons? Is this some prize to some charity donor or such? Seriously, what stupid person would want skating lessons?"

Jacob's brow furrowed. "There are many people who would want skating lessons with an Olympic gold-medal hockey player."

"Was it a child?"

"An adult."

She laughed again.

"As if you know how to skate. You've never been on the ice with me once in seven years. Adults can want to learn things too."

She rolled her eyes. "I can't imagine some middle-aged man with deep pockets giving to your little children's charity and saying 'now teach me to skate'. That's ridiculous."

"Actually, that's a great idea. I'll start offering that." Jacob's flared. "As it was, that's not what happened. All that matters is I was helping someone who needed to learn how to skate."

The silence between them felt as cold as ice until the therapist intervened. "Ameleah, how does it make you feel that he put another person before your dinner?"

Jacob began to protest, but the therapist silenced him.

"It makes me feel like... he's being a bit hypocritical with his accusations against me," Ameleah responded. "And honestly, I don't know if I can be in a relationship with a hypocrite."

"I'm a hypocrite for already having plans before you decided to have a dinner with an architect that I never agreed to meet in the first place?"

"You expected me to drop everything in Paris to give you my time, but you clearly can't do the same for me."

"Do you feel this is a fair comparison?" the therapist asked Jacob.

"No!" he cried out. "Never in a million years would this be considered the same."

"Why?" the therapist asked him.

His face contorted as he tried to find the words.

"Because it's about him," Ameleah answered for him. "Being 'there for each other' is only when I'm there for him, not when he is there for me. He never considers the pressures I face trying to make it in the fashion industry. It's not an easy road to take. There are countless deadlines, people to speak with, social media and regular media to report to, and I have to constantly decide between salad or sushi. I can't even think about a steak or hamburger."

"You're becoming self-centered because you're *hangry*?" Jacob asked her.

"I'm not the self-centered one here. I am focused on my career because no one else seems to be."

He stood to his feet. "I care about your career. But what I don't care for is that you are so *focused* on your career that you can't seem to care about anyone else."

"That's what 'focus' is, Jacob." She bounced to her feet as well. "If you're focused on something, then you really don't have time to do other things. That's how people build their careers."

"Yeah, well, not everyone. There's good people out there trying to live their dream, but not doing it at the sake of those they care for."

Her chin lifted in the air defiantly. "Then maybe you should be in a relationship with one of them."

"Maybe I should."

His response made her mouth form a small 'o' in surprise. Before she had a chance to respond, he left the therapist's office, his hands clinched in tight fists.

Chapter 10

"Have you seen the news?" Kara asked Merridy.

It was Friday morning, the date of the big event for Evelyn's coffeeshop, and the day before Merridy's audition. Several days had passed, with Jacob unable to practice with her Tuesday and Thursday due to games – which she watched. On Wednesday, they had managed a long session with much success. Already, Merridy felt easier about her audition. But Friday night's event at Evelyn's coffeeshop meant that any training session would be fleeting and late. Merridy worried that she would be unable to skate and carry her guitar, let alone play it and sing. It was all she could think about as she waited for her morning cup of coffee.

"I have not seen any news. I don't even know what the weather is supposed to be like today. Hopefully good, for Evie's sake."

"Not that kind of news... though I should probably check the weather too." Kara pushed her phone into Merridy's face. "Look at this post."

Still bleary-eyed from her state of pre-coffee-morning, Merridy narrowed her eyes to focus on the screen. It was Ameleah Antonie's social media page:

'As hard as this is to announce, Jacob Kenway and myself have decided to part ways after a beautiful seven-year relationship. I owe so many fond memories to my time with Jacob, and will treasure them always. But for the time being, it is better for us to focus on our individual careers. Thank you for everything Jacob.'

"Wow," Merridy responded. "I knew there were problems, but... I have a feeling Jacob would have preferred the breakup remain private between them."

"Wait, you knew there were problems in paradise?" Kara asked. "You were in on the gossip and didn't tell me?"

Merridy rolled her eyes. "We shouldn't gossip, Kara," she chided her friend with a smile. "Besides, I was told things in confidence of friendship. It wasn't my secret to share."

"Well with Ameleah Antonie, no secrets stay secret for long."

"Jacob is going to be crushed. I don't know... should I text him? What would I text him? 'Hey I saw your ex blabbed about your breakup? Sorry.' That sounds... awful."

Kara grabbed a muffin from the box in front of them. "You're also not sorry."

Evelyn brought their coffees to them. "Of course, Merridy is sorry. He's her friend. She doesn't want him to be heart-broken."

"Exactly," Merridy agreed. "Now, let's focus on getting everything prepared for today. If I focus on that, the right words might come to me."

They set up two tablets on Evelyn's counter that Kara had donated. Both were set up to accept orders from any guests arriving that night in lieu of an actual cashier, as Evelyn was short-handed, although Kara already stated she would fulfill the role of a second server. They also prepared as many meals in advanced as possible. Racks of baked goods sat ready in the back, and the fridge sat full of single-serve juices: orange, passionfruit, apple, lemonade, and specialty mixes now on the menu.

Merridy hugged Evelyn and Kara tightly before leaving to go to her own job. She worried that her friend would either be overwhelmed with business that she could not handle or that hardly anyone would show up and the preparation would be for naught. She hoped for the best-case outcome. Afterall, the one post from Monday night on Jacob's account led to a slight increase in business. And the digital flyer Kara created had been receiving a lot of activity on different social media sites. Despite the exposure performing would give Merridy, she worried most about her friend's business.

However, the distraction of preparing Evelyn for the event did not erase the thought of Ameleah's post from her mind. Isn't this what she wanted? Jacob to be available? Yes. But not like this. Not with a publicly-humiliating breakup with a model. She eyed the post from her own phone. Surely Jacob had seen this already. Even if not on his own accord, his friend, Terry, whom she heard plenty about from Jacob, probably had sent it to him.

'Praying for you today.'

She felt the message was the best thing she could say. She would be praying for him all day. He needed comfort more than anything. And she wanted him to know that she was there for him, supporting him in the best way she knew how: the power of prayer.

'I guess this means you saw Ami's post.'

His response was sudden and direct. She didn't know how to interpret it. It was one thing about text messages she could not stand — the inability to interpret a person's emotional state without any context clues. She worried that she was to blame for the breakup, despite his protests throughout the week.

'Yes. I guess the counseling didn't help. I just want you to be comforted and happy and... I'm here for you. If you want me here for you. I mean, if you need me. In the meanwhile, I'll be praying for you. I do care.'

She entered her office space calmly and began her morning work routine of checking voicemails and emails. But her cellphone lighting up distracted her from all of her required tasks.

'I know you care.'

'I'm really glad that you care, too.'

She tapped her nails on her cellphone screen, unsure of how to respond. Could anyone else in her cubicle-riddled office feel the awkward tension surrounding her? The thin line she walked between friendship and wanting more? But also, not wanting to be more at this time? She certainly did not want to take advantage of Jacob's vulnerability.

'I still plan on coming out tonight, for Evelyn. I'm rooting for her that this event goes well and that coffee will be flowing. Looking forward to hearing you sing live, too. So I guess, I'm coming out tonight, not *just* for Evelyn.'

Merridy sharply inhaled. Did she read too much into that text?

'If you're not in the right frame of mind to come out, we would all understand. No one should ever expect someone to go out in the public after something like this. I mean, I'm of the philosophy that these things call for chocolate ice cream and a burn-the-memories slumber party.'

'If you bring the ice cream, I'll bring the matches.'

'In all seriousness, I think coffee and live music is exactly what I need. I'll see you tonight. I'm going to hit the gym and see how my new 'angry workout' playlist does today. And Turnip Girl, thanks for the caring and prayer.'

Merridy put her phone away at the last text message. It was time to focus on her work. She needed to be extra productive if she was going to leave work early for the night's event.

Chapter 11

"You didn't have to come with me," Jacob told Terry while trying to find a parking spot in downtown South Hills.

"Are you kidding me? I'm not letting my best friend be alone after a breakup!"

"You didn't even like Ameleah."

"Exactly." Terry smirked. "Which is why I have to be with you – to facilitate the celebrations."

Jacob rolled his eyes. A narrow parking spot between two SUVs revealed itself.

"Plus, I *have* to meet this Merridy chick. You've successfully hidden her from me with every well-timed training session."

"Exactly," Jacob mimicked his friend.

"That hurts."

The two managed to squeeze out of the car and head to the coffeeshop. Sounds of music and a chatting crowd drifted down the street. "Sounds busy." Jacob stated with contentment. "Thank God."

"And smells delicious," Terry added. "I am starving." He paused outside of the shop. "Come on, selfie time. I'll tag the place. I've got way more followers than you."

Jacob reluctantly posed for the photo. "Now, come on, I thought you were starving."

The two made their way through the crowd toward the counter. Terry's eyes fixated on the glass counter display full of baked goods. Jacob, however, nearly collided with several people as he tried to obtain a clear view of Merridy as she sang. For a brief moment, the crowd parted between them, and they managed to lock eyes.

"What do you think? Papaya or passion fruit?"

"Huh?" Jacob asked.

Terry repeated. "Drink. Papaya. Passionfruit."

"Sounds delicious," Jacob responded without answering the question.

"Guess I'll get both..." Terry grumbled. He noted his friend's transfixed stare on the singer. "Shall I order one singing woman too?"

"Huh?" Jacob asked again. "No, um... just cool to see her sing in-person."

The song ended to a polite clap from the audience. "Thank you everyone. And thank you to everyone for coming out tonight. Remember, anyone who checks-in on social media tonight will get an e-voucher for a free coffee or drink of their choice." Merridy paused as she eyed Jacob once again. "I am going to take a short break, then will be back to take your requests. Thank you!"

She made her way through the crowd toward Jacob. "You sounded great," he blurted out.

"Oh, thank you," she blushed. "Thank you for coming out and supporting Evie."

"Of course..."

"Hi, I'm Terry," the extrovert introduced himself with an offered hand. "Jacob's best friend, teammate, wingman..."

Jacob frowned at 'wingman'.

"Hello. I'm Merridy." She shook Terry's hand. "Jacob's been helping me learn to skate."

"Oh, I know," Terry laughed. "I've heard all about that."

Merridy's blushing deepened. "Oh, um, well, thank you for coming out." She turned her head back to her guitar and stool.

"Merridy... wait..." Jacob started.

She paused. "Yes?"

"How long do you play until? I thought we might get one last session in before the audition tomorrow." His brown eyes slightly pleaded with her.

"I stop at eleven. And... I'd like that." She reached behind the counter to grab a water bottle. "Should I meet you there, or...?"

"I'll be staying for the whole show." They shared a smile before Merridy returned to her stool. "Man, she's..."

"Time. Out." Terry told his friend. "Don't finish that sentence."

Jacob turned around. "What?"

"Stop what you're about to say. Tell me what you want to eat and drink." He pointed to the tablet. "And then we're going outside to talk."

A protest forming on his lips, Jacob relented and gave Terry his order. They walked out of the restaurant with their ticket. "What did you want to say?"

"You *just* broke up with Ameleah. Any feelings you have for Merridy need to be suppressed. They are just being fueled by the emptiness you are feeling from everything happening with the breakup."

Jacob took a deep breath. "I don't... I'm not..."

"Yeah you are. And you know, she is a pretty and talented and nice girl." Terry pointed toward the open door. "And I don't want her to be your rebound."

"She's not going to be my rebound... she's my friend..."

"Which is what makes it so easy for her to become your rebound. I see the looks you were giving her. That's red flag stuff right there."

Jacob turned away from his friend to look through the storefront windows at Merridy inside. "That's absurd."

"I'm not saying she wouldn't be great for you to date. She might be wonderful. But if you try to make a move *now*, you would ruin it. It's too soon."

"This is absurd. Getting relationship advice... from you. You!" Jacob sat down hard at an outside table. "And it's not even a relationship. It's nothing. It's a friendship... training her how to skate."

Terry sat down at the table next to his friend. "You protest too much."

"Order number seventy-two," Kara called as she walked out onto the sidewalk with a tray. "One papaya, one passionfruit..." she paused as she noted Jacob and Terry. "Oh, my word."

"Fame precedes me again," Terry joked. "Yes, what you are thinking is correct. I am, in fact, Terry Sanger, co-captain of the Texas Twisters..."

Jacob eyed Kara. "I know you." He paused. "Merridy's friend, correct? Kara, the hockey player."

She placed the tray on their table. "Yes, that's me. And you're Jacob Kenway."

"Great! Her friend!" Terry excitedly clapped his hands together. "Listen, Kara, correct me on this, Merridy is focused on her career and not a relationship, right?"

Kara's eyes drifted between Terry and Jacob. Jacob's eyes lowered from her gaze. "You like Merridy?"

"She's my friend," Jacob reiterated.

"I see." Kara unloaded the tray. "Well, yes, she is focused on her career. But her heart would be open for a relationship... with the right person... at the right time." She tucked the empty tray under her arm. "I'd prefer to not know something that she doesn't know, by the way, in regards to a relationship. Our friendship is built on trust."

"There's nothing to know." Jacob pulled his drink toward him. "She's my friend. I've got my own broken, ended relationship problems to focus on. And tonight, I'm just here to help support this place, and listen to my friend perform." He took a sip of the orange juice. "You did a very good job getting this event together, Kara. Congratulations."

"Thank you." She began to walk away but paused. "And Terry, it's cool to meet you. I *am* a fan." She continued inside.

"Wow," Terry turned to his friend. "That friend of your friend is g-o-r-g-e-o-u-s gorgeous." He patted his hand on the table. "I have to stay focused. Focused."

Jacob ignored his friend as he continued to discuss Kara's attractiveness. His eyes focused on Merridy while she sang. He knew he had some feelings for her, but Terry was right. It was not the time.

"I've received a request for some Irish music," Merridy announced into the microphone. She noted Kara walk into the coffeeshop with a slight fluster to her step. "Here's a favorite of mine... one we probably all know, so be sure to sing along if you know the words." Her eyes danced from Kara who whispered to Evelyn to the open doorway and the view beyond the coffeeshop windows. Despite the crowd, she could make out the figures of Jacob and Terry watching her while in deep conversation.

She cleared her throat, then began to sing.

Oh, Danny Boy, the pipes, the pipes are calling
From glen to glen, and down the mountainside,
The summer's gone, and all the roses falling,
It's you, it's you must go and I must bide...

The crowd joined her in singing the popular song, and she attempted to drown in her music. An hour rolled by before Merridy announced another break in her singing. She bee-lined for the counter to secure another drink. "I am so parched," she joked to Kara. "But this crowd has been great. A lot have stuck around for awhile and keep ordering. That's good right? And there's been a steady coming-and-going of people. Great success lady!"

Kara wiped the sweat on her brow with the back of her hand. "Hopefully tonight will help kickstart enough funds for her to be able to hire help here. Even just a part-time person would be a great asset."

"Waitressing not your calling?" Merridy joked.

"Absolutely not. I don't know why these crazy people get into the food industry." She took a deep breath. "But I do love seeing this place full. You know that Jacob brought Terry Sanger here?"

"Yes..."

"Terry tagged this place on his social media, and it's blowing up. That's the best kind of organic marketing." She grabbed another ticket to start filling the drink orders. "I wish I could do this for every small business. Could save them all."

"I'm sure you'll have tons of time for that with the new project you're on at work," Merridy laughed.

"For real." Kara looked over the ticket. "I think this is for your friends outside."

"I can take it," Merridy beamed. She took the tray from Kara and headed outside. "Hello guys! Enjoying another round?"

Terry took his drinks off the tray. "Fourth round! These fruit drinks are incredible."

"Wow! Thank you, guys." She handed Jacob his drink. "Kara told me you posted this place on social media, and it's helping draw a crowd."

"We've certainly had to sign a few autographs," Terry chimed in. "Pretty fun though. Impromptu signing session."

Merridy eyed Jacob quietly. He kept his eyes on his drink. "Are you okay, Jacob?"

"Huh?" His eyes darted up to her and away again. "I don't know... maybe my situation is catching up to me."

She put a concerned hand on his shoulder. "You're going through a lot. If you need to leave and have some healing time with Porthos..."

"That's actually a pretty good idea," Terry chimed in. "It's getting late, and we have that plane to Toronto to catch in the morning."

"You're going to Toronto?"

114

"We have a five-game series against Toronto next week, and another series against San Jose after that," Jacob calmly told her. "Plane leaves mid-morning."

Merridy gasped. "You're traveling to Toronto tomorrow morning! You shouldn't be here, staying until late and then giving me another training session!" She nudged his shoulder playfully. "You need to get home!"

"Are you sure?" He stood. "Your audition is in the morning too."

She waved him off. "I'm fine. I feel confident in my skating! Go and relax! Does Porthos go with you when you travel?"

Jacob scratched the back of his head. He had hoped for more alone time with Merridy before leaving town for two weeks, but given Terry's revelation earlier, he knew that alone time was a bad idea. "No, he has a sitter when I'm out provided by the team. Um... I guess we should go so I can spend that time with him." He patted Merridy's shoulder. "So, um, good luck for the rest of tonight, and tomorrow?"

"Yeah..." she quietly responded. "And good luck, to you too?" Concerned by the awkward situation, Merridy took a step back to the coffeeshop. "I guess I should get back in. I've got another hour before this is over. I'll see you, later, I guess?" She did not even wait for his response before melting back into the coffee crowd.

"Let's go," Jacob said. He hurried away to his car without checking to see if Terry followed him.

Chapter 12

"I think this is the place," Merridy told Kara as the two pulled up to a non-descript brick building at the address on her audition notice. "Doesn't look like a skating rink."

"I don't think it is." Kara checked the address against her GPS. "But this is where it took us. And there's other cars."

Merridy took a deep breath. "Oh, I hope it's the right place. What if it's not? What if I miss the audition?" Her hands flew up to her hair in a state of panic. "Will they still let me? This is the address they gave me."

"Stop, stop, stop," Kara said calmly. "You can't focus on all that." She took her friend's hands in hers. "Back to the original plan. We're going to pray over your audition. You're going to walk in. And if you don't have to skate, so what? Because you're here to sing."

"You're right." She paused to take deep breaths and closed her eyes. "Father, please be with me today. Let me do your will today."

Kara joined the prayer. "Lord, let your daughter do her best. Soften the hearts of the judges. Let the gift you have given her shine through."

They ended the prayer, and Merridy exited the car with her guitar case and skates. Her heart pounded as she entered the building and followed the signs for the audition.

"He-hello," she greeted a young man at the door of the room.

He appraised her with a raised eyebrow. "You're here for the audition?"

"Yes. I had the 10am slot. Merridy Christmas?"

He silently scoffed at her name while checking his clipboard. "Miss... Christmas. Please enter the waiting room. You will be able to prepare there. When it is your turn, your name will be called by my partner. He will lead you to the judges." He opened the door.

Merridy looked inside and saw several people listening to headphones and singing along to their chosen song. No one wore ice skates.

"We're not going to be on ice for the audition?" she asked the man.

"That's cute," he huffed. "No."

"Oh... I guess I misunderstood the audition notice," she mumbled. She found the quietest spot in the room and tuned her guitar. She was one of the few with an instrument. Despite her concentration on her guitar, her stomach filled with grumbling nerves. "Lord, please give me strength," she whispered a prayer. She repeated it several more times until the grumblings subsided. With nerves calmed, Merridy began her vocal warm-ups.

"Christmas?" A man called out her name several minutes later. "Is there a Miss Christmas?"

Those waiting began to snicker at the name.

"That is I," Merridy called out, attempting to ignore the snickers. She reached for her purse and guitar case.

"Leave your things, security will keep an eye on it." The man frantically waved her over. "Hurry up. The judges have a full schedule."

She trotted to the door as he continued to frantically beckon to her.

"Alright, deep breath and in you go."

Merridy followed his advice and inhaled deeply as she entered the opened door.

"This is Merridy Christmas," one judge said to the others while looking at his tablet. "I like the name."

"Thank you," Merridy responded happily. "It's not always been appreciated when I was growing up."

"It's your birth name?" another judge asked in surprise.

"Yes ma'am."

"Well I love it," the third judge beamed. "And how perfectly fitting for our event! What are you singing for us today?"

"I'll be singing 'O Holy Night'." She readied her guitar.

"Ah thank goodness," the first judge sighed. "If I had to hear one more awful rendition of Mariah, I was going to cry. Please, begin."

"O Holy Night! The stars are brightly shining,
It is the night of the dear Saviour's birth.
Long lay the world in sin and error pining,
Till He appeared and the Spirit felt its worth.
A thrill of hope the weary world rejoices,
For yonder breaks a new and glorious morn.
Fall on your knees! Oh, hear the angel voices!
O night divine, the night when Christ was born
O night, O Holy Night, O night divine!"

The first judge raised his hand to stop her, and all three judges remained silent for a moment.

Merridy's stomach tightened once more at their silence. Had she done poorly?

"That was very beautiful, Merridy," the second judge eventually spoke. She nodded at the judge with the tablet. He passed the device to her. "You understand that the event is on ice, and you will be required to skate for your performance?"

"Yes ma'am."

The woman nodded her head silently.

"We will be in touch shortly," the first judged dismissed Merridy.

"Thank you," she responded. "Have a wonderful day!"

Merridy hurried back to her gear with a giant grin on her face. The positive statement from the judge replayed in her mind. She reached for her phone to text Kara but noted an unread message from Jacob.

'Hey. Boarding the plane to Toronto now. Hope the audition goes well. You got this Turnip Girl!'

'I just finished! I think it went really well! One judge said it was 'very beautiful' and another said they'll be in touch soon!!!'

She repeated the text to Kara as well, then gathered her guitar case and bag to leave the waiting room.

Kara's car was parked, ready for pickup, in front of the building; Kara, however, stood in front of the passenger door, eager to congratulate her friend with a hug. "Oh, my goodness! I saw the text! That is amazing!"

"I mean, it's not a done-deal," Merridy checked her excitement. "But the positive words are at least worthy of a little ice cream celebration, right?"

"Absolutely! Let's go!"

Part Two: The Contract

Kara sat in Evelyn's coffeeshop with numerous pieces of paper and her tablet in front of her. Several patrons sat at tables enjoying sandwiches and coffee. The sight of customers eating during regular hours, and not during an event, made Kara happy. She had been afraid that the crowds from the Friday night events would not convert to regular customers.

"Looks intense," Evelyn observed as she delivered Kara's coffee. "What is it?"

"A new campaign for my company. It's to be the national campaign for the whole new year." She let out a deep sigh. "I wanted this more than anything, and now I'm terrified by it."

"I can't imagine you being terrified by anything." Evelyn gestured toward the other customers. "You're brilliant Kara. You did this. This place was dead before your *one* idea."

"But doing that was fun... which I guess made it less scary."

"What made it fun compared to this?"

The question made Kara shrug her shoulders. "I guess, some part, was because I was helping you, and you are family. Do or die. There was no choice but to succeed because you're my sister."

Evelyn crossed her arms with a shake of her head. "Do or die isn't fun. That's terrifying to me. I know that I was terrified it wouldn't work, and not because I don't trust you. It was just a dire circumstance. And we still have a long way to go."

"It just had more meaning," Kara blurted out. "Marketing for you meant a small business surviving. Marketing for a corporate giant... I mean, it's not do or die for the company.

Who will benefit from it, in the long run? I mean, I appreciate what the company offers. If I didn't believe in what they provided, I wouldn't work for them. But I've been so busy climbing this ladder, that I think I lost sight of what was really important to me." Kara gathered the loose paper together. "Nothing I can do about that though. I have a job to do, and I'm going to do the job one way or another."

"Hello ladies!" Merridy skipped cheerily into the shop. "Loooook!" she held out the word. "There's customers!" She whispered the statement gleefully loud. "This is so exciting!"

Evelyn eyed the customers. "It does make me feel hopeful. Maybe, maybe I could make this work. I mean, it was Zeke's dream. He'd want this..."

"Zeke would want you to live *your* dream," Merridy reminded Evelyn. "His dream was coffee. Yours is baked goods and beautiful cakes. I've seen your sketches." She turned to Kara. "Wouldn't you agree Kara? Your brother would want Evie to live her passions. He was always about that. He told me if God gives you a gift, you best use it."

Kara felt her eyes water at the mention of her brother. She noted Evelyn did the same. "You seem in a good mood today, ma'am. What's got you smiling?"

She beamed wide. "They called to confirm I got the audition! I'm going to be singing at the tree lighting ceremony! There's going to be talent scouts, and... and... aaaahhhh!" At a loss for word, Merridy released her excitement with a giddy scream. Evelyn joined her, and Kara jumped to her feet. "It happened! I can't believe it happened!"

"Of course, it happened. You're so talented, Merridy." Evelyn hugged her tightly. "We're going to have a viewing party here! Gotta support my girl!"

124

"That's so sweet, Evie."

Kara silently hugged her friend after Evelyn stepped back.

"Couldn't have done this without you Kara," Merridy whispered to her friend.

"Nonsense," Kara replied. "You were faithful to the Lord. That's how you're here." She indicated the chair at her table. "Now, sit down, we have more to plan before the performance. Gotta make sure the whole world hears you sing."

Merridy plopped down into the seat with a contented sigh. "I've been working on a new song. Maybe I can do a video of it? Or should I wait until I get a record deal so I can have it as my first single? Oh Kara, can you just be my agent? You're amazing. You have business sense."

She continued rambling until Kara took her hands in hers. "One step at a time. We're going to announce on your social media that you will be performing at the event. I will email the event's marketing team to coordinate with them. And you... I wouldn't debut your own songs just yet. Something tells me you're going to want to hold those close to your heart for now."

The musician heeded her friend's words. "What can I do?" She shook her hands out from Kara's to release nervous energy. "I need to be doing something."

Kara slid her phone to her. "Record a video of yourself announcing that you'll be singing at the tree lighting. That's how we'll announce it."

She picked up her phone to start the video. "Oh hey. Jacob texted me."

"Wow," Kara responded. "It's been a few days, hasn't it?"

"Yeah, like a week and a half or something? Not since the audition, I think. I guess I should tell him I got the part, but I didn't want to come off as... you know..." Merridy shook her head. "I mean, I haven't seen him since he came out that Friday, and left on awkward terms. I don't know what happened. Or maybe it was nothing. He's been playing non-stop. He's probably just focused." She stopped talking to open the text message.

'Hey Turnip Girl. Sorry I've not reached out. I don't know if you follow the team, or anything, but we're going through a rut. I get inside my own head when we're doing bad. Have you heard from the audition yet?'

'Actually yeah. I saw that your team wasn't doing well. I'm sorry. :(I did get the audition though. I will be singing at the tree lighting ceremony! I was actually about to attempt a video recording to announce it.'

'That's awesome! I'm so happy for you. I didn't mean to interrupt your video recording session.'

'Thank you. It's really a selfie session which means it's going to take hours of

reshoots. I think Kara knows it will keep
me busy and focus my nervous energy.'

'Maybe that's what I need, not that I
have nervous energy. But something to
take my mind off everything. I really
need some Porthos time, but still a few
days away from getting to go home.'

'Traveling away from the one you love is
always hard. :) Especially when it's
someone as handsome as Mister Porthos.'

'What can I say? I'm a sucker for that
fluffy face. I'm actually going to check-
in with the dog-sitter. She hasn't
messaged me for a couple days, and I
need to confirm that big boy is behaving
himself.'

'I'm certain he is. You've said it yourself.
He's the goodest boy. Have a good day!'

'You too!'

Merridy relaxed in her seat after the exchange. Time had helped the tension fade, and their exchange felt akin to their initial, friendly, messaging.

"That good?"

She glanced up to note Kara's smirk. "What?" Merridy asked innocently.

"You were beaming with every text message that came in."

The observation made Merridy sigh contently. "It felt like it used to. Just normal, somewhat silly, conversation. Not awkward like when he came out here. I mean, he was going through a lot that day. He just needed time to process... right?"

Kara's eyes drifted down to her tablet. "Merridy, I love you. You know that, right?"

"I know that. I love you too."

"Then you understand when I say, please be careful. I don't want you caught up in Jacob to the point he uses you as a rebound. I don't think it would be intentional, but with the timing of everything... I don't want you to get hurt, or accidentally hurt each other."

Merridy quietly absorbed the statement.

"And you just got the audition, and everything is going really well right now. I totally want you to have a friend, and I would never discourage healthy friendships. I simply want to express my concern. I know it's not really my business, but I love you, so I had to say it."

"Kara, you verbalized what has been in my head this whole time. This *whole* time." She stood with phone in hand. "Honestly, it makes me feel better that you've said it. Now I know you can keep me in check. Because I want to be his friend, and I am curious if there's more there, because I have feelings. But I know now is not the time. And… it's just very complicated, isn't it?"

"That's why I don't date," Kara laughed. "Ain't got time for complicated!"

"Maybe that's the mantra I should take on. 'Ain't got time for complicated.' We should make t-shirts!" She turned her phone on selfie mode and checked her hair and makeup. "Now time to start a recording session of fifty videos making my awesome announcement before I decide on one that I actually like. Have I mentioned that I hate modeling?"

"You got this," Kara cheered her on with two thumbs up.

Chapter 14

Merridy sat on the edge of her bed as she strummed her guitar and practiced 'O Holy Night' for her performance. Her video announcement posted successfully earlier that day, after a few dozen attempts of filming it, and its reach proved higher than she or Kara had expected. The initial success of such a simple video message made her both excited and nervous.

Her wondering mind caused her to botch the lyrics, and she floundered on a chord change. "Focus Merridy, focus," she chided herself. She started to begin on the second verse when her cellphone's ringtone blasted from beneath a nearby notebook. A startled shout escaped her lips. Only her parents called; friends preferred texting.

The call was from Jacob.

"He... hello?" she answered.

"Merridy! Thank you for answering! Sorry to interrupt, and call without warning..."

The panic in his voice caused Merridy to lower her guitar on the bed in worry. "What's wrong Jacob?"

"Sorry. I just found out that the dog-sitter is sick, and she hasn't been able to check on Porthos since yesterday morning."

"Oh no!" Merridy's heart broke thinking about the sweet dog sitting alone.

"I have a really big favor to ask..."

"You need me to go check on him?"

Jacob sighed heavily. "Yes. You're the only one I know in town that I trust, and who likes dogs, and who Porthos will love. If I give you my address and security codes, could you? There's a hide-a-key in my downstairs mailbox."

"Yes. I can go check on him. Poor baby is probably scared, hungry, and really needs to pee."

"I doubt he held it in." A shout in the background distracted Jacob. "We're about to take ice. I'll send you my info first. I'll give my phone to a trainer so if you need anything..." Another shout. "I have to go so I can text you the info."

"No worries. Go win one for me and Porthos."

"Thank you Merridy. You're the best." The call ended, and, within seconds, his address was sent to her. Another text followed with a security code and mailbox combination.

She gathered her things and hurried to the address sent to her. As she drove down the expressway toward Dallas, she realized that Jacob's apartment building was not one of the more expensive high-rises in Uptown as she expected. He resided in a more modest area nearby. After parking in the basement garage, she took an elevator to the marble-and-oak-lined lobby. "Swanky," Merridy observed. She knew the building would have been top amongst the luxury apartments of the 1970s, but each decade brought 'newer', 'taller', and 'better' to the city.

Antique mailboxes with gold inlays lined a far wall. Jacob's sat in the middle. The tumbler turned with ease to the combination, and a handful of envelopes fell onto the floor from the fullness of the box.

"Oh dear." She gathered Jacob's mail for him as well as the key taped to the back of the mailbox door. Another elevator ride took her to the top floor of the building where his apartment was one of two. "Porthos?" she whispered as sweetly as possible through the door. "I'm a new friend. I'll help you, okay buddy?"

A bark greeted her. It sounded sad rather than aggressive or alert. Merridy proceeded unlocking the door. More barks from the giant bear-dog greeted her. He kept several feet away from her as he attempted to determine if she was friend or foe.

She continued to baby talk the dog. "Hi Porthos. I'm a friend of your dad's. You're a sweet boy Porthos." The security system beeped, reminding her to input the code before it alerted the police. "Have you been scared? We found out you've been alone Porthos. You don't have to be alone now."

After a few minutes of baby-talking the dog and repeating his name, he tentatively moved forward to sniff Merridy. Content that she was a 'friendly', and not an enemy, he licked her hand with a happy bark. The authorization to continue forward from the large dog allowed Merridy to put Jacob's mail down on his coffee table and search for Porthos's food and bowls. He quickly showed her the way.

"Oh, you're hungry, aren't you?"

He barked a reply and added a happy dance as the kibble hit his bowl.

"Now some water, and while you eat and drink, I will clean up those messes I can smell." She flitted around the apartment, finding Jacob's cleaning supplies, and dealt with the gifts Porthos had left. Once completed, the two left for a quick walk. Despite the size of the dog, he was well-trained, and never strained against his leash.

For Jacob's peace of mind, she took a selfie of herself and Porthos on their walk, and texted it to him.

'Operation: Save the Musketeer was a success. He's been fed, watered, and we're having a great walk! Now you better be winning because when we get back from the walk, we're turning the game on!'

True to her word, they returned to the apartment, and she turned on Jacob's television to the hockey game. "See? There's your daddy! Say 'GOOOOOO DAADDDDY!'"

Porthos barked a cheery response, then jumped on the couch to watch the television. Not ready to leave him alone, Merridy joined him. By the end of the second period, Porthos was stretched across her lap and receiving belly rubs.

"Someone is a bit spoiled," she teased. "But guess what? Your daddy's team is winning now. Isn't that good? They're going into the third period up by a goal. And you know what's even better? I know what all of that means now!"

He licked her arm in return for the commentary and rubs. Slowly, Merridy's eyes closed while she held the warm, furry creature close.

The ringtone of her phone woke her up an hour later. "Oh no," she whispered, noting that Porthos was asleep as well. "I didn't mean to fall asleep." She grabbed her phone. "It's a video call from your daddy." Wiping away any lingering sleep in her eyes, or potential drool on her face, she answered with her own video. "Hey Jacob!"

He seemed fresh out of the shower with wet hair draping his face. "Hey! Thank you so much for taking care of my boy!"

She turned the camera to face Porthos. "No worries! Say hi Porthos!"

He barked.

"That's my good boy!" Jacob cooed over the phone.

Hearing his master's voice made Porthos stand on the couch in excitement. Another bark.

After a few moments of exchanging words and barks, Jacob turned his attention back to Merridy. "Hey, Merridy..."

She turned the camera to face her once again. The exchange of sweet words from Jacob to his dog had filled her with warmth, and her cheeks blushed to show it. "Yes?"

"Thank you again. I can't say it enough. I panicked. I didn't even think how late it was, and you came through anyway. I'm on California time now, and..." He shook his head. "You're amazing."

"I did what any friend would do." She attempted to stifle a yawn. "And maybe I did fall asleep during the second intermission of the game. Did you win?"

He grinned. Merridy noted the smile lines that formed around his eyes at the action. Slight dimples could be seen despite his facial hair. "Yeah, we won. Terry got on a hot streak." He paused; a look of concern flashed across his eyes. "It's really late Merridy. Now that I'm of sound mind that my dog is okay, and the game is over, I really don't think you should drive home at this hour. Stay there at my place. Please."

"I have work in the morning," she protested groggily. "I wish I could bring Porthos with me."

The dog whined and tilted his head at her.

"He's so stinkin' cute… and this guilt he can use," she continued. "Maybe I'll just get up early to get home for work."

Relief washed over Jacob's face. "I have some clothes you can change into, if you like. I'm almost certain anything of mine will fit you and then some. Might have to roll sleeves and pant legs up."

She walked toward his bedroom with Porthos following. "Are you calling me short?"

"No! Never! I'm calling myself… tall," he chuckled. "Look in that top drawer. All my pajama pants are there."

Merridy became distracted by a picture on the dresser. "Who's this?"

"My dad, mom, brother, sisters, and me, at our first Christmas after we were both drafted to the NHL."

"You look so young."

"Hey now, it wasn't *that* long ago."

She giggled a response as she opened the top drawer of the dresser. "This feels weird, digging through another person's dresser drawer, to steal clothes… to sleep in their bed."

The observation caused Jacob to blush. "I can't wait to get back to Dallas."

"I bet. I just heard how much you miss Porthos." She found a Team Canada sweatshirt that seemed extra-long and tossed it on the bed to change into.

"It's not just Porthos I miss."

Merridy paused at the statement. "Oh," she finally whispered a response.

Jacob cleared his throat loudly. "Um, yeah, so it's late. I need to let you go so you can change and get sleep. Thank you again, Merridy." Without giving her a chance to respond, the call ended.

She tossed the phone onto the bed and turned her attention back to the sweatshirt. "What are you doing Merridy? Just go home." A whine from Porthos made her sigh. "I can't just leave him. And I can't take him with me or my landlord will get upset." She caved in, changed into the sweatshirt, and fell asleep in Jacob's bed alongside a happy Akita.

Chapter 15

"Where are you off to in a hurry?" Kara asked her friend after Wednesday night's church service.

"Going back to Jacob's apartment so I can feed and walk his dog. The dog-sitter ended up getting the flu, and she hasn't been able to check on the poor fellow, so I have pretty much taken the job." Merridy spoke quickly. "And no, don't think it's because of any of the things you're thinking. It's for the dog, Kara. Look, he's a giant, fluffy bear." She flashed a photo of Porthos to Kara. "See? I couldn't disappoint that face."

Kara sighed. "Please be careful."

"I know, I know…" Merridy blew a kiss to her best friend. "Bye! I love you! Wanna get down to Dallas before the dog has an accident on the carpet… again." She hurried away to her car and traveled the familiar path to Jacob's apartment. "Hey pretty boy!" Porthos licked her face in jubilance at her arrival. "Ready for a walk?"

The dog could barely contain his excitement as she secured his leash and walking harness.

After an hour of walking, playing, and, eventually, feeding, Merridy knelt in front of Porthos. "I really have to go. It's pretty late. But your daddy will be back tomorrow. Aren't you excited?"

In response she received the high-pitch whining of a sorrowful dog. Porthos placed one of his gigantic paws on her arm and tilted his head pitifully.

"Well… I mean, I brought an overnight bag… just in case…" Merridy confessed. She adored the dog; he reminded her of the countless dogs she had on her parents' ranch in her youth. "But I will need to wake up early for work. Okay?"

Porthos began panting blissfully to show his approval. After a quick change of clothes, they curled up together on Jacob's bed. The dog sprawled out over her with his paws in the air as she provided him with belly rubs and a serenade.

"This is a sight for sore eyes."

Merridy abruptly stopped singing and petting the dog at the sound of Jacob's voice. Simultaneously, Porthos rolled to his feet and leapt off the bed toward his master.

"Hey there, boy!" Jacob greeted him with a laugh and ear rubs.

"You're home!" Merridy exclaimed. "But... I thought your flight was tomorrow?"

"The team is flying home tomorrow. I caught an earlier flight, given the dog situation." He kissed Porthos. "But considering what I walked in on, I think he was quite happy while I was gone."

Merridy blushed. "I didn't plan on staying. I bring stuff, just in case he really needs me, and... I guess he did. Or I'm easily swayed by puppy guilt. I'm not sure."

Jacob grinned. "I'm glad you are." His eyes remained fixed on Porthos. "I mean, it put me at ease knowing he was well taken care of. And the place looks great. I imagine that, after his alone time, it wasn't quite so nice."

"Nothing bleach couldn't cure. And I put all your mail on the dining room table. It was on the coffee table, buuuuut, someone thought it would be a fun game if he took an envelope and ran away with it. Put a stop to that game."

"Sounds like him. Actually, I'm surprised he stopped the game when you changed the mail spot. And thank you, for the mail. And the cleaning. And the dog-sitting." Jacob walked into his living room. "I got something for you, to say thanks."

Merridy rolled off the bed to follow him. "Jacob, that's not necessary. It's what any friend would do. Plus, I got to spend time in this beautiful apartment. It's like a vacation in a luxury hotel. I could never afford a suite like this!" Her bare feet stopped short on the gray-washed hardwood floor of the living room. A beautiful bouquet of white and lavender roses, white carnations, and gardenias greeted her. "Oh my," she whispered.

He shrugged his shoulders. "I saw these at the airport. I don't know." He stammered over his words. "They called to me. I thought you would like them."

"They're very pretty. You didn't have to." She lifted the bouquet to smell the flowers. "But thank you."

A momentary silence passed between them: Merridy, standing with flowers in hand; and Jacob, watching her indulge in the floral aromas. He smiled at the pleasure she found in the blossoms. When he saw the airport florist, he nearly dismissed the thought. He had become accustomed to those around him needing more expensive gifts, like electronics or jewelry. But he suspected Merridy appreciated the thought rather than the price tag.

"I love these lavender roses. I've seen them a few times in pictures, but I've never been gifted them," Merridy softly cooed over the purple petals. "I looked it up one time, wondering if they were real or if they were dyed white roses. But they're real. Well, they're a hybrid." Her eyes drifted from the roses to the giver. "That makes them even more special."

"Makes sense," Jacob agreed. "Special roses for a special woman."

Merridy felt a flush on her cheeks at the sentiment. Her fingers tingled, and she felt she would drop the vase if she stood holding it much longer.

As if he could sense her feelings, Jacob reached out to take the vase from her hands. His hands brushed over hers, and, for that moment, Merridy felt time stop. It was not the first time his hands touched hers. He held her hands plenty of times for balance when teaching her to skate. But this time felt different. This time, she thought she felt a spark of electricity.

Her breath inhaled sharply.

What was it that Kara had told her? Something about timing and not getting hurt? Kara was right, of course; she always was. It had been less than two weeks since Jacob and Ameleah's breakup. And while he had told her their relationship had been sinking for some time prior, she still felt partially responsible about the ordeal. She also knew anything this soon would generate confusing emotions for him. The worst thing that could happen, she concluded, was rushing the feelings she had for him – and the feelings he had for her.

Even still, he seemed much, much closer to her than before. Her stomach tightened. The desire to close the distance between them overwhelmed her. She attempted to use all logic and reason within her to fight that desire. Was she not still in her pajamas? Was she not in his apartment? Her own mother's voice began lecturing about safety and appearances in the chaos of her mind. How could she think straight while attempting to listen to her mother, her own logic, and that deepest of desire?

"This is an interesting development."

The few inches that separated Merridy and Jacob grew in an instant. Merridy's startled hands nearly dropped the vase of flowers, but Jacob's grip tightened on it to kept it safe from shattering.

"I guess the request for relationship therapy was a simple rouse to make yourself the victim. Meanwhile, you had this... thing... on the side?"

Ameleah's sharp words cut Merridy. *Thing?* Merridy recognized she was not a Parisian model. She thought she at least qualified as more than a 'thing'. Upset by the word, upset by the accusation, and upset by the possibility of the accusation's truth, Merridy took the vase from Jacob and quickly marched into his bedroom to gather her belongings in order to leave.

"Wait... Merridy..." Jacob called after her. She ignored the plea and closed the door behind her. The statement caused him to turn back to Ameleah. "How are you here? Why are you here?" he yelled.

Her eyes rolled as she held up his apartment key. "My copy, remember?" She threw the key on the coffee table, nearly hitting Porthos in the process. "I am here because I thought maybe we could reconcile." She laughed haughtily. "What a joke."

"Reconciliation was never an option."

"Oh, I see that. You've clearly moved on."

"It's not like that..."

"Isn't it?" Ameleah lashed out. "You were handing some woman in pajamas a bouquet of flowers and about to kiss her!"

Jacob crossed his arms defensively. "I was not about to kiss her."

"No one stands that close to someone unless they're intimate or about to become intimate," she responded with another roll of her eyes. "Whatever. Do what you will in private, Jacob. But don't you dare humiliate me publicly by being seen with *that*."

"How dare you speak of her that way!" he bellowed. The anger in his voice rattled the room and sent Porthos scurrying into the kitchen. Even Ameleah, in all her arrogance, shrunk under Jacob's fury. "She is a kind, talented, and beautiful woman. I would be lucky to be seen with her *in public*. She is twice the woman you ever were, Ameleah. She is here in her pajamas because she was going to spend the night to make sure my dog wouldn't be alone while I was in San Jose. I was handing her flowers to thank her for dropping everything to take care of something I hold dear while I was away. You never once took care of Porthos while I was traveling. I had to hire a sitter. In fact, you don't even like my dog. She *loves* my dog. She understands his name. She reads literature. You only read celebrity gossip magazines. She has substance. You're all... surface." The words bubbled out of him. All of his feelings from the last two weeks, and the last several months, exploded out of him like water breaking from a dam. "You came to my home, uninvited, and now, you can leave. For good. And forever."

Without a word of response, Ameleah turned on her heel and left. Jacob stood alone in the middle of his living room. His shoulders swelled with each deep breath he took as he attempted to regain composure. He had never spoken that way to anyone. Until recently, he never would have considered it. But his words had all been truth. Prior to Merridy, he was discouraged about Ameleah's behaviors. But after meeting Merridy, he knew why that had been. The characteristics

Merridy possessed were the same ones he craved in another. Ameleah had none of them.

The bedroom door opened, and he turned to see Merridy standing shyly. Her clothes had been changed out of the pajamas, her bags were on her shoulders, and she grasped the vase of flowers firmly. "I… need to go…" she finally stated.

"Merridy… I…"

"No," she shook her head forcefully. "I heard what you said. And you're sweet to say that about me. But Jacob, you're…" She walked toward the apartment door. "You're emotional right now. You just broke up with Ameleah. And she just barged in. And…"

Defeat washed over Jacob. Minutes before he had felt emboldened by his tirade. Now he felt as though it was all for naught. "Merridy, I care about you."

"I know you do." She lifted the flowers slightly for emphasis. "Or, you think you do? Jacob, you need time to recover."

"But…"

She grabbed the door handle. "I…" she sighed. "I really have to go." With that, she scurried out of the apartment. Alone in the elevator, she placed a hand over her mouth to muffle the sounds of woeful weeping.

Chapter 16

Jacob leaned against the locker of the South Hills arena after a Saturday morning practice. Thursday and Friday passed in melancholy. His game performance suffered. Not only did he not score, but his penalties were up, his penalty box time was up, and his shots on goal were significantly down. His coach expressed disappointment at the morning practice. If he could not get his mind back on the game, then he faced getting benched.

"What is up with you?" Terry asked his friend as he slathered deodorant under his freshly-showered underarms. "You're playing like…"

"I know." Jacob slipped a long-sleeved shirt over his head. "I'm well aware how bad I am."

"Is this because of the breakup with Ameleah?"

Jacob sighed. Despite Terry being his best friend, he had not divulged a word of Wednesday night's events to him. He feared the inevitable 'I told you so' that would come. Terry had told him that if he made a move too soon with Merridy that it would ruin everything. Those words of wisdom had been true.

The silence made Terry produce a knowing "oooooh" sound. "It's the other woman. Merridy."

Still no reply from Jacob.

"Oh no. You didn't." Terry, half-dressed in his sweat pants, spun on his heel to face his friend. "You moved too soon, didn't you?"

Jacob shrugged his shoulders in response. "She, helped with Porthos. I bought her flowers to thank her."

144

"Flowers? A gift card to a burger place. Not flowers."

"They were beautiful, like her."

Terry slammed his locker shut. "No! Okay, stop. Say no more. We have to distract you from all of this." He pulled out his phone and began scanning events in the area. "Hey, there's a fall festival going on nearby. Let's go. Right now." He hurriedly finished dressing and dragged his friend out of the locker room.

The car ride was silent. Every so often Terry wanted to reiterate 'I told you so' but thought better of it. Signs pointed to parking for the festival, and he complied. "Let's bob for apples..." Terry started.

"...Ameleah showed up."

Terry put his car in park loudly. "What?" he shouted.

"I was handing the flowers to Merridy in my apartment, and Ameleah walked in." When his friend said nothing, Jacob continued, "She was rude to Merridy. So, I told her off. I told her everything I've been despising about her. And I told her everything amazing about Merridy. She left. Merridy left."

"Dude."

Jacob crossed his arms over his chest. "That's all you can say?"

"You don't want to know what else I wish to say." He opened his car door. "Come on." They crossed the street from the parking lot to the large field housing the festival. Booths with local vendors, food trucks, and carnival games greeted them. "Perfect. This will keep you busy. You need to stop thinking about Ameleah and Merridy. Just focus on having fun. Be free my man." He pointed at a vendor booth that housed a dog bakery. "Look, think about your buddy. Let's get him some treats. That dog always cheers you up."

"I do owe him some biscuits." Jacob pulled out his wallet. "Who puts this festival on anyway?" he asked the baker.

"South Hills Restoration Church."

The name of the church made his head jerk up from macaroon-shaped dog biscuits. "Really?"

"Oh!" the woman excitedly responded. "You've heard of it? I go there! It's such a great place. Have you been?"

"No. I have a friend who goes there. That's all." He handed his credit card to her. "A dozen of the macaroons please."

She filled his order and ran the card. "Whenever you want, we would love to have you at a service."

He grunted a response and followed Terry to a high striker carnival game. "Merridy's church is putting on this event."

"You have to be kidding me," Terry sighed heavily. "I bring you here to get your mind off of her, and her church is sponsoring the event?"

Jacob took the hammer from the carnie. "Maybe I'm not supposed to get my mind off of her. What if this is a sign?"

"More like a brutal coincidence," Terry moaned a response.

The hammer swung down hard, and the puck flew to the top and hit the bell. "A woman literally fell into my arms at the same time Ameleah and I are crumbling apart, and you find that a brutal coincidence?"

Terry yanked the hammer from Jacob. "I just don't want to see you hurt again. You're rushing this. I tried to tell you not to. I wanted to protect you. But you did it anyway." He crashed the hammer down onto the lever. "Your heart needs time to heal." The bell dinged to accent his point.

Jacob took the hammer back once more. "My heart is already over Ameleah." Bell ding.

The hammer changed back to Terry. The carnival game attendant attempted to secure it from the two men, but they were caught up in their heated exchange of words and ignored the man. "You think that. But when you're alone, staring at your navel, you start thinking of all the good times the two of you had together. And you miss the pre-Paris Ameleah. And if you're still thinking of *that* Ameleah fondly, then you're still healing. You're just focusing so much on Merridy so you don't have to think about what you've lost."

Slam. Ding!

"It's like Charles Lee Laban killed the old Ameleah and made a new one." Jacob grabbed the hammer. "He ruined everything!"

Slam. Ding!

"Are you boys done?" Breathing hard, both men turned to the owner of the voice. Kara stood behind them with hands angrily on her hips. "I believe you've played more than your fair share. There are others who wish to play the game." She indicated a line that had formed behind them. "The hammer please?"

Jacob handed the hammer to her. "I'm sorry, Kara," he apologized.

She passed the hammer off to the game attendant while patting Jacob on the arm. "I know you're going through some things."

The pat of Kara's hand on his arm sent a spark through Jacob. Not a spark like he felt around Merridy, which felt like electricity that ran heat through his body and settled in his stomach. The spark from Kara felt like some unknown power. He felt compelled to speak with her more, though he was unsure why. "Hey Kara," he called after her. "Can we talk?"

"What you wish to talk about is going to take more time than I can give you right now," she answered him knowingly. "You have a lot weighing on your shoulders. It's manifesting physically." She stopped walking away to face the man who followed her. Her hands fell on both of his shoulders and squeezed them tightly. "Stress, confusion, and pain is not your destiny Jacob Kenway. This is only a season. *Peace I leave with you, My peace I give to you; not as the world gives do I give to you. Let not your heart be troubled, neither let it be afraid.* Step back from your worldly problems for a week, focus on healing your heart and spirit."

Jacob felt tears forming in the corners of his eyes. "I don't know how."

She handed him a flyer from the bag on her hip. "Rest today, and come visit us tomorrow morning." A final pat of his arm, and the woman walked on to another crowd of festival attenders.

Terry stepped up behind his friend and put a reassuring arm around his shoulders. "Let's go."

Chapter 17

Six days passed with no correspondence between Merridy and Jacob. It had been nearly a week and a half since she ran out of his apartment. The flowers gifted to her sat on her bedroom dresser, slowly wilting as the days passed by. A few petals sat around the bottom of the vase.

She stared with dead eyes at the flowers. Every morning brought the same routine: check phone for missed messages from Jacob, cry with the guilt that she had ruined everything, and stare at the flowers. The time that was once dedicated to devotional reading and prayer was now spent in self-pity. Each day it worsened. Each day she felt hollower than the day before. Now, she could not even find it within her to go to work, and texted her boss to let him know she would be out sick.

Her phone lit up sporadically throughout the morning as she laid curled up in her bed. She'd glance at her phone to see if it was Jacob, but every time it would be Kara. Merridy ignored the messages. She would not even swipe her phone to read them. Instead, she would stare at the dying flowers and fall in-and-out of sleep.

Shortly after noon, a loud knock on her bedroom door and a shout awoke her. "Merridy! Are you alive?" The door opened to reveal Kara. "Merridy!"

"What are you doing here?" Merridy responded wearily. "How are you here?"

Kara held up a key. "Apartment key for emergencies." She assertively walked forward to the bedside and placed a hand on Merridy's forehead to check for fever. "You didn't answer my texts. I called your office, and they said you were sick. I needed to make sure you didn't need medical attention. That was our promise to check on each other, wasn't it?"

"I'm not that kind of sick, Kara." She rolled over to face the wall opposite her friend. "I just didn't want to people today."

"Oh." Kara's eyes drifted to the dying flowers on the dresser. "You're heart-sick today." She took a seat on the bed and began to stroke Merridy's hair tenderly. "I know heart sickness. It can hurt deeply, and make you feel worthless inside. Don't let that define you Merridy. Not when you are so close to achieving the plans God has for you."

"How can I sing when I feel dead inside?" Merridy sobbed. "I ruined everything Kara!"

"You didn't ruin anything," Kara reminded her friend. "If it's meant to be with Jacob, it's meant to be. Things will work itself out there. And I know for a fact that he's very confused about all of this as well. Just trust in the Lord to sort it out in *His* time. But what's important right now is that practice you have tomorrow for the tree lighting ceremony."

Merridy rolled over. Her puffy eyes met Kara's. "I don't know if I can. Maybe someone else should go."

"Oh, I don't think so." Kara stood abruptly and pulled Merridy halfway off the bed. "Get up and wipe your face off, girl. We're going to an ice rink. We're focusing you back on the important things."

Despite Merridy's protests, Kara proved to be stronger, and she wrestled her friend out of bed toward the shower. After a lengthy battle of wills, Kara drove Merridy to the South Hills ice rink. "Why here?" Merridy asked. "It's where *he* practices."

"He's not practicing now. But you're going to." Kara knelt to adjust Merridy's skates that were half-heartedly tied to her feet.

"Remember the reason you met him to begin with? Because you were learning to skate in order to perform and win that record contract?"

"Yeah." The response was half-hearted. "I guess."

Kara sighed. Merridy and Jacob had only known each other four weeks before the apartment-incident. Though they did not see each other often in that time, she knew the two had been in contact frequently via phone. Their bond was undeniable. She felt that in Jacob's spirit at the fall festival. She felt that in Merridy's spirit now. But she knew the record contract had the upmost importance. "God give me wisdom," she whispered as she led her friend onto the ice. "Merridy, you know that Jacob just went through a very hard, very public break-up. He is suffering as much as you are. His feelings for you are real. Your feelings for him are real. You are both scared because of the timing of it all. You're torn because as much as you want to be with him, you don't want to be a rebound. And I believe he feels the same. He does not want you to be a rebound. Therefore, while it hurts deeply to be apart from someone you have these feelings for, it will only make things better in the long run. Let God work on Jacob's heart while you work on the plans that He has for you."

"You're right. And I've known all this, all this time." She pulled away from Kara, skating on her own to center ice. "I don't like the push and pull I've felt the entire month of October. And I shouldn't let it distract me. I *know* this. But why can't I get over it?"

"Because you're not allowing yourself to get over it."

The words stung Merridy hard.

"When you focus on something, it's all you can think of." She pointed to Merridy skating. "When you were focused on the fact you couldn't skate, then you couldn't skate. But now look at you. You're not focused on your inability, and you're skating just fine. You have to stop focusing on the negative."

Merridy paused her skating to contemplate the words of her friend.

"If you stop thinking about Jacob, then you will start thinking about everything else that you have pushed away. And maybe you focused a little more on him because you were scared about your big break coming up. That's okay to be scared. But we have to refocus on it, because that practice is tomorrow. It's the only practice they are doing before the actual event."

"You're right." She skated to meet her friend at the ice entrance. "I'm going to get my guitar out and try to skate with it on."

"Good girl," Kara encouraged her. "I'm going to the restroom." Kara changed into her slip-ons and left the rink for the hallway of the facility. She eyed the entrance to the public restrooms, then eyed the double doors that led to the executive offices of the Twisters.

The fact that Jacob had not come to church on Sunday concerned her. She knew he needed the spiritual guidance; his soul and heart longed for it at the fall festival. She suspected Terry had kept him preoccupied with the normal 'worldly' ways of 'getting over a girl' – and she noted his playing that week had suffered from it. Her mind told her to simply go to the restroom and return to Merridy, but her feet marched forward to the executive offices.

"Hello," the receptionist greeted her. "Welcome to the home of the Twisters. How may I help you?"

"I was at the rink..." Kara started. "Well, I need to speak to Jacob Kenway. Is there a way to page him? I know he's off today..."

The receptionist's eyebrows raised. "Ma'am, we can't just page a player for anyone who walks in..."

Of course. Kara sighed heavily. She knew this. What had she expected? Why did her feet force her this way? "I'm sorry." She shook her head. "No, you're right. My friend has him on her phone. I'll reach out to him that way. That was dumb." She turned to leave. "I'm sorry again. My brain was not on."

"Kara?"

She froze at the voice. It was not Jacob's, or Terry's, or any other voice she would have expected while standing in the lobby of the Twister's executive offices.

"It *is* you. I thought I recognized your voice down the hall."

Sheepishly, she turned toward the speaker. A blonde woman stood there, holding an artificial Christmas tree. "Long time, no see, Elyssa."

"For real. I thought I would never see you again." She sat the tree down in the corner of the room next to boxes full of holiday decorations. "How have you been?"

Kara bit the tip of her tongue. Elyssa Brooks had been her closest high school friend. They played hockey together. Elyssa was also the reason she stopped playing the sport. "I've been okay. Found a different path in life than hockey. Do marketing for an insurance company." She shrugged. "See that you're still in the hockey life."

"Yeah, I do marketing as well, for the team." She nodded at the trees. "And I guess part-time decorator." An awkward silence

153

passed between the two. "I'm so glad I ran into you Kara. I'd love to catch up – really, truly catch up."

Weight shifted from one foot to another. This run-in had been unexpected. Kara prepared her heart to talk to Jacob, not to Elyssa. "Yeah, I guess that would be good to do. Do you see any of the others?"

"Certainly. We see Tom all the time. He bought the little indie label they used to play for, and we help him with that." She smiled hopefully at Kara. "Adrienne is helping him too. They'd all love to see you."

The names of her high school friends filled Kara with mixed emotions. She had not communicated with them in over a decade. She avoided social media in order to not reconnect. Now she was being held accountable to her past. "I think... I think I'd love to see them too."

Elyssa walked to the receptionist desk and grabbed a business card from a display. "Here's my info. Please let me know a time we can get together." She handed it to Kara. "And Kara? I know it was a long time ago, but that day has weighed heavily on my heart. I'm sorry."

"That is water under the bridge," Kara said reassuringly, though she was not sure if she believed it herself. "Thank you. I'll see you around, Elyssa." She tucked the business card in her pocket and shuffled away to the restroom.

"That was a long restroom trip," Merridy remarked to her friend upon Kara's return to the ice. "Are *you* okay?"

Kara stepped onto the ice in her slip-ons rather than changing to skates. "Yeah, I just ran into somebody I used to know while I was out there. A girl from my high school."

"Looks like I'm not the only one with something heavy weighing on them." Merridy spun around on the ice while strumming her guitar. "But at least I am fully confident in performing at the practice tomorrow."

"Excellent. Because I think we're due for some TexMex after this week."

"Amen sister." Merridy skated off the ice and handed her guitar to Kara. "So was the high school girl a friend?"

"She was my best friend, back then," Kara told Merridy. "We played hockey together. Made it to state and nationals together." She closed the guitar case. "But when we tried out for Team USA, for the Olympics, we were put on opposite scrimmage teams. And things got heated. And I was injured. She went to the Olympics with Team USA. I went home to re-think my life."

"Oh no," Merridy whispered as she put her skates away. "Your friendship was ruined over that?"

"I didn't have contact with her or any of our mutual friends after that." Kara lifted the case and her bag. "I was in a dark place. I was bitter. And I wasn't right with God. I've had to move on from there, but I guess it's always been something that I've not fully dealt with. Funny, He gave me advice for you, but forced me to deal with my own issues."

Merridy shouldered her bag. "That settles one thing."

"What's that?" Kara asked.

"We're definitely ordering the guacamole." Both girls laughed as they left the arena.

Chapter 18

The practice for the tree lighting ceremony took place at a private rink rented by the show's coordinators. The lead coordinator reviewed the order of ceremony, and the event planners allowed each special guest to perform once. Merridy went after an elementary school choir, but before an Olympic ice dancing couple. Kara, accompanying her friend, recorded the practice on her phone for further review later.

"How did it go?" Merridy asked her while taking off her skates.

"Really well. I thought you would get your nerves out in practice, but didn't look like you had any!"

Merridy giggled. "Maybe I have a future as a great actress."

"Hello... Merridy Christmas?" The two women stopped laughing in order to gauge the middle-aged man who stood behind them. He wore a designer suit, polished black shoes, black-rimmed glasses, and his peppered brown hair was slicked back. In his right hand he held a leather brief case. "I'm Casimir Alvah, from Echo Star Records. We sponsor the tree lighting ceremony."

"You sponsor it?" Kara asked.

"It's one way we find our fresh, new talent." He smiled and winked. "We've yet to be disappointed. In fact, Miss Christmas, I think once again we've struck gold."

The compliment caused Merridy to laugh happily, and she forced herself to not hug Kara. This was what she had waited on – a positive reaction from a record label representative.

"You see, before the show even happens, we like to approach the talent, give them a tour of the studios, sign a few papers, and do a little fine-tuning. That way, when the tree lighting ceremony happens, it's a great kickstart to a holiday record." Casimir waived his hand absently. "It's all rather fast-paced, but who can be slow during the holidays?"

"Wait, you're offering her a record deal, before she even performs?" Kara asked.

"More like, we're offering her a seat at the table," he clarified, "to discuss a deal."

"Oh, my goodness!" Merridy exclaimed happily. She hugged Kara. "It's happening!"

Kara returned the hug tightly. "Yes ma'am, it is. You just had to keep your faith and focus!" She patted Merridy's head affectionately then turned to Casimir. "When is this 'sitting at the table' happening? The ceremony is only three weeks away, and you mentioned an album in time for Christmas?"

"Are you her... agent?" Casimir asked. "Usually I discuss this directly with the talent."

The comment took Kara aback, but Merridy simply replied. "Kara is a dear friend who helps me out. But she is right. When does this table talk happen?"

"It can happen right now, if you'd like. I noted there are plenty of restaurants in walking distance of here that we can grab a late lunch at. I can give you a nice overview of what the agreement is, and let you look over the papers. If all goes well, then we can head to New York at your earliest convenience to begin."

"Oh wow, it really is fast-paced in the industry, isn't it?" Merridy felt herself exuding joy, but also feeling overwhelmed at the rush of everything. She wanted to laugh in happiness and cry in fear.

"When opportunity knocks, we answer quickly." Casimir answered. "Please, I would love to discuss things more."

Merridy glanced at Kara. "Yes, we can..."

Casimir turned to Kara as well. "I'm sorry, but your friend... what is your name?"

"Kara. Kara Jackson," she responded. Her arms folded across her chest. She felt a sense of unease about Casimir but could not place why she felt that way.

"Yes, well, I'm sorry Miss Jackson. Our company policy strictly wants talent-only to attend these meetings unless you're authorized legal counsel. Are... you...?"

"No. No, I'm not." Kara turned to Merridy. "This is your choice. But if you go speak with Mr. Alvah, I would like to speak with you first."

Merridy glanced between Kara and Casimir. The nerves were beginning to win; she never attempted anything business-related without seeking Kara's advice. But she knew she could not let fear stand in the way of her dreams. "Yes, I would like to grab that meal with you, Mr. Alvah. But I do want to speak with my friend first, in private."

Casimir nodded. "Of course. I will await you in the foyer." He walked out of the rink to the building's foyer, giving the two a chance to speak.

"Do you think he's the real deal?" she asked Kara. "This isn't a scam, right?"

Kara paused thoughtfully. She knew of Echo Star Records – they had produced many female pop stars. In fact, female pop star creation was their specialty. Although Merridy wanted to record faith-based music rather than pop music, the fact that they worked with female talent was a positive. It could get her foot in the door of the industry. It was not unheard of for an artist to change record labels as they grew in notoriety. "No, I don't think it's a scam. I think Casimir is what he says he is." She wondered why she had an uneasy feeling about him, but she shook the thought away. "He acts a bit like a sleezy record company guy. But I think that's the personality they look for in that position. They're about the fast-pitch and quick-sale. Think of him as a used cars salesman... and don't sign anything without a lawyer."

"Right," Merridy agreed. "I just want to hear what they're offering. I'm not signing *anything*." She slipped on her shoes. "And I will remember everything he says so I can tell you about it later."

"Correct." Kara took Merridy's guitar case and her tote with the ice skates inside. "I will go put these in the car, and I will eat at one of the restaurants you will *not* be at so I can wait to drive you home."

Merridy waived the sentiment away. "Don't worry about that. I will get an Uber after dinner. I don't know how long this conversation will be, and you have your own project you have to work on. You've been putting it off enough for my sake."

"Are you sure?"

"Of course. I can't be selfish, or a child. I need to do this, Kara."

Kara nodded hesitantly. "You're right." They left the rink to join Casimir, and Kara offered a final hug before leaving her friend behind.

"Surf and turf work for you, Miss Christmas?" Casimir offered. He smiled again. "The closest restaurant is a seafood and steak joint. Slightly high-end, but these shoes weren't made for walking great distances."

Merridy glanced at his shoes and realized they were leather designer shoes whose price tag was more than the cost of her entire wardrobe. "Oh, of course." She followed Casimir to the restaurant. "Do you live in New York, Mr. Alvah?"

"I do, in Manhattan. And please, call me Casimir."

"Wow. Manhattan. That's really nice."

"Have you ever been?" he asked, surprised.

"No. But I've seen it a lot... on TV, and... movies," she added flatly. "It looks beautiful. Especially Central Park."

"Yes, my apartment overlooks Central Park."

Merridy did not want to know how much the rent on such an apartment would be.

"And if all goes well, you can fly up to New York next week to see the park for yourself."

"Wait, really, next week?" Merridy's voice squeaked out the question. What would she do about work? Could she take vacation with that little warning or use her sick days? Did she have enough sick days? Would her current job be pointless if she secured the record deal anyway? It was a factor she had not even considered while pursuing the contract.

"Like I said, we move fast. A Monday flight would be preferable."

"I'll have to work it out with my boss."

Casimir laughed. "Merridy, if you agree to work with Echo Star, you won't need your other job. We make sure our talent is well-compensated for their efforts. Do you know some of the people under our label?"

"I'm not certain, but I think Christina Apollo and Brittany Clare were, or are? I think I'm showing my age with those two. I was a pre-teen when they were popular."

"Oh yes, we have both of them. And both of them are making a comeback, actually. You might get to meet them when you come to New York. I think they're in studio right now. And on top of them, we have Kellie Crane, Lila Winters, Alicia East, and Megan Mill. That's the last four female Grammy winners in the past four years. We're very proud of our female talent."

"As you should be with a lineup like that!" Merridy exclaimed. All of the women mentioned were mega-popstars with amazing careers. The idea of receiving a fraction of their success overwhelmed her mind. "Your label seems like it's well-versed in female talent."

"It *is* our area of expertise. Our talent team knows exactly what to do for women to prepare them for the public eye of scrutiny. When it comes to be an award-winning, platinum-selling artist, talent is only a fraction of the equation. Image and public relations are the most important factors."

Merridy's stomach tightened. She wanted to disagree with the statement, but she also remembered how much Kara worked on her social media presence and her wardrobe. Perhaps Casimir was correct.

"That is what we are offering you, Merridy. In exchange for your amazing vocals, we offer you a team that will place you among the stars." He opened the restaurant door for Merridy. "This could be the first day of your new life, Miss Christmas."

"How exciting and terrifying." The two were seated at a small table in the middle of the restaurant. When Merridy's eyes landed on the menu, she noted prices were not listed. Her stomach tensed. Could she afford anything here? She would have to select whatever she thought would be the cheapest – like a nice salad.

Casimir adjusted his glasses further along the bridge of his nose in order to review the menu. "Now, I must know, what inspired the stage name 'Merridy Christmas'?"

"Oh, that's not a stage name. It's my actual name." Merridy noted a grilled chicken Caesar salad. That was it. That was the option. Certainly not the steaks, the seafood, or even the pear, gorgonzola and candied-pecan salad. She felt the multiple specialty ingredients would drive up the cost. "It's a combination of melody and merry."

"Merry Christmas? That would have been a hard name to bear." He took his cellphone out of his pocket and typed into it briefly. "But fitting for this time of year."

The waiter arrived, and they ordered their respective beverages: Casimir, a glass of Chardonnay; Merridy, a glass of water. She smiled as the waiter walked away. "Have to stay hydrated."

"Of course." He lifted his brief case and took a folder full of papers out. "Our basic contract," he explained. "I can review it with you and explain what it would mean to you."

Merridy moved aside items on the table to make room for the paperwork. "Yes please. I would like that."

Before they had a chance to review the paperwork, the waiter returned with their drinks and took their lunch order. Casimir ordered the filet mignon with béarnaise sauce; she ordered her salad with dressing on the side.

"Now, without further interruptions…" Casimir joked. "The contract is a five-year-term with an optional resign at the end of the five years. It includes a release commitment for four full-length studio albums plus one live album. We typically do this in year four or five."

She eyed the papers that contained multiple paragraphs of legalese under headers that indicated term contracts and release commitments.

"We also offer a great signing bonus, if you look on page five." Casimir took a deep drink of his wine.

She reviewed the pages to get to page five. "Signing bonus?"

"Oh yes," Casimir laughed. "The money. That's the game-changer, isn't it? Fifty-thousand sign-on bonus."

"Fifty thousand?" she gasped. That was more than her current yearly salary – and it was just a signing bonus. "That *is* a game changer. Seems so much for a signing bonus."

"Advance for a record is no joke. We also a have an industry-standard two-percent royalty along with the advance bonus. There's standard deductions, of course, like recording deductions, production costs, packaging costs, marketing and public relation fees – the whole basic package." The waiter placed their meals in front of them. Casimir waved a hand at the filet before him. "You're an investment by the company. They invest in you, and in turn, you and the company both make a fair profit."

Merridy put the paperwork to the side. "True. I understand the company has to make their money too." She lightly sprinkled her dressing over the salad. "It's an investment like the food we eat - an investment in our health."

"We spend money on higher quality foods in order to put better nutrients in our bodies."

A chunk of romaine lettuce entered her mouth, preventing her from responding. She did not have the heart to tell Casimir that she lived on twenty-nine cent ramen noodles loaded with whatever vegetables were on sell at the grocery store. The milk she bought the night before had been a splurge. Now she was thankful she had – tonight was going to be a stress-induced, dessert-making night. Sodium-loaded ramen and stress-eaten desserts contributed to her weight. With fifty-thousand dollars, perhaps she could afford to eat healthier and lose some pounds.

"As I mentioned before, we would be rushing to get a holiday album out fairly quickly. The ideal would be in time for black Friday sales."

Merridy wiped her mouth. "But the ceremony is on black Friday. It's three weeks away..."

"We do fast. If all goes right, we can get you in New York on Monday. Tuesday will be a meeting with our image manager, and we'd get the ball rolling from there. He'd probably want to get you in hair, makeup, and wardrobe, then do a photoshoot for promos which would take most of Wednesday. Then the rest of the week would be creative meetings and studio time."

She pulled out her phone to check the calendar.

"Our marketing team looked over your social media presence before I came down here. We have a feeling of what you're going for, and they can take it over for you after the creative meeting."

"Will either of you be having dessert?" the waiter interrupted.

Casimir pushed his plate to the side. "None for me, thanks."

"Me neither. I barely finished this salad. Thank you though. It was delicious. I've never had chicken in a salad that was so moist." She handed the salad bowl to the waiter.

"Thank you, ma'am. Will this be on one check or separate?"

"Separate please," Merridy answered before Casimir could answer. She was not sure what the record company covered, but she knew without a doubt that she could not afford to cover Casimir's meal.

When the table was cleared of dishes, she pulled the paperwork back in front of her. A solid thirty pages made up the contract.

"What do you think?" Casimir asked. "Does it sound like something you'd be interested in?"

"I'm very interested, of course," she replied, with more giddiness than she intended. She shuffled to the final page of the contract to review its contents before the signature line. "There's so much to it. I'd need to read it all..." she paused to accept the check from the waiter. "Thank you." She opened the black padded guest check presenter meekly to glance at the number inside. Free water, thankfully. The salad cost a cool $18.50. She slipped her credit card into the presenter and handed it back to the waiter.

Casimir did the same. She wondered what his ticket was for wine and filet, if water and a salad cost $18.50. "Of course, we would expect you to read it all," he focused the conversation back on the contract. "There is much in it that we did not review. It discusses who your image manager would be, and his expectations as well."

"You mentioned an image manager before. What does he do?" Merridy asked. "I have a, friend, who has an agent that's developed his... image... I guess? Is it like an agent?"

"Agents do that, in part. But, with the level of playing field that you will be on, you will require a veteran of the industry who can compete with other divas."

The word 'diva' caught Merridy off-guard. She never considered herself to be a potential 'diva'. Was she flattered that she, a slightly overweight auburn-haired country-girl could be a diva, or terrified that she would be ridiculed miserably for even attempting it?

"Here you go, ma'am." The waiter returned the presenter and credit card to her.

She silently pulled the receipt out of its pouch in order to sign it. Her signature almost ran off the narrow slip of paper and onto the contract below it. "Oops, better put this away before I spill something all over it," she joked. The receipt was placed back in its presenter and the contract back into its folder. "Is this something I can take home and review, or..." Her voice trailed off as she noted a group walking past them to a table.

The host led two women, Terry, and Jacob to a table diagonally behind her. Jacob's eyes noted her, and he froze where he stood. "Merridy?"

A thousand thoughts churned through her mind: Was he here on a double date? Was this why he stopped talking to her? Was she only a temporary novelty while he dealt with his breakup?

"I didn't expect to see you here," he stammered.

Her eyes drifted to the woman who sat next to the empty chair. She was beautiful – tall, lithe, golden hair, blue eyes. In fact, she was the type of woman that Merridy visualized when hearing 'diva'. This woman could be the diva, not her. "Clearly."

Nervously, Jacob turned to look at the woman and back to Merridy. "It's not... I mean, yes, but no. Terry needed a... I... it's complicated." His face reddened at her stern facial expression. Then he noted Casimir across from her. "Though... I've apparently interrupted something as well."

Not wanting him to assume *she* was on a date like he was, she indicated Casimir with a wave of her hand. "Jacob, this is Casimir Alvah, from Echo Star Records. Casimir, this is Jacob Kenway, from the Texas Twisters."

Casimir stood and offered his hand to Jacob. "A pleasure to meet you, Mr. Kenway. The Twisters... are a hockey team. Correct? I went to a few Islander games back in my youth. As I recall, it was quite exciting."

"I'm sure it was," Jacob replied. "I'm guessing early 80's, when they won back-to-back-to-back-to-back Stanley Cups."

"Good guess," Casimir acknowledged. "It was."

Jacob turned his attention back to Merridy. "Echo Star Records? That's exciting."

"It is." Merridy made a point of turning her attention back to Casimir. "About the contract?"

"Right! It was nice meeting you Mr. Kenway." He turned to pick up the folder with the contract papers.

Merridy grabbed her purse without acknowledging Jacob.

"Please... Merridy..." he whispered. "Let me..."

She hurried away from him toward the restaurant door; Casimir hurried after her. "Former boyfriend?" he finally asked her when they reached outside.

The question caused her to pale. "No. Just a friend – if even that. Now, about the contract?"

"I'll email you a copy to review, if you'd like." He pulled his phone out of his jacket pocket. "But before we part ways Merridy, would you be interested in coming to New York on Monday? Just to look around, no strings attached. Get a feel for what you're signing up for. See the diva you can become."

Her eyes drifted to the restaurant. "Yes. Yes, I'd like that."

Chapter 19

The party chatted and laughed over lobster tails and filet mignon, but Jacob could only hear one word: *Clearly*. The tone of Merridy's comment cut him deeply. He had done everything he could to separate himself from her and give her the space that everyone recommended.

When Terry asked for a wingman, he had swiftly declined. Then Terry reminded him that the fastest way to moving on to a new relationship was to rebound with something meaningless. "What could be more meaningless than a wingman's duty?" Terry had asked.

Jacob cringed at the thought. Meaningless? *Clearly* it was not. His fingers drifted toward his phone that sat beside his plate. Should he text her? Should he explain everything to her? He wanted to be sitting with Merridy at this table. He wanted to hear all about this record company executive and the contract. He wanted to hear about her practice. He wanted to ask her what she was doing for Thanksgiving. He wanted to talk about her Thanksgiving memories on her family's ranch.

Yes, he was sitting next to a woman who seemed nice enough. But it was not the woman he wanted to be sitting with. Denise, or was her name Danielle? She had too much air in her laughter. The movements of her hands felt rehearsed. Every word spoken felt as though they were tactically planted. But Merridy: she laughed from her stomach. Her hands awkwardly fumbled with her hair, or with each other, never knowing what to do with them in such an innocent way that it made him smile thinking about it. Most importantly, her words were honest.

His phone buzzed. Maybe it was Merridy. Maybe she did not like the way things went down between them either.

'Hey Jacob. It's Kara, Merridy's friend.
I swiped your number from her phone.
You have really been on my heart lately.
I wanted you to know I'm praying for you,
and I really would like to see you at
church tomorrow. Service starts at 10,
but we offer breakfast beforehand. I
think it would do everyone some good.'

He tapped the side of his phone in contemplation. It would be a place he could see Merridy, and talk with her to explain himself.

'Yes. Thank you. I will be there
tomorrow.'

Typing the words gave him a sense of peace. Tomorrow, everything would be set right.

"Hey White Rabbit, little late to the fun?" Terry asked him. All three were staring at him. "Little rude to sit there on your phone."

"Sorry." Jacob tucked his phone into his pocket. He turned to the woman next to him. "Tell me, what is a dream you have? What do you want to achieve in your future?"

The woman's rehearsed smile faded for a moment as confusion clouded her eyes briefly. "Excuse me?"

"Don't you have a goal you want to achieve this year?"

170

She tapped a finger on her chin. "I suppose... I want to get new ski boots before a Christmas trip to Aspen. I would love for you to come with us there."

"Your family goes to Aspen for Christmas?" Jacob asked, slightly excited to hear about a family tradition.

The woman laughed. "Oh no! I go with my sorority sisters and their guys. They'd love to meet you! The lodge we stay at is low-key savage..." Jacob's eyes turned to his half-eaten meal as he tuned out the rest of her dribble about the Aspen lodge and the gifts she expected to receive from her sorority sisters. The words blurred until she asked. "You think you could come?"

"No," he answered flatly. "I always spend Christmas with my family."

"Really?" Her voice had an air of disbelief.

"Yes. My brother, Eddie, and his wife, just had their first child. It will be the child's first Christmas. It's going to be very special this year." He stood and placed cash on the table to cover his meal as well as his companion's meal. "Terry, I'm sorry... I can't... I have to go." Protests from his friend echoed behind him as he left the restaurant into the sunlight. His phone burned in his pocket. He desperately wanted to call Merridy. He resisted.

Instead, he walked to a nearby shop to find a congratulatory gift for her record deal in hopes of giving it to her the next day. His focus remained on Sunday morning. Saturday became a blur for him as he drifted in-and-out of stores to find the perfect gift. Even the greetings of Porthos and subsequent cuddles did little to distract him from the coming morning as he eventually drifted to a restless sleep.

The restless sleep culminated into a dreary morning. Everything he attempted took longer to achieve. The coffee brewed slowly. Porthos had to sniff every tree, sign, and hydrant on his walk. The elevator stopped on every floor. The shower refused to warm. None of his clothes matched. Every street light was red. Despite every circumstance that seemed to weigh him down and delay his journey, he managed to pull into the South Hills Restoration Church parking lot. The breakfast gathering and morning classes were over, but he managed to walk in a few minutes before the main worship service began.

A gentleman opened the church doors and greeted him warmly. Several others greeted him as well, and he slowly walked through the semi-crowded foyer, looking for a glimpse of Merridy.

"Jacob! You made it!"

He spun around to see Kara waving at him from a cluster of young women. He noted Merridy was not among them. "Hey Kara."

She purposefully strode to him. "You made it just in time." Her hand landed on his elbow, and she gently guided him into the sanctuary as they spoke.

"If something could slow me down this morning, it did."

"Yeah," she nodded. "The world does that on Sunday mornings."

"Is Merridy here? I have something for her... I saw her yesterday, with the record deal guy..." He lifted his right hand that held a white gift bag. Tissue paper adorned with music notes popped above its upper rim. "It's just a congratulations..." he mumbled.

"That's really sweet of you," Kara reassured him. "She's here. She's on stage. She sings with the worship team, but you can give it to her afterward. For now, just focus on the music and the message." Kara indicated empty seats. "I saved you a seat with us."

They took their seats, but Jacob felt awkward. He only ever attended church when he visited his parents. The hometown church always felt more like a social gathering to him. Here, he knew no one except the woman next to him and the one on stage. His eyes turned to the stage where the praise and worship team entered to their respective microphones and instruments. The sight of Merridy made his stomach tighten – and he wondered if coming was the right choice.

"Good morning South Hills!" the man at the keyboard greeted in his microphone. "Are we happy to be in the Lord's house this morning?"

There were claps and "amens" from the attenders. Jacob looked around. He had never been in such a vocal church before.

The man continued. "This is the day that the Lord has made. Let us *rejoice* and be glad in it!"

The response was more enthusiastic than before.

"Join us in prayer before we begin to lead you in worship."

Jacob bowed his head as the man prayed aloud. At the end of the prayer, with a collective 'amen', the music from the worship group began playing.

Merridy stepped up to the microphone while strumming her guitar. "No matter the up's and down's of life... no matter what confusion hangs over your head, whether in victory, or in defeat... there is one truth we can cling to – and that is our victory in Jesus. He is all my hope and peace." She then began singing, and Jacob found himself transfixed on her as he stood alongside Kara.

What can wash away my sin?
Nothing but the blood of Jesus.
What can make me whole again?
Nothing but the blood of Jesus.

Oh, precious is the flow,
That makes me white as snow,
No other fount I know,
Nothing but the blood of Jesus.

She stepped back from the microphone to strum her guitar during a musical bridge.

This is all my hope and peace,
Nothing but the blood of Jesus.
This is all my righteousness,
Nothing but the blood of Jesus.

Oh, precious is the flow,
That makes me white as snow,
No other fount I know,
Nothing but the blood of Jesus.

After another musical bridge, Merridy sang the chorus again before ending the song. She laughed. "I know sometimes we don't sing those old songs, but I quite like the old songs sometimes. Sometimes the new songs, they don't talk that much about the cross, and the blood, and that's okay. The new songs are good, and worthy, and have their place in worship. But sometimes I just want to sing about the cross. Is that okay if we sing about the cross today?"

Jacob was not sure what she meant about the old songs versus the new songs. He was completely lost in everything she said. But he glanced at Kara next to him who clapped and raised her hands as the next song began. He felt like a fish out of water.

On a hill far away stood an old rugged cross,
The emblem of suffering and shame.
And I love that old where the Dearest and Best,
For a world of sinners, was slain.

So I'll cherish the old rugged cross,
Till my trophies at last I lay down;
I will cling to the old rugged cross,
And exchange it some day for a crown.

Oh, that old rugged cross, so despised by the world,
Has a wondrous attraction for me;
For the dear Lamb of God left His glory above,
To bear it to dark Calvary.

So I'll cherish the old rugged cross,
Till my trophies at last I lay down;
I will cling to the old rugged cross,
And exchange it some day for a crown.

A hush fell over the church body, and even Jacob, in his confusion of everything going on, knew something special was happening. He bowed his head and closed his eyes. The air tingled with electricity. The hairs on his arms stood at attention. Then a woman further behind him spoke in a language he never heard before. Moments after the woman spoke the foreign tongue, Kara began speaking in a commanding voice to all in attendance: "Did I not say 'Ask, and it shall be given you; seek, and ye shall find; knock, and it shall be opened unto you'? You have asked it, and will receive it. You who are seeking will find. You who are knocking, My door will be opened unto you. For I, the Good Father, give good gifts unto My children who wait upon Me."

The words caused several people among the attendees to whisper 'thank you Lord' and other exclamations of gratitude. Jacob was unsure what had happened. But the words echoed in his mind and heart. Were those words for him? They spoke straight to everything he struggled with. Tentatively, he opened his eyes and glanced at the stage. Merridy stood there with a tissue in hand, crying. He wondered why she cried. He wondered many things about this experience. He closed his eyes again to contemplate.

He believed in God. His parents occasionally attended a church when he was younger, but they did not devoutly go every Sunday. He knew a few stories from the Bible, like David and Goliath, or Noah's Ark, but he had no deep understanding of the text. He did not know the songs being sung like those around him. He never prayed. He was not even sure of what happened. But something within him he felt that those words were for him. He grunted slightly in discouragement. Why would God bother speaking to him when he did not even claim to be a Christian?

Someone began playing the piano softly, and he heard Merridy began singing.

Why should I feel discouraged?
Why should the shadows come?
Why should my heart be lonely,
And long for heaven and home?
When Jesus is my portion,
My constant friend is He.

His eye is on the sparrow,
And I know He watches me.

Jacob opened his eyes to watch her. Kara lifted her hands next to him and began singing along with Merridy, "His eye is on the sparrow, and I know He watches me."

I sing because I'm happy,
I sing because I'm free,
For His eye is on the sparrow,
And I know He watches me.

The pastor stepped up to the microphone while the music continued playing softly. "Thank you, God, for blessing us with Your Presence today. Can we just take a moment to praise Him for all that He is?"

Jacob looked around as many in the congregation shouted "hallelujahs" and others clapped. He joined the clapping.

"A Word was given for someone today. Maybe for more than one of us. Maybe you are struggling with this Word. Maybe you are struggling with your faith. Maybe you don't even know your Father… but He knows you. And just like His eye is on the sparrow, He is watching you. He is waiting for you to rest in Him. If you need that refreshing of His Spirit, or if you want to take that first step in your walk with Christ, or if you just need prayer for anything, these altars are open for you. Take those few steps towards Him, and He will welcome you like the good, good Father He is." He motioned to the praise team. "Keep singing team as these altars fill."

The pastor replaced the microphone in its stand and walked off the stage to begin praying with people who walked toward the altar. Jacob watched intently as tears streamed down people's faces as they prayed.

"Let not your heart be troubled,"
His tender word I hear,
And resting on His goodness,
I lose my doubts and fears;
Though by the path He leadeth,
But one step I may see;
His eye Is on the sparrow,
And I know He watches me.
His eye is on the sparrow,
And I know He watches me.

Jacob clenched the back of the seat in front of him as he continued to observe the scene. He listened to the words of the song. How did the song seem to know exactly what he needed to hear? It was as if a voice whispered to Merridy what she should sing to encourage him. Yes. That word was for him. He knew it. He could not explain the feeling that welled up in his chest. He wanted to cry out. What should he do?

He turned to ask Kara what he should do, but she was gone from her seat, praying over others at the altar. The altar. A hesitant step toward the end of the row of seats. Another step. With each step, Jacob felt more and more an overwhelming urge to get to the altar. It was no longer a curiosity, but a longing. He wanted what these people had.

Whenever I am tempted,
Whenever clouds arise,
When songs give place to sighing,
When hope within me dies,
I draw the closer to Him,
From care He sets me free;
His eye is on the sparrow,
And I know He watches me.

He followed his feet to the front of the church that served as the altar. Unassured of himself, he bowed his head to have an internal dialogue: "Hi God. It's me, Jacob. I don't know what I'm doing. But I know I need you. I want what these people have, and I know that to get that is with You."

I sing because I'm happy,
I sing because I'm free,
For His eye is on the sparrow,
And I know He watches me.

The singer was a different voice. He paused his internal dialogue when he noted that Merridy no longer sang. Then he felt hands on his shoulders, and he heard Kara praying over him. Soon after, the pastor stood before him. "Yes, yes, the Good Father is waiting for you with open arms," he spoke to Jacob. "You want that freedom in the Lord. You want His Peace."

Jacob was surprised – how did this man know what he was wanting?

He gently took Jason's hands in his and lifted them in the air. "Are you ready to ask Jesus Christ to be your Lord and Savior?"

He breathed in deeply. Was he? Did he even know what he was getting into? His head swarmed with the struggle. In one instant, he wanted to give a whole-hearted 'yes' to the pastor; in the next instant, he wanted to run away.

Then Kara spoke from behind him, "Peace I leave with you, my peace I give unto you: not as the world giveth, give I unto you. Let not your heart be troubled, neither let it be afraid."

The same words she had spoken at the fall festival, she spoke again to him. Peace. And as she spoke the words, that struggle fled his mind. "I want peace," Jacob answered the pastor.

"Okay son. Then repeat after me." He held onto Jacob's outstretched hands. "Dear Jesus, I believe you died for my sins and rose from the dead."

"Dear Jesus, I believe you died for my sins and rose from the dead," Jacob repeated.

"I know that I am a sinner, and I ask for Your Forgiveness," the pastor continued.

"I know that I am a sinner, and I ask for Your Forgiveness."

The pastor nodded and continued the prayer. "I turn from my sins and invite You to come into my heart and life. I will trust and follow You as my Lord and Savior."

"I turn from my sins and invite You to come into my heart and life. I will trust and follow You as my Lord and Savior."

"Amen," the pastor concluded.

"Amen," Jacob repeated. The feeling in his chest from earlier felt as though it exploded, and a gentle warmness ran through his entire body. Tears formed in his eyes. An indescribable joy overwhelmed him.

The pastor and Kara began clapping. "He loves you son," the pastor told Jacob. "He wants you to have peace. He wants you to have the desires of your heart." He hugged Jacob and whispered, "That word earlier was for you too."

"Thank you," Jacob managed to whisper as tears overtook him. He understood now why Merridy cried. The pastor offered another pat on the back before he moved on to the next person to pray for. Unsure what to do, he turned to Kara who still stood behind him. "Thank you," he repeated.

She wrapped her arms around him in a tight hug. "He has such great plans for you Jacob. I'm so glad you opened your heart to the Lord."

And Jacob admitted to himself that he, too, was happy he had opened his heart to the Lord.

Kara released the hug in order to pray for another person, but he was soon wrapped up in yet a third hug. It was Merridy.

She did not speak a word to him. She simply hugged him tight through her tears. He returned her hug amidst his own happy tears. And they held each other in a jubilant, tearful embrace at the altar as the prayer continued around them.

Chapter 20

Merridy turned to Jacob after the service ended. "I am so sorry about how I behaved yesterday." Ever since she hugged him at the altar, she had stay by his side for the whole service. Her heart beamed in happiness at his decision – not because of any romantic feelings she wrestled with – but because he had chosen a new, positive journey in life. No matter what existed, or did not exist, between them, she wanted to be a resource for him as he navigated this new life. The first step to being that was to apologize for all the wrongs she committed against him.

"You don't have to..." he stammered.

"I really do. Jacob, I was catty and rude." She took a deep breath. "It is okay for you to be on a date. There is nothing between us. I just was caught off guard, because of what you said and what happened at your apartment, and then... you were there with that beautiful woman. But it's okay. You should be happy."

His brow furrowed. She had stated 'there is nothing between us'. She confirmed it. "I mean, it wasn't a real date. I guess? Terry just needed a wingman. It was very casual. You know, because of with Ameleah..." He paused. "I guess I'm just confused, that's all."

"It's not easy to navigate after a breakup. And our friendship made it more confusing." She turned her eyes away from him for a moment. Clearly, he needed something casual. She knew she should remain merely a friend. She had known that from the moment she saw his phone's screen when they first met, didn't she? "But I'm happy to be your friend. And that's why I had to apologize. I didn't like storming out like that. It wasn't right."

"You're okay Merridy. You were caught off-guard, and during an important meeting. How did that go by the way?" He looked down at her hand and became painfully aware of how close it was to his own. 'Friends', he reminded himself.

A deep sigh released from her. "I have to go home and pack frantically. I leave for New York City tomorrow morning. They want to show me around, and already have all these meetings set up for me. I wasn't expecting any of this before the tree lighting performance, but I guess they want all the ducks in a row before the big reveal."

"Sounds intense. Anything I can do? I can help… pack?" He flexed his arm muscle. "I can carry whatever you need."

She laughed. "Well Kara is coming over…"

"I will help you pick out what clothes to take. I didn't promise any heavy lifting," Kara reminded her. She stood with a different group of women nearby; yet, she had apparently heard every word. "I think it would be great for Jacob to come over. We can grab some food to go from Evie's place and have a packing party."

His eyes sparked at the suggestion. "I'm game. I mean, I'm certainly not the expert on fashion like Kara, but I can get food and carry twenty-pound bags of shoes."

Merridy's cheeks blushed. "I guess I'm outnumbered."

They coordinated food orders, which Jacob volunteered to go buy and deliver to Merridy's apartment. He tucked his present into her hands, and then the ladies left to the apartment.

"I am so confused by you," Merridy told her best friend.

Kara opened the closet door to review her friend's clothes. "What?"

"You invited Jacob to church – which I *am* glad about; my heart is ecstatic that he was saved today. But still, you invited him to a place you knew I would be, and then invited him here. Weren't you the one saying I was too focused on him?" She hurriedly packed underwear into a small bag before Jacob arrived. "That's contradictory."

"Felt like the right call. I read in a diet book that you should walk down the cookie aisle while not buying anything to build up immunity and willpower." She winked at Merridy. "Plus, you are about to go to New York City. Your whole life is getting flipped upside down. You need solid friends to surround you. And despite anything else, I know he cares about you enough to want only the best for you."

Merridy stuffed the underwear-bag into a larger suitcase. "I guess that makes sense?"

"The Twisters will be playing New York next week," Kara continued. "You'll be in the same city as Jacob for three or four days, depending on their travel. And honestly, that gives me peace of mind. I'm not totally sold on this Casimir guy. And record companies can be... overwhelming, and terrifying, but magical. We don't know what you'll be getting yourself into. Having someone nearby in the middle of it all could be really beneficial." She pulled out a few dresses from Merridy's closet and handed them to her.

Merridy quietly contemplated her friend's words while opening the gift from Jacob. A small white box sat under the music-note tissue paper.

"I know I'll be a phone call away," Kara confirmed. "But we're about to go into all these meetings on the campaign at work. I know my limitations of being highly distracted by that."

"That's true," Merridy whispered. In her elation, she nearly forgot that her best friend was also going through a major breakthrough in her career. "You're very wise, Kara. I'm blessed to have you on my side." She opened the white box to see a delicate, mother-of-pear and silver music box.

"Oh girl," Kara waved the statement away. "I'm not that wise. But that's a story for a different time."

A knock on the apartment door distracted them, and Kara left the bedroom to greet Jacob with the food. Merridy followed slightly behind after repacking the gift and slipping it into her suitcase.

Jacob nervously glanced around the apartment. While Merridy had been in his apartment several times, he had never been in hers. The décor style was entirely eclectic: from bohemian to farmhouse to antique pieces he imagined belonged in her family for years. The thought caused him to smile. It was entirely what he expected from Merridy – memories over style.

"Thank you for lunch," Merridy told him as she grabbed one of the to-go bags from his arms and laid it out on her table. "I've been eating through leftovers to clear out the fridge since I'll be gone for three weeks. All that's left is some milk and banana pudding."

"You made your special banana pudding without telling me?" Kara accused. "I'm questioning this best friend situation now."

Merridy laughed. "I made it last night in a fit of stress-eating."

"Special banana pudding?" Jacob asked. "What makes it special?"

"It's completely homemade," Kara answered him. "Com-plete-ly. The pudding. The wafers. Even the whipped cream. It's her grandma's recipe."

"It's also a great way to use up milk, because I just bought a gallon on Friday."

"Glad I have room for dessert," Jacob beamed before tearing into his panini.

Packing was put on hold as the three enjoyed a shared meal, each reminiscing about their grandmother's cooking. "I remember my Granny T used to make a sweet potato pie that would win the church's pie cookoff every year. She grew the potatoes herself in her tiny backyard garden. I've tried to make it for Thanksgiving, but it's never right. Zeke got the recipe from her. Evie tried to make it. Still missing something. I think she kept an ingredient from us. Or it's how she grew those potatoes."

Merridy laughed. "Homegrown always tastes better. What about you Jacob?"

"Well my dad's mom, whom we very properly call 'Grandmother', is from Nanaimo. She claims her mother invented the Nanaimo bar. But then again, who from that town hasn't claimed that?" He noted their blank stares. "Oh, please tell me you have had a Nanaimo bar."

"I don't even know what that is," Merridy answered.

"What?" he cried out. "It is a delicious blend of crumbly, coconutty goodness, custard, and chocolate ganache. How have you not experienced this? There are actual diners in Dallas that sell it."

She shrugged her shoulders. "I'm sheltered."

In disdain, he folded his arms across his chest. "I have to rectify this. And let me say, Grandmother makes the *best* Nanaimo bars. There's a very delicate ratio between the crumbly base, the custard filling, and the chocolate topping – and she nails it."

He stroked the stubble on his chin. "My mom's mother, Mam-o, was from Ireland. She baked everything from scratch. Honestly, hers was the only soda bread I ever liked. And she would make shortbread cookies, and a bread pudding... and an Irish coffee... yeah. I miss her. And her food. She passed away when I was fourteen, the week before Thanksgiving."

"I'm sorry to hear that," Merridy offered. "My dad's mom passed away when I was little. But my mom's mom is the one who always calls me her 'Merry Christmas' present."

"It's so stinking cute," Kara added. "I've seen it happen."

"And I would be devastated if I lost her," Merridy finished. She smiled at Jacob. "But she lives on the family ranch and has to keep everyone in line. So, I suppose she's got a few miles left in her."

"I keep hearing about this family ranch, and it makes me want to ride a horse."

Merridy laughed. "You keep talking about Canada... and it makes me remember how cold it is there."

"And you two keep talking about everything except that we finished our meals and it's time to break out that banana pudding!" Kara marched deliberately to the refrigerator to secure the trifle bowl full of the delicious and beautifully layered dessert.

At the first bite of the pudding, Jacob realized that this was the first time he ate something Merridy had cooked. 'Delicious' did not begin to describe it. His thoughts drifted to Ameleah, who refused to cook even before Paris, and even the woman he sat beside the evening before, who probably could not distinguish a whisk from a spatula. Something about this little slice of domestic-life from Merridy gripped his chest. Once again, he knew – friendship might be the current status, but it could *not* be the end goal.

Two hours passed before Kara excused herself due to her phone lighting up like fireworks on the Fourth. Work beckoned her in prelude to Monday meetings, and she reluctantly needed to respond. Jacob awkwardly stood in the living room with Merridy's three suitcases stacked nearby. "Should I go too?" he asked her finally after the door closed behind Kara. "I don't want to cause an awkward situation, or… I mean, is there more you need, or want or, is there church tonight?"

She giggled at his stammering. "You don't have to go. It's not awkward. There's no church tonight; they've made the first Sunday night of each month 'family night' for families to stay home together and bond. And… I do need company since Kara had to go. I'm actually really nervous about tomorrow. And the day after. And the day after that." Her voice faded slightly as she spoke. "And so on."

Jacob immediately noted the choke in her voice and stepped forward to hug her tightly. "You will be amazing, because you *are* amazing."

"Thank you," she whispered.

"Do you want to, to talk about it? I've got all day and night. Whatever you need from me." He released her from her hug.

She flung herself onto her couch and grabbed a nearby pillow to cuddle. "I arrive tomorrow, and then I meet with some kind of image manager on Tuesday, and then there was all this talk about hair, makeup, wardrobe, and photoshoots. Then a creative meeting. And then after all the publicity and image and clothes and outer appearance, then, *then*," she reiterated, "there will be discussion with a songwriter. It's like the music is the least important thing."

"I can see that." He sat on the couch next to her. "They are a celebrity factory."

The statement caused her to unconsciously bite on her thumbnail. Celebrity *factory*.

"That was crude. I mean, they just seem to pump out the big ones, right? I guess they know what they're doing for that industry. But it's also terrifying. I mean, image manager? Sounds like Am... I mean... yeah, that's a real thing."

Her eyes drifted to him. Ameleah. He was about to say her name. He still thought about her. Of course, he did. It had only been mere weeks.

"Sorry," he apologized as if reading her mind. "I don't *want* to talk about her. The reality is hockey players have agents that work on our images, some. But nothing like a 'celebrity maker' or 'image manager' or anything like that. *She* is my only experience with that. That's all." He waved his hand as if to wave the thoughts away. "But what's important is you. You already shine without an image manager. And as for a songwriter, that might be cool. You could collaborate with someone that's been in the industry awhile. That might be a great learning experience."

"True. I hadn't thought of that." She sat up and glanced at her nearby guitar case. It was earmarked to remain behind in the apartment as 'all instruments would be supplied' per a text from Casimir. "I've written a few songs myself, but nothing like a professional, I'm sure. I mean, imagine, all you do is write Grammy-winning songs all day."

"Sounds pretty cool," he agreed. "But I bet your songs are beautiful too."

A small sigh answered him.

"No, don't be that way. How couldn't they be beautiful? They've come from *you*."

"Thank you for the flattery, but..."

"It's not flattery, Merridy. It's honesty." A courage flared inside him, one that he had not felt since he last faced Ameleah in a rage. His hands reached out to Merridy's in earnest, and he squeezed them tightly. "Everything I said that night in my apartment was the truth, Merridy. And whether you see us as just friends, or not even friends, or you never even see my face again, I want you to know the truth. You are absolutely wonderful – creative, kind, smart, loving, and stunningly beautiful." Her face turned red in embarrassment as he spoke. "And so humble, maybe too humble. Because you can't even see how amazing you really are. I would give anything for you to see you how I see you. And I see you constantly – you're my ever-waking thought. You're in my every dream. You... consume me. And you said we're just friends, and I will abide by that... but..."

His soliloquy was stopped short as Merridy brought her lips to his. She silenced him with a tender kiss; he eagerly returned it. His hands left hers and found their way to her wild, curly auburn-hair. "You consume me too," she whispered as she pulled back.

Jacob leaned his forehead against hers and smiled. "So, you feel it, right? That we're being pulled together...?"

"I felt something the moment I fell into your arms at the skating rink," she laughed. "But you were with someone, and then I felt like an intruder, and then you broke up and I didn't want to be a rebound, and then there was the whole you-could-be-distracting-me-from-my-goals." She shook her head which caused their noses to briefly flutter against each other. "Kara is wise, sometimes. But not this time. She wanted to protect me

190

and focus me. And my own head got the better of me too. I was scared. I didn't want to get hurt…"

She began to ramble, but this time Jacob kissed her in order to silence her rambling. "I understand," he finally told her after the kiss. "Terry said the same thing about the rebound. He had plenty of Terry-esque advice, wise or not. And I didn't want to distract you. I didn't want to hurt you. And I know the timing is awful. I *know* this. But I can't ignore what I feel. It's not a rebound. Please hear me on that Merridy. You are no rebound." He lifted his lips to her forehead. "I would move mountains for you. I want the world for you. You are no rebound."

The earnest sentiment in his words caused Merridy to tear up. She had dated, yes. But never had she felt this way about anyone. And never had she felt completely at ease in the arms of a man. For the third time that day, Jacob wrapped his arms around her and held her tightly. "I believe you, Jacob."

He stroked her hair and kissed her forehead again. "Of course… all this and you leave tomorrow morning."

"Of course," she giggled. "But we have fifteen hours before my flight."

"Which is more like thirteen before you need to be in line for security… because flights."

"Because flights," she repeated. She nestled her face into the crook of his neck and inhaled deeply. The scent of his cologne filled her nostrils. The warmth of his breath on her temple as he leaned his head against hers spread throughout her whole body.

Why had she fought this for so long? Simple – she was afraid. Afraid of rejection, afraid of being used – afraid of everything that could go wrong – instead of focusing on everything that could go right. She had been shocked when Casimir told her that she could be a diva. Now, she felt a sensation of surrealism as she considered the fact that a sports celebrity was hugging her and kissing her cheek.   Two months before, she never would have considered her life being more than clerical work and living paycheck to paycheck.

Then October happened.

His finger traced her cheek.   "You are so beautiful," he repeated, in a solemn whisper. Then he tilted her chin toward him and kissed her once again. They sat entwined on the couch for some time, embracing one another in the joy of their realized attraction.   "I'll be in New York next week."   The statement blurted out of Jacob as if he suddenly remembered that he played hockey. "I mean, we usually have early practice and warm-up on game days, but we do get some free time. And maybe my free time will line up with your free time." He took her hand in his and kissed it. "I want to see you as much as possible while I'm in New York. And when we get a break, I can fly back there."

His eagerness caused Merridy to laugh. "What about Porthos?"

"He can come too." Jacob shrugged and laughed. "When I'm not traveling with the team."

She reached up to play with a strand of his hair that fell forward over his forehead, separated from the rest which was always pristinely slicked back. "I'd like that. He's a handsome fellow. A bit like his dad. Maybe drools less."

"Can't help it. He's not looking at what I'm looking at."

The comeback caused Merridy to blush again. Once again, she heard her mother's voice in her head. Even as an adult, she was keenly aware of being alone in her apartment with Jacob. She was even more aware that a slight struggle of willpower stirred within her. "Um… Jacob?"

"Yes Merry?"

She paused at the name. She actually liked it when it came from him. "Um… you know… I've never… um." How did you tell someone you have never been intimate with a man? In modern society, it was a general assumption that most adults had been intimate. "Well… I went to a *Bible college*… and, you know…"

His finger gently 'booped' her nose, and he grinned. "Yeah, I get it. Sometimes I wish I could say the same." He chuckled. "Maybe not about the *Bible college* part. I don't imagine they had a decent hockey team. But I could be wrong."

Relief washed over her. "No hockey team at all, but an *incredible* disc golf group." They shared a laugh before she laid her head back against his shoulder. "Thank you for understanding."

"It's part of who you are, and I like that about you. All of you. Every little piece of you. From the guitar-string callouses on your fingers to the family photos on the wall to the hand-embroidered towels in the bathroom. You're real. And sincere. And… just you."

"Yeah? Well… I like that you're you too. From the little chipped tooth to the art deco apartment to the French literature puppies. All of you."

His tongue traced the edge of his chipped tooth. "Hazards of the job." He glanced at the clock on the wall. "I feel like I should take you out on a proper first date."

"And yet, all my best outfits are already packed away." She stood from the couch. "But I *do* have cereal and board games?"

He lifted his fists in victory. "Please let it be Froot Loops and Clue. Please let it be Froot Loops and Clue."

"Of course! It's Froot Loops and Clue!" She bounded to the hall closet that also served as her pantry. From it, she produced a box of cereal and the game.

"Yes!" He hurried into the kitchen to secure bowls and the remainder of the milk. "I love Froot Loops. They're delicious circles that look like a rainbow. And *no one* ever lets me eat them because – to quote certain trainers – they're not healthy. Listen, I work out every day, I think I earned some Froot Loops."

She handed him the cereal box. "Then I will always have Froot Loops for you to enjoy."

"Always?" he asked with a raised eyebrow.

"Yeah," she smiled. "Always."

Chapter 21

An early morning alarm stirred Merridy. She was not accustomed to waking in what she felt was the middle of the night, but her plane would be taking off with the sunrise. Her hand slammed against her phone to silence it. She fought the temptation to go back to sleep. Then she noted a light beaming under her closed bedroom door. Right. Jacob had stayed the night on her couch. The thought caused her to smile. He wanted as much time with her as possible, including driving her to the airport himself before his morning practice.

She shuffled out of bed and stretched. Her promised career was happening today. Butterflies fluttered wildly in her stomach. "Deep breaths lady. One step at a time." She grabbed the outfit prepared for the day and her bag of toiletries in order to shower. In the hall between the rooms, she paused to see Jacob in the living room. He was already awake. Headphones on, shirt off, he intently went through his own morning workout routine. A push up, clap, another push up, then he leapt up on his feet, then back down into a push up to start the cycle over again. She was mesmerized. The mere thought of a push up was enough to drain her.

'Why is he with me again?' she thought to herself while watching him.

The voice of doubt fled as he finished his final burpee and turned to see her standing there. His smile radiated brighter than the sweat that enveloped his chest. She refocused her eyes on his smile with an embarrassed gasp. "Good morning."

"Good morning," she whispered. This was certainly a first for her. She bit her bottom lip in contemplation. "I was just going to shower and get ready."

"Right," he responded. His hand flew to the back of his head where he nervously scratched at the hairline. "I was just... hmmm... I might need a towel, at least?"

"Oh, do you want to shower?" she squeaked. "You can go first... I can wait..."

"It's your day. Your place. You get priority." He grinned. "But I would like a towel." He walked forward to the bathroom. "Before you get started. If that's okay."

"Yeah. That's okay." Her mind told her to step backwards to give him room. She stood still until he was mere inches from her. The scent of his faded cologne mingled with the fresh scent of sweat. Logically, she did not think she would like the smell of sweat. But it was *his* sweat. And that made everything different.

"Okay." He repeated the word while reaching up to her hair and pulled her into a kiss.

She wanted to resist. She was painfully aware of her morning breath and her knotted hair. But that did not phase Jacob. Hunger filled his kiss. Again, the willpower struggle consumed her being as she returned the kiss in the doorway of her bathroom. The clothing and toiletries bag fell from her hands as she placed her hands on his slick chest. She knew any other girl would be pulling him to the shower with her, or the bed, or the couch. She had seen the movies. She knew what culture dictated in the situation. But...

Jacob pulled away. "Okay," he whispered. He knelt down to pick up the dropped items. Silently, he handed her the clothes and bag before grabbing a nearby towel. "I regret to inform you I finished off the milk with the last of the Froot Loops, but will be most happy to take you for coffee and a snack on the way to the airport."

Her heart pounded in her throat. How was he able to calmly talk about breakfast after a kiss like the one they shared? She felt breathless. "Okay."

He winked. "Okay."

She slipped into the bathroom and closed the door behind her. "Okay," she whispered to herself, "get your head on straight."

After an awkward dance of bathroom shuffle, both were ready to depart. Merridy prayed over her apartment and that God would protect it while she was away. She handed her spare key to Jacob.

"I have a few plants that could use some water on occasion," she joked.

He glanced around the apartment. "You mean... your cactus on the patio?"

She shrugged her shoulders. "It might get lonely. Plus, I have the key to your place that I never returned. Guess we're even."

"Already exchanging keys." His eyebrows raised. "Right after our first date that I spent the night on. This is downright scandalous, Merridy."

"Believe me, I am already hearing my mother's voice in my head about all of this. She would have died about last night, even though you were a perfect gentleman."

"Moms are like that though." He clipped her key to his key chain and picked up her bags that were by the door. "You ready to go?"

"As ready as I'll ever be."

The two left the apartment, and she locked the door behind them. It felt strange that she was going to be away from her home for such a length of time. A little part of her felt the same sorrow that she has felt when she left her parents' home for college. She attempted to focus on all the excitement that would be happening soon. Within a few hours she would be landing in New York City and touring a record company. Since Kara was unable to take her to the airport and see her off, she was very glad that Jacob stayed to do this. Although his presence would make leaving much harder.

The hour was earlier than Evelyn's shop opened, so they settled for a drive-thru of a 24-hour burger place that happened to serve breakfast. The coffee was not as good as Evelyn's, but it would keep her awake on the flight.

"Have you ever been to New York before? " Jacob asked.

"No. I'm not very well-traveled." She sipped on the watered-down coffee and nibbled at a hash brown. "It makes me a little scared just thinking about it. There are so many people. I hope I don't get lost. But hopefully Casimir is there at the gate waiting for me."

"He should be since it was his idea to make you go so quickly to New York. That feels a little strange to me. But then again, I don't really know how the music industry works. "

"I think Kara felt that way too. She seemed a little on edge about Casimir, and me going to New York. She actually let me know you were going to be in New York next week before you did. I think it gave her some peace of mind."

"Would it still give her peace of mind if she knew I stayed the night last night?"

"Honestly, I don't know how she would feel about this.," Merridy sighed. "She likes you well enough as a friend, clearly. She invited you to church for a reason. She knew you would be in New York in a good asset. But at the same time..." her voice trailed off, "I just don't know."

"Well, I hope she eventually approves of me. I hope I get the approval of everyone important in your life. I already know you'll get the approval of everyone in my life."

"Even Terry?"

"Even Terry, " Jacob laughed. "But seriously, at the end of the day, he just wants me happy. He's my best friend."

"Same with Kara." Merridy turned to him with a wry smile. "But even if she didn't, it wouldn't matter. I think even if my parents didn't approve of you, it wouldn't matter. I like you a lot Jacob. Maybe just enough to be a rebel for you."

"Is that so?" He reached his hand out to hers while his other hand stayed on the steering wheel. "Even still, I would never ask you to do that. This time... I want everything done right. You deserve everything to be right." His thumb massaged the back of her hand. "Even this record deal. I want it all to be right for you."

"I want everything to be right for you too. Win the Stanley Cup. Win the... Art... Ross... Trophy?"

"You know about the Art Ross Trophy?" Jacob laughed a surprise.

"I've been reading."

"Reading about how my attempts have certainly been miserable for several seasons in a row?"

She shrugged. "This season will be different. This is the year."

"You know, you might be right." They drove on in relative silence save the sports talk show that played over his car stereo.

At the airport, Jacob followed her as far as he could until security. He hugged her tightly. "Let me know when you land."

"I will."

He kissed her forehead, reluctant to let her go.

"And we'll talk tonight. We have phones and internet and face time."

"I can't kiss a phone."

"Technically you could. It just couldn't kiss back."

He smiled, and they exchanged a kiss.

Merridy took a step backward. "This is it. I'm going to become a recording artist."

"Yes! You are!" Jacob lifted his fists into his 'victory' pose. He stood nearby until she cleared security, and, once she fully disappeared behind the gates, he left for his morning game-day practice.

Chapter 22

Merridy followed the crowd at JFK to the baggage claim, uncertain of where she was supposed to meet with Casimir. She grabbed her phone and sent a text to Jacob.

'Just landed at JFK and headed to baggage claim. I'm not totally lost… yet. Have not seen Casimir but about to message him.'

She then shot Casimir a message informing him of her arrival and asking where she should meet him. Then she awaited a response and her suitcases. They arrived at the same time.

'Glad you made it safely. Let me know if Casimir flakes out. I know people in New York and will have them at the airport immediately to get you.'

The sentiment caused her to smile, and she felt her unease about being alone in a new city lessen. Her phone buzzed again as she grabbed her last suitcase. Casimir had sent a car in his stead, and the driver would find her shortly.

'He just messaged me that he sent a car.
The record company must be very serious
about this... sending a car and everything.
I feel special.'

                    'You are special, Turnip Girl. Never
                                     forget it.'

The nickname caused her to smile. She found Casimir's driver at the gate with a sign reading 'Miss Christmas'. "Oh my, it's just like the movies."

"Miss Christmas?" the driver asked.

"Yes, that's me."

"A pleasure to meet you. I am Carter. I will be taking you to your hotel where you may rest before Mr. Alvah comes to meet you for dinner at seven." He shook her hand then picked up her luggage.

Carter was not one for small talk, and proceeded exactly as he stated. Her bags were given to a bellhop who escorted her directly to a suite without a need for a check-in. She wondered if this was how it worked for Jacob, and made note to ask him later. The bellhop placed her bags by the door of her suite at her request, and then handed her the room key. She was accustomed to the plastic key cards used by most hotels; this key was an antique made of metal with a tassel on the end. She held the key to her chest and spun around in excitement.

"It's really happening! It's really happening!" She jumped up and down before rushing around her multi-room suite to explore. The furniture and décor seemed frozen in the Gilded Age to match the age of the hotel, but pieces from the 1920s and 1960s also accented the suite. It reminded her of the long legacy the building had in New York City. She took her phone out and began taking pictures of everything and sent them to Kara. Her friend responded with shocked face emojis. They chatted briefly before Kara had to depart for yet another meeting.

The pause allowed Merridy to realize that she was actually very tired. The late night and early morning coupled with stress and the loss of an hour drained her. She forced herself to unpack her suitcases into the bedroom's closet and dresser. She then prepared to nap on the softest bed she had every laid upon.

'I can't believe I'm staying in a hotel that's over a hundred years old. I'm lying on a bed that royalty could have slept on – I don't know. This is crazy. But really cool. Everything is so beautiful here, and I've not even stepped outside the hotel, which is on Park Avenue. I can literally see 5th Avenue from my bedroom window right now. I don't really know what's on 5th Avenue – but I know that's a thing. Is this what it's like for you when you travel? The driver brought me to the front, a bellhop – in a uniform – took my bags and led me directly to a private elevator and room. No check in. This is mind blowing.'

Her eyes began drooping closed, but she kept them cracked to see a response from Jacob.

'Absolutely not at all what it's like when I go to a hotel. The team wouldn't spend that much money on all of us, haha. We do get nice accommodations, just not 'Park Avenue nice'. And we don't have cars pick us up. We travel on the team's private plane, then we take a bus to wherever we're staying or wherever we're practicing or wherever we're playing. It's like a school field trip – always with the group and chaperones tell you where to go and what to do. I think you're getting the royalty diva treatment. Hockey players don't get treated like divas. Can't imagine why. What's next on the agenda?'

'PS – I already miss you.'

'I'm lying on the bed about to nap. Guess we didn't get a lot of sleep last night. Plus, nerves drain me, apparently. They never have before, but then again, this is a whole other level of nervousness. I miss you too.'

'Agreed about the sleep. Think I might join you for that nap. I was pretty sluggish at practice. Need to be fresh for the game tonight. Wish I was joining you for the nap in person. O:-) Gonna have to hug Porthos really tight.'

'<3 Porthos <3 Give him smooches from me. I'm having dinner with Casimir at 7 our time. I might not get to talk to you until after your game. One, praying for you and all your goals, literally and figuratively. Two, I have my alerts set on my phone for the game so I can keep up-to-date, so just know I'm watching you in my own way!.'

'A woman who gets hockey updates on her phone? That's hot. Good luck at dinner. I'll talk to you tonight. Sleep well Turnip Girl.'

'You too, White Rabbit.'

Chapter 23

Kara glanced at her phone as a multitude of pictures flooded it. She smiled. Merridy was thrilled with the beauty and history of the hotel. She wished she could be with her friend, soaking in the excitement of the jazz age in the hotel's speakeasy-style lounge. Instead, she was putting the final touches on her presentation folios for the next meeting.

"Focus on your own gift," she reminded herself. "You were thrilled to get this assignment."

A soft knock on her door indicated that everyone was ready, and she hurried down the hall to the conference room. A face from her past caught her eye. She gulped. It had been difficult to reconnect with Elyssa – she had been her best friend in high school. But now, her high school boyfriend sat across the conference table from the door.

"Kara!" her boss greeted her. "Please come in. We're eager to hear what you have planned. We've invited Baris Market Strategies to sit in on this before we combine our forces."

Her eyebrows arched in surprise as she looked between her ex-boyfriend representing Baris and her boss. "We're combining forces with Baris?"

"Don't be so surprised, Kara." Her ex stood with a grin plastered on his face from ear-to-ear. "I'm sure we will work perfectly together. We have before."

"Oh!" her boss exclaimed. "You two have worked together before?"

"Well..." Kara attempted to clarify.

"Absolutely! We started our journey in market strategies together."

Kara shot him a stern look. "Caleb Stone," she stated coldly, "means to say, that we took sports marketing together in high school. And our individual love for marketing advanced from there. We were never in business together. Simply, high school *acquaintances*." She accentuated the last word for Caleb to hear. "But that is the past, and the only past I care about today is the legacy of this company." She smiled cheerily at those in attendance. "I have made each of you a folio to accompany today's presentation."

She passed out the folios and began her presentation. Caleb staring at her with his cocky grin unnerved her completely. What game was he playing at?

At the end of her presentation, he stood with a slow clap. "That's very interesting, Miss Jackson." He paused. "It is still *Miss* Jackson, isn't it?"

"Yes." Her reply was flat.

"You're thinking old-school." He held up the folio. "A folio? A lovely presentation on embracing the past? It's 2018. We're in a new millennium. You're thinking Flintstones, but we need the Jetsons."

She rolled her eyes. "Actually, many people believe the Flintstones are in the future in a post-apocalyptic setting. That's why they were celebrating *Christmas*." A smug smile due to her trivial knowledge settled on her hips. She held her own folio up. "While the folio, the presentation, and my ideas seem old-fashioned, they are also full of elegance and class. Just as these folios are vellum with gold inlays, our hundred and fiftieth anniversary should be a reminder of the constant security this company has been for more than half our country's lifespan. Not many companies in this industry can claim that."

"But really... the Jazz Age?" He grabbed the presentation clicker and rewound a few slides. "Speakeasies? The Charleston?" He waved his hands in a mock dance and laughed. "That might appeal to an older crowd, but you're in life insurance. You're wanting to attract the younger crowd with a nice, long life and assets to invest in this company."

She recalled the pictures Merridy had sent her earlier of the speakeasy lounge. "The Great Gatsby," she interjected. "In 2013, Baz Luhmann brought the iconic 1920s story to life, grossing over three-hundred-and-fifty-million dollars at the box office. Leonardo DiCaprio? Tobey Maguire? Those are not actors representing older generations... those are actors that Millennials *love*. And Millennials showed how much they loved it at the theatre." She turned to everyone at the conference table excitedly, ignoring Caleb's presence. "Our 150th anniversary happens mere months before 2020. What better way to bring in the next Roaring 20's than with a Jazz Age theme?"

Caleb sat down with a triumphant smile. "I told you we worked well together. You just went from dated class to a bombastic 20's party."

Kara shot him an angry glance.

"Listen," he put his hands up defensively, "Baz Luhmann did bring Gatsby to the Millennials in a way that they loved... but it was in *his* style. Not in a boring Fitzgerald way." He rolled his eyes. "Snooze fest! Anyone else get bored with it in required reading? But!" He punctuated his excitement with his hands. "The glitz. The glam. The gold. The gin. Now that was a party. Think about Chicago. Did anyone like dour little Roxie Hart, or did they like that – five, six, seven, eight – and *all that jazz* Roxie

Hart? Gotta glam it up. Celebrate your heritage, but with a little razzle and dazzle."

Sixteen years ago she had begged him to take her to Chicago the movie. Now she regretted it. "Too much razzle and dazzle, and we take away from what we are as a company." Her eyes turned to her boss. "We can't give up our image as America's most reliable financial institution by going full-Gatsby. There *is* a balance."

"Go big or go home," Caleb countered.

She pulled up a few of the photos Merridy had sent her. "Look. This is at the Roche Morgan Hotel on Park Avenue – known for its stately elegance. It has existed there since the Gilded Age, since the family it's named for used it as their city home and hosted the great four-hundred families in its ballroom. It underwent a few changes throughout its years, notably in the Twenties and Sixties, but always it retained the air of sophistication that is its core. And people from all over the world still flock to it. There is a way to maintain that balance. They found it. We can find it."

Her boss stood and paced. "I think you are both on to something. And I think you both need to collaborate on this to find that balance. We're not just celebrating our past, we are moving forward in a more digital world. Let's get both into this campaign." He tapped his finger onto his chin thoughtfully. "You're on to something about the Roche Morgan Hotel. Maybe you should go there and get a little inspired."

Kara's stomach did a backflip. She would be in New York with Merridy!

"Together."

The backflipping stomach landed flat on its face. "Sir?"

209

"Use the corporate account. Get something nice for you and Mr. Stone. Get out there as soon as possible, take about three or four days to get inspired, then come back with another presentation. Floor us with it. We'll meet in a week from today."

She nodded. "Yes sir. I will get on that right away." She quickly grabbed her materials and headed back to her office in the swiftest, most professional walk possible. Caleb still managed to follow her. "I hope you're happy," she called over her shoulder.

"Not really, no," he replied as he barged into her office after her. "I have two kids at home that I would rather not break this news to. You know, the lady at work opened her big mouth about the fancy hotel halfway across the country and now daddy has to go there?"

He had kids? Kara turned her back to him in order to hide her surprised face. The arrogant man in the conference room was more arrogant than the one she had dated in high school. It was hard to imagine him as a father. "I had to do something. The guy at work had to keep talking about 'go big or go home' and I was not ready to go home yet. Maybe tell your kids that daddy should have backed off."

"Never," he snorted. "I taught my kids to play to win."

"Well I'm sure your wife will be able to manage them while you're gone."

"My wife is dead," he responded tersely. "I'm about to go make some calls to find a nanny that can survive the twins."

"I'm... sorry," she softened and turned to him. "I really am. Loss is never easy."

He shrugged his shoulders. "It's been a couple of years."

"Doesn't make it easier."

"You're right." He turned to leave and paused. "Here's my business card. Let me know about our arrangements, and I'll be sure to arrive on time."

She took the card. "Will do." After he left, she sent a swift text to Merridy:

'I'm coming to New York!'

Merridy sat across from Casimir, his assistant Maun, and KT Tally – a former boy band pop star that now served as a songwriter for Echo Star Records. She focused her eyes on her menu in order to prevent an embarrassing 'fan girl' stare down of the man. He had once donned a poster above her bed. Now she was having dinner with him. Could her life add anything else surreal?

"We were going to wait until Wednesday to have a meeting with KT, but his schedule opened," Casimir announced.

"I like to get to know the personality of whomever I'm writing a song for so it fits them better," KT added. "It adds authenticity to an industry that can be a bit..." He paused his statement as Casimir shot a discerning glare his way.

"Calculated?" Merridy offered.

Her statement surprised Casimir.

"Excellent description," KT agreed. His blue-green eyes twinkled with his smile. "There's a lot of studies done about song length, chords, lyrics... anything to find out what makes a song a hit. Sometimes the artist can get lost in that."

"Those studies have also proven to be an excellent resource in making Grammy-award-winning artists," Casimir interjected. The statement caused KT to lower his eyes back on his own menu. "KT has several Grammy awards under his belt thanks to his meticulous use of studies as well as his own special talents. He's won a Grammy for song of the year, and best song in each genre – rock, R&B, rap, and country. Not to mention the performance awards he shared with his fellow members of NTUNE."

"Yes… I watched NTUNE win those awards," Merridy smiled. "And not to diminish Mr. Tally's remarkable song writing accolades… but rock, R&B, rap, and country aren't the only genres awarded 'best song' at the Grammy's. There's at least three others – gospel, contemporary Christian, and American roots."

Casimir nodded. "Of course. But those genres aren't known for being Top 40 material. Echo Star is a Top 40 record company."

The statement stung Merridy, and she felt KT's eyes focus on her above his menu. She was keenly aware that he was already determining her personality with this exchange. "True… which is sad, but if I recall correctly, the first American roots song award went to gentleman named Steve Martin… and I believe everyone knows who he is. That's not to mention the co-writer, Edie Brickell, who did have a couple of Billboard Top 40 songs. It may not be a glamorous genre, but it's certainly not to be ignored."

Her rebuttal caused Casimir to clear his throat and flag down the waitress to place their orders. KT smirked at Merridy. "Personally, I would love to win a Grammy in that category as well," he joked. "And the other two. I think it would be a first."

"Unfortunately, folk music isn't in your contract," Casimir reminded him.

Merridy was surprised by the statement but remained silent.

KT also seemed put off by the comment but attempted to move forward. "Who are some of your favorite artists, Merridy?"

"I guess I'm eclectic. I mean, there's a time when I would have immediately answered with NTUNE," she laughed, "and while I'm not the preteen with boy band posters in my room anymore… I do still listen to those albums on occasion. But nowadays?" She began listing a mix of Christian, folk, and country artists, with an occasional veteran of the rock and pop genres. KT wrote each name down on a small notepad by his water glass. After listing twenty artists, she paused. "I guess I could keep going?"

"I'm not stopping you. This is about *you* after all."

"I will interject," Casimir stated.

"Of course, you will," KT sarcastically replied.

"Merridy's first album will be a holiday release to play off the tree lighting ceremony. But we don't want her to get pigeon-holed as a holiday-only artist. We don't need another Bublé."

She felt that was a harsh comment; she enjoyed his non-Christmas music as well.

"That's going to be difficult with a name like *Merridy Christmas*," KT countered.

"Focus on the songs, KT. And we will do what we do best."

Their first course arrived, and Merridy ate in silence. Eventually KT spoke up once more. "What's your favorite Christmas song, Merridy?"

"Oh wow. I can only pick one?"

He laughed. "I expected as much. Okay – what are your top five favorite Christmas songs?"

"Well... I *love* 'O Holy Night' – not just the vocal range, but the words are so strong. It's what I plan on singing at the tree lighting ceremony." She noted an exchange of glances between Casimir and KT but continued speaking. "And I think 'O Come, O Come Emmanuel' is beautiful. And then of course, 'Go Tell It On the Mountain', and 'I Heard the Bells on Christmas Day'... and I really like caroling 'Joy to the World'."

KT made notes of these as well. "I'm certain each one of those have special meaning to you, don't they?"

"Of course!" Merridy exclaimed. "They're about why the season even exists."

"Do you know what Casimir's favorite Christmas song is?"

She shook her head 'no', and Casimir glared at KT. "Mariah Carey's 'All I Want for Christmas is You'. It has sold sixteen million copies worldwide," Casimir answered KT. "And it's a great, catchy number."

"How do you feel about that song, Merridy?" KT asked her.

Her face blushed as she was put on the spot. "Um... well it *is* very catchy. Can't go Christmas shopping without hearing it play."

"And I suspect when you hear it play, you roll your eyes."

The red in her face flushed more. "Well... yes... actually. I mean, the song isn't *bad*. It's just not... me? It's not how I feel. I mean, I understand really loving someone and longing for them. I really do get that." The realization made her gasp. "I do get it."

KT leaned back in his chair and stroked his chin thoughtfully. "You understand the sentiment, but why do you roll your eyes when you hear it?"

"Because, it's not Christmas. It's just another love song wrapped in Christmas paper."

He slapped his hand on the table happily. "Exactly!"

Casimir frowned.

"See?" KT pointed his finger at Casimir. "It's not a *real* Christmas song. The world craves *real*."

"Sixteen million copies sold," Casimir repeated. "Numbers don't lie."

"The best-selling Christmas song of all time isn't that song though," Merridy interjected. "It's not even the second best-selling Christmas song of all time." She cleared her throat defiantly. "Bing Crosby's 'White Christmas' is in the Guinness Book of Records. It's sold like fifty million copies. And while it's not a religious song, it is about the warm-fuzzy feelings that everyone experiences this time of year." She pointed out the red poinsettias of their table's centerpiece and the meticulously decorated trees at the hotel restaurant's entrance. "These decorations occur once a year. What other holiday gets this much attention every year at this restaurant? People long for that feeling all year long. That's what the song is about. *Dreaming. Just like the one I used to know.* It's a song about nostalgia. Everyone knows that song – even people who don't know who Bing Crosby is – knows *that* song. Because it speaks to *everyone*." She grabbed her glass of water and took a long gulp; she was afraid she had spoken out of turn to a record executive and a Grammy-award-winning songwriter. What did she know about writing songs? She couldn't even finish the one she had been working on for a month.

To her surprise, KT stood to his feet and began clapping.

"Sit down," Casimir hissed to him.

KT walked over to Merridy and extended a hand to shake. "I look forward to writing songs for you, Merridy. I think we're on the brink of something big."

She smiled and took his hand. "I think so too."

The waitress brought the main entrée out to the group. After several minutes of casual conversation over their meals, Casimir excused himself from the table and left toward the restrooms. KT took the opportunity to lean in close to Merridy. "I pushed too many of his buttons tonight."

"What?" Merridy asked. But she *had* noticed Casimir's disgruntled expressions. KT clearly upset the man.

"Too much to explain right now. When he returns, he'll be asking for the check, and will *politely* ask me to join him in his company car away from here so we don't get to speak privately. But we need to." He handed a business card to Merridy. "My home address is on the back. Come over for dinner Wednesday at seven. Meet my family, and let's talk."

"I have a friend coming in to town..."

"Bring your friend. Bring whoever... just no one from Echo Star. They don't need to know."

Merridy gulped hard. KT's eyes were earnest. "Of course."

He nodded and returned to his seat casually. Merridy slipped the business card into her pocket before Casimir returned. As KT had predicted, he asked for the check, and beckoned KT to leave with him. Merridy wished them a goodnight. To her surprise, she received a hug from KT before she left for her hotel suite.

While reaching into her pocket for the business card, she noted her cellphone flashed blue with a text message. She unlocked the screen and noted the hockey update – Twisters won 3-2. With a smile, she opened her messages.

'Game over. We won, but of course you know this as you're a hot woman who gets hockey updates on her phone. Hope your dinner is going well. If you want to talk after, then... you know Porthos wouldn't mind hearing your voice.'

She smiled. After the exchange at the table, there was no one she wanted to talk to more than Jacob. One thing about the dinner had proven true. She really did understand the sentiment of the Mariah Carey song, even if it made her roll her eyes. With a grin, she rolled her eyes at herself.

'Only Porthos wants to hear my voice?
Well, I guess he can call when he's ready.'

A few minutes after the text, her phone buzzed with a video call request. She quickly fidgeted with her hair before answering the call. "Hi," she shyly greeted Jacob.

He sat on his bed with Porthos in his lap. "Hey there." He glanced down at the dog. "Say hi to Merridy," he instructed him. Porthos responded with a happy bark.

Merridy giggled. "Hey Porthos! You being a good boy?"

Another happy bark.

"Well, that's very good. Extra pets and treats when I get back."

Porthos smiled happily with his tongue lolled to the side. Drool dropped onto Jacob's shirt. "Thank you," Jacob laughed. "Drool King."

"Saw the score. Three to two." Merridy walked over to the grand window in the suite's living area. The stars were barely visible above the New York skyline, but she enjoyed seeing the Christmas lights line 5th Avenue in the distance.

"Barely. Luckily, White Rabbit showed up."

"He's good in the clutch." She arched an eyebrow. "Did I use that term right?"

"Good enough," he laughed. "How did dinner go?"

The question caused her to turn her attention away from 5th Avenue's lights to the phone in her hand. "It was really weird." She walked to the couch in her suite and collapsed on it. "I met the songwriter. Which was cool. Guess who it was?"

Jacob grinned. "Um... Sting."

"Sting?"

"It wasn't Sting?"

Merridy smiled. "No. And I'm just... surprised by your guess."

"What? Sting is awesome. I like Sting."

They shared a laugh. "Well, it was not Sting. *But* I was very excited about it. KT Tally. You know, the 'T' in NTUNE?"

"Oh... I should have known..." Jacob laughed. "You're a boy band girl."

"Of course, I was... am." She smiled. "So that was cool, and it started off normal. But then... weird. Like there was a lot of tension between KT and Casimir. And honestly, I like what KT was saying."

"What was he saying?"

She recounted the entire dinner to Jacob, including the business card and dinner invite. "Kara is coming into town tomorrow because of her business project. I'm going to take her with me."

"I'm glad she'll be there. Wish I could. Something seems off, but I bet she'll be able to discern it. She's good at that." He petted Porthos. "What's on the agenda tomorrow?"

"I meet with the image manager."

"Right," he acknowledged with the roll of his eyes. She knew the term reminded him of Ameleah. "But what about for fun? You're in New York at Christmas time."

"Well it's like prepping-for-Christmas time," she reminded him. "They have some decorations up, but they're still putting up more. The restaurant had the centerpieces out, and the trees up at the entrance. I can tell they're prepping to do more. The hotel lobby only has a tree up, and I looked at pictures online to see years past. They do way more. I'm really pumped for it."

He grinned. "By next week, everything should be set up, and you'll get the full experience."

"I will?" she shyly asked.

"Oh yes. 5th Avenue, Central Park... Rockefeller Center."

"Ah yeah, Rockefeller Center, where I can show off my *amazing* ice-skating skills."

"Well you did have an *amazing* instructor." He winked, and they shared a laugh. Porthos jumped away from the scene, leaving Jacob alone with a patch of slobber on his shirt and phone in hand. He smiled. "I really do miss you."

"It's only been a day," she joked.

"So… you don't miss me?"

She bit her lip sheepishly. "Well… I didn't say *that*." They both grinned at each other without saying anything. Merridy wondered if he felt butterflies in his stomach the way she did. Despite being half a country apart, she could smell his cologne, feel the warmth of his breath on her cheek. *Longing*. That's what it was. She longed for him. "I miss you… very deeply," she finally confessed.

"Deeply." He paused. "I agree… but even more so. Deeply times infinite."

"Deeply times infinite," she repeated, a hint of sleep in her voice.

"You better get some rest. Big day tomorrow."

Merridy let out an airy laugh. "Honestly… every day seems like a big day anymore." She turned the living room lights out and slowly headed to the suite's bedroom.

"Are you okay with everything being… this much?"

"I guess I need to be. I mean, it's what I wanted." She rolled her eyes. "I mean, if I wasn't here, I'd just be watching Christmas movies in my comfy pants and planning to go see my parents for Thanksgiving like I do every year at this time. Shaking things up."

"Nothing wrong with traditions though."

She fell down onto the bed. "No, nothing wrong with traditions. But a little adventure is fun too."

"Wish I was there to tuck you in... that's an adventure I wouldn't mind becoming a tradition."

With her face partially buried in a pillow, she attempted to turn one eye to the camera. "I wouldn't mind that either."

"Goodnight Turnip Girl."

"Goodnight White Rabbit."

Chapter 25

A buzz of people flittered around a dressing room in the Echo Star Headquarters. On Tuesday, Merridy had met with the image manager's assistant. He took a plethora of measurements of her face, body, arms, legs, neck, and even length of her hair. The assistant then photographed her at multiple angles in order to create a digital image of her in a specialized computer program. The aftermath had been alarming as he began making adjustments in the computer that manipulated her own image into someone she hardly recognized.

Casimir assured her that it was mere speculation and an 'example' of what the program could do. However, something sat heavy in her stomach during the rest of the meeting. By the time she had arrived in the privacy of her hotel suite, she was tearfully calling Jacob. He consoled her until she fell asleep. She had been so overwhelmed with negative feelings about her body-image, that she missed Kara's flight arriving.

Now, on Wednesday, she sat texting her friend as stylists worked her hair. Anything was preferable than seeing her changing image in the mirror.

'I still feel bad about yesterday.'

'No need to feel bad. Not after what you went through. Why don't you get a say about any of this?'

'They say I do. But I feel powerless.
Whenever I bring something up, Casimir
quotes some study they've done to show
what fans like and what sells. Stuff like
that. I don't know how to argue with
statistics.'

'But you're not a statistic. You're a
person.'

'I'm also the product. Isn't this what
marketing is? Isn't that what you do
when you market a product?'

'An insurance product doesn't have
feelings. There's a right way to market a
person and a wrong way to market a
person. I really don't like this. And I
can't wait to see your face today.
Hopefully it's the same face I know. Um,
please don't let them take a knife to your
face by the way. I want to say that's a
joke, but I've heard rumors.'

'Absolutely not. I will be running away immediately. Right now, they're doing hair and makeup. That's all.'

'By the way, I can't wait to surprise you with where we're going for dinner tonight. I'd text you but I MUST see your face when I tell you.'

'Hopefully I can ditch Caleb for it. I can't believe I'm stuck on a project in NYC with my high school ex.'

'It's the most wonderful time of the year.'

'I'll try to focus on that. Because I really don't want to focus on my past. Not too thrilled with it popping up so much lately.'

'Maybe there's a reason for it, and you just don't know it yet.'

'Maybe. I hope God shows me why soon.
One flight with this man was enough to
remind me why he is firmly in the 'ex'-
category. High maintenance. He wears a
mask over his eyes to sleep. He needs
noise-cancelling headphones. He needs
his water TEPID. Who from Texas
orders their water 'TEPID' instead of
iced?'

'I am certain that Texans order their
water as sweet iced tea.'

'Exactly.'

'They're telling me I have to put the
phone down so they can do my makeup. I
will text you when I head back to the
hotel. I think it's photos after this.'

'See you soon. I'll be working away on this
project.'

Merridy put her phone away in order to lean back in the chair
and allow the stylists to start on her makeup. Layer upon layer
was applied to her skin. Her face had never felt this heavy

before. After what felt like hours, a perky stylist chimed, "We're done!"

She opened her eyes to view the mirror. The reflection looking back at her was a stranger. "Is this... right?"

"Looks great, doesn't it?"

The stylist seemed excited about her work, and Merridy offered her a smile. "You're a real artist." The statement was true. Dark liner traced her inner waterlines, frosty blue shadow with a glitter shimmer, bold blush, subtle contours, and bright red lips reflected back to her. "This is like the best of the best of 2018. Not that I know how to do any of this, but I read magazines."

"Thank you so much!" She bounced away happily as the image manager's assistant walked forward with a clipboard and an ear piece.

"Makeup and hair look great. Let's get you downstairs where they can work on lighting before the shoot."

A whirlwind of people surrounded her as they hurried down halls to the photoshoot area. Men and women worked handheld machines to check lighting before posing Merridy to re-check through the camera lens. She thought there was only one photographer, but it felt as though a dozen people frantically ran around her.

"Where's my model? Are my lights ready?" An authoritative voice boomed across the room, and Merridy noted a man in a black turtleneck and matching black slacks heading toward her – the photographer. "You. Girl. Are you my model?"

"Ye..."

"Then get in there. Show me what you have." He waved his hand to the set. Merridy timidly hurried to the area, already uncomfortable under the lights with her heavy makeup and head full of hair extensions. "Come on, pose, do something. Need to see you with some angles."

Awkwardly, she attempted to pose in ways she had seen on television and movies, but she was immediately scoffed at.

"Is this what I have to work with? Amateur hour down on the farm? Has she even been in wardrobe yet? What is this monstrosity she's wearing?"

Merridy crossed her arms over her dress. While she had not 'gone to wardrobe' yet, she was already wearing one of her favorite dresses — a cornflower blue floral maxi dress with long-sleeves.

"This is New York, not Little House on the Prairie. Can we get a stylist in here? Wardrobe!"

A woman with a rack of clothes ran into the room and frantically began pulling clothes off hangers. Another woman started unbuttoning the back of Merridy's clothes. "Excuse me!" Merridy shouted.

"Hey babe, we gotta get you out of the 1800s and into 2018," the woman replied while continuing to unbutton the dress.

Merridy jerked herself away from the woman. "First of all, I can undress myself. Second of all, I will not be undressed in the middle of a crowded room." She held a hand to the front of her dress to keep it in place. The woman had succeeded in unbuttoning enough that the dress wanted to slide forward and down. "Hand me what you want me to wear, and I will change in a changing room."

Flustered by Merridy's request, the woman turned to the photographer in a huff. Casimir walked forward and nodded to her. "Put her in that green number," he called out. "There on the end."

She turned to a short, hunter green, sleeveless dress with a tie on the side. The low-cut top of the dress, including the split in the center, gave Merridy unease. "I don't... have a strapless bra..."

While giving an 'I told you so' mock eyebrow, the woman held up silicone pads and tape. "We don't use those. Still think you can dress yourself?"

"I still think I'm not getting undressed in the middle of this room."

"Zydonna, please take Merridy to another, empty room, and assist her in changing," Casimir instructed the woman.

"And make it snappy," the photographer added. "I haven't all day. Why would anyone come here before wardrobe?"

The complaining voice of the photographer faded into the general menagerie of frantic voices as Zydonna led Merridy down the hall to another room.

"Is it normal for artists to simply strip in the middle of the shoot, or any room, like that?" Merridy asked her.

Zydonna simply grunted.

"Sorry... that's just, not me. It's not what I'm used to, or how I was raised, or what I believe..."

"Why are you here?" Zydonna snapped once they were alone in the room.

Merridy stepped back in surprise. "I... want to sing."

Zydonna laughed. "You want to sing?"

229

"It's a record company, so yes…"

"It's not just a record company. Do you know who works here? Do you know the people I've dressed… this is New York City. This isn't…"

"The farm. I get it." Merridy sighed. "I didn't ask to come here, you know. I was asked to come here." She slipped off her dress. "I'm just trying to make this my career. It's all I ever dreamed of. Didn't you have a dream? Isn't this your dream?"

The woman began applying the undergarments required for the dress. "Dream? This city doesn't believe in dreams."

Merridy frowned. "You can't let go of your dreams because of this city. What were you called for?"

"Called for?"

"Your dream. Your calling on your life."

Zydonna hoisted the green dress onto Merridy and began tucking as needed. "Whatever…" She tied the bow on the side. "I mean, when I was in school, I wanted to go into design."

"Clothing design?"

"No… interior design," the stylist sarcastically responded. "Yes, fashion. I wanted to be a fashion designer."

Merridy looked down at the dress she was wearing. The style did not flatter her figure at all, and she felt highly uncomfortable in it, especially with the amount of flesh showing in the chest-area. "Look at this… a designer made this. A man chose it to be put on me. But what do *you* think? You, not what they want you to say."

Zydonna took a step back and looked over the outfit. "Not your color. Not your cut. You need a darker shade of green, and an empire waistline that not only flatters your figure, but will give you more comfort."

"I think you're right."

"It doesn't matter though," Zydonna waived off the slight softness she had almost shown. "The boss picked this dress. Let's go." She draped Merridy's maxi dress over her shoulder and led her back to the shoot. She tossed matching heels to Merridy. "Have at it."

The singer attempted to go back into the shoot, but felt distracted by the constrictions of the dress. Her hands kept rising to her chest to cover it in her attempt to be modest. The actions caused the photographer to unleash a whirlwind of demeaning comments at her. Casimir silently stood nearby. His acceptance of the photographer's words angered Merridy.

"Stop!" she shouted. "I can't do this anymore!" She yanked on her dress to pull it up. "I'm halfway hanging out of this dress. I can barely breath in it. How do you expect me to pose naturally if everything about this is unnatural?"

Casimir walked away and snapped his finger at two interns. They swarmed around Merridy and helped to pose her despite her protests. "Trust us," one intern whispered. "They know what they're doing."

"Get the next set ready," Casimir announced. "Put her in sequins. High neckline this time."

Once again Zydonna did as she was told, though in private she admitted to Merridy the changes she would make to the dress for it to flatter Merridy's body shape better. Merridy did appreciate the mock-turtle collar of the dress and its long sleeves, even though the length of the dress was still shorter than she preferred.

Before they re-entered the set, Zydonna gently placed a hand on Merridy's shoulder. The tender motion from the woman caught Merridy off-guard.

"One moment…"

"What is it Zydonna?"

"You… seem like a good person. So, word of advice, don't yell back like you did last time. Just do what the boss says if you want to make it in the industry, ok?" She rushed into the room before Merridy could respond. She abided by the advice, however, and managed to get through the second half of the photoshoot without yelling or crying.

A company car returned her to the hotel. Casimir rode alongside her in order to list the next day's agenda. She silently listened although her heart did not feel any joy from it. Her ability to hold in her emotions left her as soon as she entered her hotel suite alone. Tears flowed for the second day in a row.

'Hope your day got better. I should be over in thirty minutes. That ok?'

Merridy stared at the text through her tears. She wanted nothing more than her best friend, and the wisest woman she knew, to tell her what to do. Kara always knew what choices to make.

'I'm eager to see your face. I'll see you in thirty.'

232

The thirty minutes allowed Merridy time to ugly cry, shower, scrape the layers of makeup off her face, and prepare for the evening's meal. Kara arrived five minutes earlier than predicted.

"What's wrong?" her friend greeted her.

"I... I'm over it. I don't want it to ruin our evening by talking about the day, especially when you hear what I have to say."

Kara arched an eyebrow. "Are you sure? You seem very, very upset. I can feel it in the air."

"It was a hard day. All of this is really hard Kara. But if it was easy, everyone would do it, right?" Merridy attempted a laugh. "I came back to my room, I cried, and I've moved on."

Her friend hugged her nonetheless. Merridy cherished the hug briefly before pulling away.

"No, really, Kara... where we're going tonight for dinner... it's worth all the tears. We're going to be dining with boy band heartthrob KT Tally of NTUNE!"

"What?!" Kara shouted happily. She clapped her hands. "Oh girl, is he still good looking? I bet he is." She squeaked. "I shouldn't even be saying that. But oh, he had some gorgeous eyes."

"His eyes are still gorgeous, but he *is* a married man now. We'll be eating with his family."

The two held hands and jumped around in circles with preteen glee. The moment allowed the day's harrowing experiences to be temporarily forgotten.

Later, a taxi ride brought them to a brick townhouse on the Upper East Side of Manhattan. "Oh, my word," Merridy breathed. "What does something like this go for in this neighborhood?"

"Millions," the taxi driver answered her.

"I can't even imagine," Merridy responded. "The cost of this place would be a thousand acres of ranch land where my parents live."

"Land is a little scarcer up here," Kara told her. "Supply and demand." They paid the taxi driver and nervously headed to the townhouse's front door. "I've never rung the bell of a celebrity before."

"Can we do it together?"

"Let's do it together."

They reached up to the tiny round buzzer for KT's door. Almost immediately, the door was opened by a tall, tanned woman with shoulder-length brunette hair. Her checkered slacks were pristinely pressed with a perfect crease, and her black, button-down shirt matched. "Merridy?"

"Yes ma'am," Merridy answered.

"Welcome!" The woman rushed forward and hugged her. "I'm Elizabeth Tally, KT's wife. He told me all about you."

"It's so nice to meet you," Merridy returned the hug. "This is my best friend, Kara Jackson."

They shared a hug of greeting as well before Elizabeth ushered them into the home. Merridy was surprised by the interior: white shiplap walls and trendy 'farmhouse' décor. The Texas trend of interior design was something she never would have expected in a Manhattan townhouse. "You have a lovely home," Kara stated.

"Thank you so much." She stopped at a stairwell. "KT! Our guests are here!"

Two preteen girls preceded their father down the stairs, and their mother introduced both of them. "Merridy, Kara, meet our two girls Cyndi and Whitney."

"Hello Cyndi. Hello Whitney," Merridy greeted them.

"I love those names," Kara added. "Whitney Houston is one of my favorite singers."

"Mine too," KT agreed.

"And Cyndi Lauper is one of mine," Elizabeth added. "Come on girls, let's head to the dining room and setup."

The three departed, allowing Merridy a moment with Kara and KT. "Thank you for having us over," Merridy stated. "Even though your invitation *was* a little cryptic."

"Hard to talk honestly around the record execs," KT shrugged. "You've been here a few days, surely you know what they're like by now." He casually finished his descent down the final few steps of the staircase. "I've been in the business since I was a child enslaved to The Mouse. It can be beautiful, but very ugly. It's important to have the right friends in the right places."

"And are you one of those right friends?" Kara asked.

KT grinned. "I thought Merridy was a spitfire at our dinner, but you take the cake."

Kara winked. "I'm not a spitfire. I'm a realist."

"She has a discernment of spirits," Merridy told KT. His confused face encouraged Merridy to continue. "It's part of our faith, a gift of the Holy Spirit. She is anointed, and can tell when people are lying."

"That's quite the super power." KT tapped his finger on his chin. "And to answer your question, yes, I would like to be one of the *right* friends. I think Merridy's one heck of a lady. I look forward to songwriting with her." He nodded his head toward the nearby living room. "Come on. Before we write songs together, I'd like to hear you sing... live."

"First time someone has asked me to sing since I've been in New York," Merridy told Kara.

KT snorted. "Not surprised." He handed her a microphone connected to a karaoke machine. "Already setup for family night, so let's have a go."

"What do you want me to sing?"

Kara sat in an oversized armchair and melted into its plushness. "Obviously some Whitney, after Whitney in there."

"Excellent suggestion!" KT agreed. He queued up a song whose title projected on the screen.

The sight of the song title made Merridy swallow hard. "I Will Always Love You?" she asked.

"You know it, of course?"

"Written and record by Dolly, reimagined into legend by Whitney? Yes... yes I know it. It's... not for the... faint of heart."

"You got this," Kara encouraged her. "You could sing it blindfolded."

Merridy took a deep breath. "If I..." she began, as the words flashed across the television. She had sung the song a million times before, both versions, and adored it. But she never understood the emotions behind it until now – love. The more she began to realize that she was in love, the stronger her voice became. By the iconic 'big note', she was lost in the words with her eyes closed.

Applause met her ending note. The sound caused her eyes to jolt open and cheeks redden. KT's wife and daughters had joined the audience.

"I knew it," KT smiled. "You have the voice." He stroked his chin. "You don't need auto-tune. You don't need their schemes. You have the talent already."

She placed the microphone in its stand. "I'm sorry, what?"

"Echo... they're just putting you in the music factory. You can do so much more than them." He eagerly sat on the arm of his couch and leaned forward with an eager grin. "With a range like that, you can sing *anything*."

"I want to sing gospel," Merridy responded. She walked over to Kara. "I don't think that's what Echo wants."

"No, of course it's not what they want. They only want pop, R&B, and some hip-hop, a dash of mainstream country. Top 40 only. That's all they produce." KT pointed at her. "Think on that."

Kara raised an eyebrow. "KT... I have to ask. You don't seem to like Echo at all. Why do you work for them?"

His eyes darted to meet those of his wife. She nodded and sent the girls out of the room. "You ever hear about people who sell their soul to the devil?"

"Yes..." Merridy tentatively responded.

"Echo is the devil, and I signed a contract with them that was out of desperation." He slowly lowered to sit on the couch properly. "It was not in my best interest. And I'm still stuck in it. Until they release me, or another ten years pass. I have been told multiple times by some of the best lawyers I can afford that it is a solid contract, and I couldn't afford the repercussions of a breach."

Elizabeth went to stand by his side and offered a comforting hand on his shoulder. "He signed it when we were pregnant with Cyndi. His solo career wasn't taking off with them as we had hoped, and they offered him the deal so he could support his family. We thought they were generous at the time."

"Now I know my solo career failed because they had me releasing *horrible* music. And they have me writing more horrible music." He glared at the floor. "Grammy-winning-horrible-music."

"That's awful," Merridy agreed. "I'm sorry you're trapped."

"You're trapped too. How many years did your contract say?" KT asked her.

Merridy put a hand to her chest. "Five years. But... I haven't signed any contracts. Thank God."

"That is wonderful news!" Elizabeth beamed. "The food is ready everyone. Let's eat and have a more pleasant conversation." She beckoned Merridy who happily followed her out of the room.

KT remained on the couch with a furrowed brow of concern. Kara tapped her chin while staring at him. "You are holding a lot more in than your own wretched contract with Echo."

"I can't lie to the lady with the superpower," he agreed. "Yes, I'm concerned. It's unusual for the company to bring someone in and invest the time and money they have without a signed contract. I wonder if they tricked her into signing something that she didn't know was the contract."

238

"I'll ask her if she has signed anything, contract or otherwise." Tense silence passed between them as KT stared at the electric fireplace flickering under fall decorations. "There's more."

"Yes." He refused to elaborate.

Kara slowly stood from her chair and walked to KT. "If I remember teen magazines correctly, you were a believer at one point in your life."

"A long, long time ago," he muttered.

"...That one day is with the Lord, as a thousand years, and a thousand years as one day..." She shook her head and knelt next to him. "He's the Maker and Commander of time. 'A long, long time ago' is but a second to God. He's working on something in your heart, KT; I can feel it. Your paths crossed with Merridy for a reason."

His face contorted with more frustration. "The things I know would destroy me."

She placed hands on his hunched over shoulders. "Hasn't He told you already to go and confront this enemy that you cower from?"

KT teared up at the statement. Power exuded from Kara's lips and radiated from her fingertips. He had never felt any power like it. "I can't. I can't do it alone."

"The enemy will be brought to light," Kara confirmed. "But it will not be done by you, and you will receive no honor from it. It will be given to... a woman." She closed her eyes and whispered a prayer.

KT closed his eyes and began crying. "I will support her then, whoever she is," he mumbled around his clasped hands which covered his mouth. "Thank you for calling me out on this, Kara."

"It wasn't me," she whispered. "It's never me."

"Dad!" Cyndi called from the hallway. "Let's eat!"

He nodded at Kara. "Go ahead. I have to shut the machine down." She followed his instruction, allowing him time to clear his tears in private.

Chapter 26

Caleb and Kara sat in the lounge of the hotel, surrounded by manilla folders and tablets. She sighed heavily as she compared photos of different architectural features of the hotel to find the balance she hoped for.

"What's wrong?" She shifted in order to ignore him, but he repeated his question. "What's wrong, Kara? You're in a worse mood than normal."

Another sigh escaped her. "Last night was rough. That's all."

He snorted. "Went out to a speakeasy for research?"

"No," she rolled her eyes. "I had a nice dinner with my best friend, who is in town, and one of her business associates."

"And that was rough?"

"I learned a bit about the business she's in, or rather, learned I don't know a lot. And now I'm worried for her." She swiped the screen of her tablet. "Being stuck with you instead of helping her adds to the misery."

"What's so bad about being stuck with me?"

"Ha," she laughed sarcastically. Her hoop earrings rattled when she shook her head. "Where do I begin? How you ruined my business proposal that I worked diligently on? How you're making each decision more difficult than it needs to be? Or how you're one more example of my past refusing to stay in my past?"

Caleb nodded his head. "Sounds like you're mad at your circumstances, not me." He took a bite of his salad. "I didn't ruin your business proposal; I challenged it. Challenging your proposal is going to make it bigger and better than you imagined. And that's why I'm making your decisions difficult. I know you. I know you are the best, and that you can produce the best, so I'm demanding the best."

She lowered her eyes to the papers. The compliments unexpectantly reached her heart.

"And I don't understand why you're upset about your past. Or why you disappeared from your past."

The ice clanked in her glass as she lifted a raspberry tea to her lips. "I'm upset about my past because I worked so hard to leave it there. I'm not the same woman I was back then. I was rebellious, angry, hurt people, and not living a clean lifestyle."

"I know exactly the kind of lifestyle you were living. I was part of it. And I remember you were a loyal friend, passionate about music, organized, creative... I think you have a warped view of your former self."

"You have the warped view," she mumbled. "I know exactly what I was, the acts I committed, and how I treated my family. And I had to change who I was."

"Which meant also cutting ties to anyone from back then? Is that why don't have social media and avoid everyone you knew?"

Kara stood from the table and gathered her papers. "I think I'll take my research up to my room."

"Avoidance isn't the way to handle this, and you know it." He reached out and took the papers from her. "You changed. We all have. We all have regrets. Why not accept the fact that the past is finding you so you can learn how those people have changed too?"

Wisdom existed in his words; Kara could not stand it. "I never liked when you were right."

"To be fair, I never got to be right very often." He calmly set the papers on the table with his own. "How about we enjoy this food and drink, and play catch up. Get to know each other in the present tense. Then maybe we can work together better."

Against her better judgement, she returned to her seat. Caleb called the waiter over to refill their glasses and present the dessert cart.

"I'll begin. I'm Caleb Stone. I'm a marketing executive at a respectable firm where I excel at consumer analysis. I previously worked in sports and entertainment marketing, didn't care much for the celebrity game, and shifted my focus to product-based marketing. I have two children, seven-year-old twins, named Aaliyah and Aaron, after the musician and Hank Aaron, respectively." He held his hand out in greeting.

She shook it. "I'm Kara Jackson. I'm on the marketing team at a life insurance and annuities institution. I also teach Wednesday-night Bible class at my church and serve on the executive ministry board there. I don't have children because I have yet to find that special someone in my life."

"That's impressive. I didn't know you were a minister." Caleb nodded his head while leaning back in his chair. "Is that why you want to distance yourself from your past so much? Because I would think that your past is something that would let you know how important ministry is."

"It does. But at the same time, when I have to face it, I still feel shame for what I've done. I know God forgives me, but I can't forgive myself." Tears hit the brim of Kara's eyes. "And that's why avoidance is easier."

"Who else are you avoiding besides me?"

The waiter returned with drinks and the dessert cart. It offered Kara an opportunity to catch her breath. An urge to ugly-cry sat in her throat, and, if she continued speaking, the urge would no longer be containable. She pointed to a piece of chocolate ganache cake. Then, she drowned herself in more raspberry tea.

"That bad huh? Must be Elyssa."

She nearly choked on her tea.

"Yep. It's Elyssa." He smiled. "I take everything back. Having to deal with both myself *and* Elyssa in a short time span? That is a lot for you to deal with." He toyed with a lemon-slice before squeezing it into his water. "Listen, what happened between you and I, I will admit, was greatly on me. I was a jerk in high school and a good bit of college. Honestly, if it wasn't for my bride, I wouldn't be the loveable guy I am today. But what happened between you and Elyssa? You both could have handled it better."

"It was all me." Kara's response was barely audible. "I destroyed our friendship."

"Nah, it wasn't all you. I remember that game like it was yesterday. She played to kill. And she did. She killed your dreams. But at the same time, you were playing just as deadly. It just happened that you were the one that got injured. The roles easily could have been reversed."

The fresh perspective took Kara by surprise. Luckily, the slice of cake arrived, and she set about savoring each bite while Caleb continued to speak.

"She's working with the Twisters now on their marketing team. I did some work with her before I switched to my current employer. She's good at what she does." The spoon for his Italian ice seemed miniscule in his large hands, yet he daintily scooped a bite. "All your friends are hustlin'. Kenny has an art studio, Mark lives at the beach, Tom owns that indie record label, Luke is on tour, Kyle recently returned from the Pacific…"

"Tom owns the record label?"

"Well yeah." The directness of the question caught Caleb off-guard. "That local one they recorded under in high school. He's been building it up. Luke is signed under it and has a few records out. You really need to get on social media. It's like you're living under a rock the size of our school."

Kara gulped a giant bite of the cake. "I think I understand what God has been doing… maybe. I have to go pray about this." She grabbed her papers. "And these too. I'll reach out in a couple of hours, and we can meet back up to review our progress."

"Alright then, but I'm finishing your cake." He slid the chocolate dessert toward him as she bound out of the hotel's restaurant. "No shame in my cake game."

'How did the first half of your day go?'

Although Kara was staying in the same hotel as Merridy, the two held busy schedules and only crossed paths when specifically scheduled. Evenings offered more free time than during the day. Still, she needed to know her friend was okay.

'Oh my goodness. It was crazy. I got an early morning wakeup call from a trainer the studio has on staff. I spent two hours at the gym. I wanted to die. I get that I'm not perfectly in-shape, but given my recent ice-skating time, I thought I was gaining some stamina. Throw that thought out the window! They have me drinking a cleanse too. Um yeah, do the math. How has work gone with Caleb?'

'You've been working out? I thought today was going to be songwriting day? And work with Caleb actually went better than expected. Some eye-opening moments I'll share with you later. We're splitting for now and will circle back later to regroup.'

'Yeah... I thought it was songwriting day too. Casimir said that they were having a creative meeting with KT this morning about the direction they want the album to go first. In the meantime, I get started on my health plan. Tomorrow evening I get to meet the actual image manager. It's like they want me prepped for it. I don't know, am I about to get inspected? I feel like a house getting ready for open house. It's weird.'

'I'm glad that the work with Caleb went
well too.'

'Who's this image manager?'

'Some guy named Charles Lee Laban. I've
not a chance to look him up. Keep
meaning too, but I forget. My head feels
like it's in a fog.'

Kara gasped at the response. She knew the name. She knew
who his clients were – including Ameleah.

'He's the guy that managed Ameleah,
Jacob's ex.'

A long pause existed between Kara's revelation and Merridy's
response.

'That's the guy Jacob blames for ruining
Ameleah. I'm now terrified Kara. Is he
ruining me? You'll tell me if I start
becoming a monster, right?'

'Of course. Just be wary Merridy. I love you. I don't want anything bad to happen to you. Okay?'

'Yes ma'am. Hopefully I'm free tonight, and we can go out and see some sights. Grab some food. I'll be starving.'

Kara put her phone aside and turned to the desk in her hotel room. "Pray for her. Leave her in God's hands. And focus on your own project," she reminded herself. "Everything will be revealed in time."

Chapter 27

The Rockefeller Center swarmed with ice skaters around the base of an undecorated tree. Merridy and Kara sat on a bench overlooking the scene as they savored hot chocolate. "A little over a month ago we were watching a skating rink with no idea that life would change this much," Kara noted. "I mean, we hoped great things for you. But we couldn't have imagined it."

"Who knew the changes a skating rink could bring." Merridy inhaled deeply. Despite a near week passing, she had not told her best friend about her and Jacob. She wanted to focus on her budding feelings for him, her nighttime phone calls and constant texts, and the release he provided from the pressures of the music industry.

"A record deal…"

"A relationship…"

Kara turned to her with a raised eyebrow. "What?"

"Well, my last night at home, after you left… Jacob stayed… and we talked…" Merridy found the words rushing out of her mouth. "We admitted things…"

Stunned, her friend stared at her with mouth slightly agape.

"We kissed, and, kissed again." Merridy inhaled deeply before recounting every detail to her friend. "We've been talking every night. For hours. Video chat, regular calls, texts…" She hugged her arms around her waist. "I get butterflies every time we speak. Kara, I'm crazy for him."

"And you're certain he's equally crazy for you?"

Merridy grinned wide. "Absolutely." Happiness radiated from her eyes, and it was the first time Kara had seen true happiness in her friend since arriving in New York. "I think... well... I'll wait until he's here. I can't wait until he gets to New York. We have a whole list of places to go for Christmas in the Big Apple."

"I'm so happy for you." Kara hugged her friend. "I know I warned against it for a long time, but he's a new person. His past is behind him, and you are before him. I really, really am happy for you."

"Thank you." Merridy felt tiny tears of joy form in the corners of her eyes. "Sometimes I just think, wow, he's with me? He's chosen me? Is this real?"

Kara chuckled. "Well why wouldn't he choose you Merridy? You're amazing."

"Yeah but look at me and look at the woman he was just with. If I bend my head down, I've got a second chin. And I have handles not made out of love. And I've got stretch marks without having ever been pregnant. My thighs touch. I inhale deep when I zip up my jeans to keep my belly fat from getting pinched..."

"Stop it." Kara put a gloved hand on her friend's face. "You are a beautiful daughter of God. Don't say such things about yourself. These physical bodies are temporary. It's who you are on the inside that matters Merridy. And what is on the inside is absolutely beautiful. Jacob knows it."

The auburn-haired woman smiled.

"Plus, your body isn't as bad as you describe. Don't let those people at Echo give you any body dysmorphia; you are lovely."

Merridy threw her arms around her best friend. "You are the best."

"I want to hear about all the places you have planned for when Jacob is in town. It better include a carriage ride in Central Park. Always wanted to do that with some prince charming – you know, tall, British, with an accent, a little quirky and funny, and then he surprises me with a single rose and a carriage ride in the park?"

"Kara!" Merridy gasped playfully. "I didn't know there was this romantic side to you. Where has it been hiding all these years?"

Her friend shrugged. "I had it buried with some other things in my past. But you know, being around Caleb this week has helped me get over those things. I gained a great work proposal and some old friends this week."

"Well then I'm happy for you too. We've had a pretty great week." Merridy melted into her hot chocolate and enjoyed the warm steam engulfing her face. "Not without it's hard times too, but a good week nonetheless."

"You haven't told me how it went last night with the image manager."

"Ugh," Merridy moaned. She held her arms tighter to her and focused on the marshmallows floating on the surface of the cocoa. "I was trying to just focus on the greatness of New York at Christmas time. Even if they're still decorating it."

Kara placed an arm around her friend's shoulders. "That bad?"

"It's like they brought me to him, had me stand there, rotate several times, lift arms up, jiggled my arm fat, lifted my hair, lifted my shirt mid-drift, put a ruler up to my thighs... I don't know. He just stood there watching me the whole time. Expressionless. They shouted all my numbers to him. Occasionally, he would whisper to his assistant. His beady eyes behind those thick glasses never stopped staring at me." She shuddered. "I hated it. I felt like a cow going up for auction with the butcher eyeing it up."

"That is awful! What is the point of it all?"

"I don't know. But he's who has made *everyone* Kara. Echo does all those studies, they hire all these people, but I heard that without Charles Lee Laban as the image manager, none of those ladies would be who they are." Merridy's face contorted. "I mean, I can't compete with ladies like Christina, Brittany, Kellie, Lila, Alicia, and Megan without changing my image. Right?" Her voice became frantic as she spoke, and she stared at her hot chocolate. "I shouldn't even be drinking this. It's too many calories."

"Hold up," Kara cut her off. "Stop, stop, stop. First of all, you aren't competing with any ladies. This is your ministry, not some competition. You sing to praise God. You're not singing to beat Christina or Brittany." Her friend stood up as she continued. "Also, why are you changing your image because some old white man told you to? Girl, you were made by the One who sits on High. Everything He makes is perfect, so you are perfect, and no reason to change. Finally, don't you dare start giving up a small hot chocolate because there are too many calories. Life is too short to not drink hot chocolate on a cold autumn night."

Merridy gazed upon her friend in silence. Then the tears began rolling. "Kara, I don't know what is happening to me." She placed her cocoa to the side in order to cover her face with her gloved hands. "Everything is going okay, and then suddenly I hear their voices in my head with all their measurements and statistics. It's like this is why I didn't want to talk about it. I just want it to be this thing that's happening to a different person, and I'm detached from it all."

252

"That is no way to live your dream." Kara knelt down next to her friend. "You deserve better than this Merridy. I don't care who these people are. You have to demand respect."

The crying continued. "I don't want to make them angry Kara. I don't want to lose my chance."

"You can't put that above your calling. When you are given an anointing, God will open a door for you. If not this one, then another." She squeezed Merridy's hands. "Don't let them tear you down. No matter what."

Merridy was unable to respond.

"I wish I wasn't flying out tomorrow now." Kara wrapped her arms around her friend to pull her into a tight hug. "I don't like leaving you when you're so torn."

"You have to go tomorrow. Your presentation is on Monday." She sniffled. "It can't be all about me." A few deep breaths later, and she managed to say, "Jacob is flying in on Monday. I won't be alone for long here. Plus, KT and his family are here. And I have the day off tomorrow. I might not leave bed. Actually, the bed… it might be all I need to recharge."

Kara tightened her hug. "Maybe. And speaking of bed, I do think I'm due for my bed. The checkout time will come very early."

The two stood, arms linked, and walked down 49th Street back to the hotel on Park Avenue.

The checkout time did, in fact, come early, but Merridy ensured that she awoke to enjoy brunch with Kara and Caleb before they departed to the airport. She hugged her friend for thirty seconds in an attempt to absorb every fiber of happiness she could from the embrace.

Alone in the hotel lobby, Merridy stared at the gilded decorations, hoping they had been enough inspiration for her friend. She prayed for her friend's safe travels, she prayed for her friend's presentation, and she prayed for the positive changes her friend had expressed the night before. She even prayed that Kara would find her tall, quirky, funny Brit with an accent.

"Are you okay?"

Her eyes opened. A woman stood nearby with arched eyebrows.

"Yes ma'am," she replied to the woman. "My friend just left, and I'm praying for her safe travels."

The woman responded with a slight nod of the head and her mouth formed the word 'ah', but she said nothing as she continued forward into the lobby.

"Praying doesn't make me crazy," Merridy mumbled. "I don't care what the world says." She turned to head to her room and talk to her boyfriend.

'How's your Sunday morning?'

She crashed on her bed, gathering the pillows and down comforter around her. The sun filled the room through the arched windows. A sigh of contentment left her lips as she enjoyed the peaceful feelings of being away from the record company.

'Church was nice. I went to the early service. Felt like something was missing though. I mean, what could it be? The praise team was a little lite.'

'Hopefully was still good though.'

'Pretty awesome. Some songs I hadn't heard before. And the sermon was good. I got a Bible. And I brought it. I'm proud of me for remembering to bring it. Now I just need to memorize the order of the books.'

'Awwwww. You got a Bible? I'm so proud of you!'

'Yep. I've been reading it too. I actually didn't know my name was in the Bible. And my namesake had some issues.'

'<3 He did. What part are you reading? Aside from Genesis. And what was the sermon about? I actually really missed

going to service this morning. But I guess
I can finally say I've had a fancy NYC
Sunday brunch. No mimosas though.
Just plain OJ for this gal. Though it still
tasted weird. Flavored OJ. Is that a
thing?'

'I don't know. I prefer my OJ to be
orange flavored. You know, the point of
it? ;) But the sermon was on Isaiah 54.
That weapons will be formed against you
but they won't prosper. It was like, yes,
bad things will come against you, but they
won't win. But the bad things will still
come. I don't know how to explain it. He
talked about Daniel and the Hebrew boys.
But I've not read that far, so I got a
little lost.'

'That's deep. Actually, I really needed to
hear that message. I'll have to go online
and watch the recording of it. I
understand, I think. God never said the
bad things won't come; He just said they
won't prosper. Like, Daniel still went into
the lion's den, but the lions could not hurt
him. The three Hebrew boys still went
into the fire, but the fire could not burn

them. Yes, sounds like a very good
message.'

          'YES! That's it. You're so smart.'

          'And pretty.'

          'And talented.'

          'And I miss you.'

'You're making me blush. I miss you too!'

She rolled onto her stomach and tucked the comforter around her with the pillows in new tactical positions. Her teeth bit down on her tongue's tip as she decided on her next message. Instead, she hit the video call button.

Jacob answered it immediately. "Hello beautiful Turnip Girl."

"Hello handsome White Rabbit." She grinned. "What are you up to now?"

The camera screen tilted briefly, revealing the ceiling, then the floor, then Porthos running across Jacob's living room, and finally settled on Jacob once again. "Sorry. We are prepping for a tug-of-war. I made a promise." He leaned in close to the phone as he made adjustments. "Trying to secure the phone in this holder so my hands can be free enough to hold this rope." He stepped back as the phone remained in place. "Perfection!" He grabbed the rope that served as Porthos's toy.

"Oh yay! Just in time for ultimate tug-of-war!" Merridy cheered. She leaned the phone against a spare pillow in order to prop her head up with her hands. "Go Porthos!"

"Traitor!" Jacob called out with a laugh.

She returned the laughter. Watching the two added to her contentment, though she longed to be with them. Her eyes darted to the magnificent display of her hotel suite. It was beautiful. But in her mind, it did not hold a candle to being anywhere with Jacob.

"Oh no!" Porthos jumped on Jacob, knocking him to the ground. He grabbed the rope that fell to the floor and ran away with it. "What have your paws been in?" Jacob yelled after him. "Look at this shirt," he directed at Merridy. The white shirt was covered in muddy paw prints. "We didn't even walk in the mud. How does he find this?"

"Maybe it's his superpower."

Jacob slipped the shirt off. The action caused Merridy to blush. "I'm going to teach him to do laundry. That's a superpower worthy of the name." He grabbed the phone off its stand and headed to his laundry room. "Think of how many hits that video would get: 'Akita Pre-Treats Stains'."

"I would certainly watch that," she agreed. His camera tilted again as he placed it on top of the dryer. "I'm ready for you to be in New York."

"I'm ready to be *in* New York. If we didn't have the pre-travel practice this evening, I would have booked a flight today. I've got a whole list of things to do while we're there. I apologize in advance if you don't get any sleep."

"Sleep is for the weak. Also, I'll sleep today to prepare. Maybe while you're out, sweating away at practice, I'll get cozy in my bed and snore."

He leaned over the camera and glared at her. "You don't have to rub it in."

She faked snoring sounds.

"They're giving you the whole day off?"

"I mean, I'm supposed to work out today too. Which I will. I'm just very sore. They have me on a two-hour workout regimen with an hour and half of cardio then thirty minutes weights. Every three days I increase the workout routine by thirty minutes, to help with endurance. I think next week I start dance classes?"

"Wow."

"Yeah, they're really serious about physical health, I guess."

"Makes sense. I guess you need endurance for those concerts. Some of those shows go for hours." He stroked his chin. "I wonder how many calories does singing burn?"

"Hmmm... Now I have to know. Let's ask Google." She typed the question into her phone. An answer immediately popped up. "Singing burns around 136 calories per hour, dependent on your size and energy used."

"What you're saying is there *could* be a thing called the singing diet."

"That would take a lot of singing. I don't know if the vocal cords could keep up with it," she laughed. Her hands grabbed the phone as she rolled off the bed to walk to her suite's bedroom window. "At least not the calorie deficit I'm expected to meet." Her face soured slightly, and Jacob noted it.

"Throw that out the window when I'm in town." He grinned at her. The trick worked as she grinned back. "Magical restaurants. Magical light displays. Carriage rides. Only the best for you."

The butterflies overwhelmed her stomach again as she thought of a carriage ride in the park with Jacob. "Can we fast forward a day?" she whispered. Her fingers began toying with a strand of her hair absent-mindedly while she dwelled on her daydreams. "Maybe skip the whole business meetings and hockey game nonsense and get down to the magic and the romance and..."

"The kissing?" Jacob interjected. He grinned sheepishly, revealing his dimples, and his long eyelashes fluttered briefly. "Sorry. It's been a week. Can't stop thinking about kissing you."

She was certain her entire face could match the red of Santa's suit. "Nothing to apologize for. I... keep thinking about it too." Merridy bit her bottom lip. "Sometimes I'm concerned that I've turned into some silly high school girl."

His grin cocked. "Nothing silly or high school about wanting to kiss you forever." He looked at his watch. "I wish I could be on this call forever. But I'll take hours."

"Hours? I might could go for that."

"Merridy Rachel Christmas... you know that these hours will feel like seconds."

She spun away from the hotel window to reach her suite's fridge for a bottle of water. "Jacob Randolph Kenway... I still have to fuel up."

They shared a laugh before moving to their next topic of choice – Christmas around the world.

Chapter 28

Zydonna handed Merridy a faux-fur muff to wrap over her arms. "I still think this isn't the right look for you," the woman protested. "Feels like they're trying to make you into Marilyn Monroe."

"I felt that way too." Merridy tilted her head for the diamond earrings to sparkle in the dressing room lights. "I hope they know diamonds aren't my best friend, I'm not materialistic, and I am *not* singing 'Santa Baby'. Not that they've had me sing *anything* yet."

"That's really strange, you know, since you're the singer." The stylist fidgeted with Merridy's outfit. "I'm told to trust the system, but a little weird that they have you doing a photo session for the album cover when you've not recorded the album yet."

"Honestly, I thought they were going to Milli Vanilli me, which wouldn't have made sense at all because I have a much better voice than image," Merridy laughed. "But I am supposed to go over songs with KT today and do some practice." The two walked out of the dressing room to the photo shoot. "I can't wait to see what I'll be singing. Christmas is my..."

The two froze upon seeing Charles Lee Laban walk forward. A woman in oversized sunglasses walked alongside him with linked arms. But the sunglasses did not fool Merridy; she knew the woman well: Ameleah Antoine. The frown that crossed Ameleah's face confirmed her identity. "What are you doing here?" she barked at Merridy.

"Now, now," Charles Lee calmly stated. He patted Ameleah's hand that rested on his arm. "Miss Christmas is my next project, my dear Ameleah."

The frown remained.

"We are sculpting her into something quite nice." He grinned and nodded. "Yes, quite nice indeed."

Merridy felt ill under his gaze. His eyes seemed smaller under the thick, circular glasses. His nose hooked like a hawk's beak. His high cheekbones and angular jaw added to the raptor-demeanor.

"Casimir assures me that Miss Christmas will be our next big star... bigger even than Brittany." He nodded his head contently. "With the right guidance."

Ameleah pouted as she looked from Charles Lee to Merridy and back to Charles Lee.

"Where is my model?" the photographer's voice echoed down the hall.

Zydonna tugged at Merridy's arm. "That's my que," she mumbled. The two scurried around Charles and Ameleah. "That was the most awkward moment ever."

"Every moment around Charles Lee Laban is awkward," Zydonna hissed back. She looked over her shoulder to ensure enough distance had been placed between the parties. "He looks like a hawk, and every one of us is his prey."

Merridy gasped. "I feel the same. I was just thinking he had the beak thing going."

"And he's very controlling of the stars' images. Like Ameleah back there... he forced her to have an abortion when she was in Paris."

The news caused Merridy to freeze. "What?"

"She was making her debut. He found out and told her to get rid of the baby before the bump showed." Merridy's heart broke. "He said a baby would kill her career before it started."

"But... it was Jacob's baby..."

Zydonna shrugged. "Maybe not. Jacob Kenway wasn't the only guy she was with at the time."

"What..." Merridy began, but they had entered the photoshoot. The chaotic whirl of assistants, lighting, effects, and the photographer took her away from Zydonna before she could get more information out of the woman. But the revelations distracted her as she attempted to pose for the album cover. She wanted nothing more than to finish the photos to get back to her conversation. *Who else had Ameleah been with? Did Jacob know? Of course he didn't know.*

"Girl! Look like you care to be here!" the photographer shouted. "You're getting diamonds for Christmas! You're getting a box from Tiffany's! You're excited! Live it up!"

She sighed and placed a fake smile on her face. She knew she had been doing that more and more with the record label. "Force yourself to think about the music," she whispered. Her smile intensified. The music was why she had come to New York after all.

"Yes! Yes! More of that!"

Honestly, she did not know what she was doing. But she continued her focus on the music to get through the shoot. After an hour of lights, posing, and flashes, the photographer dismissed her. She rushed to Zydonna. "Who else was she with?" she blurted out.

"Who?" Zydonna asked. The two returned to the dressing room.

"Ameleah Antoine. You said she was with other guys at the time of her pregnancy."

The woman spun in a circle to ensure they were alone in the hallway. "Shhh!" They entered the dressing room, and Zydonna slammed the door shut. "That is not a topic to be shouted where any ear could hear it."

"Why? Who was she with?" Merridy felt tears in her eyes. Her voice lashed out harder than she intended. Perhaps she *had* been shouting in the hallway.

Zydonna took the muff off of Merridy's trembling arms. "I never expected you for gossip. You seem... better than that."

"I'm not. Not when it involves Jacob." The quizzical look on Zydonna's face caused Merridy to shake her head. "I'm sorry. I know. I'm not making sense. I care because... Jacob and I are dating. That's why this was an awkward encounter. I'm dating Ameleah's ex-boyfriend. And she and I have had a run-in before." Merridy breathed in deeply to steady her rambling. "I just have to know that she didn't have an abortion with Jacob's baby..." The words broke her; tears streamed down her eyes. "It would hurt him. Any of this would hurt him. I don't want him hurt."

The stylist bit her lip while putting a tentative hand on Merridy's shoulder. "Wow, you really like this guy, huh?"

Merridy nodded.

"Well, deep breaths. Let's get this horrible outfit off of you while I tell you more about this place you need to know." Zydonna worked on one of the earrings. "I'll probably be fired when they find out I told you."

"If."

"No… when. They always find out." She laid the first earring on the counter. "That's why the non-disclosure agreement is in every contract for every job here. We're not supposed to talk about these things. In fact, not only can they fire me, but they can sue me."

Merridy inhaled deeply. "Then… don't say anything." Her mind quickly began to put pieces together.

"But…"

"She was in Paris. She had a baby bird, but daddy bird didn't want it."

"Oh." Zydonna nodded. "Yeah. It's a 50/50 shot."

"Oh." It was a lot of information that Zydonna confirmed. Merridy bit her lip. Her heart broke for Ameleah, to feel forced to make such a choice. Her heart broke for Jacob, who knew something changed with her in Paris, and now she knew, it was both an affair and an abortion. Monumental forces that would change anyone. And Merridy wondered how much of the affair was within Ameleah's consent, whether by force or manipulation. The disgusted feelings she had for Charles Lee Laban had been justified, one way or another. Even if he had Ameleah's consent, he had no right to demand the abortion for the sake of celebrity status.

Her phone buzzed, and she glanced at it. Casimir requested her presence at a studio for practice.

"The boss needs us to hurry up?" Zydonna asked. "They always do. No chance to breathe in this industry."

"Maybe there's a reason for that. If you're not breathing, a part of you is dying." She closed her eyes and allowed Zydonna to finish her job.

266

"I am not singing these songs."

Casimir leaned against the wall of the studio with his arms folded across his chest. His forehead frowned in anger and frustration. "Our analysts have spent a week on this list of songs, cross-checked by ten different computer systems especially made for song selection. Every. Artist. Adheres. To. This."

The list rattled as she held the printed paper. She enjoyed the songs on the list, but they were not what she wanted to sing. "Why did we even have dinner with KT, why talk about what songs are my favorite Christmas songs, if we are going to use computer programs to make a list of songs that are the opposite of what I wanted to sing about?"

KT sat silently on a couch in the corner of the room. His hands were folded together under his chin as he watched the scene unfold.

"I mean, the Mariah Carey song we specifically talked about is on this list. I am *not* singing a song that makes me roll my eyes." She began reading song titles. "'Last Christmas'. 'Santa Baby'. 'Santa Tell Me'. I mean, is this why I was dressed up like Marilyn Monroe for the album cover shoot? You're selling me as a materialistic diva?"

"Christina Apollo, Brittany Clare, Kellie Crane, Lila Winters, Alicia East, and Megan Mill. It is what the masses want," Casimir countered.

Merridy placed the paper down calmly. She inhaled deeply through her nose. "But it's not what they need."

"You need to think about if you want this or not," Casimir hissed. He left the room.

Her eyes drifted to KT. "I don't know."

"Whether you want this or not?"

"Do I want to sing? Yes. Do I want a record contract? Yes. Is this the way I want it? No." She hugged herself while she paced in the center of the room. "I get that... I can't always get what I want. I wasn't expecting *everything* to go my way. But nothing is what I want here. The photo shoots, the makeover, the thousand calorie limits to my day, the songs... some of those songs were written by you. Would I like them?"

KT smiled. "You would absolutely hate them."

She let out an exasperated sigh. "Ugh! Why don't they listen to me?"

"It's never been about *you*, Merridy. I've been trying to make that clear. Echo has a formula. A formula that has worked. And they won't change as long as the formula works."

His statement caused her to stop pacing. "I need to break the formula."

The comment received an eyebrow arch in return. "Now you sound like a mad scientist. But I like it." He bounced off the couch and reached into his back pocket. Firmly folded pieces of crumbled paper emerged. "Take these. You might need them."

She slid the papers into the pocket of her dress. "Let's get out of here. I want a hotdog, and I feel no shame about it."

They linked arms and left the studio.

Chapter 29

The pages from KT sat scattered around Merridy's bed for her to review. He had written songs for her in private, away from the prying eyes of Casimir and the record company. A note accompanied them: 'They can never know I wrote these. They own everything I officially write.'

She loved the lyrics and hummed the notes written. Regret at not bringing her guitar seeped into her. A buzz on her phone distracted her.

'The eagle has landed.'

Her eyes darted to the clock on the bed's nightstand: eight in the evening.

'Eagle? Or Rabbit? And... I know it's late.
But...???'

'Rabbit. Late. Story of my life. BUT.
Once we check-in at the hotel, I will be
free to do whatever you wish. Dinner.
Dancing. Foot rubs. Whatever your
heart desires.'

'Wait... foot rubs? I'm sold.'

269

'I need a guitar. I don't know where to
get one this time of night.'

'The record company doesn't have a guitar
for you? And darling, this is NYC. It's
the city that doesn't sleep. We can find
you a guitar anywhere.'

'Just need access to a guitar away from
the record company. I have a theory I'm
working on with KT. And you're right. I'm
not used to this 24/7 town yet. Let's
have a musical adventure.'

'In that case, I should be there in thirty
minutes. And after I kiss you, I will get
us a cab to hunt a guitar.'

Merridy threw her phone on the bed and rushed to the suite's
bathroom in order to prepare herself for Jacob's arrival. It had
been a week since she had last seen him, despite talking to him
daily, and her nerves made her knees shake. He wanted to kiss
her. Kiss *her*. The thought still overwhelmed her.

Then she recalled all that she had learned from Zydonna.
Nerves turned into fear. Should she tell him tonight? Would it

ruin his focus on his upcoming games? Would it ruin their time together? Would not telling him be selfish?

Her stomach rumbled in stress. "No, no, now is not the time," she chided herself. Deep breaths helped her regain her composure long enough to freshen up and dress for her first official date with her boyfriend.

Forty minutes later, a knock sounded at her hotel door.

"You're late, White Rabbit," she joked while opening it.

He grinned. "I wouldn't be me if I showed up on time." Jacob leaned forward and wrapped his hands in her hair to bring her in for a kiss. Merridy felt as though she melted into his embrace. "This week has been too long," he whispered between kisses. He closed the hotel door behind him while still leaning into a kiss.

"Oh, first you stay the night at my apartment, and now we're in my hotel room alone," Merridy joked. "My mom is probably having a heart attack right now, feeling this in the air."

Jacob held his hands up innocently with a grin. "I swear to be a gentleman."

She giggled and wrapped her arms around his neck. "A practical Prince Charming." Her eyes twinkled as she locked her gaze with his. Wrinkles formed around his eyes from smiling. "Jacob," she whispered. "I... I want to be completely honest with you."

His eyebrows arched. "And I with you..."

"Well," she sighed. "Okay, let's say I know something, and I want to tell you, but if I tell you, it could ruin our evening?"

"Hmmm," he frowned. His fingers traced the outlines of her face. "It has nothing to do with you wanting to end our relationship, does it?"

"Absolutely not!" she gasped. "I... I... really like you. And I've been practically imploding until you arrived. But it's still something important, to you, and your past."

"Oh." He spun her around and wrapped his arms tightly around her waist. His nose buried into her hair. "Let's leave the past in the past for now. That's not worth ruining our evening over."

She blushed. The world's most handsome man was hugging her tightly from behind – she felt like she was on the cover of a romance novel, though far more modestly dressed. "Okay," she whispered. "But when you're ready to know, I will tell you everything I know."

"Agreed." He swayed slightly; Merridy, still in his embrace, moved with him. "I got you a ticket to the game tomorrow night, by the way. Right on the glass, right next to the box by me."

"Jacob, I don't want to distract you..."

"You won't. I suspect that with you there, I'm going to have the best game of my life."

His hand lifted up, placing her hair behind her ear. Goosebumps covered her arms at the feeling of her neck exposed under his breath. The chills intensified as he ran his pointer finger over the exposed skin delicately.

"That is, if I can ever let you out of my arms again," he whispered. "It has been a very, very long week."

She spun around and kissed him, more passionately than before. "It really has," she finally agreed with heavy breath.

"I'll be honest... I don't know how to proceed tonight," Jacob confessed. "Dinner first? Dancing? Guitar hunting? Foot rubs? More kissing? I'm good for all of them, even if it takes me all night."

"All night, huh?" She felt as though her smile was so large it reached from ear to ear. "Well, let's start with the practical mission, the guitar, and then we grab pizza – I've been in New York City a week, and I've yet to have a slice. Then we come back here to eat, dance, rub feet, kiss... you know, whatever."

"Whatever?" he repeated. "That leads the door wide open Miss Christmas. I mean, we could go wild and end up playing a five-hour long game of Monopoly with that kind of agenda."

"Never. I don't let my Monopoly games drag out. I'm a land baron in training." She winked. "I'll go get my bag."

They happily walked arm-in-arm out of the hotel to a flagged cab. They cab took them to a string of pawn shops to find an appropriate guitar for Merridy. Several shops offered electric guitars, which she found lovely but not suited for the task at hand. After the fourth shop, she began to despair.

"Maybe I should wait until morning when the regular guitar shops open. I just really wanted to practice these songs tonight... for you... to tell you my plan..."

Jacob rubbed her back. "Don't give up yet. There is bound to be hundreds of pawn shops in this town. We're just going to keep going until we reach Little Italy for that pizza."

The last pawn shop on their list before Little Italy proved to be the jackpot. A well-maintained acoustic guitar stood on the wall. The shop owner behind the counter eyed Merridy as she stared at the piece. "This is an older Gibson, from like the forties," she told Jacob. "It's very beautiful."

"How do you know it's from the forties?"

She pointed to the logo on the headstock. "It's italic, which is early Gibson, but not too early, because it would say *The Gibson*. The italics are thick and the word is slightly tilted, which distinguishes it from the thirties." She smiled. "My dad favors Gibsons. It was the first guitar he ever bought me."

"You have a good eye," the pawnbroker commented. "That guitar is part of history."

"Every classic guitar is," Merridy responded. "But it is a nice piece."

"Looking to buy it? Because you should know, this is not any Gibson, this is *the* Gibson J-50 that Bob Dylan used to play."

Merridy sighed. She finally found a nice guitar, and the owner was trying to upsell it with outlandish claims.

"If you had proof that this was Dylan's guitar, then I'm sure it would be sold at auction. Not here... no offense," Jacob countered. "Do you have a certificate of authenticity?'

The pawnbroker seemed frustrated at the response. He pulled a vinyl record out and pointed to the guitar Dylan was holding on it. "Very same guitar. Look for yourself."

"Certainly, the same model," Jacob agreed. "But can't confirm that it's the exact same guitar. How about this, since you don't have a certificate of authenticity, we will purchase this guitar with the respect of its antiquity, rather than celebrity authenticity. It's *still* a Gibson from the forties, which makes it unique on its own. And to sweeten the deal, I will sign a hockey puck or stick, or whatever you might have here, and you can film me signing it as proof. How would that work?" Jacob removed his baseball cap in order for the man to see his face.

"You! You're Jacob Kenway!" The pawnbroker smacked his hand on the counter. "I have a couple of sticks and a puck. Plus $4,000 for the guitar."

"I know my autograph's worth. I'll give you $3,500, sign both sticks and puck, and I assure you that my value is going up this year."

Merridy's eyebrows raised. She was intrigued by the negotiator that Jacob proved to be.

"It's a gamble for me." The pawnbroker folded his arms across his chest. "Your value might be more in Dallas than New York."

Jacob grinned. "I am winning the Art Ross and Stanley Cup this year. Trust me, my value will be just fine in New York." He nodded at the guitar. "Assuming that has a nice case with it?"

The pawnbroker stroked the stubble on his chin. "I like your confidence, even if I'm partial to the Rangers myself. The guitar has an excellent case. You have a deal." He secured three generic hockey sticks and an authentic NHL puck for Jacob to sign while filming him. "Can't wait to post this online," he stated after securing the merchandise behind his counter. "Let me get you that guitar." He secured the instrument into its case for Merridy and exchanged it with Jacob for his credit card.

After the transaction, Jacob carried the guitar out to the awaiting taxi for Merridy.

"You are amazing," she exhaled. "That's a very expensive gift you just purchased me. I mean, I should have got it. I was just stunned by that negotiating I witnessed."

He grinned. "It's a gift, but also an investment, because I believe in my girlfriend's dreams." He punctuated the comment with a kiss on her cheek. "Plus, I want to hear some singing tonight."

The request caused her to giggle. She lovingly stroked the guitar case with one hand while holding Jacob's hand with her other one. "Pizza time?"

"Best pizza in Little Italy please."

The driver led them to a pizzeria with an outdoor patio lit elegantly by stringed lights around the beams of the pergola. The duo eagerly bound up to the counter to order, deciding to eat on the patio rather than taking the pizza all the way back to the hotel.

"I'm so excited," Merridy whispered to Jacob as they sat at a corner table. The guitar case sat firmly between her legs in a protected position. "I'm about to eat New York style pizza at a restaurant in Little Italy with my hot boyfriend." She smiled sheepishly. "This is what dreams are made of."

"I can think of only one thing that can top it," he agreed. "And that's the night I'm having with my beautiful, talented, lovely," he leaned forward to kiss her hand, "girlfriend."

Merridy blushed.

"Got a slice of pepperoni and a slice of sausage," a waitress announced as she brought the plates to their table. She noted the guitar. "You a musician?"

"Yes ma'am," Merridy softly answered. A tint of blush formed on her cheeks.

"She's underselling herself," Jacob intervened. "She's got the voice of an angel."

A man from another table called out, "Sing for us, Angel Voice. The sound system at this place is busted." He was a heavier-set man who ate his pizza with a fork and knife. Nine others sat at his table. She assumed they were his family.

"Um…" she looked at the waitress. "Is that…?"

"Fine by me." The waitress glanced at the man, then back at Merridy. "You probably should do it. I'll bring you some water, for your pipes."

"Okay, then," Merridy agreed. She pulled the guitar out. "We just purchased this, so please, let me tune it real fast. What would you like to hear? Any particular song?"

The man nodded. "Yeah… something by Frankie… for my gorgeous wife." He winked at the woman next to him.

"By Frankie… yeah, I can do that." She tuned the guitar as quickly as possible, for it was certainly out of tune, before strumming the first few chords of the only Frank Sinatra song she really knew.

Why do I do just as you say,
Why must I give you your way,
Why do I sigh,
Why don't I try to forget?
It must have been that something lovers call fate,
Kept on saying I had to wait,
I saw them all,
Just couldn't fall 'til we met.

The man stood and offered his hand to his wife. The two began slowly dancing in the limited patio space. He pressed his cheek against hers. "Ah yes, this is our song, *cara mia*."

Seeing the two sharing the moment caused Merridy to smile as she strummed the guitar before the chorus.

It had to be you,

It had to be you,
Wandered around,
And finally found,
The somebody who,
Could make me be true,
Could make me blue.
And even be glad,
Just to be sad,
Thinking of you.

She ended the song, to the applause of those at the patio. "Bravo!" the man held his wine glass up to Merridy. "Your partner was not lying, Angel Voice. You have my gratitude for indulging my request. And doing it so well." He kissed his wife who giggled at the action. "We've not danced to that song in…"

"…decades," she finished his sentence.

"Very true, in fact Sinatra might have been singing that song last time we danced to it," he jested. Merridy wondered if the statement was true despite the chuckle that accompanied it.

"Well I am very glad that it served as a spark for the both of you," she sheepishly stated while glancing at Jacob. "It's always validating when my music brings others happiness."

"What's your name, sweetheart?" the man's wife asked her.

"Merridy Christmas, ma'am."

"You not only have a good set of pipes, but you have manners," the man stated. "I like you, Merridy Christmas. We're gonna keep an eye on you."

She bowed her head. "Well thank you very much. Is there another song…?"

"Nah," he waved a hand. "Enjoy your dinner, Angel Voice." He winked at his wife. "We're not the only spark that happened when you sang."

Merridy turned to see Jacob shyly smiling. "He's right," he agreed. "I can't wait to get my own private performance."

They finished their meal in silence. Eager glances and shy smiles passed between them. A cab ride later brought them back to her hotel room where she readily showed Jacob the pages KT had given her. "Aren't they wonderful?"

Jacob eyed over one of the pages. "This... is you."

She grinned broadly. "Right! I thought so too! Here, let me play some of it for you." She secured the guitar into her lap, and Jacob lounged back on the bed to listen – a content smile plastered on his face.

"Good morning beautiful." Jacob kissed Merridy's forehead.

She smiled with her eyes still closed. "I must be dreaming." He stroked her face while she kept talking. "I hear Jacob's voice, but he's thousands of miles away in Texas."

"Wrong day. This is Tuesday. And I'm here now." He leaned across her and moved KT's papers to the nightstand. "You just passed out. Songs everywhere. Guitar on the floor."

She chuckled. "We're not young anymore. Two in the morning might be our limit."

"Must be." He continued to remain leaned across her. His hand no longer placed papers on a nightstand, but stroked her hair instead. "This is a view I could get used to... every morning."

One eye opened. *"Every* morning?"

He nodded. "Every morning." He kissed her forehead. "Is that... too soon to say?"

Both eyes now opened, Merridy smiled. "I guess some would tell us, yes, but... no. I don't feel like it is. I mean, its... well... I'm not very good at this Jacob."

"Me neither." He grinned. "All I can do, is be honest, with you... and myself... and..." His hand took hers. "My heart feels like it wants to beat out of its chest." He lifted her hand to his chest. "Do you feel that?"

"Yes," she laughed. "And you're a well-trained athlete."

"No amount of training for this." He lowered himself down to press his lips against hers. "I love you, Turnip Girl."

Her breath felt as though it had left with his kiss and confession. "I love you too, White Rabbit," she gasped.

He kissed her again. "I *don't* want to leave for morning drills," he whispered between kisses. "Can I call in? Bad food last night?"

"That would be lying," she reminded him, "and lying is wrong."

"Ugh." He kissed her once more then laid his head down on her stomach. "Love sickness is a type of sickness, right? I'm so sick in love, I can't leave her side..."

She played with his hair. "I don't want to leave your side either. I don't even care about whatever they have in store for me today. I don't even want to show up. Like, what are they going to do, fire me? I haven't even signed a contract. I was told this was no strings attached. Let's put it to the test."

Jacob closed his eyes, enjoying her fingers in his hair. "At the very least, you said you wanted to reach out to Kara and tell her your plan. You can work on that today."

"Yeah, something to do, while you're at drills, then practice…"

"Then the game day nap."

"Of course, the very important game day nap." She smiled. "You might even see your own hotel room bed?"

"I don't know… this bed seems much nicer than that one." He rolled over, perched up by his elbow. "The pillows alone are way better." He poked her stomach teasingly.

"Dork," she tittered back. "Would you like some coffee before you go?"

"Allow me." He rolled off the bed to start the coffeemaker. "Nice selection of brews here." He held up the mini gourmet bags of coffee. "I'm getting jealous."

She wrestled her hair into a ponytail. "If you want to go to the gym with this insane trainer, please, have at it. I mean, I know you can do the physical part of it. That doesn't even bother me… though it kicks my butt. It's the psychological mess."

"What happened to 'no strings attached' and putting it to the test?" Jacob joked. He decided on a red velvet blend. "Stick it to the man, Christmas."

"I guess my bark is louder than my bite." She walked to the hotel room dresser to find workout clothes. She still wore the same outfit they had gone out in the night before; her jeans dug into her sides. "The trainer comes here to the hotel to get me going, takes me down to the gym… I mean, he's coming whether I want him to or not." Her eyes rolled. "Might as well get a solid workout in." She disappeared into the bathroom. "He'll probably be here soon too. He *always* shows up early."

Jacob glanced at his watch. "Yeah, we gym rats like our early morning workouts. Maybe tomorrow you and I will wake up earlier and hit the gym as a couple. How would your trainer like *that*?"

"I don't care what he would like, but, despite my general non-fondness for morning workouts, for *you*..." she opened the door to the restroom in her leggings and tank top, "...I would face that kind of punishment for. A couple workout? That's... new. I like that kind of new."

He smirked. "Look how cute you are in your workout gear and morning bedhead."

"Oh, hair..." She turned back into the bathroom to brush her hair. He stole a glance at the frantic woman in front of the mirror and sighed blissfully. Every unruly curl of her hair brought him a happiness he could never explain.

A knock on the hotel room door broke his concentration on Merridy.

"He's here," she huffed. "Could you answer for me?"

"No problem. I would love to meet this guy." Jacob walked to the door with his most charming grin. "Hello there."

"Um..." the trainer frowned. "This is supposed to be Merridy Christmas's suite?"

"It is," Jacob answered him. "She is wrestling her hair and can't come to the door right now. I'm the boyfriend."

"The boyfriend?" The man chortled. "Oh, this is great. She goes around like some sanctimonious woman at the photoshoot: *no I can't change here, I need a private dressing room because of my moral values.* And here she is, having a sleepover with you." The trainer continued laughing. "Women, right?"

Jacob sarcastically joined in with the man's laughter as he walked into the hallway, "Right." He closed the hotel door behind him. "First of all..." He pushed the man against the wall opposite the door and pinned him tightly. "That woman in there *does* have impeccable moral values. I'm astounded by them every day. And a couple can have coffee together in the morning without breaking any values. I assure you, anyone who questions her, will receive much pain from me. Understand?"

The trainer, fear in his eyes, nodded his head.

"Second of all, I've been hearing about your training methods. I'm all for physical fitness, but if I hear that you call her fat or lazy or any other demeaning comment about her looks or weight ever again, your head will be mounted in this room here, because I will be ramming you through the wall. Got it?"

"Yes... yes sir."

Jacob smiled. "Good. Because I've broken a lot of people's bones in my day, some of whom I call friend, so to me, you would be no problem." He stepped back, allowing the trainer to catch his breath. "Now, come on in."

"Jacob?" Merridy called as the two men entered the room. "Is that him?"

"Yes darling, it is him," Jacob called back. "No rush, take as long as you need."

The man stood tactfully away from Jacob. "Jacob? So, it is you... Jacob Kenway, the hockey player." He nodded at Jacob. "Ameleah's ex. I used to be her trainer too, you know. Oh, the stories I could share."

"She's in my past. Far, far in my past." Jacob filled his coffee cup with the red velvet blend and took a sip. "Not as sweet as I imagined. Interesting."

Merridy came bounding out of the bedroom. "I'm ready," she announced to the trainer.

"Good, let's go," he roughly stated.

"I left my extra key on the table," Merridy told Jacob. "I'll see you at the game?"

Jacob smiled. "Of course. And you know you can reach me anytime. I love you."

She returned his smile. "I love you too."

Chapter 30

"Nine goals," Jacob shouted in the locker room. He tapped his stick nine times against the locker and let out a cheer. "Nine! Boys, we were on fire!"

"At least a few of us were," Eddie joked. "You scored more goals in one game than most teams did tonight."

Jacob shouted again.

Terry sat down hard in the chair nearby. "Five goals. Bit of a show off."

"You had two yourself," Eddie reminded him. "Say a good night all around."

Jacob hurriedly began to strip off his equipment. "An excellent night all around," he agreed. "Best game I've had yet."

"That lucky charm must be working," Eddie told Terry. "You protested before the game, but she is apparently the key." He punched his brother's shoulder. "And you're happier than I've seen you in a long time."

"I feel happier," Jacob agreed. "I can't wait to take a shower and get out of here back to her. Diane is escorting her down to the player exit…"

"Psh," Terry hissed. "You know you're going to have to do a press conference after a game like this."

The comment made his friend frown. "You're not wrong. But it needs to be a fast one. We have a date lined up." He rushed away to the showers. Within minutes, he was clean, in his after-game outfit, and headed to the press release area. His agent caught him in the hallway to whisper in his ear. "Yeah, let's keep it limited to a few questions. I need to get out of here."

"Jacob! Jacob!" Journalists shouted as he entered the conference room. "Great game tonight!"

He held up a hand and leaned toward a microphone. "Thank you everyone. Want to keep this quick and to the point tonight. Let's go first with... Harrison, there in second row."

"Five goals in one night. What caused the change in performance tonight?"

Jacob laughed a response. "Was my performance so awful before?" he joked. The crowd chuckled with him. "Let's just say, my performance has improved, because my mindset has improved. I'm in a great place in my life, and it's showing in my work on the ice." He pointed to another journalist. "Ben?"

"Is the mindset change related to the rumors about your new girlfriend?"

He inhaled deeply. He had not spoken with Merridy about public acknowledgement of their relationship. Then again, omitting was lying, and lying was wrong. "Yes," he confessed. A murmur ran through the crowd. "Yes, I have a new girlfriend. Her name is Merridy, and she is the light of my life. Having her here at the game tonight may very well have given me the luck I need." The murmur grew louder with the celebrity gossip. "Anyone have any questions *not* about my love life?" he joked.

Another reporter raised her hand, and Jacob called on her. "Communication on the ice between you and Terry Sanger seemed off today. Is it true you are both competing for the Art Ross Trophy?"

He arched his eyebrows in surprise. "He's not mentioned anything to me about it, but at the end of the day, more goals for a player means more goals for a team. I know one promise I made myself and my team is that I will never sacrifice teamwork and assists in an attempt to score a goal myself for this award. This pursuit is a challenge to myself to make *my* shots more accurate and *my* playing cleaner and more aggressive. But if I don't have a clear shot, and a teammate does, I'm making that pass. If communication is off, it's just off... it's nothing more than that." He glanced at his watch. "I'm sorry, I only have time for one more question." He nodded to a man. "Roy?"

"In the off-season, your coach said his number one priority was to build up the team's defense. The numbers are still showing that you are giving up a lot of shots. How will you continue to build the defense if you're focused on offense?"

Jacob smirked. He wanted nothing more to be gone from the microphones and cameras. "I guess if I'm busy controlling the puck and taking shots, that's less time for the other team to take shots, right? Sounds like a great defensive strategy to me," he added the last sentence with a hint of sarcasm. "Excuse me." He stood and left the room.

An assistant that worked for the team stood nearby with his bags ready for him, and he rushed down the concrete tunnel to meet his girlfriend and agent. When Merridy saw him, she squealed and clapped her hands. "That was such a great game! You were amazing!"

He laughed and kissed her. "*You* were great. I saw you yelling and screaming. Not bad for your first live hockey game?"

"Yeah, it was really fun. Plus, when you weren't on the ice, I got to see you right there at the bench with just that little glass between us." She pecked his cheek. "And I was trying to give you all my positive vibes."

"Must have worked. I was on fire." He leaned his forehead against hers. "I can't even explain how much joy it brought me to turn and see you there at the game, cheering me on. Merridy, that means the world to me."

Her fingers fiddled with the collar of his shirt. "I will *always* be there to cheer you on. Even if I'm not in person for whatever reason, I will still be cheering you on in my heart." She tilted her head up to kiss him once more. "I mean..." she joked as she pulled away, "...I have push notifications on my phone for hockey. I never would have guessed that a year ago."

Jacob could not contain his smirk. "And I watched a livestream of some lady singing a song in her hotel room during my pre-game naptime today. Never would have guessed that either."

Linking arms, the two sauntered down the rest of the hallway to an awaiting car. "You watched? What did you think? I was so nervous, but Kara told me to just turn on the camera and start singing. She would do the rest, when she could, because the company totally liked hers and Caleb's presentation, and they've hit the ground running."

"How much caffeine did you drink during the game?" he laughed at her rambling.

The response received was a tongue stuck out. "Neh!" Her shoulder pushed into him. "A lot of caffeine. Also, I'm excited - about tonight, about everything."

"Where to then?" he asked as he opened the car door. "Hopefully dinner? I'm starving."

"Yes. Dinner. I made us reservations for a meal and a show tonight." She leaned forward to whisper to the driver. When she settled back into her seat alongside Jacob, she grinned at him. "It's a surprise though."

"Oh?" He glanced down at his jeans and long-sleeve black shirt. "Am I dressed appropriately?"

"We match." She indicated her own casual jeans and hoodie. "And I'm certain it's appropriate for this show." The car exited the stadium's underground parking garage. Merridy slipped her hand over Jacob's. "I hope you like this."

"I know I will." He leaned toward her, allowing his lips to caress her neck as the car continued to its destination. By the time they arrived at their destination, the driver had to clear his throat numerous times to gain their attention. Both blushed in embarrassment. "Sorry," Jacob whispered. He helped Merridy out of the car and offered an extra tip to the driver. "Again, sorry. We've had a lot of separation and pent up…"

The driver accepted the cash tip with a chuckle. "No apologies necessary, sir. I have been in love. I know what it's like."

Jacob reddened.

"Don't let her go. Ever," the driver advised.

"I never will." Jacob stepped back to allow the driver to go. He noted the restaurant the car had brought them to. "A pub?"

She giggled. "A really nice one. And they have live music tonight, and the best soda bread this side of the Atlantic, per the internet. And amazing bread pudding, and Irish coffee… and everything else your Mam-o used to make." Her hand lifted up to the pub. "I thought it would be a nice place to come and honor her. You said she passed away a week before Thanksgiving."

Tears welled up in Jacob's eyes. His memories of his grandmother flooded over him and were followed by the thought of Merridy's consideration. "This is… thank you so much Merridy." He pulled her into a tight hug. "I love you so much."

"I love you too." She nodded her head to the door. "Come on, let's go in. I'm freezing out here."

They hurried to the front door. "You really would freeze in Canada."

"I would just have to wear a lot of thermal underwear." She nodded at the hostess. "Hello, reservations for Merridy Christmas?"

The woman smiled. "It *is* you."

"I'm sorry?" Merridy asked. "Have we met?"

"No," the hostess grinned. "When you made the reservation, I thought that name could *not* be real. I looked you up online in curiosity. Found your website and live stream. I liked your singing. Brought it to the owner's attention. She'd love to get you to perform here sometime."

Merridy gasped. "Oh! Wow, yeah, I would love that. Tell her to just reach out on the site."

"Certainly!" The hostess led them away from the main entrance to a side staircase that led upstairs where more intimate booths overlooked the stage area. "Your waiter will be right with you."

With one arm wrapped Merridy, Jacob opened the menu. "I'm going to be honest. After a game like tonight's, I could eat one of everything on the menu."

She smiled at him. "That's one way to taste everything." Her hands lowered to his. "Pretty good seats, right? Look at that view right over the stage."

His eyes searched over her face. "I'm not going to be looking over a stage tonight," he whispered. "Not when I have my arm around the most thoughtful, sentimental, beautiful woman in the world."

"How am I lucky enough to have everything I want? Right here, right now, with you…"

Before they could kiss, the waiter arrived for their drink order. "She's going to want a hot chocolate, I need a coffee, plus waters, and can we also get those Rueben egg rolls and some soda bread with the beer cheese? I'm starving…"

"Coming right up," the waiter responded.

Merridy giggled as he left.

"What?"

"You really are going to order the whole menu, aren't you?"

He winked. "I might. It's much better than downing a dozen Big Mac's though. I've done that one too many times."

"Ladies, gentlemen, and everyone else," an announcer on the stage began. "Join me in welcoming… all the way from County Tyrone… The Logues!"

The two clapped with the rest of the audience as the band took the stage. "All the way from Ireland," Merridy whispered to Jacob. "Might be the only ones further from home than us."

"Three-thousand miles from home," he nodded. "Land or water, doesn't matter. It's a long way." He leaned his head against Merridy's as they listened to the band cover a Bruce Springsteen song. "Speaking of home… what do you think of heading out to Vancouver next month for Christmas? Or around Christmas? We have the day before and after the break off, too, this season."

"You want me, with your family, for Christmas?"

He winced. "I'm not stepping on your family plans, am I?"

"I don't know. In a normal year, I go to the ranch for Thanksgiving *and* Christmas. I don't think I'll be making it for Thanksgiving this year... and honestly, I heard them mentioning a Christmas special too..."

Jacob sat up straight with a look of concern. "They want you to perform on both holidays? Merridy, I know how important those days are to you, and how important your family is to you..."

Her head lowered. "Yeah. Those are important to me." She sighed. "I really don't know what to do anymore Jacob. If I go with Echo, then I get that record contract. I get sold-out concerts, world tours, platinum albums, Grammy awards..."

"Are those what you want?"

"I want my voice to be heard..." She shook her head. "But I guess that's the problem with them, right? I want *my* voice to be heard. Not some diva clone they're trying to make me."

"You can walk away from this," Jacob tentatively told her. "I don't want to push you one direction or the other, ever, but I do want you to know that I will always support you. If that means you don't like the deal you're getting with this Echo Star Records, then you can walk away. We will find you a better deal. Money is not an option..."

"I don't want you throwing all your money away to secure me a record deal."

He took her hands into his own. "Merridy, I believe in you. It's not throwing money away. It's making your dreams come true, just like my parents helped Eddie and I become professional hockey players. It's an investment of love. That's what I want for you, but with singing."

292

The bottom lip of Merridy began to quiver. She bit it fiercely to keep from crying.

"But as much as I want you to sing, I also want you to live the life you love. And the life you love includes your faith, your values, your family, your friends… I don't want you to lose those."

"Thank you everyone," the lead singer of the band called out. "We're honored to be here tonight. This next song was written by our very own Loguey here on the whistle." The whistle player grabbed his suspenders and bowed dramatically. "This is called 'No Place Like Home'."

Merridy turned to the band. "A fitting song," she mumbled. "Maybe it's a sign."

The waiter arrived with the drinks and appetizers. "Are you good with these for now, or would you like to order more?" His eyes drifted to the 'starving' Jacob.

"Do you know what you want, love?" Jacob asked Merridy.

"I'm starting to think I do," she responded absent-mindedly while watching the band.

He nodded. "I'm going to take a gamble and order for us both," he told the waiter. "We'll just get a few different entrees. Fish and chips, shepherd's pie, and the bangers and mash." He handed the menus to the waiter. "Oh, and those mussels too. Haven't had that in forever."

The waiter laughed. "Starving customers are the best," he joked. "I'll put this in to the kitchen."

"Here love, it's your hot chocolate." He slid the drink over to her. "Let's try some of this soda bread."

She turned to him. "Of course, for your Mam-o. That's why we're here."

"For Mam-o." They held aloft two pieces of soda bread and clinked them together as if they were toasting champagne glasses. "Thank you for this Merridy. I can't say it enough."

She smiled. "This is just part one of tonight."

"Part one?"

"Part one." She pecked his cheek before turning her attention to the hot chocolate and Reuben eggrolls.

"Got to admit, I'm enjoying part two." Jacob and Merridy held hands as they skated around the undecorated tree at Rockefeller Center. "Especially now that you're not falling into my arms."

"Yes," she agreed. "Though I wouldn't mind falling into your arms once more." She skated in close for him to wrap his arms around her. "Just glad your legs are still working after the game."

"You know me. I could live on ice, even loaded down with Irish pub food."

Merridy spun out of his arms. "You eat two appetizers, three entrees, countless Irish coffees, and a dessert, and that's a normal evening. I have to maintain only a thousand calories, burn thousands more, and it's still not good enough."

"You need to eat more darling." He skated up to her. "Eat what makes you happy." His hands grabbed her waist and pulled her in tight. "You are beautiful just the way you are."

She forced a smile. "That's a concept I'm working on."

"Here, let me remind you." He dipped her down into a passionate kiss. "That help?"

Her hands folded around the back of his head. "I don't know. Maybe once more."

Jacob obliged her before noting a few other skaters around them had their phones up. "Who needs paparazzi when you have the general public looking for hits on social media?" he whispered. "Guess this is what happens when you announce you're in a new relationship to the press."

She giggled as he helped her stand upright. "Opening those cans of worms," she joked.

"Better to be open and honest with the press than clandestine." He led her away from the ice to swap back into their shoes. "Speaking of which, what was it you wanted to tell me yesterday?"

"Hmmm?"

"The dark thing, that you were worried about ruining our evening." Jacob helped her to her feet. "You can tell me now. Nothing can ruin our evening." He jumped onto a concrete bench. "If this was a musical, I could burst out singing right now."

"Improvisational singing?" She jumped onto the bench beside him, albeit less gracefully, and swung her hand out to Tiffany's in the distance. "Gold and diamonds are not what I need," she sang. Her other hand pointed further away to FAO Schwarz, "when I can have a teddy bear decked out in tweed."

Jacob laughed at her.

"Some people have hearts of greed, but I come from a different breed..." She stopped singing and jumped down. "I always did like musicals," she confessed. "But this news is too grim for that."

He hopped down next to her. "What is it?" Concern ravaged his eyes.

Her hands lowered to her stomach. "It's about Ameleah." Jacob darkened at the mention of her name. "You were right, she did change in Paris. She had been cheating on you before then though, with several people. I don't know the names of all of them." Her voice croaked when she saw the heart in his eyes. "I do know one name though... and I know the man..."

"Charles Lee Laban."

"Yes."

He hung his head. "I always suspected it. It's disturbing. He's old enough to be her..." he shook his head.

"Grandfather," Merridy tersely responded. "Yes. It disturbed me. But that's not all." She reached out to his hands. "She was pregnant in Paris. And she... lost the baby." Merridy could not bring herself to tell Jacob that Ameleah had gotten an abortion. As much as she did not care for Laban or Ameleah, she knew *that* knowledge would destroy Jacob.

"What?" he cried out. He took off running toward FAO Schwarz.

Merridy took a deep breath before running after him. "Jacob!"

He fell onto his knees in front of the closed store's window display. Tears streamed down his red face.

She stopped short of him, giving him space to cry.

"I could have been a father!" he called out. "Why?" He screamed the word over and over.

Tentatively, she stepped forward and placed a hand on his back. "I'm sorry Jacob." Hunched over, he continued to cry. Merridy wrapped her arm around him and laid her forehead against his shoulder. "I'm so sorry."

"How did she lose the baby?" he eventually choked out.

"Jacob..." Merridy whispered. Tears filled her eyes. She did not want to lie to him, but she did not want to add fuel to his fire.

"Please, tell me Merridy. Tell me the whole truth. You promised..." He sat up partially to meet her eyes. "Please."

Sorrow filled her eyes. "Jacob, it... was... not a miscarriage."

"So she?"

"Yes." Merridy sighed. "I can't say the words Jacob. It's too awful. But please know, from what I heard, her hand was forced."

He buried his face against her and continued to cry. "I could have been a dad," he whispered between his tears. Merridy stroked his hair. "She chose that stupid career over us, and our future."

"I know. I'm sorry."

He sniffled as he attempted to stop crying. "Let's get back to your hotel room. I need away from, here." He looked up at the iconic FAO Schwartz Bear Soldiers in the window. "I should be buying that now."

Merridy helped him to his feet and flagged a cab. The night felt officially ruined.

Chapter 31

Merridy sat on her hotel suite couch with Jacob's head in her lap. Her fingers traced over the tufts of his brunette hair delicately. "Would you like some coffee, dear?"

He did not respond but continued to stare numbly into the distance. He had been that way since they returned to the hotel the night before. When the driver dropped them off, Jacob wanted to return to his own hotel. Merridy felt nervous about his frame of mind and convinced him to stay the night in her room. He crashed on the couch, and there he remained.

"I'll get you anything you want. Say the word."

Ten more minutes of silence passed between them. "I want answers," he whispered. "I want my child."

"Oh sweetie." She ran her hand down his arm. "I wish I had the answers for you. Only Ameleah can give you those. All I can say is… these people she's had to deal with, they can mess up how you think. They've been working me over in just a week and a half. She was with them much longer. Maybe she's deserving of some grace. Though…" She still could not imagine doing the same as Ameleah, but she also recognized one simple fact. "No, no *though*. She deserves grace. Scripture says *all have sinned and fall short of the glory of God*. We're all screwed up, and *have* screwed up, in our own ways. We need to show Ameleah love, grace, and kindness. No matter how hard that is. It's what we were called to do."

He set up. His red eyes were puffy and dark circles surrounded them. "You're a better person than me."

"No, I'm not." She placed a hand over his heart. "He who lives in me, lives in you. And that's where you're going to find the strength to overcome this." Her eyes lowered. "I'm so sorry about all of this Jacob. I should have never brought it up to begin with."

His hand covered hers. "Don't feel sorry. I needed to know." His lip quivered. "I needed to know that I have a child waiting for me."

Their hands squeezed together tightly at the sentiment. Merridy never knew that Jacob had such a deep desire to be a father. She knew that family was important to him. Children had not been discussed though. "I love you Jacob. And one day... we'll have children."

The statement seemed to snap Jacob out of his comatose. "Our children?"

"Our children." His hands abandoned hers in order to grab her hair and pull her into a passionate kiss. "Jacob..." she panted. "You've never kissed me like that."

"You've never talked about our future like that." He ran his fingers through her hair. "I love you. And..." Shame crossed over his eyes. "I said that it wouldn't ruin our evening. Then I did."

"You didn't ruin anything."

"I cried in front of you."

"Oh honey," Merridy stroked his cheek. "I would have been more concerned if you hadn't had cried. And I need to tell you... today I'm telling Casimir that I don't want to be with Echo Star. You were right. I need to be somewhere where *my* voice can be heard without sacrificing my values."

He hugged her tightly. "We will find you a better way."

"The trainer cancelled this morning's session yesterday. He told me another trainer would take over for him starting Thursday." She grinned at Jacob. "He seemed to be terrified of you."

"Well," Jacob snorted, "we talked a bit yesterday morning. Maybe it allowed him some much needed self-reflection."

"He did seem less... crude. I suppose I should thank you." She pecked his cheek. "But it's also time I start fighting my own battles." She stood from the couch and headed to her guitar which leaned against the suite's desk. "My weapon is a melody."

He followed her to the desk. "Doing another livestream?"

"Yeah, thinking of doing one this morning and one this afternoon." She sighed. "I'll need to figure out a hotel situation and how to get back home. I doubt they will pay for anything when I tell them no. Man, I hope they don't make me foot the bill for everything when I say no." She winced. "They wouldn't do that, would they?"

"I... would hope not. But don't worry about any of that. It will work out. Let's go get ready for this livestream."

"Did you just include yourself in my livestream?" she teased.

He picked up his phone from the desk and logged into his social media. "In fact, I'm about to share your stream from yesterday."

"Alright, well there's not really another chair..."

"I'll just lounge on the couch." He sauntered toward the restroom to freshen up. "You can see it from the camera. I'll just wave and request my song from here."

"A song request?" She headed to her dresser with a mischievous gleam in her eye. "I hope it's one I know."

"You know it." He closed the bathroom door. "Everyone knows it." The two prattled about in their morning routines in order to prepare for the camera. By the time Merridy was finished and taking her seat at the desk, Jacob was lounging on the couch and drinking a hotel-brand bottle of water.

She nodded and turned to her laptop. "Hello and good morning everyone!" she greeted the livestream crowd. Her smile widened when she noted Jacob share the livestream. "It's bright and early here in New York City. What better way to start the day than with a song?" Lifting her thumb over her shoulder, she indicated Jacob on the couch. "My sweet boyfriend has already announced he has a song request, so I guess he's getting that before coffee – which to me, is quite surprising." She lifted her guitar. "Mr. Kenway, what song would like this morning?"

"The classic which everyone knows," he began while partially sitting up. "And one my Mam-o once sang often when I was little, 'Amazing Grace'."

"Awww," she responded. For a moment, she forgot she was on livestream. "Of course, I will sing that for your sweet Mam-o." They exchanged a genuine smile before she remembered the computer. "Mam-o was Jacob's maternal grandmother who passed away this time of year a while ago, and we've been celebrating her legacy. This is a perfect tribute. Dear Mam-o, I wish I had been able to meet you. Thank you for your wonderful grandson. He would make you proud." She flashed one more smile over her shoulder for Jacob before singing.

Amazing grace how sweet the sound,
That saved a wretch like me,
I once was lost, but now I'm found,
Was blind but now I see.

It was grace that taught my heart to fear,
And grace my fears relieved,
How precious did that grace appear,
The hour I first believed.

Through many dangers, toils, and snares,
I have already come,
This grace that brought me safe thus far,
And grace will lead me home.

She sang the chorus again, and Jacob softly joined her from the couch. The sentiment nearly caused her to miss a few words as she smiled happily. For the briefest of moments, she pictured the two of them singing over a cradle.

When we've been here ten thousand years,
Bright, shining as the sun,
We've no less days to sing God's praise,
Than when we first begun.

Merridy repeated the chorus one last time before ending the song. She bowed her head at the camera. "Thank you for tuning in this morning. I will be back later today once I get some affairs in order. Look forward to featuring another original piece that I wrote in October. Have a great day everyone!" She clicked off the livestream and closed the laptop. "That was so sweet," she told Jacob. "I love how much you loved your grandmother."

"We're both attached to our grandmother's, I believe." He walked toward her holding out his phone. "Did you see how many active viewers you had during that livestream?"

"No, I was focused on the song and the meaning behind it…"

"Two-hundred, Merridy. You had two-hundred people watching you live, early in the morning, before the sun has rose in many places. They're watching you, without Echo Star doing any promotion of any kind." He knelt down in front of her excitedly. "You and Kara have got this… without them. People like *you*, the real you. Not a diva clone."

"I actually needed that confidence boost before I go to the studio and tell them no." She lowered her guitar in order to hug Jacob. "Thank you."

"I think we should have breakfast and a carriage ride before I have to go to practice and you go talk to them. Not that I want to procrastinate but… after last night… I think we just need… or I just need… you."

She kissed his forehead. "I think we both need each other, and I think this is a good idea."

Chapter 32

"How did it go?" Kara asked Merridy over the phone.

Merridy paced in her hotel suite while talking on the phone. "it went... more cordial than I expected. I told Casimir this isn't right for me. He quietly nodded, stroked his chin, then said he would give me the night to think it over. In the morning, if I still felt this way, they'd send me home to Dallas."

"That does seem *really* cordial. As much grief as they've been giving you, and they're just like, 'sure you can go'."

"Right, I thought the same thing. And it's not like they said we would move forward with a different direction more to my liking. It was just like he expects me to magically change my mind tonight."

"Maybe they'll be sending a bribe up to the hotel room?" Kara asked. "That's not unheard of in the corporate world."

"Why bribe me with whatever when they could simply let me be true to myself?" She plopped onto her bed. "I was hoping they would see that my true self is enough. I looked at my numbers from the livestream this morning. They are *really, really* good." Her free hand fiddled with the hem of her shirt. "Jacob said we would find a different path. I believe him. I just don't want him getting me a record deal by buying me a deal."

"You know..." Kara slowly stated. "I think there's another way, and it didn't occur to me until now. I'm beginning to believe that all of these run-in's with my past had a purpose. Let me reach out to some of those people, and get back to you. By the time you're back in Dallas, I should have you an audition lined up."

Merridy sat up excitedly. "Really?"

Kara laughed. "Really. And don't forget, even though you're not going with Echo Star, you already have that contract for the tree-lighting performance. That's happening regardless of anything happening in New York. You will have a record deal, the right way, and a Christmas album that makes you happy."

"Yes!" The singer jumped to her feet. "I think it's time I start planning that album out. It will give me something to focus on, especially when their bribe shows up. I mean, at least until Jacob gets here."

"Good luck. I will call you in the morning with a report on that record deal."

"Awesome. You're the best Kara. I love you."

"Love you too sweet friend."

Merridy hung up the phone and rushed to her desk. While her laptop booted up, she began scribbling song titles on a notepad.

'O Come, O Come Emmanuel'

'O Little Town of Bethlehem'

'While Shepherds Watched Their Flocks'

'We Three Kings'

'Go Tell It On The Mountain'

'O Holy Night'

She paused writing when the laptop's password screen appeared. "Yes, I'm loving this list so far. Plus, the songs I wrote, and the ones KT made..." she whispered. "They can't bribe this feeling away." Her eyes drifted to the clock on the computer screen. "Jacob's practice should be over. I should text him before I start this livestream." She clicked her tongue against her teeth in contemplation. "Nah, I'll do this one on my own."

A few mouse clicks, and the screen opened. Before she could begin her livestream performance, however, a knock sounded on the door.

"That's probably Jacob." She sat her guitar back down and rushed to the door. "Hey sweet..." Her voice froze when she noticed the men on the other side of the door. "Casimir? Charles Lee? Why are you here?"

Casimir gently pushed the door open wider. "I talked with Mr. Laban about your change of heart. He insisted on coming over today to convince you otherwise."

The dark look in Charles Lee's eyes caused Merridy to take a step back. "I feel very content with my decision."

"But dear, Miss Christmas... you don't understand," Charles Lee began. "Women come to us, beg to *us*, to make them stars. We *never* beg. But that's how much potential you have." His hands reached toward a tuft of her hair. "Your absolute *innocence* makes you more unique than you know."

Merridy stepped backward again before Charles Lee could touch her hair. "Please, leave."

Casimir closed the door behind him. "Not until we get your agreement to stay, I'm afraid."

She shook her head. "What do you think you can do to get me to stay?" She continued to back away from the duo. "Are you going to threaten me into signing some contract? How do you think that will even work in your favor?"

"To be fair, we already have paperwork with your signature on it." Casimir opened a folder in his hand and pointed to the

306

contract he had shown her at the restaurant. A signature similar to hers was on the dotted line. "This is what I've already shown to the executives. That's why they're paying for all of this." He indicated the hotel room. "Do you think a giant like Echo Star would give away so much to someone who hasn't agreed to their terms?"

"What?" she shouted. "I didn't sign anything, ever."

"You signed your lunch receipt," Casimir shrugged.

Her brow furrowed at the realization. "You forged my signature based on the lunch receipt?" She threw her hands to her hair in exacerbation. "What? How would that ever hold up?"

He put the signed document back into the folder. "I have an idea on how to make it right."

"Enough of that," Charles Lee interjected. "You get your signature after I get to know Merridy better." His hands reached out to her once more. She inhaled sharply and cringed away from his wrinkled talons attempting to grab her hair. "It's okay my dear. This is how I get to know all of my clients. It's the beginning of their ride to stardom."

Jacob entered the atrium of the Roche Morgan Hotel with a wide grin on his face. He had received a text from Merridy that simply stated: *I did it*! He was eager to celebrate with her. The anticipation was short-lived when he noted Ameleah sitting on a plush chair in the lobby.

"Ameleah?" His voice hardened. Although he wanted nothing to do with her, he also needed answers. His entire practice had been a combination of rage, regret, and prayers for closure. The woman's presence felt like an answer to that prayer.

Her eyes shot up to him. "Jacob?" A smile briefly flitted across her face, but a frown hastily replaced it. "Ah… you must be here because of Merridy. I've never known you to stay at an establishment such as this, but it does have the refinement of Charles Lee." Her arms folded defiantly while her eyes traced the gold details of the atrium.

"Oh yes, that *is* a word to describe Charles Lee Laban, isn't it? Refinement." Jacob sat hard in the chair next to her; his bag crashed to the floor. The loud noise startled Ameleah who leapt a little in her chair. "I know about you and Charles Lee, Ameleah. I know you cheated on me with him."

Silently, she stared at Jacob. Her lips grew thinner as he spoke.

"I know there was a child – a child you aborted in Paris. I need to know why. Why would you abort our child?" He choked on his words in order to prevent crying. "How could you?"

"It wasn't your child," she whispered. Her eyes lowered. "I did the math before… before I made any choice."

"So it was…"

"His. It was Charles Lee's child, and it was not a child born out of love." Her voice hardened. "In this industry, there are many hard choices to make when one is a woman. You wouldn't understand. Men control *everything*. Your path to fame? Easy compared to a woman's path. I mean, where is the women's professional hockey league? Aren't their talents equal to your own?" Her crossed arms tightened around her. "Your team's marketing girl, Elyssa? She has three gold medals. How many do you have? One. The world has declared her more talented

308

than you. But she exists to market *you*. Tell me how that's fair."

Jacob remembered what Merridy had told him about giving Ameleah grace. He swallowed hard before stating, "I am sorry, Ameleah. I understand that the deck is stacked against you."

"It's not just me the deck is stacked against. It's every woman... including your precious Merridy. If she wants to achieve the fame she seeks, then she will have to make the hard choice every woman before her has made."

"No," Jacob told Ameleah. "She already confirmed she doesn't want the fame. She wants her real voice heard, not the voice Echo Star was making for her."

"Are you sure?" Ameleah asked incredulously. "No one just gives up the life that Echo Star can offer."

He lifted his phone to Ameleah to show the text Merridy had sent him earlier. "She did. She went to the studio to tell them she's refusing the contract and going home."

"Refusing the contract?" Ameleah rolled her eyes. "She's already signed the contract. That's why they brought her here."

"Listen to me," Jacob stated matter-of-factly. "Merridy has never signed a contract with Echo Star. Casimir told her to come here to see if she liked it. She decided she doesn't like it. She's out."

"That doesn't make sense," the woman scoffed. "If she's out, then why is she having a meeting with Casimir and Charles Lee right now?" Her face frowned. "Unless... they're not even giving her a choice."

"What are you saying?" Jacob asked.

Ameleah stood to her feet. "When I went to Charles Lee to advance my career, he didn't just want payment in the form of money and future royalties. He wanted more. He wanted... me. I didn't cheat on you because I was attracted to Charles Lee. I cheated on you because... that was the payment to achieve my goals."

Jacob stood to his feet. "He forced you..."

"He forced my hand. It was say 'yes' to Charles Lee, or 'goodbye' to fame." She sighed. "It was, some sort of choice, I suppose. Not that anyone has ever told him 'no' before. Until today. Until Merridy turned them down."

"He went up there to..." Realization dawned on Jacob's face before he set off at full speed.

Merridy stepped further back from Charles Lee. "I told you no. I don't want you, him, or anyone at Echo Star to take me to stardom. That's not what I want. I wanted my voice to be heard, the right way. Why can't you understand that?"

"Why can't you understand that no one tells us 'no," Charles Lee lashed back at her. His hooked beak intensified under the rage of his dark eyes.

Two hands grabbed her shoulders, and she realized Casimir stood behind her. "Easy there, Miss Christmas. Things will go smoother if you simply calm down and say yes to our demands."

"Get off of me!" she yelled. Terror struck her heart. Casimir's grip was strong. She attempted to wiggle free from his grip, but with both hands he proved too much. "Anything you do today will be brought to the police. You won't get away with this!"

"Too bad you won't remember," Charles Lee coolly stated. He nodded at Casimir who released his grip on one of Merridy's shoulders. "I've been at this game far longer than you have."

"This is no game!" With Casimir holding only her one arm, she managed to push him off of her. She dashed forward to the art deco lamp that sat on the stand beside the couch. "You will not touch me!"

Casimir brandished a syringe. "Hard way then."

"No!" The man rushed at her, and she swung at the side of his head. The blunt object hit its mark, and the man landed on the couch with a sick thud. She turned to Charles Lee who backed away.

"Now, Miss Christmas, lower your weapon…"

"You came to me… threatened me…"

"I want to help you, Miss Christmas. I want to help you land among the stars."

A shout arose from outside the hotel suite. "Where is Charles Lee?" The suite door burst opened to Jacob. "Charles Lee!" he shouted. He moved to strike the man, but the image manager fell to his knees and held up his hands in a defensive position. Jacob's fist hovered above the man. Pain washed over his face as he attempted to make a decision on whether or not to strike.

"Jacob…" Merridy cried out. She stood above Casimir her hands still clutching the lamp; tears streamed from her eyes.

"Merridy," his voice softened. He bypassed Charles Lee to rush to her side. "It's okay. I'm here now." He wrapped his arms around her trembling body. "I'm here now."

Noting the distraction of the two, Charles Lee began to scamper out of the room. However, Ameleah appeared in the doorway. "Enough."

"My dear Ameleah," Charles Lee began.

"No. Enough." The woman held her head high. "I'm saying now what I should have said years ago." Her eyes darted to the couple that stood behind Charles. "Perhaps my life would be... happier. But I'm saying it now. Enough."

Charles Lee attempted to push Ameleah aside, but she held her ground.

"He's here, officers."

Several police officers walked into the room. Two detained Charles Lee while another pair moved toward Casimir.

"I... I hit him," Merridy confessed. She held the lamp out to the nearest officer. "I panicked. He was stronger than me, and I grabbed the closest thing..." The officer took the lamp from her. "He's not... dead is he?"

Another officer checked the pulse of Casimir. "No, not dead. Unconscious." He checked the wound on the side of his head. "But this blunt force trauma could cause brain swelling. We need to get him to the hospital." He called for an ambulance over his radio.

"How did you get here so fast?" Jacob asked the officers. "I didn't call..." He looked up at Ameleah. "Ami?"

She shook her head. "It wasn't me. When you hit the stairs, I had my phone out, but then they arrived in the front doors."

"We received a call from someone in South Hills, Texas," the officer told everyone. "She saw the events happening online."

"The livestream!" Merridy gasped. "I didn't realize I started it!" She hurried over to the computer and stopped the stream. Tens of thousands of viewers had watched the scene. Comments were flooding the video. "Oh, my Lord…"

Jacob cautiously walked to her. "It's okay. This is good." He pointed to the laptop. "That saved you. Everything that happened in this room was just announced to the whole world. These men are going to be held accountable for *everything* they attempted to do to you." He kissed her forehead. "It will all be okay."

The next few hours passed in a blur as the officers processed the scene and asked her a multitude of questions. Ameleah remained in the room as well, offering her testament of Charles Lee's previous actions to the detectives who had arrived. The NYPD jumped on the case in an instant given the public nature of the offense and the high profile of those involved.

It was not until the clock showed ten in the evening that Merridy and Jacob stood alone in the hotel room. She nearly collapsed into his arms. "I want to go home," she whispered to him. "I don't want to be here anymore. I can't be in this room. I can't… this city…" Tears, which were held at bay during the questioning, now flowed freely. "I need to leave. I want to go home."

He squeezed her tightly. "Yes. We will get you out of here." He bent his knees and lifted her into his arms. "Come love, let's go get you packed up. We will take you back to my hotel room for the night. And tomorrow, we're going home."

Her face buried into his shoulder. "You have a game tomorrow."

"Not anymore I don't."

"But... you're trying..."

He sat her on the edge of the bed gently. "Tomorrow, we're going back to Texas. Together." He cupped her face in his hands. "I am not abandoning you, my love. I will pack your bags. I will call my coach. I will call Kara. Rest here as best as you can." He kissed her forehead. "Do you want... to call your parents? Do you want to talk to them? I'll get your phone."

Merridy looked down at her hands. She had kept many things from her parents with the hope of sparing her mother from worry. She knew that her mother would see the livestream by tomorrow, if she had not watched already. More than that though, "I want my mom." The statement rang with solid truth. She needed her mom.

"Alright. Let me go get your phone." He hurried away to look for her phone that had disappeared in the chaos. "Found it." He brought it back to Merridy's shaking hands. "Here... I can dial it for you?"

She nodded.

"Okay..." He held up her phone and searched her contacts for her mom. He clicked the button, ensured that the line began to ring, then held it up to Merridy's ears. "You got it?"

She nodded again. Jacob walked away to the bedroom's closet to retrieve her suitcases. "Mommy?" Her voice came out shaken and timid.

The sound of her voice broke Jacob's heart. He retrieved his phone from his pocket and scrolled down to 'Diane'. "Hey," he whispered into the phone when she picked up. "I need you to make some calls for me. I'm going to need to be out some games due to... family emergency. Go to Merridy's page and look at the last livestream. Do it now, before it's taken down. It

314

will answer everything. Also, I need two plane tickets back to Dallas tomorrow. As private as possible. I have another call to make; let me know when the situation is handled."

"Mommy, I want to come home. To the ranch." Merridy began crying into her phone.

Jacob turned back to her. He did not realize when she said 'home' she meant her childhood home. Regardless, he meant to stay by her side.

Part Three: The Performance

Jacob stared at the ceiling of his hotel room. Merridy's head rested on his chest; she slept curled up by his side. He offered to sleep on the chair and ottoman that sat in the corner of the room. She insisted he stay as close to her as possible. He could not refuse.

The whole incident made him question his behavior toward Ameleah. If she had refused Charles Lee, then her fate could have easily been the same as Merridy's. In fact, it would have been worse. He was not nearby to rescue her like he had been for Merridy. He had failed Ameleah as much as she had failed him. They were both at fault, but he recognized the pressure she had faced. He understood now. Pressure could break anyone.

His eyes drifted to Merridy. She had been right. Ameleah deserved grace, kindness, and love. He would reach out to her tomorrow. There was no going back for them. Their time was in the past. His heart belonged completely to Merridy. She stole it the day he met her. But at the least, he could correct his attitude toward Ameleah.

At the moment, his agent was preparing a short press release to announce that he would be out for a week of games due to a family emergency. He was certain the news about Merridy would spread like wildfire and be tied to his statement. Good. The world needed to see Charles Lee Laban and Echo Star Records for what they were. He made it clear to Diane that that story was what mattered most, however she determined this might affect his image.

Merridy's hand reached up to his cheek. He turned his face to kiss her palm. "You're up early," she whispered.

"I'm a morning person," he whispered back. "You should know that by now."

"Yeah, I really should." She paused. "When we stay up late texting… do you still wake up early?"

"I drank a lot of coffee and energy drinks on those days." He kissed her palm again. "One-hundred percent worth it."

Her face tilted up to look at his. "I've never done this."

"Honestly Merridy," he traced his hand over hers, "I haven't either." He smiled down at her. "Except when we passed out in your room Monday. But I'm not counting that. It wasn't a *pajama party*… an innocent pajama party. Never done this. It's nice."

She smiled. "You don't feel…" she struggled to find the right words, "…deprived?"

He chuckled softly. "No." The arm that was wrapped under her wiggled a bit to allow his hand to stroke her long, auburn curls. "I am quite happy with this. Smelling your shampoo. Hearing you breathe. Honestly, this is the way it should be. The way I should have been doing things all along." His tracing hand reached down to her elbow. "Not that the women I was with… would have gone along with it. Superficiality does that."

"Yeah, I guess it does."

"Also, after… everything… that topic should be the furthest from your mind. Because I would never…"

"I know you would never." She lowered her hand to hold his. "That's one of many reasons why I'm right where I am."

"One of many, huh?" He rolled to his side to face her. "Do share the others." He attempted to use a girlish voice. "This is a slumber party after all."

His voice caused her to giggle. "First, you make me laugh."

He turned his eyes upward and made a silly face.

"Like that. Second, I feel safe. Third, I feel loved. Fourth, I like the way you smell…"

"The way I smell?" he interrupted. "I smell like locker room soap."

"Or as I call it, eau de Jacob." She smiled. "And I love it."

"Hmmm… we should bottle it. I could have my own fragrance line." He winked. "I mean, if Terry can launch his own cologne, why can't I?"

She laughed. "Thank you for this: for picking up my broken pieces at the Roche Morgan, for packing me up, for bringing me here, for getting me to sleep, for… just thank you."

"Thank you for reminding me to get my gear bag from the front desk though." He lifted her hand to his lips. "Even if it was a delirious reminder that I had to piece together. It got the job done."

"Guess we complement each other very well."

"Guess we do." They both stopped talking as they gazed into one another's eyes. Jacob could feel the electricity between them, and he gulped hard against it. "How am I so lucky?" he whispered.

She smiled and lowered her eyes to stare at their clasped hands. "I ask myself that every moment I look at you, or talk to you."

He reached up to her chin and tilted her lips toward his. "I'm never leaving your side, Merridy Christmas. Not during any of this. Not ever."

"Jacob, you have games…"

"I've put in an official week out due to family emergency. I'm going with you, home. All the way to your family's ranch. And we will stay out there through Thanksgiving, or longer. Whatever you want, I will do it."

She pressed herself closer to him. "Thank you."

He wrapped both of his arms around her. "I've got us first class tickets out of here today. Flight leaves this morning, so we can get back as soon as possible. I can make some coffee…"

"Not yet." Her lips reached up to his neck and grazed slightly against it. "Just a little longer in your arms."

His eyes closed. "I can't argue with that."

Chapter 34

Kara met Merridy and Jacob outside of Merridy's apartment. She hugged both with tears in her eyes. "My sweet, sweet friend... I can't... I can't imagine... I'm just so glad you're safe now."

"Thank you for calling the police," Merridy whispered.

Jacob and Kara exchanged a glance. "I didn't sweetie," she admitted. "I was actually in a meeting with a friend about a record deal for you when this happened. I wasn't even watching the livestream. I didn't know anything about it until Jacob called me last night."

Merridy looked at both in confusion. "But the officer said someone from South Hills called..."

"I don't know who. I took the livestream down before really reading any of the comments. There were hundreds trying to warn you about things happening. But I didn't look closely. My main concern was getting that offline."

"I'm sure it's gone viral in some other capacity," Jacob remarked. "Things like this always do."

"Good," Merridy reminded him. "The world needs to see that. Those men can't hide their wicked deeds."

"No arguments here. I told Diane the same thing. Speaking of which..." He pulled a business card from his wallet. "You need this because when we go disappear, I'm counting on you and my agent to handle everything." He handed the card to Kara.

"Of course, whatever y'all need." She pocketed the card. "I'll reach out to her this afternoon."

"Let's head inside," Jacob advised. "Before a passerby takes out his phone for his own viral video."

"Good thinking," Kara acknowledged.

He used the key left with him to unlock the front door before allowing the ladies entry. He began piling luggage inside as the two women walked to the bedroom for a private conversation.

"Tell me, are you truly okay?" Kara asked. "Be honest with me, don't hold anything back. Jacob isn't here."

Merridy shook her head 'no' and began crying. Kara wrapped her friend into a hug. "I want to be okay. And he's really, really helped me, Kara. He's been so strong, and he loves me, and he protects me, and takes care of me. But... I'm still... I can feel Casimir's hands on my shoulders, and I close my eyes and see that predator hawk-face swooping in to take me. It's awful."

"Of course, lady, it hasn't even been twenty-four hours. Women who face this go through a lot of counseling. And that's okay. In fact, I really think you should look into it."

"Right now, I just want to get home to the ranch. I just need fresh air and an escape from all of this."

Kara slowly nodded her head. "I will do everything I can to handle the public. Don't think about any of this until you're ready."

"Thank you." Merridy hugged her friend again. "I know you went out of your way to reach out to people to help me with a record deal..."

"Don't worry about that honey. They will be quite understanding. Everyone will be very understanding." Kara squeezed her friend's hands. "No matter what you choose to do. Perform, not perform. Record, not record. This is your timeline. No one else's. Okay?"

Merridy bobbed her head. "Okay." She inhaled deeply. "I don't know what's going to happen next anyway. They arrested those two, and the detective said they were going to look into Echo Star. They're going to find out who was aware of these happenings, who was partaking in them and who were the victims of them..."

"KT," mumbled Kara.

"KT?" Merridy repeated in confusion. "KT wouldn't do this."

"No," her friend agreed. "But I think he knew something was going on. He was trying to warn us that night at his house. I knew there was something heavy on his shoulders. I didn't think it was this. This is why he was warning you to leave."

"I doubt he thought this would happen. Apparently, no one has said 'no' before." Her nostrils flared as she thought of KT. "I wish... why wasn't he more direct?"

"I don't know. I shouldn't have brought him up," Kara chided herself. "Actually, I'm going to reach out to him. He did try to help you, in his own way, with the songs. I just don't know why... well, anyway." She forced a smile to her broken friend. "I'll handle him. Him and many others." She patted her friend's hair gently. "I also need to know... are you okay with Jacob going with you to your parent's ranch? If you need alone time, then he'll understand."

Merridy shrugged her shoulders. "I really don't want to be separated from him. I mean, like this is fine. He needs to go to his own apartment tonight, I'm sure. He needs to pack. Get the dog. But, no, I need him this coming week. I need my parents, and I need my..." Merridy faltered.

"Boyfriend?" Kara attempted to help.

"Kara, do you believe in soulmates?"

Her friend laughed. "I think you're asking the wrong person. The only people who believe in soulmates, are the ones who have found theirs." She smiled. "Do you think Jacob is your soulmate?"

"Is that weird to think?" Merridy questioned. "I've known him only..." she began counting on her fingers. "I've known him forty days."

"Forty days?" Kara smiled. "Forty is a very interesting number. It's always marked a period of testing, trials, and probation. You've given the man a forty-day trial-period. What does your heart say?"

Merridy smiled. "I love him. And I can't imagine my life without him."

"That says everything Merridy." They shared another happy squeeze of the hands. "You deserve love."

A soft knock on the bedroom door interrupted their conversation. "Ladies, I have brought all the luggage in. I have used the restroom. And I've had two glasses of tap water. I'm running out of ways to pretend you're not whispering about me in there."

The girls giggled. "Come in," Kara called out.

Jacob walked in with an impish grin. "It took all my power not to hold my ear up to the door." He fell onto the bed next to them. "Kara, did she tell you all about how she likes the way I smell?"

Kara laughed. "We hadn't gotten to that part of the conversation yet. But I'm not surprised. Your best friend has a cologne line. Why shouldn't you?"

He sarcastically placed a hand on his chest. "That's exactly what my sentiment was."

"Maybe we work on that at the ranch," Merridy told him. "Plenty of horses out there for you to make your ads with. Cologne ads always have horses, or yachts."

"Very true," he agreed. "Speaking of which... I need to head to my place. I've got to pack up myself, Porthos, and rent an SUV for our little family road trip. When did you want to head out?"

Merridy inhaled deeply. "Let's head out... tomorrow."

"Are you sure?" he asked with genuine concern. "I thought you wanted to get out there as soon as possible."

"Yes, but honestly? I'm exhausted. I really just want to curl up in my bed, and sleep for the next sixteen hours."

Kara nodded in agreement. "I think you have earned it." She jutted her chin out to Jacob. "I'll take you home Jacob. Merridy, gal, actually do take a nap. I will circle back at dinner time with food for you... because you *do* need to eat something today. Then we can pack together before you put in the rest of your ten hours of sleep."

Merridy smiled. "Agreed." She hugged both of them before they stood to leave.

"Hey love, your key," Jacob handed her the apartment key. "Be sure to lock up before you fall asleep."

"I will."

He grabbed his gear bag and suitcase before following Kara out of the apartment. "How is she, really?" he asked Kara.

"She'll survive. You've definitely helped." She inhaled deeply. "Thank you."

"Of course. I would do anything for her." He tossed his bags into her open trunk. "You know, if anything legal comes up while we're out there, reach out to me first. I'll be able to gauge when to bring it to her attention. Know what I mean?"

"Yeah, that's a good idea." They piled into the car. "And maybe you can gauge where she's at for the tree-lighting performance."

He nodded solemnly. "Yeah, I've been thinking about that. Not that I want *her* thinking about it. She doesn't need to be rushed into anything. But I don't want her to lose that opportunity because of *this*."

"You... are a good man, Jacob," Kara admitted. "I'm sorry I ever convinced Merridy to not pursue you sooner."

"Nah," he waved his hand. "You were right. My mind wasn't in the right place yet. This timing was much better. Outsiders may still see it as rushed, but... it was just right." He ran his fingers through his hair nervously. "She mentioned to me that you had a friend and possible record deal?"

"I do. Whenever she's ready, they'll be ready." She turned to face him when they reached a stoplight. "Do you know Elyssa, in your accounting department?"

"Of course. Three-time Olympic gold medalist, stuck in our marketing department instead of a lucrative professional career." He sighed. "I was reminded of that fact recently. What about her?"

"She and I played hockey together in high school," Kara stated matter-of-factly. "We fell out of contact until recently, my fault. But she brought to my attention some activities of our other high school friends. One of them happens to own an indie record label right here in South Hills."

"Really?" he exclaimed. "That's fantastic!"

"They don't have the reach of Echo Star... but they will let her be true to herself. And that's what's important."

"It is. The reach comes with time... and money." He stroked his chin. "And don't tell her I said this, but this whole situation going viral... it's going to get her name out there too."

"Yeah, I thought the same thing. I was never going to mention that to her. It's not how she would want it done."

"Of course not. But a bad thing can be used for good, right?"

Kara nodded with a smile. "True. With God, all things are possible."

Chapter 35

Merridy leaned her head against a pillow strategically propped against the passenger-side door of the SUV they took to her family's ranch. Christmas music chimed over the radio. Pants from Porthos huffed in time with the music as he happily watched the scenes pass by his backseat window. Jacob softly sang along with a line or two of the song. She noticed he sang more with the music when he stopped thinking and relaxed, especially when it was nothing but open road in front of them.

"Dashing through the snow, on a one-horse open sleigh…" He nodded his head with the jazz beat of the classic song's remake. "More like a one-dog closed SUV, right Porthos?"

The dog barked a reply.

"You two are terribly cute," Merridy commented from her cozy position.

Jacob grinned at her. "He does most of the cuteness."

"That's true," she agreed with a wink. "I know I slept a lot yesterday, but I could pass out again."

He lowered the music's volume. "If you need to sleep, then please do. I have the GPS set to the Perry Ranch in Meseta. We'll be quiet."

"No, that's okay." She reached for the warm pumpkin spice latte in the vehicle's cup holder. "I need to stay awake because I want to enjoy our first road trip. What's more perfect than you, Porthos, Christmas music, and a steamy PSL?" She took a sip from the drink.

"Actual Christmas." He leaned back against the headrest. "I love it."

"I remember." She took another sip from the coffee cup. "North Pole. Santa's village. And a German market that transported you right into Europe like the first part of the Nutcracker."

"Heh, you *do* remember." He grinned. "I told you all of that the first time we met."

"Yes, you did." She cradled the coffee in her hands. "I should have remembered more from that conversation. When I started *receiving* the nice things like a fancy hotel room... I should have remembered one truth about me."

He knew what she referred to. "No, don't be down on yourself. Even a *giver* like yourself can get excited about new experiences. There's nothing wrong with that." He coughed slightly and grabbed his own coffee. "Not to change the subject... but you realize this will be my first American Thanksgiving, right? I'm at a loss at what to expect down here."

"All your time living in Texas, and you've never been part of an American Thanksgiving?"

"Well, we often play on Thanksgiving, though this year we're not on the schedule for Thursday." He shrugged his shoulders. "Plus, certain people weren't into a holiday that centered on family. Not her style."

"True, I guess. Well, for us, a lot of the extended family come to the ranch. Depending how far away they are, they might come in Wednesday and leave Friday. Some of my aunts, mom, and cousins get up early on Friday and drive to San Marcos to shop Black Friday deals. That was never for me. It is way too crazy at that mall to be doing that." She sighed. "Plus, I... I might be singing that day at a different mall."

"Do you... want to sing there?"

She did not answer him immediately. A piano-instrumental of a Christmas song passed before she finally told him, "We'll see in a few days."

"Okay love." He turned onto a state highway per the GPS's instructions. "Who all lives at the ranch normally? Just your parents and grandmother?"

"I have a few cousins there too. They help out my dad." She shifted in her seat. "I should draw you a family tree so you know who's-who."

He chuckled. "That's actually not a bad idea." He noted her pulling a notebook out of her bag. "Oh, you're really doing it."

"I really am."

"When we go to Vancouver, I'll have to return the favor." He finished the last of his coffee. "If you're down for that."

"Are you going to take me to the North Pole and Santa's Village and the German market?"

"Of course."

"Then absolutely." She quickly began scribbling out names on the paper. "My dad has two brothers and one sister. One brother and the sister still live in England, and they rarely come stateside, certainly not for Thanksgiving. His other brother lives in San Diego. He usually does Thanksgiving with his wife's family. My dad's side is from the UK, and it's not a holiday for them, kind of like for you. Therefore, I'm not really including them on this. I doubt you will have any immediate dealings with them."

"And I was looking forward to meeting Holly and Jolly," Jacob joked.

She giggled. "Well no worries. Because my mom's got plenty of siblings, and the ranch belongs to that side of the family. They all come in to see my grandma, especially since my grandpa died."

"How... many siblings?"

"Eight."

"Eight?!" he exclaimed. "That is *a lot* of people."

"Yep. Hence the paper. You should see my Christmas card list too." She shook her head. "I really should already be working on those."

"I love that you send out Christmas cards." He grinned. "I only manage a handful a year. I would love to send more out. There's just something special about receiving a Christmas card, you know? Even if it's from your insurance guy. Makes me happy. I need to be sending out that happiness too."

"Especially to little kids. They *love* getting mail. With everything digital, it makes a card or letter even more special to those little ones. They puff out their little chests and act grown-up because they received *mail*."

"See, I visit the kids at the children's hospitals for Christmas, but what if I sent a Christmas card beforehand? Ah yes, nice, a card from that crazy hockey player. But then I show up and sing them the best version of '12 Days of Christmas' ever, which I haven't written yet, but would like to. Something funny."

Merridy laughed. "Let's do it."

"Write a hilarious version of the '12 Days of Christmas'? Because I thought about asking you..."

"No sweetie, all of it."

"All of it?"

She took in a deep breath. "The Christmas cards to our family, friends, the kids, visiting the hospital... all of it."

"You want to do Christmas cards, together?"

She cringed. "Too soon?"

"No," he replied softly. "I like the idea. Maybe we should stop on the way and grab some cards from the store. Between all those people, we'll need hundreds."

"Yeah," she agreed happily. "This is going to be a fun project."

They continued the last two hours of the trip discussing holiday traditions, singing along with the radio, and stopping for more coffee, Christmas cards, and to walk a very patient Porthos.

Chapter 36

The Perry ranch included a winding driveway from the ranch-to-market road to a carriage house. The carriage house matched the main periwinkle-blue ranch house. A Texas flag and an American flag flew side-by-side on two poles between the buildings. In the distance, Jacob could make out more buildings and herds of cattle grazing in the brush of the Edward Plateau.

"Sweet Merridy!" A woman ran onto the wrap-around porch. The screen door slammed close behind her. "Oh, my baby."

Merridy eagerly clung to the woman's hug. "I missed you mama."

The scene caused Jacob to smile. He opened the backseat door and whistled for Porthos to follow him. The obedient dog leapt out with a gleeful tail wag. Upon noting Merridy hugging a stranger, he charged forward with a happy bark. He smiled up at Merridy's mom with expectations of his own pets.

"Why hello," she greeted the dog. "And who might this ferocious guardian be?" She knelt down to properly pet him.

"This is Porthos," Merridy introduced the dog. "He's Jacob's dog."

Her mom glanced up to see Jacob approaching. "Porthos," he called out. "Don't be rude. I'm so sorry..." he began to apologize.

"Nonsense," she waved it off. "He's a perfect little angel. And it's good to finally meet you, Jacob."

"It's a pleasure to meet you as well, Mrs. Christmas." He held a hand out to her.

She hugged him instead. "Please, call me Patti."

"Yes ma'am."

"Now come on in," she told them all. "We'll get the boys to unload the luggage."

"I don't mind hauling luggage in," he protested.

"Nonsense. You're our guest. Come on in." She led the three into the house. "I already got supper in the oven. Jacob, you're not allergic to any food? You eat meat, right?"

"I eat everything, ma'am," he promptly answered her.

Merridy wrapped her arms around his and offered him a smile. "And he eats a lot of it."

"Very true," he laughed. Porthos trotted further into the living room where he discovered two sheepdogs sleeping in front of the fireplace. Happy to meet friends, he greeted them. The two older dogs, curious at the interloper, stood and began sniffing him. "Behave yourself," Jacob reminded him.

"Tonight, we're having King's ranch casserole, enchiladas, taco salad, refried beans, and rice. Is that alright? I still need to make the guacamole and queso..."

Merridy followed her mom into the kitchen. "Let me help, mom."

"No dear, you just got here. Relax a little. Everyone will be here shortly." Her mom threw on a worn-down apron. "Y'all go in the living room and sit a spell."

"We've been sitting for the last six hours," she reminded her mother.

Jacob leaned against the bar-top counter that separated the kitchen from the breakfast nook. "Why don't you give me a tour? Then we can come back and help set the table."

"I can tell you're a peacemaker," Patti commented. "Coming up with a compromise so quickly."

He laughed. "I have never been called a peacemaker in my life. But I do want to see this ranch I've heard so much about."

Merridy took his hand. "Okay then. Let's go." She pointed to a door off the breakfast nook. "That's the mud room attached to the laundry room, the downstairs bathroom, and a garage that dad turned into his woodshop."

"Your dad does wood-working?"

"He dabbles."

Jacob repeated, "Your dad does wood-working, and his last name is Christmas?"

Merridy pulled Jacob back through the living room. "He's not Santa Claus, if that's what you're hinting at."

"Whatever you say. But if I find reindeer on this ranch, I'm blowing the whistle," he jested.

She pointed to a split hallway that existed to the left of the fireplace. "That leads to mom and dad's room on the right, and the office-slash-library-slash-music room on the left." She led him to the latter room. "I already know what you'll say, 'a music room? Tell me more.' So here it is. Not much." She began describing everything as Jacob looked over the room. The corner to the right of the doorway held multiple bookcases that expanded from floor to ceiling. Hundreds of volumes set on the shelves; some appeared as old as the ranch itself. A closet door sat open, revealing more books on custom shelves. "My grandfather was a bit of a book collector," Merridy admitted. An L-shaped desk filled another part of the office. A computer monitor sat on the side against the wall, but an antique typewriter sat atop the other section. An assortment of vinyl records sat on a shelf above the desk. A banjo, mandolin, and fiddle hung on the wall. "My guitar used to hang up there too. But I took it with me."

"Can you play these other instruments?"

"The mandolin and banjo I can. Not the fiddle. I have some cousins who can play the fiddle though." She led him out of the room. "You'll see that on Thanksgiving. There's always music. It's usually after we eat, depending on when the game is... or how bad the game is going."

He glanced back over his shoulder at the instruments. "That sounds, magical."

They rounded the corner to go upstairs. "Up here is the guest room to the left, and my room on the right." She opened the door next to the top of the stairs. "This is where you will be sleeping." White shiplap covered the high walls of the room; thin, white linen curtains allowed natural light to flow in. A metal-frame queen bed sat between two rustic nightstands. The nightstands held an antique alarm clock, a stack of leather-bound books, and a lamp made of repurposed copper pipes and fittings. A wooden sign above the headboard stated 'Amazing Grace' in italics. The sight made him smile. "Yeah, I thought you would like that sign."

"This is a beautiful room." He leaned forward to touch the comforter of the bed. "That is unbelievably soft."

"It's mohair," she informed him. "Angora goats. We have them here on the ranch too. It's not just *all* cattle." She patted the blanket. "Chances are my grandmother made this. She can shear a goat, turn it into wool, make yarn, dye it, and either crochet or knit it. She's the goat lady."

"Where does she stay? She's here at the ranch, right?"

Merridy nodded. "She has her own house, further back on the property. Close to her goats." She pointed to two doors across from the bed. "The left is the guest bath, and the right is the closet." He followed her back into the upstairs hallway. One wall consisted of a giant curio cabinet. A variety of antiques graced the shelves. "This is the family museum, as I like to call it. Some of the pieces in here date back to when the ranch was first settled."

"When was the ranch founded?"

"As the Perry ranch? 1882. It's not as old as some others in the area, certainly. Some in this area pre-date the Civil War, and even Texas Independence. There are very old families in Meseta. In comparison, the Perry family is 'newer'. They came here from Tennessee. Purchased half of another ranch that was falling on hard times. Been here ever since." She pointed to a family portrait. "That's the first Texas Perry... the baby. First one born in the state."

Jacob smiled. "I love this. Who put this all together?"

"My grandpa, of course. He built this whole display. Typed up the little displays on his typewriter that we have downstairs." She smiled. "I remember him doing all that when I was a little girl. Loved the sound of that typewriter just clacking away." She nodded to her bedroom door. "This is my bedroom, unchanged since I left for college."

"Talk about a museum. I can't wait to see this ode to the last decade." He opened the door excitedly. "Oh, my goodness. Pink walls. Boy band posters. Stuffed animals. Dolls. This is what I was hoping for. Yes, yes, your trophies on a shelf. These I have to look at." He hurried to the white corner shelves that held a variety of different trophies. "You were in dance when you were little?"

"For one year. That's probably a participation trophy, which is why it's low down and in the back."

"No, no, it says third place. Very admirable. And some softball trophies. You were racking up those trophies when you were little. Turned all to ribbons and medals when you got older. Choir, musical theatre, some church camp awards, academics…" He looked over his shoulder at Merridy who stood in her doorway. "I knew you were a winner."

She laughed and sat on the foot of her bed. "I guess I *did* win a lot of singing competitions around here. Made it to all-state. Music has always been my calling."

He sat on the bed beside her. "Wait until you see my room – also untouched." He reached over to pick up one of the Teddy bears next to her pillows. "Not quite as adorable though." He made the bear dance for her. "I love that you still have all of these."

"Guess I assumed I would pass them on to my own children."

"Good idea. Not that our children won't be drowning in stuffed animals." Before he could react, Merridy reached over and kissed Jacob. The force of the sudden reaction knocked him back onto the pillows. Stuffed animals flew to the floor. "Wow," he breathed after she kissed him. He pulled her back down for another kiss. His hands became lost in her hair as they rolled over on the bed.

"I've never made out with a guy in my bedroom before," she whispered impishly.

He lifted himself off of her, though he remained at the ready position. "I am very happy to fill that role."

She grinned at him. "Guess this concludes the first part of our tour."

"Best tour ever." He lowered himself to give her a softer kiss. "Probably should go help set the table. Make sure Porthos is behaving. Bring the luggage in. All that."

"Right," she sighed. "I'm enjoying this though."

"I'll be sure to pick it up later this evening then." He nodded to the door. "My room is just across the hall. I have a feeling our paths will cross again." He stood up and headed toward the stairs. Merridy followed slowly. "I'm going to go grab our luggage first. I'll put the dog bowls up in my room and show them to Porthos. He can eat when we eat." He held his hand up to Merridy to help her down the last few steps. "Then I'll come help you set up, if that works for you?"

"There's a rare sight in these day and times. A gentleman helping a lady down the staircase." An elderly woman walked forward from the living room to the foyer. "Makes this old heart happy, especially to see my Merry Christmas."

"Grandma!" Merridy rushed forward to give her grandmother a hug. "I didn't hear you come in."

The woman patted her granddaughter's back. "I brought the golf cart from my house up to the back through your father's *workshop*." She turned her attention to Jacob. "And is this the young man I've heard so much about?"

"Yes ma'am. This is Jacob Kenway, my boyfriend."

Jacob stepped forward to accept her hand. He gently shook it before she reached forward to give him a hug as well. "Aren't you a tall one?" she chuckled. "How tall are you?"

"Six feet, two inches, ma'am."

She nodded with narrow eyes. "And you're a hockey player, right? Got all your teeth?"

"Grandma!" Merridy gasped.

Jacob laughed. "Yes ma'am." He smiled as dashingly as possible. "I knock *other* people's teeth out. They don't get to mine."

"That's the spirit!" Merridy's grandmother responded. She clinched her fist and shook it victoriously. "I like you Jacob Kenway. Let's go eat." She turned toward the archway that linked the foyer to the formal dining room.

Merridy walked alongside her grandmother to help her to her seat. "Mom, how many for tonight? I'll get the plates ready."

Jacob slipped out the front door in order to get the luggage. From the front porch, he noted the oranges, pinks, and purples settling across the grand sky above him. He stepped forward to the rental savoring deep breaths of the fresh air. It had been many years since he had been removed from a metropolitan area that was not covered in snow. It refreshed him.

"Need help there?"

He looked up to see a middle-aged man in a plaid button-down shirt, jeans, and boots walk forward. The man wiped his hands on a red handkerchief that he then returned to his back pocket. "That's a lot of luggage there, but then again, Merridy never could pack light."

The comment caused Jacob to laugh. "That's why I rented the largest SUV they had."

The man shared in the chuckle and offered his hand to Jacob. "James Christmas."

"Jacob Kenway." They shared a hardy handshake; this seemed to satisfy the older man. "Beautiful ranch you have here."

"It's the wife's ranch," he responded with a wave of his leathered hand. "I just try to keep it from falling apart." He helped Jacob slide Merridy's giant roller-bag out of the vehicle. "It is beautiful though."

"That sky," Jacob commented. "I always thought the sky in Dallas was beautiful, but it's clearer here. The colors are crisper."

"Yeah, less pollution out here. Just... cow farts," he snorted.

Jacob chuckled. "Right." He slipped his gear bag over his shoulders then attempted to strap additional duffle bags to himself.

"See you brought your hockey sticks. 'Fraid we don't have any ice down here, son."

"I understand. I have several balls I use to practice stick work. There's also a seventy-five-pound Akita inside that gets his morning workout when I get my *ball* practice." Jacob picked up the last bag. "I can't get rusty in my downtime. I'm an up-before-the-sun kind of guy."

"You'll fit in here." James shut the hatchback and picked up the rest of his daughter's luggage. "Wake up early and go to bed late. Man has to do what he has to do to get it all done."

"Exactly right." They carefully entered the house. "You can leave those at the foot of the stairs, James. I'll take them up. Thank you for the help."

Merridy paused with the place setting as she watched the scene unfold.

"No worries, son. And call me Jamie." He lowered the bags and continued forward to the dining room. "Smells good, Patti!" he called out.

"Daddy," Merridy whispered. She lowered the rest of the plates on the table and hugged her father. "You like him," she continued to whisper.

"Young lady, if you think I didn't see everything that happened in New York, then you're quite mistaken." He pointed upstairs where they could hear Jacob depositing her bags into her room. "That man was willing to kill for you. He's a good one." He patted her back. "Now I gotta go wash up if we're eating at the nice table."

Merridy grinned at her father, and then turned her attention to Jacob as he descended the stairs to get the next group of suitcases. "Thank you," she told him.

He responded with a confused face. "Of course. You're welcome." He chuckled. "This bag weighs more than I do. Someone has to get it up all these stairs." He winked before continuing his task.

"Go put a record on," her grandma called from the dining room. She picked up the plates Merridy had been laying out. "Put that Bing Crosby record on. Little mood music for dinner."

"Yes Grandma." Merridy departed to the office.

"Little mood music for an engagement," her grandmother whispered to herself with a confident grin.

Chapter 37

The family sat around the many couches and arm chairs in the living room after dinner. The fireplace cackled calmly. Perry Como sounded from the phonograph in the corner. Porthos and his new friends slept on a rug in front of the fire. Jamie sat nearby on well-worn leather recliner; his eyes were heavy with second-helpings. Merridy sat between her grandmother and mother on the couch, looking over a photo album spread out in her lap. Two male cousins who lived on the ranch, as well with their young families, had also come for dinner.

Derrick, the older cousin, and his wife, Sadie, sat curled up on a loveseat near the photo-engulfed women. Their twin five-year-old sons, Joshua and Caleb, sat on the floor with Jacob, in order to teach him a game involving plastic spaghetti noodles. The other cousin, Darren, also sat on the floor with the spaghetti-gamers. His wife, Ashton, sat in a rocking chair cradling their four-month old daughter.

No television was on, although it existed. Everyone simply enjoyed each other's company and the calm holiday music from the crooner on vinyl.

"Darren," Ashton whispered. "We might want to get back and put her down." She nodded at the baby in her arms.

"Right." He turned to Jacob. "It was nice to meet you."

"Same here."

"That might be our que too," Derrick told his wife. She nodded in agreement. "Hey grandma, let us take you back to your house. It's too dark out there for your golf cart."

"Nonsense," the elder woman waved him away. She turned the page of the photo album in order to dismiss the notion completely.

"Listen to the boy Judith," Jamie grumbled from his recliner. "You're seventy-six years old. You shouldn't be running around a ranch on a golf cart at nine-o'clock at night."

She glared at her son-in-law. "You're no spring chicken yourself." She nodded sternly at him. "Let's go Derrick." She defiantly walked out of the house.

"Nice meeting you," Derrick told Jacob with a laugh in his voice. "Come on boys."

"You'll be here tomorrow, right Jacob?" one of the boys asked him.

"Yes sir," he answered them. "I'll be here through Thanksgiving."

"Score!" The twins high-fived each other before running after their parents.

Silence restored to the living room. Jacob placed the plastic spaghetti noodles back to their box and stored it on the shelf full of boardgames near the phonograph.

"When was this?" Merridy asked her mother about a particular picture. Jacob noted the young Merridy in the picture and settled in the seat vacated by Judith. "I don't remember this dress at all."

Her mother reviewed the image. "You were… three. You hated that dress. Threw a fit whenever I'd put you in it. I gave it away to the church for the yard sale."

"Guess that's why I don't remember it."

Jacob looked at the pink and purple dress. "Why did she hate it? I mean, she's quite cute in it."

"She said it was too itchy," Patti answered with a roll of her eyes. "This girl could always find something to complain about at that age."

"Mom," Merridy chided her.

They shared a chuckle as they reviewed the album more.

"Wow, look at all those Christmas decorations," he stated. Photos of the ranch showed wreathes and lights adorning the entirety of the iron gate and fence that lined the main road. Every building's exterior also displayed a hefty amount of décor and lights. "How many trees do you put up?"

Patti grinned broadly. "It used to be just the one in here, in that area where the phonograph is. But then I added another one to the entry way. With the vaulted ceiling in there, I use a two-story tree." She clasped her hands excitedly. "I call that my themed tree. Each year, a special theme."

"The tree that goes here in the living room is the family tree, with all the meaningful ornaments, like hand-made ornaments, or antiques passed down in the family. With the foyer tree, she gets to unleash her inner designer."

"It's so much fun. Oh, and Merridy, have you heard about these pencil trees? They're *thin* Christmas trees, so you could put them in places they normally wouldn't fit. I was thinking a few in the dining room, and the breakfast nook, and the office." Her eyes were glowing with the thought of all the trees.

Merridy's face darkened. "I think I need to go to sleep." She kissed her mother's cheek without meeting her worried look. "Goodnight dad. Night Jacob." She sulked to the staircase and disappeared from view.

"What... did I say?" Patti asked Jacob.

He noted Jamie's eyes were also open, fully awake from his pre-sleep nap. "It's nothing you said," Jacob reassured her. "This happened on our flight, and a few times on the drive out here. A conversation happens, and it makes her think of something, and she gets into her head." He shook his head. "It could easily be that she started thinking about Christmas trees, and... the tree-lighting ceremony? Or, I think she was a bit disappointed in not seeing the tree at the Rockefeller Center all decorated. And honestly, I think that tree is somewhat ruined for her too right now. The whole city is." He shook his head. "She just needs time to heal."

Patti closed the album. "Maybe I should go talk to her."

"Now Patti, she's a grown woman..." Jamie interjected.

She stood up. "A grown woman who still needs her mother." She marched upstairs.

Jamie sighed. "You drink hot cider?"

"Of course."

The rancher stood. "Come on." He led the younger man into the kitchen where they secured two coffee cups of microwaved cider. "I like it better from the slow cooker," he revealed. "But no time for that." He walked through the door that led to the mudroom and onward into his woodshop.

Sawdust's distinct odor filled Jacob's nose upon entry. "This is fantastic, Jamie." He surveyed the myriad of tools and planks of wood. A few unfinished projects sat on a table in the middle of the shop area. "Those look like toys to me." His eyes landed on a substantial tarp-covered object further back in the shop. "That's a sleigh under there, isn't it, Mr. Christmas?"

The implication caused Jamie to laugh heartily. "A few more of Patti's pumpkin pies, and my stomach will shake like a bowl full of jelly." He sauntered over to the tarp. "It's actually a carriage I'm repairing for the town visitor's committee. Trying to get it ready for the season. They make a bit of an effort to get the town looking good for the holidays, and offer carriage rides around. Not much traffic, but who knows. Sometimes small towns get a wave of curious folks when they find out a star is from there."

"You think Merridy is a star?" Jacob asked. Her ran his hands over a partially made sign.

"I know she is."

"That makes two of us... three of us if you count her best friend back home." Jacob sighed. "I think she's afraid to think that now." He put his coffee cup down, harder than expected. "Those stupid jerks up at Echo Star got so deep into her head, they messed her up. They tore her down. All they wanted to do was break her spirit so they could replace it with some cookie-cutter pop-diva clone."

Jamie calmly listened as Jacob vented.

"She is *so* unique, and they couldn't see it. They just knew she had a great voice, and that's the one thing they can't clone. So, they used her. And I didn't see it until it was too late." He punched his own hand. "As soon as I heard about that trainer, and the words he said, I should have known it was Charles Lee. I didn't see it though. I didn't know Charles Lee was her image manager until I got to New York. And even then... even then I didn't pull her out. I should have protected her." His punched hand went to his chest. "It's *my* fault."

The rancher gently put his coffee cup down next to Jacob's and took a fresh handkerchief from his pocket to offer up.

348

Jacob silently accepted it. He turned his back in order to keep the man from seeing his tears. "I have a failing record," he mumbled.

"Son," Jamie finally spoke. "Now that you've gotten that off your chest. I want to tell you what I've seen. I watched the video. I wanted nothing more to get on a plane and put a 9mm in both of those men. It's not Christian of me, but I'm a father." He let out a long sigh. "But I didn't have to. Because you were there. You were ready to kill that man, too. But you did something that I probably couldn't have done, you showed him mercy." He folded his arms and leaned back against the counter. "You did something else I couldn't have done either. You're letting her fight her battles. You're not letting her fight them alone, but you're letting her fight them her way. She needs that. It ain't easy on the rest of us, who love her, and just want to make everything better for her, but she sure needs it."

Jacob faced the man once more. "I just want her to get her dream. I don't want those..." He bit his lip and his eyes bulged. "I don't want what happened in New York to ruin her chance at her dream. I want to keep encouraging her to go for it. I want her to sing at that tree-lighting ceremony. I want her to record a Christmas album. I want her to make music videos, and win Dove Awards, and Grammy Awards. I want her voice to reach millions across the world. I want all of those things for her, but I don't even know if she wants them for herself anymore. That's how far they got into her mind."

"She still wants them." Jamie nodded his head. "You just got to remind her, gently, that she does." He lifted his coffee cup full of lukewarm cider. "What better place to do that than on a ranch that's about to be buried in Christmas decorations?"

"You're right." Jacob gazed at the carriage. "What better place to restart than home?"

Chapter 38

A sharp knock sounded on the front door of the ranch house while the family ate their Saturday morning breakfast. Jamie silently stood from the table to answer it. Merridy absent-mindedly poked at her scrambled eggs while watching him walk away. "Who comes out here this early?" she asked her mother.

"No clue." Her mom pushed a bowl of fruit toward her daughter. "Eat your eggs honey, you need your strength."

"I just don't eat that much in one setting anymore," her daughter responded.

Jacob added more triangles of French toast to his plate. "You know the caloric deficiency they had you on was not healthy, right?"

"I know, but I got used to it, okay?" she bitterly responded.

He sighed and exchanged a glance with Patti. "I understand love. I'm just trying to… help. Eggs are really healthy. That's only like a hundred-and-seventy calories, but sixteen grams protein. You would walk those eggs off in less than an hour." He stopped himself. "Sorry. Your breakfast, your choice." He silently drizzled syrup over his French toast and commenced to eating in silence.

Patti offered him a smile of appreciation. She patted Merridy's hand gently. "You just let me know whatever sounds good to you, and I will make it for you."

"Merridy, you have visitors," Jamie announced as he reentered the breakfast area. A man and woman followed him. He wore a khaki button-down and matching khaki Stetson. A badge was pinned to his shirt. She wore a white button down and white

Stetson; her badge, different than his, rested on her belt. "You remember Joseph Parker. He's the Meseta County sheriff now."

"Hi Joey," Merridy greeted him. Her voice came across flat, and she appeared annoyed at herself for it. "I'm sorry," she mumbled. "Rough morning."

He removed his hat and slicked back his black hair. "I understand. It's not been an easy time for you." His eyes darted to Jacob. "That's why I'm here, Merridy. The NYPD reached out to us to check-in on you."

"Was I not supposed to leave New York?" she asked. "They never told me I couldn't."

"No, no, it's not that. The video evidence made it apparent that you acted in self-defense. There's no criminal case against you. In fact, the detectives in New York are building up a case against your attackers and the company they worked for. That's why they reached out to us." His fast talking stopped abruptly. "Um, some of the questions are rather personal. I don't have a woman in the sheriff's department, except our secretary, so I reached out to my colleague." He indicated the woman nearby. "This is Lana Hardin, she works for the Texas Rangers, out of the Meseta office."

"Pleasure to meet y'all," she greeted the family.

"Likewise," Merridy responded. Her tone still did not reflect her normal jubilancy.

"Is there someplace we can talk in private?" Lana asked her. "It won't take long. I don't want to keep you from breakfast."

"Mama, can you come too?"

Patti turned her surprised face from Merridy to Lana. "Is that, okay?"

"Yes ma'am. Whatever makes her feel most comfortable."

The three women departed for the office. Merridy took the desk chair in the office; Patti stood behind her with her hands on her daughter's shoulders. "What is this about?" Merridy asked.

"These are follow-up questions about the actions against you that were not on camera. It will cover any interactions you had with the two assailants before Wednesday evening's events."

"They want to know if this was a one-off fluke of two depraved individuals, or if the entire company runs this way," Merridy countered.

Lana nodded. "As an officer of the law, I cannot speculate. As a woman, I would agree with that statement."

Merridy nodded. "I will happily tell you every detail from the moment I first met Casimir, and every detailed interaction I had with everyone associated with Echo Star."

Meanwhile, Joseph stood awkwardly in the kitchen holding his hat.

"Sit down Joey," Jamie instructed him. "I'll get you a coffee. Want something to eat?"

Joseph sat as instructed. "Just the coffee would be great. Thanks Mr. Christmas." He nodded his head at Jacob. "I have to say, I'm a big fan of yours."

"You like hockey?" Jacob responded eagerly. He knew he was in football country, and the slim hope there was a hockey fan in the area excited him.

"Yep." Joseph chuckled at Jacob's lit-up eyes. "I have a Blackhawks jersey signed by Fred Sasakamoose that my father got back in the day. He was very proud of that jersey. Always told me that the world sees hockey as a white-man's sport, but the First Nations were playing field hockey long before the white man ever arrived." He accepted a cup of coffee from Jamie with a nod of appreciation.

Jacob responded with a grin. "That is a very true statement. And that is an amazing piece of hockey history that you have. Sasakamoose is a freaking legend." The two began talking about hockey while Jamie read the newspaper over his breakfast. After a thirty-minute discussion, wailing from the office interrupted them. Jacob sprang to his feet and raced into the office. "What's wrong?"

Merridy sat doubled-over on the floor with Patti kneeling nearby. The desk chair was smashed against the wall. Lana held a recording device in her hand. She blankly stared at Jacob's intervention. "Merridy has gone through a traumatic event." She put away her recording device and escorted Jacob out of the room. She closed the office door softly behind them. "You have heard of post-traumatic stress disorder, correct?"

Realization dawned on Jacob. "Merridy has PTSD? Merridy has PTSD. I mean, that makes sense. I just... I don't know what to do for her."

"I know a doctor in Austin who specializes in non-military PTSD. He owes me a favor. I can ask him to come out here Monday and meet with Merridy." Lana lifted her phone to make a note. "In the meantime, keep doing what you have been doing, love and support her." She left him at the office door to return to Joseph in the kitchen. "I asked all of NYPD's questions and received a full recap to transmit to them. She needs rest now. That was hard for her."

Joseph nodded. "Thank you, Lana. It was good seeing you again, Mr. Christmas."

354

"Wish it had been under better circumstances," Jamie offered.

"Agreed." Joseph returned his hat to his head. "We'll see ourselves out."

Jacob stood in front of the office with his hand on the door handle. The sounds of Merridy's crying continued to fill his ears. "What do I do?" he whispered. He turned his eyes upward. "What do I do?" he asked again. A scripture from Genesis popped into his head. He opened the door. Merridy was pushing her mother away with one arm while burying her face in her other arm. Purposefully, he walked forward and scooped her into his arms. She resisted with all her might, but he proved too strong. "Come on, Merridy, I'm taking you to a safe space." He carried her out of the office and up to her bedroom. He laid her on the bed, tucked her blankets around her, and handed her one of the Teddy bears. "I love you, Merridy. If you want to cry, cry. If you want to scream, scream. Whatever you want to do, do. But do it knowing you are in a safe place, and that you are loved."

She buried her face against the Teddy bear and continued to cry.

"Do you want me here, or do you want to be alone?"

Her hand reached out to his. He held it tight and remained calmly on her bed.

Patti joined her husband in the kitchen where he was putting away food and dishes. "I had no idea what my daughter was going through in New York," she confessed. "I should have been nosier. I knew something was happening, and I just trusted her to come to me. I didn't think she would just, allow herself to get manipulated like that."

"I don't think she allowed it," Jamie corrected his wife. "I think she was focused on getting that record deal and achieving her goals. That's what we raised, an achiever. Everything else blindsided her. Isn't that how the enemy works? A little whisper at a time so we don't even notice him?"

She picked up the bowl full of fruit from the table. "What am I supposed to do, James? My baby came home because she wanted her mother, and I could do nothing for her when she broke. Jacob had to pick her up and take her upstairs. I stood there, dumb and useless."

"She asked for you to go with her for the questioning. She needed you then. She needs him now." He hugged his wife. "Be glad he's a good man, and that he's here for her. And don't go blaming yourself for any of this. The only people to blame are the ones who did this. That's it." He patted her back. "I gotta go meet the boys to work on some fence line. When she's calmed down a bit, send them down to the Frio to relax. And then maybe have her start working on those Christmas decorations."

"The tree put her in a bad mood last night," Patti responded. "I'm afraid to bring it up again."

Jamie walked into the mud room. "Her name is Merridy Christmas. It's in her blood. She can't give those bad men any power over her love for Christmas."

"Jacob?" Merridy called out after an extended silence that followed her crying.

Still holding her hand, he leaned down alongside her. "Yes love?"

"Thank you."

"Of course. Anything for you."

She paused. "Can we go for a walk?"

"Certainly. Where to?"

"I have a treehouse that overlooks the Frio River. I want to go there."

He nodded. "Alright. We will go to your treehouse."

"And Jacob?"

"Yes love?" he repeated.

"Um... I'm kind of hungry now."

He smiled. "I'll pack us a picnic." He kissed her cheek and ran downstairs to the kitchen. "Patti, she's hungry, and she wants to go to her treehouse!" he announced elatedly. "I need to make some sandwiches... or something."

She clapped her hands in excitement. "She's wanting to eat and go out! That's progress." She began opening cabinets. "I'll make the food. You go get the picnic bag and blanket from the entryway closet. It's on the shelf. And then look in the ottoman in the living room. There's some pillows and blankets in there that you'll want to take. The treehouse hasn't been used since she left. I'm sure it's full of who-knows-what. There'll be no place for her to be comfortable. Oh, and there's a foldable wagon in the deck's storage room. You'll need it to carry everything."

Jacob rushed around attempting to do as Patti instructed him. She busied herself with making lunch in world record time. By the time Merridy made her way downstairs, he had the wagon fully stocked with comforts, food, sporting goods, and drinks. "Ready?" he asked her.

The sight caused her to smile. "Yes." They set out on a worn-down trail with Porthos trailing behind. "This is how to get to grandma's house."

"That means it's *toward* the river and through the woods to grandmother's house we go?" Jacob joked.

"The dog knows the way to go run and play with the frisbee we do throw," Merridy sung the next line. She picked up a frisbee from the cart and tossed it out between the trees. Porthos eagerly ran after it. "I'm sorry about earlier. And last night."

"You don't have to apologize for anything Merridy." He followed her off the worn trail to an overgrown trail. "Your feelings are valid. I just hope to help. Whatever you need from me."

Her hand traced over low-lying branches whose leaves continued to fall to the ground. "I wish I could just act like none of it happened. And I really, really want to be able to move forward like that. Just poof – that memory is gone. But then it hits me like a flood. I guess, I just want to distract my brain from it. Is that possible?"

"I'm no expert, but I can certainly help with distractions." He watched the slight breeze whip at Merridy's broom skirt as she retrieved the frisbee from Porthos. Her hair whipped around her face. The moment felt peaceful; no one would suspect the underlying hurt. He trotted forward to walk alongside her. "Your mom said the treehouse hasn't been in use for some time. We might have to clean it out."

She tilted her head. "Great. Probably full of gross things."

"Nothing I can't handle."

"Well, in the meantime, we can setup near the treehouse, if it doesn't smell like dead animal." She began walking faster, and in the distance, he could hear the sound of water over stones. The sound spurred Merridy. She ran forward down the faded path.

Jacob hurried behind, as fast as the cart would let him. "Easy tiger!" he called out.

She paused next to the last tree before a gentle slope led down to the calm Frio River. The tree held a little two-story house around its trunk complete with a deck. Its pink and white paint were faded with the years. "This is it." She turned to him. "My childhood treehouse. The place where I learned to swim." She pointed down to the river. "The Frio."

He set the cart up next to the treehouse deck and climbed into it. He abruptly climbed out. "Yeah, you don't want to go in there right now." He reached into the cart to retrieve the picnic blanket. "But I can set us up out here."

After a strenuous game of frisbee between Merridy and Porthos, the picnic was setup. The trio calmly ate on a mound of blankets and pillows overlooking the river in serene silence.

Chapter 39

The next few days went by calmly. They attended church with the family, enjoyed a large Sunday meal in between services, and walked the ranch. On Monday, the doctor from Austin drove out to the ranch to meet with Merridy. He spoke with her privately in the office before speaking to the rest of the family on how to interact with her as she healed. The rest of the day remained uneventful save for the stack of Christmas cards she began to tackle with Jacob. Tuesday saw more cards completed, along with a great undertaking of decorating the ranch with Christmas cheer.

Jacob spent his time between helping Merridy, practicing and exercising, playing with the twin boys, and working with Jamie around the ranch. In addition, he developed a love for Jamie's workshop, spending late nights and early mornings in it with the man's permission.

Wednesday morning, he walked into the breakfast nook, still drying his hands from the mudroom clean-up. To his surprise, Merridy was awake and sitting at the breakfast table. She sipped on hot coffee and wrote quietly on a small notepad. "Hey darling," Jacob greeted her. "You're up early."

She smiled. "You are too."

"I'm *always* up early." He poured a cup of coffee for himself. "Hence, I have no need to explain myself. What about you?"

"I woke up with thoughts. And I needed to write them down."

"Understandable." Jacob slipped into the seat next to her. "That's what wakes me up too. Thoughts."

"Thoughts like," she attempted a masculine voice as she continued, "time to drink my protein shake and lift some weights!"

"Exactly." He reached out to rub her forearm. "What are yours?"

She put her pen and coffee down. Then she inhaled deeply. The dramatic effect caused Jacob to lower his own coffee with great interest. "Before… things… I was writing a song list of pieces I wanted to make into an album. One thing that the record company kept lording over me was they had access to *so many copyrighted songs*, like 'Blue Christmas' and 'All I Want for Christmas is You'. But I don't *need* those songs to make an album. There are plenty in the public domain, and I have a few I've written."

"Plus, the ones that KT wrote," he added.

"Eh…"

"Have you talked to him? I think Kara's been reaching out. I didn't know if you have."

Merridy shook her head. "He's reached out. I just haven't answered my phone."

Jacob did not know how to tell her that he was certain that Kara had reached out to KT. Kara downloaded the whole situation to him. KT suspected that Echo Star leadership pressured their stars for illicit sexual 'favors' in exchange for their promising careers. He had no proof which was why he could only warn Merridy to be careful and not sign on with Echo Star. He himself had been a victim of blackmail from the record company, and he agreed to testify in the case the State of New York was building against the corporate giant. "You remember how you knew something, and didn't want to keep it from me, so you told me whenever I was ready to hear it? I have something similar. Not child-related. But it might upset you, potentially."

"Then tell me, later. Because I want to tell you what else I was thinking about this morning." She smiled broadly. "I'm going to sing at the tree-lighting ceremony. I know that they reached out to Kara to confirm. She told me they needed to know this morning. I just texted her the greenlight."

Jacob let out a shout of happiness and hugged her tightly. "I am so glad to hear you say that. I didn't want you to lose this opportunity that you worked so hard for... and it's the reason we met." He kissed her forehead. "There's also something I want to show you. I've been working on it the last few days. In light of this news, I think it's time to reveal. You know, before the family coming in today arrives."

"I do like a *good* surprise."

He stood and reached his hand out to her. "Let's go."

He led her outside and down the trail to her treehouse. She noted the trail was more worn than when they journeyed down it on Saturday. Porthos walked ahead of them. He knew exactly where to go. "What have you two been up to?" she joked. She received a bark in reply before Porthos rushed forward. It did not take her long to see the surprise.

Her old treehouse sat restored, improved, and expanded. The faded pink paint had been replaced by a bright white coat with black accents. A barn-style door supplanted the empty doorway from before, and matching shutters surrounded new windows. The deck and staircase were restored with water-sealed, solid wood. A wooden sign that read 'The Treehouse' sat at the staircase's base.

"Oh Jacob…"

"Go inside. There's more." He helped her up the staircase. "I made it one-story, so it's tall enough for us to enter without breaking our backs in-half, which is why I expanded it out, to make up for the loss of square footage."

Merridy entered to find the interior painted a calm sage-green. Built-in shelves held waterproof, clear boxes with classic children's books inside. Other shelves held bins with a variety of toys and props for every make-believe adventure imaginable: pirates, cowboys, astronauts, knights, and gladiators. An armoire opened to matching costumes. Lounge chairs covered in pillows and blankets sat nearby the bookshelves to make a reading nook. Bunkbeds were built into the far wall, though there were no mattresses to compliment them.

"It's not quite finished yet. I need to go to town today to get a few things. Like, these pillows and blankets on the chairs I made are actually from your mom's living room ottoman stash. I brought them over this morning hoping I could reveal this to you today. And the toys and costumes are from some of the twin's toys that they had in the storage closet off the deck. Patti gave the go ahead to bring them out here where they'll get used." He tapped the books. "You can guess these. They were part of your grandfather's collection, in the office closet. Permission received to use them of course. But I made sure this was a waterproof bin. Your dad was using it for some wooden bits in his workshop, but he liked this idea better. As long as I buy him a new bin when I go to town." He walked over to an empty area. "I have a toy chest I'm building in the shop still. I'm going to put it here. Then I'll get some outdoor toys to put in it."

Merridy stood in stunned silence watching him lay out his visualization for the rest of the treehouse, which included stringed lights – inside and out – that ran on weather-proofed batteries that he researched, lounge chairs on the deck, and an elaborate pulley-system up to a side-window – just for the fun of it.

"What do you think?"

"I think it's... wonderful. Jacob, this must have taken you so much time. When... when have you been doing this? You've been helping me, and dad, and watching the boys..."

He shrugged. "Get up early. Go to bed late. A man has to do what a man has to do for his family."

The answer overwhelmed her with emotion. She sat on one of the chairs and wrapped herself in a blanket. "That's my daddy's words. Jacob... this means, more than I can say."

"I wanted a place for you to come to when we're here, and also a place for our kids to come play when we're visiting their grandparents." He slid the other chair next to her in order to hold her hands. "In the meantime, I thought it would be fun for Joshua and Caleb to come out here to play."

"And I think that is lovely." She kissed his cheek. "What did I ever do to deserve you?"

He shook his head. "You have that backwards. I thank God every day that He had you literally fall into my arms." He kissed her hand. "Want to head back? We can get ready and head into town early, before the stores close for the holiday."

"I'm down. We need more Christmas cards anyway."

"Yes, we do." He inhaled deeply. "I also think we need some photos together, to put in the cards. That's what couples do, right? Nice, holiday photos. And what better place than a ranch that's decorated for the special day?"

"I don't really have a photographer around here." She laughed. "Then again, my grandmother would make a better photographer than the last one I had."

He tapped his chin thoughtfully. "Oh yeah, that's the other part of the surprise. I invited a friend for Thanksgiving. She's a clever marketing guru who's pretty skilled with a camera. I've seen some of her work, and I must say, I am not disappointed. Though she did work with a subject matter I'm *highly* interested in."

Merridy squealed. "You invited Kara out for tomorrow?!"

"Yeah, but she's driving in this afternoon."

She jumped to her feet. "Then what are we waiting for? We have shopping to do! Plus, I'll need something nice to wear for our pictures. I didn't pack anything for that."

"Whatever your heart desires."

She clapped her hands gleefully and ran out of the treehouse.

Jacob pulled the SUV in front of Meseta's general store. "This place has been here forever," Merridy told Jacob. "When I was a kid, dad always brought me here after school on Fridays to get candy – if I had done well in school that week."

"Which I imagine was every week."

"Almost. I could be a rebel sometimes, though." She hopped out of the vehicle. "Might get myself some candy today."

"I could go for those sour gummies, if you see them." He opened the door for Merridy. A bell chimed above them.

"Welcome in!" the shop clerk announced with a long drawl. He rounded a corner to see them. "Well I'll be, Merridy Christmas. It's been a long time since I've seen you in my shop."

"Yes, it has, Mr. Thompson." She walked directly to the candy section. "Good to see the layout has remained the same."

"Mr. Thompson," Jacob repeated the name. "I'm Jacob Kenway. We spoke on the phone."

"Yes, Mr. Kenway." The middle-aged man shook his hand. "They arrived last night. I got them in the back."

"Perfect. I can circle around to load up, if that works? After we buy some more things," he eyed Merridy filling a small paper bag with sour gummies, "like candy."

"That would be just fine.""

Jacob began grabbing a hodge-podge of toys, lights, blankets, and pillows off the shelf. After securing plenty of candy, Merridy moved on to Christmas cards and decorations. Mr. Thompson began ringing up items before the duo finished shopping in order to stay ahead of the massive amount of purchases.

"Well, if I wasn't closing my store early for the holiday, I would be doing so just to restock," he joked. "Your vehicle has enough room for this and two mattresses?"

"This we have room for. It's when Merridy goes clothes shopping next that I worry about." They shared a laugh.

Merridy brought a stack of Christmas card boxes and extra ornaments to the counter. "I heard that," she warned Jacob with a wink. "I'm going next door to the boutique. I'll try not to buy-out the place as well." She bounced out of the store with her phone at the ready.

'Jacob just told me that you're driving out here for Thanksgiving. I'm so excited!'

'Wouldn't miss it for the world. I'm bringing Evie too. I hope that's okay.'

'Of course, it is! The more the merrier! And it feels like it's been forever since I've seen her. I'm about to go into a boutique to get something nice and Christmasy to wear for photos with Jacob. He wants to get photos done while we're out here for our Christmas cards.'

'Joint Christmas cards? Wow, big step! I do like the idea of photos of you at the ranch all decked-out in Christmas attire. Good thing I'm bringing the camera. You should pick a few outfits out. I have an idea up my sleeve.'

'I won't turn away the opportunity to buy some clothes.'

Merridy slipped her phone into her pocket in order to enter the rustic teal door of the downtown clothing boutique. "Welcome in!" a woman announced with her back turned to the door. She wrestled with a mannequin from the back of the store. "Anything I can help you with today?"

"Something Christmasy, in plus size, that looks okay on a plus size instead of like a sausage casing."

The woman put the mannequin down. "Specific, let's see what we can do. I have a decent plus size section." She walked to a corner of the boutique. "What's your usual dress size?"

"I can run from 16 to 20, depending on the cut. I err on the side of larger since it's the holidays." Merridy folded her arms over her waist. She hated to announce the numbers. They indicated the truth of her weight; a subject she did not relish in. Merridy stepped forward to help the woman look through the dress options. Most just appeared to be a wider version of the regular-sized dresses, which never fit right for her. Finally, a long-sleeved dress with an empire waistline and long, pleated skirt presented itself to her. The cranberry color and intricate design of the lace sleeves made it seem like a holiday-worthy dress. "Can I try this one on?"

"Certainly, the curtains in the back. I'll keep looking for some other options."

Merridy doubted the woman would find another option. The plus-section was not as 'decent' as she stated. Luckily, the dress fit. She stepped out of the curtained changing booth to check the three-way mirror.

"You look beautiful." Jacob stood at the store's entrance with a goofy smile on his face. "Absolutely. Beautiful."

The compliment caused her to blush. Even when she felt at her lowest about her looks and weight, this man lifted her out of her negative self-image. This man, who dated fashion models, chose to be her boyfriend with a great attraction and passion toward her. "You like this for our cards?"

"Absolutely." He came to stand next to her. "And more."

"They don't really have more here," she replied, crestfallen.

He put his hands on her lace-covered shoulders. "I don't mean and more clothes... I meant, I like this for many reasons more than the Christmas cards." He kissed her cheek. "And if you want more clothes, we can always have it special-ordered. Whatever you want."

She smiled. "I think I know the perfect designer for it."

He turned to the boutique clerk. "Do you have anything for men that would match this? I notice it is mostly women's clothes here. I have black jeans, black shirt, and black coat that I brought. Anything with a touch of this... red?"

"Cranberry," Merridy corrected him.

"Is that why you look so delicious?"

"Oh my." She blushed and went back into the changing room. Jacob grinned after her.

The woman presented him with a cranberry tie and handkerchief. "This will do," he thanked her. He glanced at a nearby display of jewelry. A teardrop-style necklace made of silver with red and clear crystals set upon a black velvet bust. "And I'll take that too." He nodded at the changing room. "Before she gets out."

"Understood."

The secret purchase was slipped into his pocket, and the rest was carried back to the full SUV. "Anything else you would like?" Jacob asked her. "Or shall we head back to the ranch?"

Merridy glanced around at the small town she grew up in. "I'm good. Let's get back, have some hot chocolate, then unload this stuff to the tree house before people arrive."

"Only if we can have the hot chocolate on the porch swing." He opened the car door for her and offered a hand. He managed to steal a kiss on her cheek during the transaction.

"Deal," she giggled before returning another kiss to him.

Chapter 40

The buzz of a phone caused Jacob to grunt. He sat wrapped up in a blanket with Merridy overlooking the Frio. The completed treehouse cast its shade over them. She buried her face against his side. "What is that noise?" she groaned sleepily.

"Your phone," he whispered. "I think it's in your back pocket. Should I get it?"

She chuckled. "It's not in my pocket."

"Maybe I should check, to be sure." He shifted his arms under the blanket. "You're right. No phone."

"Mhmm." She began to kiss him, but his phone began ringing. "Maybe we're being sought."

"Let them look." He wrapped the blanket around them tighter before returning the attempted kiss. "We finished that treehouse. This is our reward."

"More like, you completely re-did that treehouse, and this is *your* reward," she whispered. Her fingers ran through his hair. "I love you."

"I love you too." He shifted his hands behind his head. "And I love when you play with my hair."

Merridy smiled. "I could do this forever." She noted the missed call notice on Jacob's nearby phone. "Though now I know who it was calling us. I bet Kara has arrived."

"That does make sense." He closed his eyes. "I bet some other family members have arrived too. The responsible, adult-thing-to-do is head back."

"Probably." More time passed between them before Merridy threw the blanket off of them. "Okay, we really should go."

"Yes." He sat up with Merridy sitting in his lap. "Right." He kissed her neck. "I want to spend every day of my life doing this with you."

"Me too."

They begrudgingly returned the blanket to the treehouse before walking back. Kara and Evie sat on chairs on the back-porch deck along with Patti and other family members Jacob did not recognize. "Hey, I'm going to pop into your dad's workshop real quick." He kissed her forehead before veering into a side door. The fresh scent of sawdust filled his nostrils, and he smiled. The workshop became his favorite place on the entire ranch. Jamie stood above a project; calmly, he sanded the curves of the rocking horse. "Good afternoon, Jamie."

"Afternoon, Jacob." He adjusted his glasses. "How did the treehouse turn out?"

"Fantastic. I wanted to thank you for all of your help with it." He strode forward to uncover the carriage. "She's ready to show the twins tomorrow."

Jamie grunted approvingly. "Thinking of taking out the carriage?"

"I've been thinking about it all week. Her friends are here. They might want to make a girl's night of it." Jacob shrugged. "We've been content walking."

"Only walking?"

Jacob coughed at the question. "I mean, we've been enjoying the views."

372

"Nice, wholesome views, I hope." Jamie lowered the sandpaper and picked up a brush to remove the dust. "Nothing I would disapprove of."

"I've not taken any liberties, if that's what you're concerned about. Merridy was very clear about that, and I'm in agreement with her." He found a screwdriver to check a few joints of the carriage. "I do want to ask your permission, though, for another matter."

The brush stopped moving in response.

"I love your daughter, with all my heart. I want to spend the rest of my life with her..."

"You asking permission to marry my only daughter?"

"Yes sir." Jacob walked to Jamie to look him directly in the eyes. "I would like to propose to Merridy, sooner rather than later." Jamie scratched his chin in thoughtful consideration. He walked out of the workshop, leaving Jacob without an answer. "That's... not good?" Jacob asked the rocking horse.

The door reopened. Jamie led Patti into the concrete room. "Jacob here, asked me an important question, Patti. And I don't want to answer him without you being here." He repeated the question to his wife. She gasped and nodded her head. "I guess that is a yes from her. And a yes from me. But son, when you ask, we have to be there."

Jacob nodded. "How do you feel about a Canadian Christmas?"

Patti and Jamie turned to each other with a smile.

Merridy excitedly hugged her friends amidst squeals and greetings. They curled up on the deck's couch with oversized knitted blankets and hot cider provided by Patti. The three nearly spoke over each other in their eagerness to catch up on the week's events. All carefully ignored New York in their conversation, each unsure how to approach the subject after Merridy's week of healing.

"How's the coffeeshop doing?"

Evelyn sighed reluctantly. "I mean, it's doing better with all that Kara and you have done." She shrugged. "I guess I was deeper in the hole than I thought."

"That seems absurd," Merridy shook her head. "The landlord sounds awful."

"It's just the problem when you have faceless corporations based out of California or New York running these things." Evelyn froze after her statement. She mentioned New York; she feared Merridy's reaction to the reminder.

Instead, her friend smiled. "That's very true. I'm sorry it's not what we hoped for. But hopefully, soon, you can find a person to sublease from you."

"In the meantime, I've decided to sell the house."

"What?" Merridy gasped. "Oh no, Evie, I'm so sorry."

Jacob walked out on the deck with a smile. "Hey ladies." He reached to hug Kara.

"White Rabbit," Merridy sighed, "strikes again."

"Uh oh, what did I do?" he asked, stopping mid-motion. "Or rather, what did I come late to?"

Merridy handed him her empty cider mug. "Evie was telling me that her sales have improved, but it's still not enough. She is having to sell the house. It was her and Zeke's house. They put all their memories in it…" She turned with tear-rimmed eyes to Evelyn. "I'm sorry."

"It's okay, Merridy." Evelyn stood to hug Jacob. "Our memories are there. Our memories are in the coffeeshop. And you know what? It's okay to move forward because I know in my heart-of-hearts, that's what he wanted. He told me after the doctors said there was nothing more that he wanted me to grieve then move on with my life. He told me I was young. I couldn't stop living just because he was moving on." Her voice began to shake with her tears. "And I'm trying to do that. I'm trying to figure out how to move forward while tying up these loose ends."

"Man, I'm so sorry Evie." Jacob pulled one of the deck chairs up to the couch. "I mean, I can lend you…"

"No," she cut him off. "You are very kind, Jacob. But I don't want a hand-out or charity or…"

Merridy took her friend's hands. "It's not charity. You're our friend. It's what friends do for each other." The three women continued to talk about the situation as Jacob mused over the situation. "It's such a beautiful house too. If you could keep it, you could rent it out and have an income to help you with your future needs."

"Do you have photos of the house?" Jacob asked. She opened pictures on her phone and handed it to Jacob. Images of a gray and white craftsman house popped up. Four white columns with brick bases created a wide front porch; three ceiling fans spanned the width. "Three bedrooms?"

"Yeah. Zeke worked with an architect to make it the way he wanted. Shotgun-style to remind him of their grandparents' home."

Kara smiled at the memory of her grandparents' home.

"And there's a formal living room, and a den. Plus, a downstairs office. The three bedrooms are all upstairs. The kitchen has double ovens, my favorite part." She smiled. "We were going to add a deck, and a garage, in time. It's on a good-sized property. Was thinking a pool at one point and still have land for a playhouse for the kids."

"There was a future there," Kara agreed. "And we will never understand why things went the way they did. I just want you to be happy."

Jacob handed the phone back to Evelyn. "Ladies, how about you go get refills of your drinks and meet me at the front of the house. I know just the thing you need." He disappeared into the workshop once more.

"What is your man up to?" Kara asked Merridy.

"I've no clue. But I'm very curious." The ladies walked into the kitchen to refill their cider. Merridy found a clean travel mug to pour Jacob some as well. "He's already done some amazing things this week. Tomorrow, when it's light out, I'll have to take you to my childhood treehouse. It was dilapidated, and he restored it to something *beautiful* for my cousin's twin boys to enjoy."

"That is stinkin' sweet," Kara agreed.

They walked to the front porch to await Jacob. The sound of horses neighing from the side of the house aroused their curiosity. "Hello ladies!" he greeted them from the seat of a horse-drawn carriage. "The Meseta County Carriage is back in action, and I thought you could enjoy the first ride."

The group giggled amongst themselves as they hurriedly boarded the carriage. He led the horses slowly down the winding driveway of the ranch; the pace allowed the girls to enjoy more gossip. They admired the setting sun and the white lights that now adorned the trees lining the drive. "When did the lights get put up?" Merridy asked. She shook her head. "I helped mom with the inside of the house, but I didn't know she did anything out here."

Kara caught sight of Jacob grinning over his shoulder; she realized he was the man who put the lights on the trees and ranch fence. She suspected he did it specifically for this carriage ride.

"It's very beautiful," Evie happily commented. "Christmas lights. Horse-drawn carriage. Hot apple cider. This is perfect."

"Yes, it is," Merridy responded. As indigo took over the sky, the lights shined bright around them. "Reminds me of the magic of Christmas. Reminds me of why I love it so much."

"Needs some caroling," Kara added.

Merridy smiled broadly and began to sing "Have Yourself a Merry Little Christmas". Her two friends leaned against her as she sang the Judy Garland classic. Their own troubles all began to drift away into the night as the words comforted them. Jacob nodded at the appropriateness of the song's lyrics. He turned the team back to the ranch house to finish the short trip.

The porch lights accented the garland and red ribbon wrapped around the front porch's columns; they also marked the end of Merridy's singing. Jacob helped all of them out of the carriage. Merridy exited last, and he held her close before kissing her deeply. "You have the voice of an angel. You know this, right?" he asked her.

She blushed. "You keep telling me this. I might start believing it."

His eyes smiled at her. "I have a question for you." He glanced over his shoulder to ensure the other two were far enough away to not hear his whispers. "What do you think about buying Evelyn's home?"

"You mean, us?"

He nodded. "I mean, we're talking about our future all the time, Merridy. Let's start with the house. It's gorgeous. I'm a sucker for craftsman homes. Cozy place in old South Hills. And it's got all that room to grow. It's perfect."

She bit her lip as he continued to speak.

"Plus, it's helping Evie. She won't take any hand-outs, right? But she can take a payment for her house. And since *you* would own it, she could come visit you anytime if she's wanting to be nostalgic. Keeps it in the family."

The thought overwhelmed Merridy; butterflies enflamed her cider-filled stomach. "I do want that future with you, Jacob. But I can't just... move in with you. I mean, I know we've, shared a bed together, to sleep, but... moving in?"

He nodded solemnly. "Right. You're right. It's too soon, and it's completely inappropriate. We're not married yet. I think, I just got excited." He stepped away from Merridy in order to take the driver's seat once more. "I have to go park this and handle the horses. I'll see you inside for dinner."

"Jacob..." Merridy began. But he continued forward without acknowledging her. "Ladies," Merridy called to the other two.

"Let's go up to my room. I need girl advice." She took them by the hand and led them upstairs to her room where she repeated the entire conversation to them both and whole-heartedly received the advice of both.

Kara took Merridy's hands in hers. "At the end of the day, stay true to your values. Chances are Jacob is not upset at your decision. He is most likely upset at himself for making the suggestion knowing how you felt. This is how he's processing it."

"Still… he does want to help Evie," Merridy turned to her other friend. "This really could help you."

"Don't let me factor into this," Evelyn answered her. "This is between you, Jacob, and God."

Merridy breathed in deeply. "You're right. I'm going to put it out of my mind. There's so many other things to worry about." She turned to Kara. "Like you. How is the project with Caleb going?"

Her friend arched her eyebrows. "It's going great. I received a nice bonus too. No problems here to worry about. Merridy… we need to talk about the elephant in the room. I confirmed with folks on your behalf that you will sing Friday, which is great, but I don't think you realize how far your name has gotten."

"No, I guess I don't. I've stayed away from social media." She grabbed one of her pillows to cling to. "How bad is it?"

"Bad?" Kara shook her head. "It's only bad for the perpetrators. Merridy, you did nothing wrong. There is so much support for you right now."

"When I was watching the livestream, a lot of people were also watching and freaking out in the comments," Evelyn advised her friend. "That support has only grown from there."

"You watched the livestream?" Merridy asked her.

"Evie is the one who called the policy," Kara informed her friend. "She had been sharing your livestream at the coffeeshop."

"My customers freaked out."

Kara pulled her tablet out of her bag. "Look how many hits you have on your videos. This one of 'It Is Well' has reached over five-hundred-thousand. Merridy, you are viral. People genuinely want to know that you're okay."

She let out a barely audible scoff in response. "Guess I proved in the end I could market myself without doing things *their* way. I can get out there and milk this, couldn't I? That's what Casimir would have said," she added bitterly. "But I don't want to build my career as the girl-who-was-victim."

"No," Evie interjected. "You are a woman who worked hard to make it in a competitive industry, and you've survived an ordeal that could have prevented you from succeeding. But you're overcoming it."

"Everything she said," Kara agreed. "I'm not bringing this info about you being viral for a marketing angle, Merridy. I want you to see the support you have. That's all."

A soft rapt on the door interrupted the conversation. "Ladies, dinner is ready. Patti wanted me to let you know." Jacob cleared his throat. "Also, I moved my bags down to the office, and brought Kara's and Evie's bags up to the guestroom. Thought they would prefer the queen bed rather than the pull-out downstairs." His footsteps sounded his quick retreat.

Chapter 41

The pre-Thanksgiving dinner had been lite – casserole and salad – in order for everyone to save their appetites. Patti remained in the kitchen long after, accompanied by Evelyn, to prepare the side dishes for the next day's meal. Jacob assisted Jamie with the turkeys and pork in the backyard smoker. Other early-arriving family members meandered off to the separate houses of Judith, Derrick, and Darren to settle down in their respective guestrooms. Kara disappeared to the guestroom's clawfoot tub for a 'brainstorm bath'.

Merridy sat in her room alone. The piano keyboard she purchased in middle school beckoned to her from its dusty corner. She obliged. The sleeve of her shirt wiped away the layer of dust. To her surprise, the power still worked along with all of the keys. The feel of the plastic 'ivories' under her fingers transported her back to a simpler time. Old songs memorized for Christmas gatherings and church services made their way out of her. Calmer after playing the piano, she noted her nearby laptop.

"Take a leap of faith," she told herself. Once the laptop was powered on and in position, she pressed the button to start recording a livestream. "Hello everyone," she began. "It has been awhile since we last spoke. I've been spending quiet time with my loved ones in seclusion deep in the heart of Texas. It has been a time of healing, and a time of reflection. I am so grateful for those closest to me in helping to keep it all together. Or as best as one can keep it together."

She quickly wiped the tears that threatened to escape her eyes.

"There are so many mixed and contradicting emotions that occur for a person who goes through a traumatic event. I never realized that until now. Like, I've gotten mad at myself for being broken up about the ordeal. I actually told myself that I was lucky to have not been raped, that I survived the assault. And there is truth to that – it could have been worse. But that doesn't invalidate the feelings I have. All my feelings are valid, because there are so many levels to this."

Her fingers instinctually began playing on the keyboard while she spoke.

"I am afraid. I am afraid that this may happen again. Not just to me, but to anyone trying to make a name for themselves and held hostage by this demand. I fear for those who feel like they can't say no. And I fear for those who say no but are forced anyway. I am angry that this is even a situation. How long has this been going on? How many stars are only stars because they were forced to compromise their integrity? How many more talented persons said no, were desecrated, and their abilities forsaken in their grief?"

More tears escaped, and she paused playing in order to wipe them away.

"I'm confused. I'm hurt. I had lost hope that I would be able to sing again. I thought maybe it was a sign that I should give up. I mean, I didn't even want anything to do with Christmas, and that's my last name! It's such a big part of who I am. Those two men, actually, that whole company, messed up my mind. It made me question my identity and values. Not just from what happened that night, but my entire time with Echo Star. I was put on a highly restrictive diet, which I've now found out from my athletic boyfriend was not healthy at all. They coupled that with a trainer who constantly ridiculed me for my weight. It got into my head that I needed to change everything about me in order to be successful: wear the clothes they wanted me to wear; sing the songs they wanted me to sing; be the person they wanted me to be. I can't imagine how much more twisted my mind would have been by them if I didn't have friends helping to offset some of those evil lies."

She paused a moment to catch her breath.

"This week has been a mental cleanse. It has been me trying to return to normal. But most importantly, it has given me a chance to get alone with God in my prayer closet. I yelled at Him. I cried. I demanded answers. But now, I realize, the best thing I can do is surrender *everything* to Him. That is what He wants. He is the Good Father who wants to carry your burdens. We just have to let go. I know that sounds crazy. We think that's giving up, or not working through it in a healthy manner. But that's not what I'm doing. I will continue with therapy. I will continue with legal action against Echo Star to hold people accountable. But I'm surrendering the weight of my burdens to God so that I may move into peace."

The random tune she had been playing on the piano changed and she began singing.

I surrender all,
I surrender all,
All to Thee, my blessed Savior,
I surrender all.

All to Jesus I surrender,
All to Him I freely give;
I will ever love and trust Him,
In His presence daily live.

I surrender all,
I surrender all,
All to Thee, my blessed Savior,
I surrender all.

All to Jesus I surrender,
Lord, I give myself to Thee;
Fill me with Thy love and power,
Let Thy blessing fall on me.

I surrender all,
I surrender all,
All to Thee, my blessed Savior,
I surrender all.
All to Thee, my blessed Savior,
I surrender all.

She inhaled deeply at the end of the song. "Thank you all. I hope everyone has a great night. Have a wonderful Thanksgiving tomorrow. And I will see you in Dallas for the tree-lighting ceremony." She clicked off the livestream.

Her hands returned to the piano keys. The burden that had been weighing her spirit felt lifted, true to the words she had spoken. When she stopped looking for God to take action and started focusing on her *faith* in Him, He was finally able to move. A song she had been working on since meeting Jacob came to mind.

You said You'd give the desires of my heart,
And I thought that it meant whatever I want.
When the world around me began to fall apart,
The faith I had was shaken and dropped.

My eyes turned from seeking Your face,
All I wanted was Your hand,
But it turned my life away from Your greater plan...

She noted the lyrics on her laptop. A slight knock sounded on Merridy's door in the post-livestream silence. "Hey, it's me," Jacob whispered. "You don't have to open the door. I just want to let you know I'm sorry. I shouldn't have suggested the house. I just got caught up in the moment."

Merridy turned off the keyboard. "You can come in."

The door creaked slightly as he slowly opened it. He noted her sitting at the keyboard with the nearby laptop. "Sorry if I interrupted..."

"No, I just finished." She turned to face him, and he could see she had been crying. "I got some stuff off my chest and gave the world the song put on my heart."

"I'm really proud of you." Jacob pulled her into a bear hug. "You're so amazingly strong."

"And you're amazingly sweet. You don't have to apologize. We both approached it wrong." She pulled back from his hug to hold his hands. "I would love to grow our future in that house. I've been to it. It *is* gorgeous. Therefore, why don't we buy it, and you live in it now. Once we're married, I can join you."

He contemplated the proposition. "It *would* put me much closer to you. And... I could get started on a few projects in it."

"A few projects?" she smiled. "Like what?"

"Trophy cases for all the awards we're going to be raking in, obviously."

"Obviously."

He began to swing her arms. "And a gym, that way I can stay at home for my morning workouts. And a music room, for you, with all the equipment you need or want. And a fence that can contain an Akita."

"I like what I'm hearing."

The two shared a smile; the smile developed into a kiss. "I'm glad we could work this out," Jacob admitted. "Especially since it was really awkward laying on the couch downstairs with Porthos while your mom and Evie were still cooking in the kitchen. I felt like I wasn't being helpful, but I also thought I'd probably be in the way if I tried to help. Much nicer to be up here, talking with you."

"Guess the living room isn't quite as cozy when there's frantic folks in the kitchen." Merridy released her hold of Jacob's hands in order to turn to another dust-covered piece of nostalgia: a boombox. "It's not the downstairs phonograph, but it will do."

"Sounds great to me." He began singing along with a Dean Martin Christmas classic. "May I have this dance?"

She accepted his hand, and the two began waltzing in her bedroom. Kara entered the open doorway to check on her friend, but noted how enamored the couple appeared in each other's arms. With a smile, she stepped back into the hallway and closed the door behind her.

Chapter 42

Merridy awoke to the sounds of Christmas music still playing from her bedroom boombox and laughter from downstairs. She felt a warm body wrapped in the blankets next to her and discovered Porthos snoozing comfortably. His eyes partially opened when she petted him behind the ears. "When did you end up in my bed, sweet baby boy?' she cooed to him.

His response was a giant tongue to her face. She laughed and kissed him back.

"I guess I better get ready and go downstairs…" she trailed off. A card and wrapped box sat on her nightstand. "What's this?" She opened the card. A scenic Thomas Kincaid cabin covered in snow greeted her; a long note sat on the inside.

Merridy,

I know gifts on Thanksgiving aren't customary, but I couldn't wait until Christmas to give this to you. You'll get plenty more for Christmas anyway. I think it will look nice with your new dress. Hopefully. I'm not the most fashion-conscious human. Also, I know gifts aren't your love language, but sometimes, they just need to happen, especially this time of year.

Please know, you really do mean the world to me. You've changed my life, for the better. Before I met you, I was living in absolute misery. I lied to myself all the time. Some mornings, I didn't want to get out of bed. Now, I don't want to get out of bed for a different reason… you know, if you're with me. People around me felt dull, predictable, boring, and shallow. Then here comes this auburn-haired whirlwind of talent, humor, compassion, faith, and intelligence. Wow. You're just so fantastic. I really didn't stand a chance. Which is fine by me.

I look forward to the day when I can wake up by your side every morning. I got the taste of that in New York, not for the reasons we wanted, but, waking up with your hair in my face... that was special. I hold it close to my heart. I look forward to watching your career grow, and your talents be used the way you were called to use them. I look forward to so much more that I can't put in writing in case your dad saw this and decided to kill me. But yes, I look forward to every aspect that comes with our future.

I love you Turnip Girl.

Your White Rabbit

The ending of the note made Merridy blush. She never realized that he thought of more intimate moments with her. She looked at herself in the mirror. "Yeah, I need to knock some pounds off before... the honeymoon," she concluded. Her hand drifted to the box. Inside, a beautiful necklace with red and clear crystals greeted her. "Awww."

Porthos jumped out of bed to assist with her morning routine. Occasionally, she would reexamine herself in a mirror, the sentiment of Jacob's card still in her mind. Stretch marks everywhere. Muffin top. Thunder thighs. Jiggling upper arms. All of which he would know nothing about thanks to carefully selected clothes. But what would happen once they were exposed? She frowned at her image. The words of her trainer echoed in her mind. Perhaps he had been partially right.

"Good morning," she announced to her family and friends downstairs upon finishing her morning cycle. "Thank you for my gift." Merridy hugged Jacob. "And that card," she added with a whisper in his ear. "Got a little scandalous."

He grinned. "It could have been much, much more." His eyes hungrily gazed at her, and she blushed again. "Want some breakfast?"

She lowered a hand to her stomach. The last thing she needed was holiday weight. "Maybe just coffee, or something."

"Or something... so eggs." He winked. "Please, please, try this." He pulled her into the breakfast nook. "I attempted an eggs benedict from scratch. I promise, it's not too heavy. It won't ruin your appetite for later."

"I shouldn't eat too much. I mean, I'm trying to lose weight."

The comment caused him to pause. He lowered his voice. "This isn't about what they told you up in New York is it?"

"No. It's about that card. You know. You will see me..." She waved her hands at her body. "Me. And it's not pretty, and if I could lose..."

"Merridy, you are beautiful just the way you are." He put his hands on either side of her head. Locking his fingers in her hair, he stroked her cheeks with his thumbs. "This woman here? She's the one who drives me crazy. Nothing else matters. Do you believe me? Please believe me."

She nodded.

"Good. Now, please try this awful attempt at eggs benedict. I used dill. Starting to think capers would be the way to go." He fixed Merridy a plate and sat alongside as she ate. "Capers. Right?"

"It's good. But yes, capers would make it better." She did not want to admit it, but the food tasted superb. Worrying about her looks, which apparently did not matter, nearly deprived her of the meal. She realized then that, while she wanted to begin a healthier lifestyle, she did not want to live a life of regret. "Like the ham though."

"Canadian bacon," he corrected her.

They were joined at the table by Kara, Evie, and a few of Merridy's cousins who all helped themselves to Patti's pumpkin pancakes. "After breakfast, do you two want to change into your fancy clothes so we can take some photos around the ranch?" Kara asked. We can knock out the photos before any singing or the big meal... or the big game."

"I'm down," Merridy agreed. "I have the perfect outfit." Her eyes darted to Jacob. "With the perfect embellishment."

After breakfast, the duo gussied up and headed outside to pose under Kara's directions. Jacob could hardly keep his eyes off of Merridy and told her several times how stunning she looked in the cranberry-dress. Seventy-five different locations and poses later, Kara released them to change back into comfortable clothes and join the festivities of the day. Jacob immediately joined a game of tag football.

Merridy joined other cousins on the deck overlooking the game. Eventually one person requested a song, and others agreed with the request. Soon, an uncle was hurrying to the office to secure the instruments from the wall. Merridy went to her own room to retrieve her guitar. The game dwindled to a halt once the music began.

"Sing for me, my little Merry Christmas," Judith instructed her granddaughter. "Sing my favorite."

"Yes ma'am," Merridy answered her grandmother. She turned to her cousins on the porch who held the banjo, mandolin, and fiddle. "Let's play grandma's favorite." She led with the guitar, and the other three instruments began to catch up. An uncle began to keep a beat on a box he sat on, and Jacob soon realized the box's purpose was to be an actual drum.

There's a land that is fairer than day,
And by faith we can see it afar;
For the Father waits o'er the way,
To prepare us a dwelling place there.

The entire family began to sing the chorus. "In the sweet," Merridy sang.

"In the sweet," others sang back.

"By and by," she sang.

"By and by."

We shall meet on that beautiful shore.
In the sweet by and by,
We shall meet on that beautiful shore.

We shall sing on that beautiful shore,
The melodious songs of the blest;
And our spirits shall sorrow no more,
Not a sigh for the blessing of rest.

In the sweet by and by,
We shall meet on that beautiful shore.
In the sweet by and by,
We shall meet on that beautiful shore.

To Jacob's surprise, Jamie produced a harmonica from his pocket to perform a solo before Merridy sang again.

To our bountiful Father above,
We will offer our tribute of praise,
For the glorious gift of his love,
And the blessings that hallow our days.

In the sweet by and by,
We shall meet on that beautiful shore,
In the sweet by and by,
We shall meet on that beautiful shore.

Jacob found a seat next to Evelyn. She grinned at him. "Isn't this amazing? I've heard Merridy and Kara talk about the Perry family singing at their gatherings. But it's something else to see so many generations singing like this. Even the children."

Even the children. She was right. This was something he wanted his future to experience. He wanted them to sing along with their mother, and grandparents, and great-grandmother. This was a tradition he wanted continued throughout the ages. He adored his own family's traditions, but this tradition had a specialness to it he could not explain.

Another gospel song began. He noted Judith sat in her rocking chair, happily clapping her hands to the beat, though she shivered slightly. Jacob stepped into the living room to retrieve a blanket from the ottoman. "Oh Jacob, can you take this out to my mother?" Patti called from the kitchen. A warm mug of cider sat on a tiny piece of free counter real estate. "She's going to catch her cold out there."

"Yes ma'am. I was taking her this blanket too." He picked up the cider-mug and managed to avoid Patti's accolades in order to return to Judith and the singing. Kneeling next to Judith, he handed her the cider and tucked the blanket around her legs. Her shaking hand patted him gratefully. "Warm up with that drink," he whispered the instruction.

Merridy smiled at him from her position nearby. "He gave sight to blind Bartimaeus, he gave peace to the crazed and stricken.

No matter what he'll be there for us. Whether we're tired, broke, or sick and... I know I'll shout my praise," she sang.

"She wrote this," Judith said to Jacob, proudly. "She writes such good songs."

After an hour of singing, the instruments were put away. The family gathered inside where the food lined the counters, the breakfast table, and the dining room table. A beautiful cake sat in the middle of the breakfast table, courtesy of Evelyn; the extended family whispered in admiration of the dessert. "We want to thank everyone for making it out here for Thanksgiving," Patti announced. "We haven't had a gathering of this size in many years. It is good to have so many friendly faces brought together." She turned to Judith. "Mama, did you want to say anything?"

"I'm hungry," Judith replied back. The statement was met with laughter. "Where's Aaron? He's a pastor. Say grace over this food so we can eat."

Merridy's uncle stepped forward and spoke an eloquent grace over the food. Once the prayer was completed, a free-for-all occurred with everyone grabbing plates, silverware, and attempting to secure their favorite dishes.

"What should I be going for?" Jacob asked Merridy.

She silently tugged him away from the main crowd in the dining room. "Listen, most everyone goes for the main courses first. Those are always in the dining room because it's the biggest table. But the room itself gets way too crowded. Best option is to score some dessert first, polish it off, then get the other dishes once people have moved on to dessert."

"Ah, a clever tactic. Plus, we get sweets first." He ended up with thin slices of pumpkin pie, pecan pie, buttermilk pie, and coconut cream pie. Due to his curiosity, he also ensured to have a slice of Evelyn's cake. "Hope I have room for the rest of the food."

"I'm sure you will," Merridy joked. "Now, if you want a good view of the game, and a comfortable seat, then you don't want to eat down here at all." She pointed to the stairs. "My room. My television should be hooked up still."

Jacob followed her lead, and they curled up with their sweets just in time for kickoff. "Happy Thanksgiving, Merridy Christmas."

"Happy Thanksgiving, Jacob Kenway." They toasted each other with a clink of cider mugs. For the time being, she could forget about what the next day would bring.

Chapter 43

Late Thanksgiving Day, after the game, a nap, and revealing the treehouse to the delighted twins, the Dallas group headed back home. Jacob led the way in the SUV. Merridy slept in the backseat with Porthos. Kara drove the second car while Evelyn perused cakes on social media pin boards. Classical Christmas music played over the SUV's radio, and Jacob hummed along with the tunes in order to remain awake. Turkey, pulled pork, cornbread dressing, deviled eggs, green bean casseroles, and a hundred other dishes made his stomach heavy. It threatened to put him to sleep.

Yet the two-car caravan made it to the metroplex in safety. They arrived at Evelyn's house where everyone decided to sleep until the early wakeup hour to prepare for the tree-lighting ceremony. Jacob managed to carry Merridy upstairs to a guest bed. He passed out next to her with Porthos at their feet.

The alarm seemed to sound instantly.

"Ugh," Merridy responded. She reached over to hit the alarm. To her surprise, she instead hit Jacob in the chest. "Where am I?" she groggily asked.

"Evie's," he answered her, half asleep himself. "We made it back late last night, or rather early this morning."

"Oh." She sat up excitedly. "Oh! It's the day!"

"Yep," he rolled out of the bed. "Time to get ready for your big performance." He stumbled to the door. "Bags are on your side of the room. I'll see if the other ladies are up."

Porthos followed him out of the room. Merridy felt instantly awake. Her seven-week journey had led to this very day. This was her performance to the world. Grabbing her toiletry bag, she jumped into the bathroom.

By the time Jacob returned to the room, she was wrapped in a towel with white stripes over her teeth, a corrective mask over her face, and a wet brush combing her hair. He sipped his coffee. "I probably shouldn't be seeing this, but you didn't shut the door."

"No time. Performance day." She nodded to her hanging bag. "Can you pull the cranberry dress out. Ask Kara if it will be okay to use that one again."

"No, no," Kara announced. She entered the room past Jacob. "I already brought a dress and everything you need to Evie's before we left to Meseta. That's why I told Jacob to come here. Perfect staging area." She entered the bathroom to help Merridy with her hair. "Jacob, your job is to drop off your things and Porthos to your home now. We will meet you at the mall."

He saluted. "Aye, aye. Anything else you need?'

"If we think of something, we will text you."

Jacob slipped out of the house to follow her instructions.

Within hours, Merridy found herself waiting anxiously in a room off the plaza's ice-skating rink. Kara stood nearby talking with the event organizers. "After the skaters finish, we'll introduce Merridy. The audience is really looking forward to seeing her," the organizer told Kara. "I'm sure you saw the comments online."

"I did." Kara turned to look at Merridy. "She's ready to perform."

Merridy wrapped her guitar strap securely and played a few warm-up chords.

The organizer began walking out as the Olympic skater routine came to a close. "Ladies and gentlemen, give it up to our Olympic gold-medalists Ken Vaughn and Kelly Bell!" The crowd applauded. "They are simply beautiful on ice, aren't they? Next up, we have a musical talent from right down the road in South Hills, Texas. With over one-million views on social media, the Dallas Plaza is proud to present Miss Merridy Christmas!"

A roaring cheer greeted Merridy as she skated onto the ice. Her stomach tightened when a small voice in the back of her head said, "They're only cheering for you because you're a victim."

Despite the negative thought, she attempted to smile broadly and thanked the audience. Her voice nearly wavered, and she paused briefly to look down at her guitar. Her fingers felt frozen over the strings.

"You got this Merridy!" a voice shouted above the murmur of the crowd. The voice belonged to Jacob.

Another shout joined him. "Come on Merridy!" Terry accompanied his friend.

The combined outbursts stirred a cheer from the crowd. Merridy's fingers began to move. Knowing Jacob, and even Terry, were in the crowd, supporting her, helped.

"O holy night..." she began. The song swept away any remnants of the negative thoughts. Focusing on that night, thousands of years ago in Bethlehem, she remembered the gift given to her both then and now. The first chorus swept her along. Many in the audience sang with her. As she entered into the second verse, she felt a stirring in her spirit; her voice carried out stronger and louder than before.

Truly He taught us to love one another;
His law is Love, and His gospel is Peace;
Chains shall he break, for the slave is our brother,

And in his name... all oppression shall cease.

Her hand lifted from her guitar as she sang the last line. She could feel that God was ceasing the oppression on her spirit as she voiced the words. She continued acapella.

Sweet hymns of joy in grateful chorus raise we;
Let all within us praise His Holy Name!

She hit the word 'name' at a higher note than she had rehearsed, surprising herself and the audience. They began to wildly cheer her as she finished out the song at the higher octave.

Fall on your knees, Oh hear the angel voices!
O night divine! O night when Christ was born.
O night divine! O night divine!

Tears streamed from her eyes as the song finished. The organizer skated out to her. "Wow! What an incredible version of that song! Just wow!" She clapped, encouraging the audience to applaud more. "Merridy, we are so honored that you joined us today. I don't want to really go down that path, but just know that all of us have been supporting you and cheering you on. Our hearts are with you. You are out there leading a cause that's been swept under the rug for decades. You're an absolutely courageous woman. Thank you so much for being here today."

Leading a cause? The comment struck a nerve with Merridy. She really did not feel like someone leading a cause. She was merely someone who survived an ordeal. She barely felt like a survivor. She lived as a recluse at her parent's ranch for a week after the event. Most of the 'leading' had been done by Kara and Jacob. She simply... existed. Meekly she simply replied, "Thank you." Her skates could not get her off the ice fast enough. "Why are they calling me a leader?" she whispered to Kara. "I'm not a leader. You are. KT is. I'm not doing anything."

Kara put her hands firmly on Merridy's shoulders. "You struck the first blow," she reminded Merridy. "That puts you front and center. I'm certainly *not* leading anything. I am just relaying your messages to detectives and lawyers. KT is helping me with the legal team. But he's not in the public's eye. I'm not even a known factor outside of closed doors. It's all about you. Whether you like it or not, people are looking toward you."

"I don't want that." Merridy shoved her guitar in its case and speedily escaped her skates. "I just want to sing."

"Oh Merridy." Kara knelt down to help her friend. "Singing is how you're leading. What did they try to take from you? *Your singing*. They wanted *their singer*. Being yourself and moving forward is exactly how you're going to lead." She held a hand out to her friend to help her to her feet. "And with that in mind, there are some friends I want you to meet."

A part of Merridy wanted to run away to her parent's ranch once again. She thought she had reached a place of healing in order to move forward with life; but the words of the organizer and the faces of the crowd, affected her in a way she had not expected. "Not now..." she whispered.

"If not now, when?"

The question hit Merridy hard. Four weeks and a handful of days sat between now and Christmas. Prospects of releasing a Christmas album for the year looked dim now that Echo Star was out of the picture. Legal matters would take even more of her time. If not now, then would she have to wait another year? Would she start with a non-Christmas album? Is that what she wanted? "I don' know," she mumbled.

"Just meet them. One step at a time."

Merridy glanced out as the crowd began a countdown to the tree's lighting. Three-two-one... the four-hundred and fifty-thousand lights of the ninety-five-foot-tall tree blazed to life at the push of a button. Her eyes lit up in sight of the country's tallest indoor Christmas tree brought to life by holiday spirit. "Okay."

Kara led her down a hallway and into a restaurant that sat nearby the skating rink in the plaza. "I booked us all a private room to celebrate how well your performance went, and the season, and... well, hopefully more."

The restaurant's hostess led them into a room where they were greeted by Jacob, Terry, and three others Merridy did not recognize. "Merridy, this is my friend, Elyssa Brooks... well not a Brooks anymore, old habits die hard. She leads the marketing department for the Texas Twisters."

"Small world, right?" Jacob grinned at his girlfriend.

"Very," she agreed.

Kara turned to the two others. "I would also like to introduce two old friends from my high school days, Tom Fontenot and Adrienne Lopez. They are co-owners of Golden Eagle Entertainment, a local record company."

"It's nice to meet you," Tom offered a handshake to Merridy.

Adrienne shook her hand as well. "I wish it was under better circumstances. Sometimes, life gives us lemons. Hopefully, we can make some lemonade." Something in the tone of her voice made Merridy believe that Adrienne understood better than most how she felt.

"We want you to know up-front that we are a small operation," Tom candidly stated. "We don't have the reach of bigger companies, but we also don't have the pressures other companies present as well. We give our artists much greater freedom."

Kara indicated the table. "Come on. Let's all sit with some food and drink before we discuss the hard stuff." She placed Merridy between herself and Jacob. Elyssa, Tom, and Adrienne sat across from the three. Terry, ceremoniously, took a seat at the end of the table between Adrienne and Jacob.

"Tell me when it gets to be too much, and I will pull you out of here," Jacob whispered in her ear. He reached under her table and squeezed her thigh. "You're my top priority."

"Thank you." She pecked his cheek. Turning her attention to Tom, she began, "I appreciate your directness with me, Mr. Fontenot. There are less than five weeks to Christmas. My original plan with Echo Star was to have an album releasing today to couple my performance. Clearly, that has fallen through and any thought of having an album out before Christmas seems insane now. I'm not even sure if any of this is relevant."

Tom's folded hands sat calmly on the table. "What if I told you that we could have an announcement today, pre-orders online, and an album cut in a week?"

"That's a bold claim," Kara stated.

He arched his eyebrows. "I'm a bold man. You know that."

Kara laughed. "No, the *boy* I knew is quite different from the man talking now." She turned to Merridy. "*Tom* was the joker. It's hard to swallow this claim."

"We're a small operation," he restated. "Which means we can focus more in crunch-time. If Merridy is willing to crunch with us, it's doable. But I'll be honest. We don't own an arsenal of copyrights like a big company. It will limit song selection because getting the rights will take extra time. But the songs you lean toward seem to be more classic songs, many of which fall into public domain, taking that burden off of us. We already have skilled recording musicians to back you up. And honestly, Adrienne and I discussed that we're willing to hire extra help with marketing to hit this as hard as possible."

Merridy folded her arms. "You have to forgive me if I'm skeptical after everything I've gone through."

"I don't blame you," Adrienne agreed. "It also feels a bit callous discussing this so soon after, but with the Christmas season upon us, if we don't discuss this now and make a decision, this album isn't happening this year. That's the bottom line. We will not push you to make a rushed decision that you are uncomfortable with. We just want to present everything up front with you, in open communication. If you prefer to wait, we can wait. If you prefer to look elsewhere, we understand that as well. I just hope you can hear us out. That's all we're asking."

The two women exchanged a long glance. Merridy nodded. "I will hear you out."

"Our initial term is only for one year with a subsequent option period and optional renewal," Adrienne announced. "We want to ensure that you find us a good fit and vice-versa. We don't want you to feel compelled to live out your creative life with us if you don't want to. Within the one-year initial term, there is a release commitment for two studio albums. This would cover the Christmas album and one other album. There is a zero-dollar marketing and production spend for *you*; the full cost of marketing, recording, and producing the albums will be on us. That means no deductions from your royalties for the actual creation of the albums. Any marketing by you would be organic marketing on social media which is up to your discretion." She glanced down at a notecard. "We usually offer brand new artists a ten-percent royalty, but given that you now have public notoriety, we decided that a twelve-and-a-half percent royalty would be fairer."

Nearby, Kara made notes of everything Adrienne said. "Twelve-and-a-half percent royalty?" Merridy repeated. She recalled Echo Star only offered a two-percent royalty. "I thought industry standard was much lower."

"There's a lot of scum out there who like to say one-to-three percent is standard. It is absolutely not." Adrienne turned back to her notecards. "I'm sorry, I didn't bring an actual contract here because if felt crass. I have to rely on notes, because there's so much legalese." She took a sip of the sparkling apple cider the waiter poured for the table. "We don't offer a signing bonus because of the zero-dollar spend for the artist. I know that sounds bad, but a lot of other companies like to say they offer a signing bonus, but it's really an advance with a lot of quote-unquote standard deductions, such as recording, production, packaging, marketing, and public relations. We don't process those deductions from the artists. That is our company's cost of doing bonus, or rather, our investment in our talent."

The comment once again reminded Merridy of the signing bonus promised by Casimir, and his subsequent list of standard deductions. She never felt more confident in not signing the absurd contract.

"Also, you maintain creative rights to songs you write. That's very important to us," Adrienne stated. "I know you're probably not aware of this, but Tom and myself were both formerly in bands since we were... fourteen, fifteen? We've been in this industry awhile, and it's very, very important that an artist retain a copyright to their creation. If you write a song, it is *your* song, not the record company's song."

"You also earn a different set of royalties when you record a song you have written. We have calculators for that because it's very regulated by the federal government," Tom added. "We can send you, or all of you, a more detailed chart and explanation of the songwriter royalties."

"And in regard to master recordings," Adrienne added, "we operate under an equal shares concept – the master recording is evenly split between the company, the recording artist, and the songwriters. For example, if you record a public domain song from the nineteenth-century, the master recording is owned fifty-fifty by Golden Eagle and you. But if you record one of your original songs, then you are the sole writer of, you would own two-thirds of the rights of the master recording. It was the Big Compromise we created years ago when we tried to decide where it fell. Our equipment and funding, the artists' and songwriters' talents... this is what it boiled down to."

The waiter arrived to take orders, allowing Merridy time to process everything. The numbers sounded better than Echo Star's, but she was afraid to move forward without knowing if it was in her best interest. Everything felt like a trap anymore.

Adrienne flipped to a new notecard. She chuckled to herself. "I made notes about how streaming royalties work, but I don't want to ruin this meal. The whole system is so convoluted. I don't know if you've read about streaming services and the push for them to change their payouts. It's been very difficult in working that out within our company given how little we are. We do *rely* on streaming services to reach audiences that we can't with FM or satellite radio. So, we like it, but we just don't love it." Another flipped notecard. "Performances. We do have a woman on staff who coordinates performances, events, and tours for our artists. She is paid directly by us, not a royalty from you. I know that's a bit different as most artists have agents and booking royalties, but this is part of being a small operation." She shrugged her shoulders. "We do have one tour of fifteen shows built into the one-year-term contract. The timing of that tour is negotiable. Honestly, for this situation, I would recommend the tour go with the second album, not the holiday album. This holiday album will be better suited with guest appearances and performances, if we can swing those."

"That is something I can agree with," Kara chimed in. "What kind of special appearances are you thinking?"

Adrienne smiled at her friend. "We have a whole list that we've brainstormed. Or rather, our lady at the office and Tom have brainstormed. I don't have a marketing bone in my body." She turned to Merridy. "Honestly, this is why we agreed to hire on more marketers to rush the word on your album, if you signed with us. We know our intellectual shortfalls."

Kara looked over her long list of notes. "I'm actually impressed. Ever since I saw the contract Echo Star tried to push on Merridy..."

"You saw that?" Merridy wondered how. She had not even seen a copy of the contract since the original meal with Casimir. "Where is it?"

"In an evidence locker in New York City. But the lawyer sent me a copy to review with you. We just... haven't yet." She shrugged her shoulders. "Plus, when I read it, I started researching. It was horrible. What they offered, plus what they demanded in return. I can see why they're using it as part of the legal proceedings, aside from the forgery." She nodded at Adrienne. "The numbers Adrienne have given are much more palatable."

Merridy nodded. "I just want to be *sure*."

"If you like what you hear enough to want to go into further detail," Tom told her, "then let's go into further detail. We can go straight to the office after this, have our legal meet with your legal and get you the best deal. Then we can work on the music."

Silent so far, Elyssa finally spoke up, "I have no skin in this game, but I just want you to know Merridy… these guys… it's about the music for them. Before anything else, it's about the music. They want to create and help you create."

"You should also know, we've talked to KT Tally. He's coming down to meet with us as well after Kara introduced him to me over the phone." Tom ran nervous fingers through his black hair. "I'm actually pretty excited. I was a major fan of NTUNE, and I'm not ashamed to admit it. But KT… with Echo Star not controlling him anymore… he's looking at getting in some low-key recording and songwriting. He just misses performing. And we miss him performing. If it all goes well, maybe we can reunite the two of you on the album."

"I actually do like the sound of that." She turned to Jacob with a smile. "What do you think?"

"I think… I see a spark in your eyes that had disappeared for quite some time, and I do like seeing that."

"Alright." She nodded. "Let's do this."

Part Four: The Album

Chapter 44

Merridy stepped forward to a condenser microphone behind a window in the Golden Eagle recording studio. Her stomach performed an elated backflip. *Recording* – the one task she never achieved with Echo Star, and the one she wanted to do more than anything.

On the other side of the window, Tom, Adrienne, and KT sat at the sound boards with headsets on. She discovered that Adrienne and Tom not only owned the company, but proved to be quality producers for albums. This helped them keep costs down by not having to hire special producers. They did, however, bring KT on as an employee, though they continued to discuss a recording contract with him. He felt torn on recording his own album. His days with NTUNE had left a sour taste in his mouth, and Echo Star only worsened it.

He did agree to feature his vocals on Merridy's album for one of the songs he wrote. It would be his first time behind a microphone in over a decade.

"Let's take it from the top," Adrienne announced. "Start with the vocals, fade in the music," she told Tom. "I want to capture the dire feelings of this song. Lament with the captive Israel, Merridy."

Merridy nodded and awaited her que. Her eyes closed, and she held her hands to her chest.

O come, O come, Emmanuel,
And ransom captive Israel,
That mourns in lonely exile here,
Until the Son of God appear.

Rejoice! Rejoice! Emmanuel shall come to thee, O Israel.

O come, Thou Rod of Jesse,
Free thine own from Satan's tyranny;
From depths of hell Thy people save,
And give them victory o'er the grave.

Rejoice! Rejoice! Emmanuel shall come to thee, O Israel.

She paused. Was she expressing enough longing in her voice? Her thoughts raced as she heard the music in her headset; plucked notes on Middle Eastern ouds and qanuns added to the flair of the song. Her suggestion in their creative session was to make the centuries-old tune sound as though the children of Israel cried out for their Savior in the last century BC. Excited at the idea, Adrienne delved into music of the era.

O come, Thou Dayspring, from on high,
And cheer us by Thy drawing nigh;
Disperse the gloomy clouds of night,
And death's dark shadows put to flight.

Rejoice! Rejoice! Emmanuel shall come to thee, O Israel.

O come, Thou Key of David,
Come and open wide our heav'nly home;
Make safe the way that leads on high,
And close the path to misery.

Rejoice! Rejoice! Emmanuel shall come to thee, O Israel.

She paused once again, and this time Adrienne cut the music. "What's wrong?" Merridy asked in a panic. She knew there was one more chorus to sing in which the Israelis cry out to Adonai, the term used by the Hebrews to refer to God as His divine

411

name became too sacred too utter. She did not want to leave out the last verse as many people often did. To her, it felt like the most time-and-geographically appropriate verse of them all.

"Nothing. You sound beautiful." Tom turned to Adrienne. "What are you thinking?"

"Replace the chorus. Let's use a Hebrew translation for all subsequent choruses after the first time, do the last verse in Hebrew, and then the final chorus back in English."

Tom nodded. "Sounds great in theory. I, personally, don't speak Hebrew. I barely speak what little Urdu I learned from my mom."

"I'll find someone to translate for us." She tapped on the glass to Merridy. "Let's transition over to 'O Holy Night'. We'll take a break after that."

The recording session lasted for several more hours before the group ended for the day. Merridy's voice felt tired. She understood the rush they underwent. The day before, she had stayed up past midnight with the studio musicians to record their parts. The current day would also require late hours. She headed to a 'Giving Tuesday' benefit concert that Jacob and Elyssa helped secure.

Jacob would be attending a different 'Giving Tuesday' banquet without her. The thought saddened her. Soon, their schedules would conflict more and more. She realized how precious their time together had been during her week of seclusion, and she eagerly looked forward to their upcoming Christmas break.

Until then, her schedule consisted of practices, recording sessions, special appearances, and events. Thursday, she knew she would see Jacob as she had promised to join him at the children's hospital for their special performance of "The Twelve

Days of Christmas". Tom and Adrienne would attend as well in order to record the live song for a bonus track of the album.

"Merridy?"

Hearing her name took Merridy out of her tumbling thoughts. "Sorry. In my head, again."

Kara smiled at her friend. "I received your dress today." She held up the red velvet dress with white faux-fur trim. "Zydonna knocked it out of the park."

In light of her former stylist losing her job with Echo Star, Merridy had ordered a few custom-made dresses from the young woman. Rather, Jacob ordered the dresses against Merridy's protests. She hated feeling indebted to him and insisted on paying him back with her first royalty check. He insisted the young stylist needed the capital to jump-start her own clothing line and that 'indebtedness' did not exist between a couple.

"It *is* pretty," Merridy agreed. "Reminds me of what Rosemary Clooney wears in *White Christmas* at the end. Always loved those dresses." She held it up to herself. "But cut just for my shape. She's good. I knew she would be."

"Let's get you ready. The show starts soon."

The two began preparing Merridy for her performance. She enjoyed the relaxed environment of only two in a dressing rather than a whole team circling her like a pack of vultures. It felt natural. She did not *want* to be a diva. She just wanted to sing.

And for the next two hours, she sang.

Jacob and Merridy sat on her couch reviewing pictures of Evelyn's house. The paperwork officially signed, they were now homeowners, though Evie would remain in the home through the month. "The Christmas tree would go here," he told her. "The lights will twinkle through the bay windows. With a big enough tree, we could keep the curtains open and the whole neighborhood could enjoy while we still enjoy privacy."

"Mhhmmm," she sighed. "Wrap the front columns with garland."

"House smelling like gingerbread." He kissed the top of her head. "And not just from the candle burning. Actual gingerbread, in the oven."

"Don't hate on my candle." She glanced at the candle melting on a warmer. "I barely have time to see you this week, let alone bake cookies."

"I know. Anyway, gingerbread is a group activity." He nuzzled her hair. "Tomorrow is the final day of recording. Are you excited?"

"I'm terrified." She swiped the picture on the tablet to another view of the house. "Three days of recording. Is that enough? I don't want it to sound rushed. Most professionals spend hours and hours and weeks in the studio to record. How are we getting this done so fast?"

"To be fair, you're spending many hours in the studio, and I bet Adrienne is spending even more hours mixing everything. She seems to run on coffee and adrenaline." He lowered the tablet and turned his attention back to Merridy. "The album will be fantastic. You will be able to breathe again. You will watch the sales roll in." He stood to reach into his pocket and pulled out a squished sprig of mistletoe. "Now..." he held it above his head, "let's focus on the current situation."

"I'm certain that's basil in your hand, not mistletoe," she jokingly commented. "But I'll give it to you." She bounced to her feet. "I have to say, you're one of my favorite Christmas gifts."

He tossed the plant onto the coffee table to wrap his arms around her. "You're certainly one of mine."

A buzz from Merridy's phone threatened to interrupt them, but they continued enjoying each other's embrace. Another buzz. A third buzz caused Merridy to sigh and pull out of Jacob's kiss. "What is happening?" she whispered. "It's fifteen minutes to midnight. Can we get some quiet time or not?"

"I'll look." Jacob bent over to glance at Merridy's phone. "Oh wow. Merridy... get ready to scream."

"What?" She took the phone from her boyfriend and squealed.

'I know it's late but I have AMAZING news, and I could not delay in telling you. And I needed to tell you before I even told Tom. Just reviewed the numbers of preorders for your album. Brace yourself.'

'We're at 500,017 preorders. PREORDERS. Your album just went GOLD and we haven't even finished it yet.'

'I think we need to bring Kara on for permanent marketing. You and she make a killer team. Hope this brings you some momentum for tomorrow's session. Good night Miss Christmas!'

"How have I sold half a million copies? It's not even out! Do you realize how many people that is?" she shouted. "Oh my.... Oh my... it's for a Christmas album, Jacob. Those don't sell in those numbers. Christmas albums don't go gold." She sat hard on the edge of her couch. "I don't understand. How? Why?"

"People want to support you, Merridy. This is their way of showing support." He gently sat on the coffee table. "And think about it, if *you*, named Merridy Christmas, couldn't sell half-a-million Christmas albums, who else could?"

She began crying joyfully and wrapped her arms around Jacob's neck. "Thank you, Jacob. This all started when you caught me."

"Nah, love, this all started when you believed in your gift – your Merry Melody." He winked and kissed her forehead. "Guess this means the launch party is also going to be a gold record party."

The first of December marked the end of the week and the album's launch party. Tom and Adrienne secured an event hall in downtown South Hills. The hall's brick walls were adorned with gold curtains and twinkle lights. Banquet tables sat on either side of the hall, loaded with sparkling ciders and gold-flaked hors d'oeuvres and desserts. A screen at the end of the hall played video montages of Merridy's performances-to-date. Pencil Christmas trees sat in the venue windows decorated with pearl and golden ornaments to tie the theme of the album and the theme of the party together.

The attendees ranged from friends to studio musicians to local radio personalities to other creators to a variety of concert and charity organizers. The crowd mingled and talked amongst themselves, all keeping an eye on the live count of the pre-orders measured in the top corner of the screen: 517,832. Kara stood with Adrienne and Elyssa in a corner, eyeing all the guests in order to strategize their next marketing steps. Tom nervously paced the back of the room near the screen to await the guest of honor. KT, along with his wife, stood with Caleb Stone to discuss KT's future return to music.

Headlights flashed across the venue's windows. A silver, luxury electric vehicle parked in front of the door. Jacob, decked out in an all-black tuxedo, exited the far side of the car. He walked around the car, fidgeting with his suit jacket, before dramatically opening the passenger door. Merridy stepped out. Her golden gown rose up around her left shoulder in a Greco-Roman style; her naturally curly hair fell down around her face in calm ringlets. Under the lights of the venue, she cut a shimmering, elegant figure.

All those in attendance applauded when she entered arm-in-arm with Jacob. The reaction caused her to blush. "Thank you everyone," she timidly responded. "Thank you. I don't deserve this. You're too kind."

"Our lady of the hour!" Tom called out. He joined the applause. "Our company's first gold record, one of the fastest selling Christmas albums, and on pace to be one of the fastest selling albums." He beckoned to her. "Merridy, come join me up here. We have a present for you."

Jacob continued to lead her forward two-thirds of the way through the hall before releasing her arm. "It's all yours, Turnip Girl," he whispered. "I love you."

"I love you too." She smiled at him. Slowly, so as to not trip over the floor-length gown, she made her way to Tom. He greeted her with a hug. "Thank you for everything Tom."

Tom brought forward an item covered in black cloth. "No, thank you for everything, Merridy. We want to officially announce, today, on December 1st, at ten o'clock at night, the release of your first album, *A Merridy Christmas*." He removed the cloth to hold a vinyl album high in the air. The crowd exploded.

The sight of the album brought warmth to her heart. She sat on a backless, green velvet settee with gold legs and embellishments. Nearby a fire blazed in an ornate, Victorian fireplace. A massive Christmas tree took up the background. Victorian ornaments adorned the thick needles to add to the antiquated scene. She wore a burgundy taffeta gown that appeared to be straight out of a Dickens novel, and her hair sat in ringlets to match the time period.

"The very first copy... for you." Tom handed Merridy the album. "The rest have already been shipped out to all the preorders we've received, and any new ones received today will be shipped out tomorrow. Digital copies go live at midnight eastern time." He glanced at his watch. "Which is now fifty-two minutes away. How does it feel?'

Merridy hugged the vinyl tightly to her. "I feel giddy. I can't even describe it in words." She breathed in deeply. "Honestly, I'm surprised we're here. You know, many of you know, that I was skeptical that this would happen. We made an album from inception to delivered *in a week*. That's unheard of. And it took *all* of us working tirelessly to make it happen. I am so thankful for all of you." She turned to her best friend. "Thank you, Kara Jackson, for pushing me from the start. Thank you for guiding me in the times I needed it most, and for always listening to God so that you can help all the rest of us." She indicated Caleb and Elyssa. "Thank you to your friends who helped you with all the relentless marketing this week that led to these crazy pre-sale numbers. You have been amazing. Can we give them a round of applause?"

The audience obliged her.

"Thank you to KT." Merridy turned to the man. "You helped me at Echo Star. You've endured many more years of torture than anyone, and you've endured it in silence. Now your songs are forever entombed on this album, and I'm so happy to have a duet with you."

He bowed in response.

"And Tom and Adrienne…. Thank you for this opportunity. A week ago, I was ready to walk out on you. But you were insistent and forthright, and that led us here."

"A gold record is thanks enough," Tom joked.

"Finally," she turned to Jacob. "Thank you to the man who was kind enough to help a stumbling girl on ice. He taught me how to skate so I could perform on ice. Luckily, in doing so, we formed a friendship that turned to something much deeper and lovelier. And honestly, I don't think I would be here without him. God has perfect timing. He's proven that with this match. When we needed each other the most, boom – perfect timing."

Jacob beamed at her statement.

"Thank you, Jacob Randolph Kenway." The crowd cheered the couple who found each other in an embrace. "Let's put this record on!" Merridy shouted. Everyone shouted an agreement back.

Tom queued up the album, and the first notes of "O Little Town of Bethlehem" sounded out of the hall's speakers.

"Look at this," Jacob beamed. He took the vinyl record from Merridy's hands and held it aloft to examine it. "Look at this. Turnip Girl's first record." He wrapped his arm around her waist and pulled her close. "I'm so proud of you." He kissed the top of her head. "So very proud of you."

She reached up to kiss him. "I meant what I said."

"I know you did. And I mean what I say, when I say, I couldn't ask for a better partner." He returned her kiss. "Now, is it appropriate to dance to Christmas songs, or do we just hit the food table? I admit, I'm a little hungry."

"Food table first, then." They meandered to the tables in order to sample every dish available. "Is this your first album launch or no? Ya know, since you're a big shot celebrity athlete and everything?"

"Terry did drag me to a rap album launch. It was much, much different than this event. Not nearly as classy." He held up a gold-flaked truffle. "And the food wasn't on level either."

"We do try to make things classy," Adrienne interrupted them. "Well done on your speech, Merridy."

"Thank you, Adrienne."

"I just came over to let you know I received a text from our event coordinator. They want you on the Helena Troy show Monday morning." She grinned and turned her eyes to Jacob. "Both of you. I know it's not a game day for you, but I didn't know about your practices. I've not reached out to your agent yet."

Jacob pulled out his phone to look at his calendar. "I'm game." He chuckled. "I've never done daytime TV before. This is going to be fun."

Chapter 45

The green room of Helena Troy's talk show offered pyramids of fruit, lines of pastries, and every brand of soft drink and bottled water imaginable. Merridy nervously sat on a couch, bouncing her legs in anticipation. Jacob stood over the spread of food, popping grapes in his mouth to the rhythm of his humming. The show's team had already visited the duo to provide insight on what was to be expected.

"How are you not nervous?" she asked him.

He rolled up the sleeves of his button-down shirt. "I mean, I can't make a bigger idiot of myself than I have in after-game interviews." With sleeves secured, he reached into the ice for a caffeinated beverage. "Last night, I asked that reporter 'what goal?'. I forgot about a goal that *I made*. It can only go up from there." He popped the can open. "No spewing. See? Heading up."

"Five-minute warning for Christmas," a production member called out. "She's calling you out after commercial."

"Then again, they don't want to hear me sing," Jacob continued on. "Those live performances are reserved for children."

His jovial attitude calmed Merridy. When the production team retrieved them, she managed a genuine smile during the walk-out. Multiple women reached out over the railing for high-fives and handshakes. She obliged. Jacob trailed several feet behind her. His goofy personality surfaced in the public eye, much to the amusement of the applauding audience.

Helena Troy, in a mauve pantsuit and matching chunky heels, loomed above Merridy. The model-turned-television personality brushed her long, blonde locks to the side before reaching a hand out to greet the singer. Previously, women like this intimidated Merridy. Over the course of the last month, she discovered that this was due to her own insecurities – insecurities that Echo Star preyed upon. "Welcome to the show," Helena indicated one of the plush chairs near hers, "please be seated."

Merridy followed her instruction. Jacob, still high-fiving audience members with his beverage in hand, noted the two women sitting and hurried to the other free chair with a laugh.

"Thank you for joining us," Helena laughed.

"He can't help it," Merridy mused. "It's a chronic condition."

The audience chuckled at her statement.

"So, you're not just the White Rabbit on the ice?" Helena asked him.

Jacob grinned. "Nope, I'm pretty much always late."

"Except when it matters the most," Merridy reminded him. "Since day one."

His mischievous grin softened upon turning to his counterpart. "Very true."

Helena leaned forward with her chin on her fist. "This sounds like we're leading to my very first question – how did you two meet? It was well before Merridy was in the public eye, from what I can tell."

They exchanged a glance. "Well, I was minding my own business on the ice, reflecting on issues I had going on in my life, and this woman with no grace fell in front of me. Out of instinct, I caught her before she crashed."

"Yep, that's pretty much it," Merridy agreed. "I was trying to learn how to skate before I auditioned for the Dallas Plaza tree lighting ceremony. Turns out, I didn't even need to know how to skate for the audition." She nodded at Jacob. "But I'm glad I didn't know that at the time because that fall worked out in my favor."

"In both of our favors," Jacob agreed. "When she told me that she was trying to learn how to skate for an audition to sing on ice, I agreed to help her learn." He turned to the audience; his mischievous smile returned. "She had *no idea* who I was, by the way. And I didn't let on."

"No, he sure didn't. And I knew nothing about hockey."

"I believe the exact phrase was 'I don't know that puck-thingy from a turnip', which is when I started calling her Turnip Girl." The crowd laughed at their story. "But at that time, it was all platonic. We literally met for skating practices and simply talked as friends."

"We were definitely friends first," Merridy agreed. "We were friends for a while; the rest blossomed from there."

"I love it. You two are so sweet." Helena leaned back into her chair. "Now there is an elephant in the room we need to discuss. I know you don't want to, but it's what everyone wants to know."

Merridy's hand instinctively went to her stomach in anxious anticipation.

"Two and a half weeks ago, a tragedy occurred. A major record company has been exposed because of it, as you were luckily livestreaming at the time of the occurrence. This is a big win for women's rights." The audience clapped in agreement. "What does that mean to you?"

While the production team told Merridy that the incident was going to arise in the conversation, they had not told her it was from the perspective of women's rights. It was an aspect she still struggled to comprehend. "Well... Helena... I don't see it as an issue of women's rights." Her carefully articulated statement caught the audience off-guard. "Honestly, by labeling this as only a woman's issue, it undervalues the full scope of these crimes." Merridy closed her eyes briefly; a silent prayer left her lips. "You see, first, it only paints the woman as a victim; whereas there are many women culpable to these actions. There are women on the board at Echo Star. Are they victims or co-conspirators? We don't know yet, and I'm not claiming either way. The problem is, if we enter into this saying that all the women are victims, then those who are equally guilty will be able to get off using this victim label."

She noted some in the audience nodding in agreement.

Her hands moved on their own accord as she continued speaking. "I don't want a guilty person to be able to say, 'Oh, they forced me' if they weren't forced. Because that takes away from people who *had* been forced. Furthermore, if we say *only* women can be the victims, that takes away from men who are victims too."

"Such as your friend, KT Tally," Helena offered.

"KT went through many awful things over his career that I'm not at liberty to discuss, nor would I share his pains. But I think of this: if we recognized that men can be victims too, would he had suffered in silence for so long? Would he had felt empowered to speak out? There are many in the entertainment industry who are men who have been sexually assaulted and sexually harassed. When they do speak out, it disappears, and suddenly, they're no longer performing." Her fists clinched so tightly that her knuckles turned white. "This isn't about women's rights, or any of that. What this is – is a movement against the abuse of power in the entertainment industry. I don't care the gender identity of the perpetrator or the victim – what I care is that those in power are using that power to solicit sexual favors from those seeking to *make it*. They *must* be called out."

The crowd applauded.

"And it's not just Echo Star. These people exist in other record companies, in other industries. I'm not alone. We're not alone. And the more people who come out, the stronger the survivors become and the weaker the abusers become."

The statement created a standing ovation.

Jacob nodded his head to Merridy. "Well said," he whispered.

Her eyes told him 'thank you'. She felt the air leave her, and she sat back in the chair.

"That was beautifully said, and so true," Helena agreed. A serious streak crossed her face. "This is something I don't speak about, have never spoken about to anyone before, but I have also been faced with this power abuse."

Breaths escaped each audience member.

Helena's hands shook as she began to speak; Merridy reached out to take her hand. "It's okay," Merridy whispered. "You don't have to say anything you don't want to."

"I... want to." Helena shook her head. "There's something about you Merridy. There's like a light within you that brings something out in others." She turned to the audience. "Do you feel that?" Without waiting for a response, she turned back to Merridy. "When I first began modeling, I was a child. I was fifteen. I had just... developed, came into my own. There was one photographer who was well known for kickstarting the careers of teenage girls, but he notoriously wanted parents away from the set as they were considered distractions." Tears welled up in Helena's eyes. "That's not why he wanted parents away. And he made it clear that if I said anything, my career was ruined."

"Oh Helena, I'm so sorry." Merridy walked over to offer a kneeling hug. "No one should go through that, especially a child."

The hostess frantically wiped her tears away. "That photographer died many years ago. But he set me up with an expectation of 'shut up and take it'. And that's not okay. Now I'm sitting here wondering, are there other girls out there just like me?"

Merridy eyed the production team off-camera making signs to cut to commercial. This was not the episode they had hoped for. She understood; the show was called 'The Helena Troy Show', but it was the people behind the camera who controlled it. "All we can do is raise awareness," Merridy offered, "...for people to know it's not okay. They need to speak up to their parents or another trusted authority figure. And we need to pray for these young souls, to give them courage to take that stand, and pray for protection over our young people."

The audience verbally agreed with Merridy's statement while they also offered sympathy to Helena. A sign lit up to let them know they had cut to commercial break. "What was that?" a man hissed as he walked onto the set. He flayed his arms around for makeup to fix Helena's tear-stained face. "That is not what we discussed." He was sure to talk in angry whispers. He did not want the live audience to hear what he had to say to Helena. "We talk about the assault, we get the audience engaged and into it, then we move on to the soft talk."

Jacob stood up. "That's not okay," he told the man. "This is her show. Let her speak."

"It is *not* her show," the man turned to Jacob. "She is replaceable..."

Helena stood. "It's okay... everyone. I said what I needed to say. After commercial, we can move forward." She looked at Merridy and Jacob. "Please."

Merridy put a hand on Jacob's arm. "Yes, we can move forward." They resumed their seats.

"Welcome back to the Helena Troy Show," the model announced upon que from a production member. "I have with me Merridy Christmas and Jacob Kenway. In this segment of the show, we would love to talk about your new album." She reached to the side of her chair and produced the vinyl record to show the audience. "*A Merridy Christmas* is available in digital format, CD, and, my favorite, vinyl. There is something a little extra about vinyl. The tone it produces is comforting. Reminds me of the holidays at my home."

"Same," Merridy agreed. "My parents have a phonograph they keep in the living room and play all the classics on it: Nat King Cole, Bing Crosby, Dean Martin, Frank Sinatra..."

"...Merridy Christmas," Jacob added. "I'm sure they play yours on repeat now."

"And yours is certainly a classic," Helena agreed. "I mean, just look at this album cover. Looking at it makes me want to enjoy a Dickens Christmas." She turned the album around to the track listing. "Most of these songs are older hymnals, I believe."

"Correct," Merridy answered. "I hand selected those that told the story of Christmas for me, from the longing of the children of Israel for Emmanuel to come, to his arrival and the nativity

428

story, all the way to the hope we have with 'I Heard the Bells on Christmas Day'. I wanted this album to be first and foremost, a projection of my faith. Because it's been my faith that has gotten me through *everything*."

"And I believe you are singing one of the songs for us today?"

Merridy nodded. "Yes, I will be singing 'I Heard the Bells on Christmas Day' based on a poem written by Henry Wadsworth Longfellow during the Civil War. Imagine, a time when brother fought brother on the battlefield and everything was falling apart around people. The hopelessness everyone felt knowing nothing would go back to normal, and this song about hope comes out of it. I think it's one of the most beautiful songs on the album."

"And I just learned about a Christmas song I've heard countless times!" Helena exclaimed.

"This woman is a Christmas encyclopedia," Jacob chimed in. "It's in her name."

"Which leads us to a question everyone wants to know. Is this your real name or a stage name?"

Merridy blushed. "It is my legal name given at birth. My father's family is from England where it is a surname. And my first name is a combination of 'merry' and 'melody'. The holiday and music are both important in my family."

"I can also vouch for that," Jacob joked.

Helena leaned forward. "What are some holiday traditions your families have? Both of you?"

"My family lives on a ranch," Merridy responded. "They decorate it with lots of lights and wreaths. My mom has two trees that she decorates before Thanksgiving. The family tree in the living room is really the same every year, but it's always fun to see how she'll decorate the foyer tree. It's a different theme each time. This year she chose a Victorian theme, and it actually inspired the album cover for me." Merridy turned to Jacob. "The town has a carriage they use for evening rides and caroling, and this guy helped my dad fix it for the season. Then he took my friends and I for a ride at Thanksgiving around the ranch. It was lovely."

Jacob grinned. "Merridy has a big family that gathers for holidays. A *huge* family. I've only met the non-English family that gathers for Thanksgiving. It's apparently doubled for Christmas. And on her mother's side, there are a lot of skilled musicians and singers who like to gather around and sing. They sing a lot of gospel music. It's actually really amazing to watch."

"Yes. In December, my family gathers at the church the Sunday before Christmas, and they sing while the community has a big Christmas dinner." Jacob tilted his head in interest. She had not previously discussed this tradition. "It's a wonderful time. Hopefully I will get to enjoy those in the future. When possible."

"And what about you Jacob?" Helena asked.

"After the Christmas tree is put up at my parent's home, we have the glorious task of setting up a giant Christmas village with a train running through it. I'm always on train duty while my siblings and their families work the village. Now, since Eddie and I are usually on the road playing when that happens, they set everything up except the train for me, and Eddie gets a corner of the village all for himself to setup. Usually the section in the corner that no one can see anyway." He shrugged with a laugh. "Then we always hit Vancouver's Christmas Market, which is a huge German market, and we go up to the North Pole, the kids meet Santa, we do some skiing, and close it out

430

with the lights around town. Vancouver is a wonderful place for Christmas traditions."

"Those all sound lovely," Helena commented. "My family's big tradition is a pajama party on Christmas Eve where we binge watch all the Claymation classics while eating cookies and drinking hot chocolate. Since so many of us are on the road or busy all year, it's our one night to just pause and enjoy family time."

"That's beautiful," Merridy agreed.

Helena noted her producers. "It's time for a break. But when we come back, Merridy Christmas will be performing 'I Heard the Bells on Christmas Day'. Stay tuned."

During the break, Merridy stepped to a side stage where a studio band waited for her. "We'll follow your lead," the piano player indicated. "Don't worry. We're professionals."

Helena welcomed back the television audience and re-introduced the duo before announcing the song once more. A cameraman in front of the side stage made motions to the piano player. A red-light went off on top of his camera. The music began. Merridy quickly found her place in the song.

I heard the bells on Christmas Day,
Their old familiar carols play.
And wild and sweet the words repeat,
Of peace on earth, good will to men.

And in despair I bowed my head:
'There is no peace on earth,' I said,
'For hate is strong and mocks the song
Of peace on earth, good will to men.'

A celloist performed the solo from her album admirably, and Merridy stepped back to enjoy the skills of the instrumentalist. She stepped forward once more to the microphone. The power of the song filled her torso.

Then pealed the bells more loud and deep:
'God is not dead, nor doth He sleep.
The wrong shall fail, the right prevail,
With peace on earth, good will to men.'

She wiped a tear from her eye.

Till ringing, singing, on its way,
The world revolved from night to day.
A voice, a chime, a chant sublime,
Of peace on earth, good will to men!

Peace on earth. Peace on earth.
The bells say,
Peace on earth, good will to men.

The crowd applauded the song. The show cut to another commercial which marked the end of their time with Helena. She shook Jacob's hands and hugged Merridy tightly. "Thank you for coming," she whispered. "I hope we can speak again soon."

"Anytime," Merridy promised. They left the studio to enjoy a day in Los Angeles before their evening flight back to Dallas.

Chapter 46

Two NYPD detectives led Merridy and Kara to a room in the courthouse. There, they met with a member of the district attorney's office.

"KT Tally is on the stand, currently," the lawyer advised. "He's doing exactly what we're advising you to do. Recount every detail of every incident you can think of. The DA has a list of those incidents you previously gave, so she can help encourage you along if you freeze on the stand."

Merridy felt her gut burn. "What about... what about the defense's attorney?"

"They will do everything they can to undermine your credibility. They'll question your character. They'll question your choices. The DA will object whenever the defense crosses the line, but expect them to not hold back. You're the face of this movement. If they can destroy you, then the whole thing crumbles."

His response brought Merridy no comfort. In fact, she felt more dread now than before she asked.

"But the good thing is, today isn't a trial." The lawyer smiled; Merridy wanted nothing more than to wipe the smile off his face. "The trial won't be until next year. This is going before the grand jury. They will hear key testimonies, such as yours, and present the evidence, such as the forged contract and video of your livestream. After they receive all of that, they will deliberate whether the case moves to trial. We have no doubt that it will."

"And this is just the criminal case against Casimir and Charles, right?" Kara asked. "Your office mentioned a case against Echo Star as well."

"Yes. We believe there is enough for an extortion case against the company. You'd even have enough for a class action lawsuit by all those done wrong. A private attorney will need to lead that charge. We only pursue criminal offenses."

Merridy attempted to calm her internal systems. "No cross examination," she repeated. "No cross examination."

"So, this isn't the extortion case, but you're questioning others besides Merridy?" Kara asked. "I'm sorry. I didn't grow up watching *Law and Order*, so I'm trying to figure out how this all goes."

"We are questioning the others to establish a trend. We want to show premeditation for the assault."

"Oooh," Kara nodded. "Because premeditation means longer sentence." She turned to her friend. "This will be good. It will get you used to telling your side of things in a legal setting. It will prepare you for the real trial."

They were led to another hallway and stood outside a door. KT exited from the room. Without a word, he hugged Merridy. "Just be honest," he whispered in her ear. He released her to hug Kara. "It won't take long," he added, louder, to Merridy. "Then we'll head out to Zydonna's place and practice at Radio City Music Hall." He grinned. "Focus on the positive."

She offered a thumbs up and entered into the room with the grand jury.

"How bad was it?" Kara asked. The trio descended the iconic steps of the New York County Supreme Court to an awaiting taxi. "I've never even served jury duty."

"Really?" KT asked. "How have you managed that?"

She shrugged. "I've never even gotten a summons."

"Honestly, it wasn't bad," Merridy looked up and answered her friend's question. "Like KT told me, be honest. The hardest part was just reliving everything. It's like, replaying a nightmare in your mind over and over. You know it can't hurt you, but it still gives you cringe feelings." She turned her attention back to her phone.

'How did it go Turnip Girl? Are you okay?'

Merridy recounted the entire Grand Jury hearing to Jacob while the trio piled into the taxi. KT directed the driver to Soho.

"Which is really weird, because whenever something amazing happens, it also feels like a dream. But a good dream that I want to last forever. I feel like there's a bit of fog around each thing though. Like, I'm sitting next to KT Tally. And I met him a month ago, but it still hasn't quite sunk in?"

"We're performing live together tonight for the first time, so I hope that fog goes away," he joked. "Though, I do get that feeling. I'm still not believing that I'm back to… performing. I've been *just the songwriter* for over a decade."

"A pretty amazing songwriter," Kara reminded him. "And honestly, what you've written without all of those surveys, test audiences, and formats that Echo Star had you doing is way better than what you wrote with them. I mean, I don't know many duets between Mary and Joseph, especially one as powerful as yours."

"Thank you." He looked out the taxi window. "It just came to me."

"It could be part of a musical. A Nativity musical. And not a cheesy one, like a good one."

Merridy giggled at the thought. "Maybe you can add some Tony awards to your Grammy's."

He shrugged. "Maybe I will. I never thought about writing a musical. That could be fun."

The taxi stopped in front of Zydonna's small shop in Soho. They tumbled out of the vehicle in eagerness to visit the new store. Merridy was surprised to see herself in a window-sized poster wearing one of Zydonna's dresses. "Guess that's why she requested the photo."

The designer greeted the trio at the front door. "Come inside! I have at least a dozen dresses you are going to love Merridy." She led the woman in by her hand. "Honestly, I've hit a market that most designers ignore. And honestly, it's a shame. You would think with the body positivity movement, more designers would be there for plus-sized ladies. But they're not."

"Yep. We're everywhere. And we need clothes," Merridy joked.

"Oh my goodness. I have another celebrity client now too. It's really amazing," Zydonna continued. "Look, I just put up a picture of you on Helena Troy's show wearing that Stuart plaid number I made for you. Keep rocking my threads. I need it on the red carpet." She led them into a backroom where many mannequins in luxurious dresses greeted them. "It's so much better doing this in person than over video chat. How was the gold dress for the release party?"

"It was fantastic. It felt way more comfortable than I would have thought," Merridy confessed.

Zydonna clapped her hands enthusiastically. Merridy loved seeing the previously dour woman burst with fervor. "It feels like I'm the personal designer for a celebrity. This is so much fun."

"I mean, you kinda are," KT told her. He walked around a candy cane inspired dress. "You're not finding this in stores."

"That's for tonight!" She led Merridy to it. "It's the most important one right now. Let's try it on and make sure you can move about comfortably in it." She focused on her client while the other two viewed the different dresses.

The garments varied from the traditional waistline placement to allow a more flattering cut for Merridy. Embellishments also encouraged the eyes to places on the body that Merridy preferred rather than the waist. One dress even included peacock feathers as the skirt. "This is amazing."

"I want a peacock outfit," KT sighed. "All my suits are black on black on black, oh hey here's white. Girls get the fun stuff."

"That's unfortunate," Zydonna called out to him from behind the changing curtain. "I made Jacob a suit jacket to match that dress. It's got the feathers embroidered on the lapel. They can match on the red carpet."

KT shrugged. "Alright. I need something for Elizabeth and I. She likes orchids. Can we do something with orchids?"

"I can do anything," Zydonna responded confidently. She escorted Merridy out of the changing room. "What do you think?"

Kara beamed. "That's cute. And looks good on you."

"Makes me want a peppermint mocha before we head to practice," KT agreed. "Nice."

Merridy smiled. "Let's get my other dress for tonight, and then we do need to hurry to practice. I don't want to mess up tonight's show."

A big band played a piece of *The Nutcracker Suite* as Merridy and KT waved at the audience of Radio City Music Hall. They bounded off to stage left for their exit amidst the thunderous applause of those watching. The sound of the music and audience made Merridy forget the early morning testimony she had given. The cringe of the nightmare had been overshadowed by the surreal fog of performing with the Rockettes and KT at an acclaimed theatre.

KT hugged her and disappeared to his dressing room. She hurried to find Kara. "Kara!" she called out to her friend. Stage technicians and wardrobe changes nearly drowned her out. "Kara!" She noted her friend talking with a group of men in suits. "Can you believe I just did that? Like, how did I get to the point I performed with *the Rockettes*?"

Kara smiled at her. "I believe our friends here are to thank." She indicated the men in suits.

Merridy immediately recognized the man in the center. He had been the gentleman that requested a song "by Frankie" for his wife at the NYC pizza place. "Hello again!" Merridy greeted him sincerely. "How is your *gorgeous* wife?"

"Fine, fine, my dear. She's back in our seats, enjoying the rest of the show. I wanted to come back here and congratulate you myself." He lifted his arms to casually hug Merridy and offered a kiss on each of her cheeks. "You were *exquisite* on the stage tonight, Angel Voice."

"Thank you very kindly. Kara mentioned... you are the one to thank for this?"

He grinned. "It was nothing a few simple calls couldn't arrange. I was happy to do it for someone who once graced my wife and I with a simple request out of the kindness of her heart." He turned to the other men in suits near him. "This young lady performed for us at Dino's. She didn't even know my name. That's true kindness. Something so lost in this world."

Merridy exchanged a curious glance with Kara. "I'm so sorry. I still don't know your name, sir. I feel ashamed for missing this."

"No worries, Miss Christmas." He bowed slightly as he introduced himself. "I am Leone Cicconi." He snapped and one of his men handed a wrapped box to Merridy. "This is an early Christmas present from the Cicconi family to you, Angel Voice."

"Oh but..."

"I insist," he politely, yet sternly, asserted. "Please, open it with our blessing, and know that your album has been gift enough. My wife plays that vinyl every day right between Nat King Cole and Dean Martin."

She gasped. "I am certainly flattered." Her fingers nimbly opened the wrapped present. A wooden plaque sat inside, engraved with Psalms 23 and an image of a shepherd. A gentle scent lifted from the wood, and she bent closer to smell it. It reminded her of black licorice. "This is beautiful."

"Knowing how important your faith is to you, as it is to us all," Leone continued, making a symbol of a cross with his hands, "I had this made out of Jerusalem pine. It was laced with myrrh from the Holy Land as well. May it remind you not of the

439

suffering you have endured, but *how* you endured it. We said our eyes would be on you, and, I assure you, your transgressors will not get away with their evil deeds."

"Thank you very much," Merridy responded in stunned reverence.

He nodded to the men who began to leave the backstage area. "It is time to return to our wives lest we find *ourselves* in trouble. A pleasure to see you again, Angel Voice."

After the disappearance of the men, Kara let out a heavy sigh. "You never told me you had dealings with Leone Cicconi."

"I didn't know I had dealings with Leone Cicconi. I don't even know... what that means?"

Kara leaned forward in order to whisper in Merridy's ear.

The singer's face went pale with the realization. "Then I'm glad... I'm on his good side?"

"Yes. Be glad you sang the song he asked you to sing." Kara sighed deeply. "I suspect there will be future performances for him from you. That's not a tie easily cut."

Merridy glanced at the wooden plaque in her hands. "Well, even Mr. Cicconi needs to hear about The Gospel, right?" She grinned and led Kara to her temporary changing room. "Let's get to the pub and fulfill my promise to perform. Then we're done with New York for some time."

"I don't know. We have time to shop in the morning before we leave. I feel I didn't have sufficient shopping time in New York the last time we were here together." Kara giggled. "This is a thing now. We can get on a plane to go shopping wherever we want now."

"I guess… so? I mean, I did go see Rodeo Drive while we were in Los Angeles. Honestly though, they can't live up to shopping in South Hills and Dallas. That's always going to be our home base."

Kara nodded. "We do have everything there, don't we?" She grinned. "Let's go. I am starving and fish and chips sound really good."

Chapter 47

The sound of skates sliding across ice comingled with the mellow tune of "The Waltz of the Sugar Plum Fairy". Porthos sat on the couch of Merridy's apartment. His pronounced eyebrows raised up and down while he watched Merridy wrapping presents on the floor.

"I know. Your daddy went off to play hockey in Minnesota, and left me to wrap all these gifts." She shook her head. "He's lucky I'm an expert at it." Her eyes glanced up to the television. A glimpse of Jacob flashed by amid the fast-paced action of the game. "And he's lucky he's so cute in that uniform." He rushed forward on the ice and checked a Minnesota player against the glass. "Also, maybe a little crazy."

Porthos barked a reply.

"Good to know we're all in agreement." She pulled a box forward from the giant stack of gifts nearby. Between Los Angeles, New York City, and Dallas, the duo had secured Christmas presents for all of their family members and dearest friends. While she loved shopping with Kara – whom she shopped with when purchasing Jacob's Christmas presents – there was something extra special about securing presents with her soulmate. It made her even happier when she signed the gift tags "From Jacob and Merridy" or "From Merridy and Jacob", depending on the relation with the recipient.

"Uh oh, looks like words are going up between Kenway and Donato," the announcer commented.

Merridy jerked her head up to see Eddie and an opposing player going nose-to-nose in a yelling match.

"I think Uncle Eddie is about to throw his gloves on the ice... oof, yep, there they went." She calmly turned to Porthos. "Now, we don't condone violence, but... go Eddie go!"

She paused with a gift for his two-month old baby in her hands in order to watch the fight. The fight escalated when the referees attempted to break it up, and the Minnesota player pushed the referee away. Jacob rushed forward to help break up the fight and was met with a punch. His gloves fell to the ice. Teammates from both sides joined the fray.

"Okay, so Jacob will have a nice black eye when he comes back home tomorrow." She sighed. "Can't wait to hear all about this fight over, and over, and over." Porthos barked an agreement. The fight finally ended with multiple players being sent to the box on both sides. The announcers were in a tizzy over the whole situation. Merridy returned to the baby's present. "And that's why I play Christmas music during the game."

A majority of the gifts were successfully wrapped by the end of the game. They overwhelmed her small pencil tree, and she secretly could not wait until they owned a magnanimous tree in their future house for all the presents to fit under. The buzz of her cellphone sounded from under the excess wrapping paper and ribbon.

"Hello sweetie," she answered it. "How's the eye?"

"You saw that, huh?" Jacob sighed. "Yeah. It got heated out there today."

"I wasn't expecting you to call before the post-game Q and A."

"I'm... not doing one. Terry is going to do it. I'm actually with the team doctor getting some stitches done."

"That's not good." Merridy settled on the couch with Porthos. "Your fur child was nervous for you."

"Was he? Tell him I'm okay. The other guy looks much worse." He sighed again. "I miss you."

"I miss you too. When is the flight home tomorrow?"

"Nine in the morning. I'll get a ride to your place. You don't have to come get me."

She stroked the top of Porthos's fluffy head. "Maybe I want to?"

He chuckled. "You know you always sleep late when Porthos is in bed with you. He's a giant teddy bear."

"Guilty." She glanced at the gifts. "I'm almost done wrapping the gifts. And we got several cards. I'm leaving them on the kitchen bar to open together."

"Wow. Thanks for wrapping." His voice winced slightly due to the stitches over his eye. "I can handle shipping them out. I can at least do that much."

"You don't have to, but, I won't say no." She tilted her head. "We were going to head over to Evie's house tomorrow evening to help her pack. I was going to invite you, but after this fight, you might want to stay home and sleep."

"Actually, you might be right. I'll help her with the big stuff when the time comes. Whoa..." he faded slightly. "I might be going to bed early tonight."

"You don't have a concussion, do you?"

"I don't know. Maybe. Hey... did you get that email I forwarded you with the kids and their wish list? I wanted to get those before Thursday so I could deliver them, but tomorrow... I don't know. I think my body needs a rest day."

"I can get the gifts for you, and then we can hit some Angel Trees together. That'll make you happy?"

"Yeah it will. I love you Merridy. I need to go."

"I love you too. Rest up, and listen to the team doctor." They hung up, and she nervously kissed the top of Porthos' head. "I don't like how he sounded."

Merridy entered Jacob's apartment and unleashed Porthos. "Sweetie, we're here."

"Bedroom," he grumbled.

She put a few canvas bags on his kitchen table before entering his bedroom. "Jacob? How are you feeling?"

"I've been worse, much worse." He rolled over to face Merridy. "They kept me awake all night because of the concussion. Now I'm sore and exhausted. That's all."

"That's all?" She sat on the edge of the bed and stroked his dark hair. "I brought some groceries. I'll go make you lunch, and then after you eat, you can take a really long nap."

"Mmm-hmmm," he agreed. Porthos jumped on the bed with him. Jacob mumbled a greeting to the dog then quickly fell asleep. He awoke again to the smell of chicken and dumplings. Stumbling out of the bed, he made his way to the kitchen. "Smells good." He noted the stack of unopened Christmas cards on the counter. "And you brought the cards. Best girlfriend ever."

She moved the pot from the burner. "You mean that?" Grabbing two mitts, she opened the oven to reveal a tray of cornbread muffins.

"I do." He leaned forward to better view the muffins. "Those are pumpkin cornbread muffins."

"Those are." She placed the cookie sheet on pot holders. "And you can have one when they're cooled down."

"Hmmm..." Jacob pulled the unopened Christmas cards toward him. "Guess that means we have time for these."

"Yes, we do." She put another tray into the oven and set a timer. "Let's do it."

"Wait, what was that?"

"Surprise."

He pulled her in tight to sit in his lap at the kitchen bar. "You're the only surprise I need." He kissed her cheek. "Ready to open some cards?"

The two enjoyed going through the stack of Christmas cards they received. After reading each, Merridy pinned them to a card board Jacob had propped up next to his tree. "By the way, I also brought a bunch of the presents. Not all, because Porthos. But the ones I could fit in my trunk and my front seat."

"Maybe we should go check out those car holiday deals." He kissed her jaw. "I'll go get a few of the presents, and then maybe the food will be cool enough to eat?"

"I'll help you." They emptied her car of the presents and placed them under his tree. "I can bring the rest over later."

"I can go get them from your apartment," he offered.

She shook her head. "You really shouldn't be driving until your feeling yourself again." Her hand stroked his face with extra attention to his injured eye. "Sit at the table, and I'll make you a bowl." She dipped him a heaping bowl of chicken and dumplings with two cornbread muffins on the side. "Before you say grace, I need to take the surprise out of the oven." Upon her statement, the timer sounded. She pulled the sheet out before Jacob could catch a glimpse of it.

"Curiouser and curiouser," Jacob joked.

"You'll see soon. It should be ready once we finish the main dish." She hurriedly made her own bowl and sat next to him. "Okay."

They held hands, and Jacob prayed over the meal. "These muffins are amazing." He downed the first muffin before he even had the chicken and dumplings. "Did you make plenty? I'm having these tonight."

"Plenty of food for tonight too." She spun her spoon in the dumplings. "After here, I'm going to get the gifts for the kids at the hospital. I can take them home and wrap them before I go to Evie's. Bring them to the rink after practice tomorrow?"

"Perfect. After we hand out the gifts, let's go do some random acts of awesomeness."

"What did you have in mind?"

He dropped his spoon into his empty bowl. "A few things I do every two weeks before Christmas – strip a few angel trees, go to some mom and pop stores and get the gifts, plus some extra toys for Toys for Tots, drop the things off. Then go look at the trains while drinking hot chocolate."

"I like this plan." She lowered her spoon. "Maybe we should also add some light gazing. I know a few neighborhoods that

447

are pretty decked out." She went to the kitchen and began working on the surprise.

"Yes." He smiled. "I can't wait until we get to Canada. You're going to love the lights." He leaned back in the chair to see what she was doing. "I can't wait anymore. What's the surprise?"

She held up a piece of a cookie bar. "I attempted a Texas-version of a Nanaimo bar, but with cookie dough, dulce de leche, and pecans."

He held up his bowl. "I'll take ten please."

Boy band Christmas songs drifted throughout Evie's home while the three girls sat about packing small items into cardboard boxes. "What's your plan Evie? I mean, you've not found someone to sublease yet. You don't have to move out until you're ready. Jacob won't force you to."

Evelyn wrapped a photo frame in bubble wrap. "I'm actually going out on a leap of faith." She placed the frame into a box and walked to Merridy. "I found an empty place in a little town east of here, not far from the Louisiana border. It's little enough to be calm, but just enough people to support a bakery." Evie opened a drawer in the kitchen. "I have everything in this folder." She handed a purple folder to Merridy. "Kara's already looked over it. I didn't trust myself. But she thinks it's a good idea."

Merridy looked over the folder. "Oh wow, so you get the store and the apartment that's above it?"

"Yep, both are *for sale*.   I'll be my own landlord - no skyrocketing rent. And since I'll be living upstairs, my commute time is maybe thirty seconds.   Every second counts when waking up at three in the morning." She sighed happily. "Also, the town has a lot of little boutiques and antique stores. They get tourists on weekends for shopping, apparently. That will be great for a little boost from the everyday sales."

"This is amazing." She continued looking over Evelyn's business plan. "Are you sure you can afford the payments on the new place if you're still having to pay rent here in South Hills?"

Evelyn sighed. "I would prefer not to, but the money from selling the house will help. Hopefully, the bakery will do enough business to keep me in the green. I'm just going to keep praying for a Christmas miracle in finding someone to sublease the place."

"And I'll keep praying right alongside you." Merridy handed the folder back to Evelyn. "I am really excited for you Evie. This place looks adorable. I can't wait to help you decorate it. Plus, we can help you host a grand opening."

"Yes!" Evelyn jumped excitedly. "That would be amazing!"

"Ladies, come quick!" Kara shouted from the family room. "You need to see this!"

The two rushed to join their friend. She stood transfixed in front of the television. 'URGENT NEWS' flashed across the screen. A reporter, in a garish hot pink dress, made a stern face. "Authorities in the US have been notified of an international abduction that happened yesterday evening in Stockholm, Sweden. American Brodie Mayer of South Hills, Texas was taken by an unknown assailant after attending the Nobel Banquet."

449

"Oh no!" Evelyn shouted. Her hands instantly went to her mouth to muffle her screams.

"Mayer is best known for making headlines as the nanny to the Royal Family of Sweden. There has been no official comment yet from the royal family on how they are proceeding with this matter, but we have it on good authority that the FBI's international division is involved in solving this abduction."

Kara muted the television and turned to her friends. "I can't believe this has happened to sweet Brodie."

"What is happening to our friends? First Merridy, now Brodie. Why are we under attack?"

Merridy took her two friends by the hand. "Whatever the enemy means for evil, God will use it for good. He did that for me. He will do that for Brodie. We just need to pray for her." The packing-session became a prayer meeting. The girls held hands and prayed for their friend.

"Ladies, would you mind a sleepover tonight? I just... don't want to be alone right now," Evelyn confessed. "This is making me really doubt my plans."

Kara hugged her friend tightly. "We will stay the night with you. But know this, sweet sister, doubting your plans is exactly what the enemy wants. I'm more convinced than ever that you are being called to that little east Texas town for more than just baking cakes."

"That's right. We're going to keep packing, keep praying, and once we're in some jammies, we're going to doodle some sketches of your store front to get your momentum up again." Merridy squeezed Evelyn's hands. Upon heading back to her packing zone, she sent a quick text to Jacob to update him on the situation.

Chapter 48

"You know, a few months ago, I had never even been on a plane. Now, I'm flying first class everywhere. I really like it," Merridy confided to Jacob. "I don't think I could sit like a sardine can when this is an option." Her eyes widened; she did not want to tread down an entitled road, real or perceived. "Though it's legitimate to sit like that! Prices are crazy! I'm just blessed that I don't have to."

Jacob laughed. "I'm not going to judge you for enjoying first class flight. I firmly believe in doing it if you can afford it. Eddie and I spent many flights like sardines when we were in junior league. We're very blessed that we don't have to anymore." He kissed Merridy's cheek. "And I'm glad that you're blessed as well."

"I'm just glad my friend is safe." She sighed. The previous evening news confirmed that authorities rescued Brodie from her Swedish abduction. The three girls immediately called one another to celebrate. Then the three flooded Brodie's phone with well-wishes. Merridy regretted that her own life's chaos had kept her from being a better friend in the last few months. "My friend is safe, we've had a lot of fun doing Christmas things like the angel trees and the children's hospital, and now I get to go meet your parents and family. You don't have a game the day before the official NHL Christmas break, which makes it an extra-long break. I'm happy."

He took her hand. "I'm glad you're happy. At first, I was happy we could get this flight after the game, but now I'm a bit sore. I shouldn't have skipped my cool down ritual." He wiggled in his seat. "Maybe for Christmas I could have a nice massage."

"Spa day?" Merridy asked eagerly.

"What?" He laughed. "No, no, I am not bathing in mud and putting cucumbers on my eyes. I was thinking… a massage."

"Oh, I know what you're thinking. But I think bigger. Spa day." She winked at him. "Now I want to see you with cucumber on your eyes."

"Maybe we settle for massages at the lodge in the North Pole for now, and spa day for Valentine's Day?"

Merridy let out an excited squeak. "Valentine's Day? We're already talking about Valentine's Day?"

Without responding, Jacob stared down at her hand in his. His thumb slowly drifted over her fingers. "Yeah, Valentine's Day," he whispered.

A flight attendant interrupted the conversation to advise everyone to return to their seats for landing. Soon, they disembarked from the plane and headed to luggage claim. "Is someone picking us up?"

"Nah, it's too late, even with the time change. I thought we might rideshare through some tunnels of Christmas lights? I think you'll enjoy."

She grabbed her suitcase. "That sounds amazing!"

The two soon found themselves in a tunnel of blue, red, and green Christmas lights. "What do you think? It's not even the best lights in town."

She stared out of the window in child-like fascination. "It's pretty magical." She reached back to squeeze his hand while her eyes remained fixated on the lights. "I wish this tunnel would go on forever."

"We can always circle through again, if that's what you wish. Anything for you."

"That's okay. I expect the next two days will be full of magic and lights." The car meandered through the city to outlying neighborhoods, all alit with lights and animatronic decorations. It stopped in front of a craftsman house whose front yard seemed to be themed as 'Candy Cane Lane' given the red and white lights on the pillars, the candy cane lights leading down the walkway from the sidewalk to the front porch, and the giant candy cane pillars in the yard. "Wow," Merridy breathed. "Your parents really are into the holiday."

"Yeah, I think our families are equally matched." He carried both of their suitcases to the door and fumbled through his keys. "My parents go to bed early. They're morning people."

"Are you telling me that we're sneaking in and need to be quiet?"

"I am." He slowly pushed open the door. The house stood silent and dark save the lights of the Christmas tree. "Would you like something to eat and drink? I'm asking because I know for a fact my mom is going to have eggnog, fudge, and cookies in the kitchen."

"Absolutely." They abandoned their suitcases in the foyer to partake of the sweets. "It's not really Christmas until you steal eggnog and cookies from your parents," she joked.

"Wait until you try this. It's her chocolate and peanut butter fudge." He held a piece up to Merridy's lips. "You can thank me later."

The rich chocolate made Merridy moan in culinary satisfaction. "Yes, thank you."

He laughed. "Ready to make tomorrow happen?"

"I don't know. This night is still pretty good." She glanced at the mistletoe above the kitchen doorway. "See?"

He grinned and kissed her.

A final check in the guest room mirror confirmed Merridy was presentable to officially meet Jacob's parents over a Kenway family breakfast.

"You're perfect," Jacob announced. He lounged on the guest room bed reading a magazine. "I'm hungry. Let's go."

"You didn't have to barge in my room this morning," she reminded him. "You could have gone straight to breakfast."

"Nope," he responded. "Because they would see me and say 'oh where is your lady friend', and I would have to say 'probably in her room looking in the mirror for the twentieth time'. And that sounds bad." She tossed a pillow at him and headed to the door. Jacob hurried after her in order to arrive downstairs together. "Mom! Dad! We're here!"

"The breakfast table," a man called back. A small bark followed.

Jacob took her hand and led her to the breakfast nook of the kitchen. "Mom and dad, meet Merridy Christmas. Merridy, this is my mom, Becky, and my dad, Isaac, though he goes by Zak."

"Pleasure to meet you both." Merridy sat down in a chair next to Becky. "Your house is lovely. The candy cane theme outside is adorable." She knelt toward the Jack Russel Terrier staring up at her. "And you must be D'Artagnan!" The dog barked a response with a tail wag. He received an ear scratch from Merridy in return. Immediately, the small dog began sniffing her. The canine attention made her miss Porthos who had remained in Dallas with Jacob's agent.

"Thank you. We kept it simple this year," Becky responded.

Zak chuckled. "Usually she wants enough light to send a Bat-signal into the air."

"That should be your theme for next year!" Jacob exclaimed. He dipped scrambled eggs onto two plates. "*A Very Gotham Christmas*. You can make Arkham Asylum for Halloween, then jazz it up with lights and wreaths."

Becky sighed and continued eating her eggs. "Merridy, you seem like a fine lady. Are you sure you want to date that sarcastic boy of mine?"

"I get it honest," he responded. He set the plates at the table. "Plus, I do think Merridy likes my sense of humor."

"I do," she beamed at him. "*Most* of the time."

Jacob laughed while shoveling eggs into his mouth. "When is Eddie getting in?"

"I thought he told you, Snickerdoodle," his mom responded. "He hasn't told us."

"Nah, I ran out after the game so we could fly in last night. Wanted to maximize our time here." He uttered each sentence between mouthfuls of scrambled eggs. "Got a lot to show Merridy. Did the tunnel lights last night. Thought we could go to the Christmas Market after breakfast. Want to go with us?"

Zak folded the newspaper he was reading. "Your sisters are coming in today. We were hoping to all go up to North Pole together."

"Today? I thought they wouldn't come in until tomorrow," Jacob moaned. "They're coming in to tell Merridy all of my embarrassing stories, aren't they?"

"Yep," Merridy told him. "You saw all my photos and heard stories from my grandma. It's my turn." She noted the mischievous sparkle in his eyes. "I'm certain you have a whole slew of embarrassing stories."

"I do. But I'm hoping that I'll keep you so busy snowshoeing, skiing, skating, and feeding reindeer, that you won't get a chance to hear them." He stood to get a second helping of eggs. "And they better have eaten before they get here. I'm not leaving a bite for them."

"Save your appetite," Becky told her son. "We're taking the train for the kids. Candy Cane Station will have all your favorites."

Merridy grinned. "Candy Cane Station? A train? Alright, Vancouver is magical. Cold, but magical." Her statement was confirmed when D'Artagnan leapt into her lap. Everyone at the table laughed in response.

Between the Kenway sisters and their families, Zak, Becky, Jacob, and Merridy, chaos erupted onto the train platform. The fourteen members of the group all wanted to go separate ways, including the adults. Jacob pulled Merridy toward a giant display of candy. "The kids know what's up." He indicated his nieces and nephews who rushed the candy displays with frantic parents following them. "Look at this. This is on a Meseta General Store level, right?"

"I mean, the taffy selection is a little weak, but their gummy game is strong." She held up a package. "It's a sushi pack... all made of gummy. Oh, look! They have little hamburgers and hotdogs. I didn't know gummies came in so many shapes. I thought it was just bears and worms."

"They have the bears," Jacob agreed. He pointed to towers full of gummy bears. Each tower held a different color bear. "Look at all the flavors."

"I thought they only came in like five flavors. I have been deprived of great gummy goodness all these years."

He grabbed a paper bag and began filling it up with the bears. "Get you a bag too. We can have a *very, beary Christmas Eve-Eve*."

"I can't say no to something that cute."

Each of the children also secured candy bags before being loaded into the train. They made it a point to sit near their Uncle Jacob, leaving Merridy alone with his sisters. "It's so nice to see him babysit," the oldest sister, Sarah, whispered. "Gives mommy a chance to enjoy her candy canes and hot chocolate."

"I can imagine," Merridy agreed. "You have quite the herd."

"Four and done," she responded. "Emily over there wants a few more though."

The other sister shook her head. "Nope. I learned from you, and I am good with two. It's going to be Eddie that has like ten children. He always said he wanted a whole hockey team."

"Has Jacob mentioned kids?"

The two sisters grinned at each other. "Yeah, he wants to be a dad," Emily answered. "Are you wanting to be a mom?"

Merridy smiled. "I do. Maybe not... ten. But two is good, like you said." She watched Jacob with the kids. "He does have fun with kids. At Thanksgiving, he spent most of his time with either my dad in the woodshop or with my cousins' kids. And his heart is at the children's hospital."

"Yep, that's Jacob. I think he likes kids cause he's still a big kid himself," Sarah commented. "He's the baby of the family. I actually changed his diapers, we have that much of an age gap."

"Wow. You had to help raise him then, huh?" Merridy tapped her chin with a finger in thought. "That's interesting. I'm an only child, so I never had those experiences."

"When I got my license, I got put on hockey practice duty. Dad was working longer hours, and mom had surgery. I can't remember why…"

Emily chimed in, "She broke her leg on ice."

"That's right. Well that meant, I drove, and Emily helped wrangle the younger two to all their hockey practices, which were a lot. They were on several leagues."

"I remember we always had to insist on Jacob taking a shower after practices. He would smell *rancid*," Emily added. "Then he'd want to go around the house like it was okay to smell that way. Absolutely disgusting."

Merridy giggled. "He got over that. He's very particular about how he smells nowadays." She opened her candy bag. "Did he do anything else weird when he was a kid?"

"She's wanting the embarrassing stories," Emily told Sarah. "Let's give the lady what she wants!"

Jacob chimed up from the ruckus of the children around him. "You better not be saying anything bad!" he yelled at his sisters.

"We're only sharing what's true." Sarah waved a dismissive hand at him. "Let's talk about his potty-training days."

The girls laughed over countless embarrassing stories until the train arrived at the mountain. Once at the mountain station, the children instantly went to their parents begging to see Santa. The parents obliged by heading to Santa's village.

"Santa? Skiing? Snowshoeing?" Jacob took Merridy's hands. "I think there's even sleds."

"Let's visit Santa with the kids. You know you're going to want pictures of your nieces and nephews with the Big Guy."

"True. I need to sit on his lap too. I have a Christmas wish to make."

They followed the rest of the family. Jacob ended up with his youngest nephew sitting on his shoulders as they waited in line for Santa. "What's your favorite Christmas song?"

"Jingle Bells," the child answered back.

Jacob began singing the song. The kid joined him. He nudged Merridy's shoulder, and she sang as well. By the time the group reached Santa, all of the kids were singing with Jacob and Merridy.

"Ho, ho, ho," Santa called out at the group. "This group is full of Christmas spirit. Who wants to visit Santa first?"

The nephew on Jacob's shoulders squirmed wildly, and he lowered the boy. The child clamored to Santa. Jacob eagerly took photos of each child sitting with Santa.

"Thank you for coming," one of the elves told the group.

"Wait! Santa." Jacob bounded over to the man and sat in his lap. He whispered in the man's ear, pointed at Merridy, and whispered once more. It caused Santa to laugh. "Thank you, Santa!" He followed his family away from Santa's village. "Nice guy, Santa."

"What did you wish for?" Merridy asked.

He bent down to pick up snow. "Guess you'll have to wait and see." He tossed the snowball at her. "Let's go ski."

She chased him with a snowball of her own to the ski lifts. Having never skied a day in her life, Merridy required him to show her how. The mountain staff offered beginner courses for adults and even a personal trainer, but she declined in order to have the one-on-one time with Jacob. He managed to teach her to stand in the skis. Then they moved forward about fifty yards on a bunny trail before Merridy fell over. Laughing, Jacob joined her in the snow, and they shared a kiss before heading up the trail to try again.

After another hour, Jacob's stomach growled. The duo left the ski trails for a nearby coffee bar. They shared holiday-themed hot coffees and pumpkin maple muffins. Sitting in front of the coffee shop's fireplace, Merridy was able to warm her nose. It was not accustomed to the frigid temperatures of the far north in winter. Her counterpart made fun of her by placing whipped cream from his coffee onto the frozen nose. A laugh was shared before they moved on to sledding.

Midday brought them together with the rest of the family for lunch at a mountaintop bistro. The group talked for a length of time after the food disappeared. Jacob decided that snowshoeing a hiking trail would be too much on the heavy stomach. Instead, they casually skated on a giant pond with the rest of the family.

"The kids are getting tired," Sarah announced. "Probably need to hit the train back down and get them home."

Jacob held Merridy's hands. "Are you ready to go, or... you want to stay for the lights?"

"More lights?"

He smiled. "Let's go do some shopping until the sun starts to set." He nodded to his family. "We'll see everyone tonight. Per his texts, Eddie should be there for you when you get back."

The group headed to the train station while Jacob led Merridy to a menagerie of stores and alpine outfitters. They shopped for some time, and Merridy managed to find thermals to help her adjust to the colder temperatures. They enjoyed another snack for Jacob with the setting sun. Then the Light Walk turned on.

He held her hand. "This is some real magic." They walked through tunnels of lights that cut through snow-laden trees. Reindeer trotted in jingle bells. Tourists offered carrots and hay to the creatures in between the lit pastures. "Happy we stayed?" he asked her.

"Absolutely."

"And these lights are nothing compared to the lights I'm going to show you tomorrow night. But first, we have to get home for dinner and sleep because we're going to the German market first thing in the morning."

Chapter 49

Jacob and Merridy walked arm-in-arm down a row of vintage street lights that paved the way of the VanDusen Botanical Garden. Swarms of lights flooded the darkness with festive spirit. The cold Canadian night nipped once again at Merridy's nose. She lifted her cup of cinnamon hot chocolate to her lips, allowing the steam to work its magic.

The morning promise of the Christmas German Market had been fulfilled. Jacob had bounced from stall to stall, purchasing every imaginable delicacy to share with his love. Half of their time at the market was spent eating potato dumplings, red cabbage, apple and sausage stuffing, schnitzel, Stollen, chocolate-covered Lebkuchen, marzipan, and gingerbread. The other half was spent finding hand-crafted ornaments and decorations for a future shared tree.

After the market closed at midday for Christmas Eve, they spent the afternoon with the entire Kenway bunch at the craftsman home. The group baked cookies, sang Christmas carols, and decorated gingerbread houses. Jacob insisted on Merridy playing with the family village and train with him, once its official setup was completed by he and Eddie. His enthusiasm over the model train delighted her. It was one experience when he viewed the trains at the mall in Dallas; it was another experience seeing him crawl on his belly in his parent's living room to 'play conductor'. He even owned a proper hat for the job.

"Alright, favorite part of a Vancouver Christmas so far?" he asked her giddily.

"Hmmm…" She considered the current light display. "Okay, probably the German Christmas Market, because I've never experienced anything like that before. And the food was *so good.*"

"I could eat strudel for days," he agreed. "Also, the mulled wine hits different. It has a weird taste, but I do like it. Though the hot chocolate was also good. It tasted, darker, thicker."

"Right. Also, I must admit, I have a new fascination for nutcrackers after that place. They literally have a nutcracker for every profession, every country, every... character. It's amazing. I might have to start collecting."

He chuckled. "Okay, but we must have room for a train and village too."

"True." She leaned hard against his arm. "Guess we could remove all furniture from the living room and make it a Christmas corner. I mean, there's a family room in Evie's place."

"You mean, our future place."

"Correct." She skipped over to a display of lights in a gazebo. "Look at this. I can't believe it's empty. I mean, I know it's Christmas Eve, but I thought there would be some people soaking in that last little bit of magic."

"It really is a magical night." He followed her into the gazebo. "You can see all the different paths of light from here." He took her hands in his. "Might be the most magical place in the whole gardens. The hedge maze is down that way, the water features are over there..." He leaned forward. "And the most beautiful woman in the whole world is right here." He kissed her forehead. "Merridy, I love you."

"I love you too," she replied. She felt transfixed under the white lights of the gazebo with her hands held tightly by Jacob.

"I know we've only been dating for a short time... I mean, we've only known each other for a short time... But we've been through so much together. I feel like I've grown closer to you more than anyone else on this planet." He raised her hands to his lips. "And I'm hoping you feel the same."

"Of course I do. Jacob, you're my best friend. I talk to you more than... literally everyone. I tell you more than everyone too."

"That's good, because..." he released her hands and knelt down to one knee. The action caused Merridy to gasp. "I'm ready to start living that future we keep talking about, that we keep planning. We were just talking about nutcrackers, trains, and villages, and turning a room in a future house into a Christmas corner. Why not a Christmas corner next year? Why not a Mister and Misses Kenway next year?" From his pocket he produced a red velvet box. "Merridy, will you do me the honor of being my bride?" He opened the box to display a diamond ring accented with garnets. The white gold band was intricately carved, appearing as though two roses wrapped around the diamond setting. The garnets severed as the rose blossoms. "My forever bride?"

Merridy cried. Her hands covered her mouth. The overwhelming tears prevented her from answering verbally. Instead, she bobbed her head rapidly.

"That's a yes?" Jacob joked.

She bobbed again.

He laughed and stood. Taking her left hand delicately, he slipped the ring on her finger. "I love you Turnip Girl."

She buried her face into his neck. "I love you White Rabbit," she mumbled.

"By the way, I invited a few people. I hope you don't mind." He wiped tears from her face as she pulled back.

Bewildered, Merridy peered into the darkness beyond the lights of the gazebo.

"Congratulations!" She heard Kara's voice in the darkness. Others joined her in well-wishing as they entered the gazebo to hug the couple. Kara, Evelyn, the entirety of Merridy's family, and the entirety of Jacob's family filled the gazebo and surrounding area. "We're so happy for you," Kara continued on. "I've got it all on camera for you to remember forever and ever."

Merridy hugged her friend. "What are you doing in Vancouver?" she managed.

"Jacob brought me out here. He brought all of us out here in secret."

"Well that was risky," she stuttered. "What if I said no?"

He laughed. "I had a really good feeling you were going to say yes. I asked Santa for a 'yes' when I sat in his lap." He kissed her forehead once again. Jamie and Patti stepped forward to hug both of them. "Thank you for helping me get everyone up here."

"You footed the bill," Jamie joked. "We were happy to send out the invites."

Patti held her daughter tightly. "This is why you wanted to ship the presents out," Merridy pointed at Jacob. "You knew everyone was going to be up here."

"Guilty. I shipped everything to my parents' house. All the gifts are hidden in the basement for tomorrow morning." He hugged his own parents and siblings. "That way we can spend our favorite holiday with all of our favorite people."

"You're the best." She wrapped her arms around Jacob's neck. "You really, really are the best."

His eyes lit up. "I've been inspired by the best. Thank God I found you." They shared another kiss at the applause of all in attendance.

Chapter 50

Christmas morning brought a mountain of people to the Kenway's craftsman home. Children from both parties tore away at pristine gift wrapping to uncover new toys, clothes, and books. Parents handed boxes to their adult children, dismissing every "you shouldn't have" thrown at them. Jacob handed out presents to Kara and Evelyn.

"Look, both of their names on the tag," Evelyn whispered to Kara. "She was definitely going to say yes."

"The Christmas cards were the first clue," Kara laughed. She opened her gift to find a smart notebook. "Wow! You can write in the notebook and it uploads digitally too. This is *way* cool." She scanned over the words on the back of the box. "Thank y'all. This is going to be so handy with all my upcoming projects." She hugged Jacob and Merridy.

Evelyn opened her gift. "An airbrush set! Now I can *really* decorate those cakes! Thank you!"

"There was also a sugar blowing thing," Jacob confessed. "I left it at my apartment. Sorry."

She laughed. "That is okay. And those are really amazing gifts - slash investments for my new business."

"We look forward to buying you out on opening day," Merridy joked.

Jacob grinned. "Plus. We'll need a wedding cake."

The pastry chef inhaled deeply. "Yes! Yes, you will!" The girls shared an ecstatic giggle.

"This is for my boys," Becky announced. She handed identical boxes to Eddie and Jacob. "I picked this especially for you."

All those gathered laughed as the two hockey players unwrapped helmet visors. "Mom, we're not required to wear these," Eddie argued. "We grandfathered out of that rule…"

"I don't care," Becky responded. "You're wearing them. Look at your brother's eye. The scar is still there."

"Yes ma'am," Jacob grumbled. He placed the visor up to his face. "This is like when I had to wear that awful helmet at the skating rink and the other kids made fun of me."

Merridy shook her head. "I don't know. I'm agreeing with your mom on this one."

"Me too," Rosella, Eddie's wife, chimed in. "You're a dad now. Time to be responsible, Edgar." She popped the visor onto his forehead.

"They're outnumbering us now, brother," Eddie told Jacob. "You tipped the numbers in their favor."

Jacob winked at Merridy. "Wouldn't have it any other way." He handed a box to Merridy. "Merry Christmas, Merridy Rachel Christmas."

"Are we certain the ring last night wasn't my Christmas present?" She opened the box to find a turnip and a hockey puck. "Nope, this is fitting. This is very Jacob Randolph Kenway," she laughed.

He held up the two items. "Now you can tell them apart. This is a turnip." He held up the turnip. "And *this* is a hockey puck." He twirled the puck between his fingers. "They're very similar. I can see where the confusion would be." He nodded at the box. "You also might want to dig under all that tissue paper."

"More?" She pushed the tissue paper aside to reveal a book. "This is… *The Three Musketeers*. A very old copy of it." She pulled the antique book out and opened to reveal its gilded pages. "This is beautiful."

"First, I want to say, that it is *not* a first edition of the book, because those go at auction for twenty-five thousand dollars. That's a lot of things for the children's hospital; I couldn't do it. I hope that's okay."

"Certainly," she smiled.

"Second, I saw that in a used bookstore, and reminded me of the first time we truly connected. When I told you about Porthos… and D'Artangan… wherever he is." He waved a hand at the chaos of Christmas morning. "We both realized there were layers to the other. And I think we both realized we wanted to get to know more. I think we stayed awake until like two or three in the morning just to talk to each other."

"Yeah, we did," she laughed. "This is really special. Thank you." She hugged the book tightly to her chest. "I feel bad Porthos isn't here now."

Jacob shrugged his shoulders. "I told him everything we were going to do. He was okay with missing it. He hates being in the cargo area of a plane when traveling, and I hate it for him too. He's much happier being with my agent today."

"Still, lots of pets and treats when we get back." She handed Jacob a box. "Merry Christmas."

His jovial smirk disappeared upon seeing his gift. A FAO Schwarz soldier bear sat at attention in its box.

"I know it's not a night we need to linger on, but I remember how you looked up at those bears. I'm making you a promise: that you'll get to give this to your child, someday."

470

He smiled. "Thank you, Merridy. We'll give it to our child…
together." He kissed her cheek. "You're going to be an amazing
mom someday."

"And you'll be an amazing dad."

A squeak from Evelyn distracted the two. "What is it Evie?"
Merridy asked.

"Brodie just messaged me." Her smile beamed from ear-to-ear.
"She found someone in Sweden who wants to sublease from
me. He's coming to South Hills in a few days to look at the place
and sign the paperwork. I knew it! I had faith! God came
through: right at the end of the month."

Jacob pulled Merridy into a tight hug. "If there's one thing I've
learned, it's that God has great timing."

But they that wait upon the LORD shall renew their strength; they shall mount up with wings as eagles; they shall run, and not be weary; and they shall walk, and not faint.

Isaiah 40:31

Author's Notes

The creation of Merridy Christmas and her Canadian hockey player (whose name has changed several times) began over six years ago. The world has changed much in those six years! Sometimes, it is hard to remember the pre-pandemic world. This book is set in 2018, the same year as "The Swedish Bodyguard", and thus it references that world and people alive in 2018 who are no longer with us.

A great example of this is the legendary First Nations hockey player Fred Sasakamoose who was taken from us by the COVID-19 virus. Whenever I read Jacob and Joseph discussing this great man, I become mournful in reflection of everyone we lost during the pandemic, whether from the disease or other reasons.

The last few years have truly been a time of loss, sadness, anger, confusion, anxiety, and depression.

What a great time to release a book about a girl named *Merridy Christmas*.

Even though Merridy faces a very serious issue in the entertainment industry, and one which needs to end, I want the reader to realize they can overcome anything with God's help and in *His* timing. Sometimes, we want to overcome our problems immediately. I understand the impatience. But often times a bigger reward is down the road if we simply hold on. We do not know the future, but He does. We ask "but why", and He says, "Trust me and I will show you."

Right now, we are asking why did the whole world go through such a dark time? I do not have that answer. No man or woman on this planet does. But I trust that God knows. A great reward is coming, in some form or fashion.

Is it hard to cling to that hope? Absolutely. I am human too. I have been that impatient person. I have been that confused person. In fact, I am both of them right now. I need people around me to lean on. I need prayer time. I need time in God's word. I need a church family. I encourage you to do the same. Please, find a great community to be a part of, because whatever you are struggling with is easier to handle when you have a support group.

Acknowledgements

This book would have never come to light if not for the support of my closest family and friends. A special thank you to my husband, Jason, who took on extra work in order to free up my time to write. Another special thank you to my mother, Joy, who I bounce ideas off of and who helps me edit my work. Also, to the two very important editors, Dixie and Zephyr, whose furry presence are constantly needed.

Inspiration for the Jael-moment (where Merridy hits Casimir with a lamp in the head) is credited to Ariel Hardy. Our lovely friendship began with a Facebook comment – "if you don't love me at my Judges 4 and 5, you don't deserve me at my Proverbs 31". Not only did I appreciate the play on a famous Marilyn Monroe quote, the sentiment was how I felt. God uses women of both types, and sometimes one woman having to be both – like Merridy. Thank you for the joke that went further than you could imagine Ariel!

Another acknowledgement due is to Kiel Cathers, Justin Logue, and the other members of The Logues. They were the last concert I attended before the world shut down, and subsequently provided great entertainment during the subsequent years. Many passages of this book were written while listening to their music, and it only felt right to include them within my story world.

Thank you to my web developer Jim Cole for handling my website and taking that burden off my shoulders. Maybe one day I can pay you what you are worth!

Love to my dearest gal pals who are my mental soundboards. Even when it is not about my book, but my anxieties and worries, these ladies listen to me, talk with me, and pray for me.

I love you Brittany O., Brittany B., Jessica, and Audrey. You ladies have been there through my engagement, my wedding, my dad's diagnosis and subsequent passing, a pandemic, and more layers of loss and drama than a few years should hold. I would go crazy without our friendship.

Finally, thank you God for your continued goodness and promise-keeping. You called me to write, and you keep making a way for this calling. With You, all things are possible.

Appendix: Song Credits

All songs either referenced or quoted in this book, by order of first appearance.

Note: Every song quoted in this text is part of the public domain.

Adam, Adolphe. **"O Holy Night"**. 1847. Translated by John Sullivan Dwight.

Spafford, Horatio and Philip Bliss. **"It Is Well with My Soul"**. 1873.

Weatherly, Frederic. **"Danny Boy"**. 1913.

Lowry, Robert. **"Nothing But the Blood of Jesus"**. 1876.

Bennard, George. **"The Old Rugged Cross"**. 1912.

Martin, Civilla D. and Charles H. Gabriel. **"His Eye Is on the Sparrow"**. 1905.

Traditional. **"O Come, O Come, Emmanuel"**. 8th century. Translated by John Mason Neale. 1861.

Traditional. **"Go Tell It on the Mountain"**. 19th century. Compiled by John Wesley Work Jr. 1865.

Longfellow, Henry Wadsworth. **"I Heard the Bells on Christmas Day"**. 1863.

Watts, Isaac. **"Joy to the World"**. 1719.

Carey, Mariah and Walter Afanasieff. **"All I Want for Christmas is You"**. *Merry Christmas*. Columbia, 1994.

Berlin, Irving. **"White Christmas"**. Performed by Bing Crosby. Decca, 1942.

Parton, Dolly. **"I Will Always Love You"**. RCA, 1973. Performed by Whitney Houston. Arista, 1992.

Michael, George. **"Last Christmas"**. *Music from the Edge of Heaven*. Columbia/Epic/CBS, 1984.

Javits, Joan and Philip Springer. **"Santa Baby"**. Performed by Eartha Kitt with Henri René and His Orchestra. RCA Victor, 1953.

Grande, Ariana, Ilya Salmanzadeh, and Savan Kotecha. **"Santa Tell Me"**. *Christmas Kisses*. Republic, 2014.

Kahn, Gus and Isham Jones. **"It Had to Be You"**. Brunswick 2614, 1924. Performed by Frank Sinatra. *Trilogy*. Reprise, 1980.

Logue, Justin. **"No Place Like Home"**. *Tough at the Bottom*. 2011.

Newton, John. **"Amazing Grace"**. 1772.

Brooks, Phillips. **"O Little Town of Bethlehem"**. 1868.

Tate, Nahum. **"While Shepherds Watched Their Flocks"**. 1700.

Hopkins Jr., John Henry. **"We Three Kings"**. 1857.

Hayes, Billy and Jay W. Johnson. **"Blue Christmas"**. Performed by Elvis Presley. *Elvis' Christmas Album*. RCA Victor, 1957.

Pierpont, James Lord. **"Jingle Bells"**. 1857.

Martin, Hugh and Ralph Blane. **"Have Yourself a Merry Little Christmas"**. Performed by Judy Garland. *Meet Me in St. Louis*. Leo Feist, Inc., 1944.

Van DeVenter, Judson W. and Winfield S. Weeden. **"I Surrender All"**. 1896.

Maureena, Ashley. **"Seek Your Face"**. *Merridy Christmas*. 2022.

Bennett, S. Fillmore and Joseph P. Webster. **"In the Sweet By-and-By"**. 1868.

Maureena, Ashley. **"I'll Shout My Praise"**. *Merridy Christmas.* 2022.

Traditional with additions by Frederic Austin. **"The Twelve Days of Christmas"**. 1780.

Tchaikovsky, Pyotr Ilyich. **"The Nutcracker Suite, Op. 71a"** and **"The Dance of the Sugar Plum Fairy"**. 1892.